A BLIND EYE

DIANE EAGLE

TWO BIRDS PUBLISHING

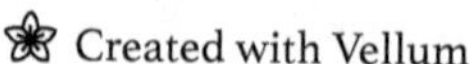 Created with Vellum

For Koji

1

Consciousness drifted like fog through her dreams until bathroom tiles hard against her cheek insisted she waken. Her breathing came in gasps and her eyes were crusted shut from dried tears. Her tongue felt swollen and coated with chalk. She spied a section of chipped tile. *Shit! I must have spent the night here . . . on my face!* Nausea heaved; she shoved it back down.

Eleanor Ketcham lurched upright and tripped over a mostly empty Mekong Whiskey bottle near the sink. Staggering into the bedroom, she pushed through the dense, humid air already heating up the sultry, cloying odors of the Orient. Odors she'd struggled to tolerate when she first arrived but that were now a part of her daily life. She looked down—still in last night's jeans and a torn, blood-spattered yellow T-shirt. Fragments of memory flashed—his yelling, his windmilling arms, fast-pitch windups, and his vicious painful punches. She touched the bump on her forehead, her swollen nose, the stickiness hardening in her matted hair.

An explosion boomed in the street below. The building shook. The floor vibrated. She wobbled from the jolt, saw dust puffing up from between the floorboards and bits of ceiling sifting down. Instincts surged. She grabbed her cameras off the sofa, a pair of black-bodied Nikon Fs prepped with wide angle and telephoto lenses, and burst out the door of the apartment.

Racing down a set of steep rickety stairs, she entered the panic raging on Le Loi Street. The sulfurous smoke of a Vietcong bomb filled the air, stung her nostrils, and watered her eyes. Chaos strangled the area. Wounded lay on the ground drenched in blood and gore; people bent over them trying to help. Others cried or fled, caught in the throes of hysteria as they rummaged for safety. She raised a camera to her eye and panned the bedlam in a staccato of motor-driven clicks.

Choking on the fumes, Ellie leaned over and coughed bloody mucous onto the ground.

Oh crap! I'm bleeding.

She spit out more blood then wiped her mouth on her arm and looked past it to the café across the way, obvious site of the explosion. Splintered chairs and tables lay all over the street amid broken glass and shattered bodies. A bloodied Vietnamese man in torn Western dress staggered out of the café through flames, smoke, and floating cinders, waving his bleeding arms and yelling in a trinity of languages, "Get away. Bomb! Bomb!"

She ignored the warning and made a dash for the blazing ruins, only to run straight into the path of a speeding emergency wagon.

A stiff-legged man, head haloed in snow-white hair, dove in front of the ambulance and knocked her out of the way. He goggled at her in recognition, then in horror.

"*Diu dannazione!* Goddammit!" he hollered in Corsican, picking her up off the ground. "Ellie! Great gods in heaven! What has happened to you?"

"Huh?" she asked, casting a gape-mouthed stare at him,

unsure how she'd gotten to the street and stunned from nearly being struck by the ambulance.

"Here is Romo to the rescue," he said gently, a cigar stub bobbing between his lips as he spoke. He cradled her face in his hands, peered into her eyes. "*Ma pauvre*, my poor little one, it is your face, purple, bloodied, and a brutal cut on your lip. Do you know this?" Romo stared harder into Ellie's face.

"*Merde!* That asshole did it to you again, did he not?" Romo shouted in anger. "Last night? Oui, the blood on your face is dry, you were not in the blast. I must get you to hospital. Your nose, she is looking crooked."

If Romo was there with her, Ellie was safe. Her shoulders sagged in relief but her ears grew hot, and blackness moved in from the edges of her vision. She was overcome with embarrassment, suddenly recalling everything that had happened last night. Her eyes opened wide, and she hoped he couldn't see the vision she saw, but there was no hiding the truth from Romo.

"No, no. I'm fine," she managed as her eyes closed and her legs buckled. She collapsed into his arms.

2

FIVE MONTHS EARLIER, NOVEMBER 1967, NEW YORK CITY

Ellie Ketcham gazed at her image in the window of Schrafft's restaurant in the Hotel Carlyle. She, a green photojournalist, was about to meet with the famous author, Ben Stryker. She hardly knew him, having met him in her uncle's office, and now he'd asked to meet with her today to talk about something important. What in the world did it portend?

She arrived early and checked her coat before being shown to a table in the elegant dining room. She smoothed her red plaid slacks and adjusted the collar of her butter-yellow blouse beneath her forest green Hong Kong sweater. Green was her favorite color; it complemented her strawberry blonde hair and creamy complexion.

A young waitress approached. Her auburn pageboy framed porcelain skin. As she offered Ellie a menu, Ben lumbered in looking like Pig Pen with all his thoughts in a dust storm swirling around his head.

"Well, Ellie," he roared in his booming baritone, "I'm glad you could make it." He turned to the waitress.

"Ah, Mary Margaret." Even those words echoed throughout

the restaurant. *Does he have no other voice?* He shed his navy cashmere coat and sank into a chair. "We'll have two hot coffees and two butterscotch sundaes with your insanely rich coffee ice cream."

She curtsied and left.

"Lovely girl, Mary Margaret, helped us with *Hedgerow Dreams*," he said.

"I read the galleys of your book, Mr. Stryker."

"Call me Ben."

"Not only was your book engaging, but it was also informative. I hadn't realized the depth of the schism in Northern Ireland."

Ben nodded at the compliment. "The Irish have been coming to this country since the potato famine in the nineteenth century." He waved his arm, indicating the whole restaurant. "Almost every waitress you see here is from Ireland."

Mary Margaret returned and set down silver footed bowls in front of each of them, placing heavy white cups and saucers to the right, and poured strong steaming coffee before curtsying and walking away.

Ellie unfolded the heavy napkin and laid it across her lap as she eyed a large, perfect scoop of coffee ice cream, hot butterscotch sauce slumping over it, and whole toasted almonds sprinkled on top.

"Behold, perfection." Ben held his spoon up then plunged it into the sundae.

She rolled her eyes. "Between ice cream and the surprise of being interviewed by Ben Stryker, I feel like the young teen I was when my parents brought me here. . .

"What was the occasion? Your birthday?" Ben interrupted.

"No, it was after the winter I won five downhills and was being courted by the U.S. Alpine Ski Team. A celebration."

Ben nodded, scooping big bites of sundae into his mouth. She wasn't sure he was listening. The man obviously had a big appetite, and he created characters who were far bigger than life, as she'd discovered in the few novels of his she'd read. Her uncle Julian had introduced her to Ben and his wife, Sarah, in his office at Harcourt, Brace & World a couple of weeks earlier. The four of them had spent time together getting to know each other somewhat.

He leaned his chair back onto two legs, a serious look on his face.

"I'll not beat around the bush any longer, Eleanor Ketcham. I'm offering you an exceptional opportunity to have a role in the making of history."

She opened her mouth to speak. He held up his hand. She closed her mouth. Sounded like a bit of an overstatement.

"We've gotten a sense of you during the past weeks here in New York—both through getting to know you a bit and your uncle's recitations of your accomplishments as a freelance writer. Both Sarah and I are impressed with you. And of course your being the niece of my editor doesn't hurt, either. I've done my research; your journalism is high level. I'm a great judge of character, if I do say so myself, plus I've read your articles on war demonstrations, and Sarah and I have scrutinized your excellent photographs. We've reached the very definite conclusion you are exactly the right person at precisely the right time to take on the Vietnam portion of this book project for me."

He clattered his chair back down to four legs, punctuation for his comments.

She almost choked on her ice cream.

"I am especially impressed by your descriptions and word choices." He flapped a hand in the air and quoted: 'Vietnam, a nation openly displaying her wounds ...' Your reports and interviews with returning veterans are exemplary, not to mention that article on the father who lost his son in Da Nang. So touching. I could feel his grief. Your grasp of human nature when it comes up against, difficulties, shall we say, is incredible."

She was about to thank him for the offer and the compliment, but he spoke so fast she could hardly grasp what he was saying. His enthusiasm was pinging off the walls. She was riveted.

"At twenty-five, you're young enough to see through fresh eyes, yet old enough to have a solid background in journalism." He pointed a finger at her. "With you feeding me interviews and portraits, I'll have enough to complete my nonfiction book, *In Other Words*."

"Excuse me, but I can't imagine that I could fill your book with my interviews. This sounds like a stretch."

"Ah, you're thinking. Good. The bulk of the book is already completed with the discussions I've had with my own generation of colleagues with whom I've plodded through countless wars. All I need is the input from this new crop of thrill freaks who call themselves journalists, and *In Other Words* will be complete." He ran his hand through his thatch of salt and pepper hair.

Ellie considered his comments. "Why are you farming out an assignment that might fall short of your high standards? I'm curious as to why you're not going yourself?"

"With you on board, I won't have to leave home while my wife is pregnant," Ben said with a taste of hesitancy in this voice.

"Sarah's pregnant? Congratulations."

"I was hoping to keep that within the family, but you ask good questions. That's why she isn't joining us today, feeling a bit sluggish, sends her best."

Mary Margaret refilled their coffee cups. He splashed in three sugar cubes and cream and stirred noisily, holding Ellie's eyes without blinking.

"We've been planning a trip to Saigon for months. Sarah's pregnancy is the best news since pickled onions, but it also means she must stay in this hemisphere. I'll not leave her at her age. Complications are compounded for older mothers, and she's 37.

"Timing is everything, they say. I was bereft when that one door closed on me but then, bang, out of the blue, along comes Eleanor Ketcham. I don't know whether I have a guardian angel or your uncle to thank, but you've been brought into our lives for a reason. This assignment is right up your alley. I'm thrilled to underwrite your trip to Saigon to photograph and interview journalists for their perspective on the war. Shouldn't take long. Coupla weeks. I suspect you'll be at home among the pantheon of those brave and daring war journalists. Pay close attention."

He lit two Camels, handed her one, and sucked down a big drag.

She puffed on the strong, unfiltered cigarette and sipped her coffee. Her pulse quickened. To see the other side of war protests, to actually be working in a war zone, hanging out with other journalists, brave superstars, this was a once-in-a-lifetime opportunity. Her heart was beating so hard she looked up to see if he'd noticed.

He sat in silence, squeezing his cigarette between thumb and forefinger, and leaned in to level his solemn gaze directly at her.

"It's quite amazing how the stars have aligned, Ellie. You haven't realized it yet, kiddo, but you and I are kindred spirits. You have courage, intestinal fortitude, endless inquisitiveness, common sense, and most of all, balls. That's almost everything you need for this assignment."

"Excuse me, balls?"

He snorted. "I know how you fought your way through a police barricade into a riot between peaceniks and hawks and got battered pretty good. That took *cojones*. You paid the price for some hot-shit photographs. That gleam in your eye, same as mine. Our bellies burn with fire. You are exactly the right person at precisely the right time to take on the Vietnam portion of this project for me."

"You already said that."

"Seize the day."

"Ah," she said. "You say I have almost everything for this assignment. What am I lacking?"

"Experience!" He scratched his jaw. "That's something you're going to attain really fast by paying meticulous attention in a war zone. You have to listen to the people who matter. Understanding who they are is part of the learning process."

She held his gaze while her belly churned. "I've read the bylines of Stanley Karnow, Michael Herr, Seymour Hersh; I've seen the graphic photos of Tim Page and Sean Flynn. They're awe inspiring, but for a greenhorn far from the conflict, it's going to be a definite challenge to hold the attention of seasoned veterans."

"Don't be ridiculous. A good interviewer, and that is exactly what you are, can pull gems out of the most reluctant subject." Ben sat forward in his chair. "It'll be a whole new world for you. Nothing easy about war, but I've got you covered. Sarah and I have a colleague in Saigon, name of David Jenkins. Old hand. He'll brief you and make introductions. He knows everyone. He knows war. He'll point you in the right direction."

Ellie wanted to hold nothing back. "You're aware, Ben, that I lean a little to the left regarding our involvement in Vietnam? I gained empathy for the men who fight in this war when I inter-viewed veterans."

"Yeah, sure, more than aware of your slant. Your last piece in the *Village Voice* was heavy-handed about the brutality of this war and how it's subduing people into submission. And the piece where you implied that our forces use torture to find enemy strongholds and weapons caches. Wow."

He leaned back as if he were pleased with himself. Clap-ping his hands together, he pointed at her chest, lowering his voice to a confidential level. "I shall repeat myself, young lady, something I'm not inclined to do. Pay close attention. I'm not asking you to report on the war; your assignment is to report on the *people* who report on the war." He drew his napkin across his mouth and dropped it on the table.

"There is just one other issue. I'm sure it will please you even though you're quite impulsive. I promised your uncle that you will *not ever* enter any battle zones. Do we have an understanding and an arrangement?"

Ellie shivered at the thought then extended a hand across the table, which Stryker grasped firmly. "Absolutely."

"Here," Ben said as he pushed a folder across to Ellie. "Just some notes I made for you: a few warzone buzz words that might come in handy, and a list of preferred journalists if you can find them."

Ellie took the folder. "Thank you. We can discuss salary and details later, after I've cleared my calendar and completed the assignments I'm committed to. Thank you, Ben."

"Thank *you*, Ellie."

3

DECEMBER 31,1967, SAIGON

Ellie had been up in the sky for so long she fantasized she was an Arctic tern flying among the clouds on her long migration. She felt weightless in the slow drift. Pan Am Flight 247 floated forever in its approach over the braid of tributaries snaking through the Mekong Delta. The landscape glistened in the sun as the plane descended through thick, tangible heat waves and landed at Saigon's Tan Son Nhut airbase.

Ducking her head, she stepped through the doorway of the DC-8 and halted mid-step. Her throat filled to gagging with the heavy fumes of engine oil and jet fuel mixed with hints of cooked fish, rotting foliage, and excrement. She crinkled her nose and sipped a shallow breath of the suffocating air. The rank dampness was gauzelike, as if the air were filled with cobwebs.

The scream of jets blasting off mingled with the thunder of propeller-driven engines setting down. Huge mastodon aircraft taxied on a runway and landed, distended bellies hanging beneath their wings like giant alien insects. They disgorged endless troops, jeeps, and Howitzers from gaping rear maws.

Sleek, sharp-nosed jet fighters sped down another runway and slanted sharply into the sky. Smaller planes stacked up waiting for clearance from the concrete control tower that poked up like a square silo above a prairie. P-38s with bombs hooked to their bellies looked too heavy to take off, like an eagle Ellie once saw trying to lift a beaver out of the water and into the air. Beyond, gigantic Chinook helicopters with propellers front and back drifted down from the sky, some emblazoned with Red Cross emblems.

Uniformed men ran around like windup toys, loading and unloading cargo. GIs sat on their rucksacks in the shade of aircraft wings trying to stay cool.

Clearly one of the busiest airports in the world. She ached to pull out a camera, but passengers behind her were antsy to get down the steps.

Red camera rucksack on her back, she hitched her duffel to a shoulder and descended to the tarmac. Out of the tangle of people and passengers below, she heard her name being called. A sinuous man moved toward her, almost in slow motion. Mink-brown hair pulled back in a ponytail; a week's growth of beard feathering his olive skin; tall, lean, muscled body. *Woof.*

"Eleanor Ketcham?" he called.

"Yes," she said. "David Jenkins?"

"No," he replied when he reached her. "Nick Burrows. Jenkins had an assignment. Couldn't make it." He lifted the bags from her shoulders. "Welcome to Saigon."

He led her into the terminal and through the throng of uniformed men, civilians, Vietnamese adults and children.

As she breezed through customs, she noted Nick's astonishment.

"How'd you manage that?" He tossed back a glance at the customs officials.

"My boss told me he'd take care of it. He must've pulled strings with the US Embassy." She held her bags in her hands.

"Nice work if you can get it."

A child in camouflage shirt bumped into the back of Nick's knees, crumpling him to the floor. The boy leered at Ellie as he snatched her knapsack and bolted toward the entrance.

Ellie screamed after him. "My cameras." She stood rooted to the floor in shock.

Nick scrambled to his feet and ran after the kid. With his long legs, it took only seconds to close in on the boy. Grabbing him by the scruff of the neck, he retrieved the knapsack, pushed the boy away, and returned to Ellie's side. He held her bag out to her, big grin shining.

She hugged the knapsack. "Thank you." She trembled. She hadn't even gotten out of the airport before a near catastrophe struck. "I'd be lost without my cameras," she managed to mumble.

"Disaster averted," Nick said. "Shall we go?" He started walking then turned back to her. "If that happens again and you lose your stuff, Hong Kong's just a short flight away. You can get top-of-the-line cameras at a discount there."

At the curb, a rusted powder-blue Mercedes waited, driver's side door hanging open. "Your chariot, Mademoiselle." A smile sparked in his hazel eyes. Eyes that were startling and clear. Eyes that shot into her core. While he stashed her duffel in the back seat, she gazed at the terminal building, a wide, two-story structure with windows running its width, awnings above the second-floor windows punctuated by flags. It looked like almost any airport she'd seen, but she'd already learned it wasn't. Gripping her pack, she got into the car, Nick creaked the door shut, jumped in the other side, and drove off.

The sensation of having landed in an alien and hostile world dizzied her as he navigated the car through several checkpoints, stopping at each one to show their I.D.s then passing through when the bar lifted. Road signs were a jumble of symbols that looked like algebra sequences. Tall palms leaned lazily against the hazy sky, fronds fluttering like fizzling fireworks. He finessed the swarm of cars, bicycles, motorcycles, taxis, and rickshaws, sliding in and out of caravans of olive-green army trucks and jeeps.

"Ewww." Ellie wrinkled her nose at the muggy reek that was no longer masked by the stifling fumes of aviation gas exhaust.

He glanced over at her. "Ahhh, the bouquet of the Orient. Makes you want to reach for a gas mask, doesn't it? You've got your smoke from fires cooking mystery meats, rotting vegetation, fishy *nuak mam* sauces, and the stench of compressed humanity stewing in this godawful humidity. When I first got here, I could hardly breathe. The good news is you'll get used to it."

She liked the sound of his rich baritone voice as he pointed out landmarks: Presidential Palace, a twin-spired cathedral that looked like Notre Dame; Rex Hotel; opera house.

"I'm not a fan of the French Colonial rule," he said, "but there's no question they brought the elegance of their architecture to this backwater pocket of the world."

The sleepy Saigon she'd seen in an outdated travel guide of Southeast Asia was now rife with trucks and jeeps, old Renault taxis, and motor scooters that belched exhaust while rushing past graceful tamarind trees that shaded sidewalks. Men in black pajamas pedaled bikes transporting stalks of sugar cane in rear baskets as well as crates of ducks and other squawking creatures.

"Surreal parade," she murmured. Her head was on a swivel. Delicate women carried parasols, dressed in spanking white *ao dais*, the long, graceful mandarin-collared tunics worn over narrow slacks. Flower sellers decorated every corner with their vivid blooms.

"It'll be old hat in no time for you, Eleanor," he promised, braking to a stop in front of the Continental Palace Hotel. Its architecture was classic French, its name emblazoned in art deco lettering.

"It's Ellie," she corrected.

He reached across her and pushed open the rusty passenger side door. Hoisting her duffel from the back seat, he ferried it into the hotel, dropped it at the front desk, and stepped back. When she finished registering, he picked it up again and led her to the elevator. She kept a solid grip on her knapsack.

They walked side by side down the second-floor hallway to her hot and musty room. She released her grip on the pack and set it on the bed. Nick dropped her duffel on the floor.

"How about a cold drink?" he suggested, hitching his thumb toward the hall. "This way to the bar, a clever open-air gathering place."

"Let me just splash some cold water on my face. Meet you down there?"

He nodded and took off.

She stood below a ceiling fan with oversized blades that moved the humid air in ceremonious and leisurely revolutions without any detectable effect. She tilted her head up, mesmerized. It was testimony by an ineffective force—a metaphor for the American presence in Vietnam?

AS THE SUN gave up the day, a slight coolness wafted through the hotel. Ellie found Nick in the terrace restaurant that was open to Tu Do Street through tall arches.

"What's your pleasure?" he asked.

"Scotch and soda with lemon, please."

He ordered that and a vodka tonic with lime for himself. "Plenty of ice," he told the waiter.

"First, Ellie, this is iodine," he said, holding out a handful of tablets. "It'll keep you from getting sick. Swallow two with your drink and then whenever you have water. If there's no water or ice in my drink, I don't take the iodine. Seems to be fine. I haven't gotten sick."

"I appreciate it, thanks, but I'll pass."

They sipped in companionable silence for several minutes, savoring the coolness of the drinks.

"Alcohol on ice cures just about everything." Nick upended his glass and slipped off his barstool. "I've got a meeting, but let's meet up for dinner and celebrate New Year's Eve." He flashed her a bright smile. "How 'bout it?"

"Sounds good."

"I'll reserve us a table. See you here at nine."

She watched him walk away, his rhythmic gait loose and long-legged.

WHITE TABLE LINENS, an arrangement of votive candles, and a bucket of champagne greeted Ellie as she entered the terrace restaurant at nine. Nick stood and bowed then pulled a chair out for her. She scanned the terrace. *Who are all these well-dressed diners? Tourists? Nope. They don't look to be military. Businesspeople? What kind of business is done in a war zone?* She turned her attention back to Nick.

"So, Ellie, tell me, what in the blazes are you doing here? You some kind of war freak?"

Nick poured the bubbly and handed her a glass.

"Serendipity. I had a meeting in New York City with Ben Stryker, who in case you don't know, is a legendary war correspondent and novelist." The sounds of street traffic and foreign languages from the tables around them were a distraction. She spoke louder to maintain her focus. "He works with my uncle, who's his editor, at Harcourt, Brace & World. Something about

Stryker was irresistibly intriguing. When he discovered my yearning to seek out the furthest limits of any experience, he said I had to come to Saigon on his behalf and interview journalists for his new book on the personal side of wartime coverage."

"Hold on." Nick held up a hand. "You meet a guy and the next minute you're on a plane to the Vietnam War? Why did you want to come to this shithole in the first place?"

Ellie thought about the comment. "It does sound kind of odd, doesn't it? His wife Sarah is pregnant, and he didn't want to leave her alone. Little did he know he was offering me a challenge I have always craved: to dig into something substantive."

"Seems we both have generous uncles," Nick commented as if he hadn't heard her words about why she'd arrived. "They're part of the family, protective and loving, yet distant at the same time."

Curious statement. Too personal and a bit negative. She let it slide.

As waiters delivered an elaborate *prix fixe* menu, she thought about what to tell him. Simplicity, she decided. "I'm an only child. Gentle mother, authoritarian father who let nothing get in the way of his goals."

"You too?" Nick blurted. "I've got an autocrat for a father, who never had time to listen to me or to what I wanted to do with my life."

Irritation filled his eyes, bushy eyebrows lowered like storm clouds. He was so transparent with his feelings; he wore them on his face and in his eyes.

"Change of subject?" she suggested.

He reached for her hand, squeezing it. "You're breathtaking, Eleanor Ketcham. I can see there's more to you than you care to reveal."

"There might be a compliment in there somewhere, but I'm not sure."

"Definite compliment, Ellie."

Time shimmered and telescoped through the hours. They laughed and shared thoughts about life, made crystalline by the glasses of champagne they drank. The bubbly contributed to Ellie's sensation of philosophical flight as their words lifted into the sky and became stars. She couldn't tell where her words ended and his picked up. It wouldn't take much for her to swoon. How had she found a like-minded soul right off the bat in this foreign land? Was it Kismet they had so much in common? Both came from New England stock, both had over-bearing fathers and protective uncles, and attuned political outlooks. Dazzling man. Being with him was thrilling and comfortable at the same time. Might make her assignment interesting.

4

———

"Feelin' groovy." Ellie sang Simon and Garfunkel's cheery song as she swept aside the mosquito netting and leapt out of bed. "I am ready for this project. Bring it on."

After what passed as a shower with its trickle of tepid water, she followed the concierge's directions to a quiet garden in an interior courtyard of the hotel. Met by the sweet aroma of tropical flowers, she canted her nose up and inhaled appreciatively.

"You're smelling the plumeria," Nick said, strolling up to her. "I don't even smell it anymore." He pulled out a chair for her. "Tell you what, let's start the new year off with fresh-from-the-oven French bread and strong coffee."

She beamed at him and sat. "Graham Greene stayed in this hotel. I read *The Quiet American* on my flight over. There's a strong sense of the past here."

"You're right; although to me it's the musty fog of oppression."

Ellie ignored his doom and gloom. As she spread rich French butter and raspberry preserves on her baguette, she wondered what had brought such disappointment to him. She preferred looking to the positive. "I think I'll take a walk down to the river after breakfast."

He checked his watch. "Brunch, more like it. Want some company?"

"No thanks, I'd prefer to explore on my own."

"Enjoy but remember what happened at the airport. Leave your purse here and stuff whatever you need deep in your pockets."

"I understand."

She strolled the few blocks to the Saigon River and back then a few blocks beyond the hotel. Sensory overload. A nap was called for.

Later in the afternoon, he showed up at her door.

"It's almost five," he announced.

"Okay. And the significance is?"

He snorted. "Significance? Five O'clock Follies. Ritual briefing session for the press. New Year's Day is no exception." His tone was smug. "Come on. I'll explain on the way."

She grabbed her camera bag and hung her credentials around her neck, saying a silent thank you to Stryker for providing them.

"You don't need cameras for this."

She ignored his comment and followed him out the door. "Stryker told me about the Follies. Is it true it's all bullshit about progress made in the war?"

"You'll see." He picked up his pace. A couple of blocks away, at the corner of Le Loi and Nguyen Hue streets, he flashed a pass to a Marine guard at the Joint United States Public Affairs Office (JUSPAO) building and led Ellie through a confusing maze of hallways. In an air-conditioned auditorium, journalists slouched in theater seats, cigarette smoke roiling around their heads like cartoon dialogue balloons. They were crammed in, like squeezing into a dress two sizes two small, she imagined.

Nick found them a spot against a side wall and pointed out a few of the correspondents.

"There's Halberstam, *New York Times*." Her eyes tracked where he pointed, and she put faces to names she recognized from bylines: "Richard Pyle, UPI bureau chief; over there, the team from Reuters; and oh, there's Jenkins, UPI. Guess he's back from his assignment."

His pointing stopped at a curly haired man dressed in a white, open-collar Oxford shirt tucked into jeans. They were belted, pulled tight. Like he was wearing an older brother's pants. Brown-and-white shoes stuck out of his pants.

Nick followed her gaze. "Really? You're a fan of saddle shoes?"

"Let's go meet him. Ben and Sarah told me so much about him." She started toward Jenkins.

Nick tapped her shoulder. "Not now. The fun's about to begin." He settled against the wall. "Lean back and enjoy the show, where intel is so far off the mark of reality it's ludicrous."

Richard Pyle, sitting in an aisle seat near them, swiveled his head at Nick's comment and smirked at Ellie. "Welcome to the longest playing tragicomedy in Southeast Asia's theater of the absurd."

She was amused by the skepticism, which, she found, often masked true opinions.

"This is supposedly the official report of the day's happenings," Nick said. "First, we get news of civilian interest then briefs by each of the military branches." An Army major marched to the well-lit podium, cleared his throat, and began reading from a sheaf of papers in his hands.

"American casualties have reached 10,000, compared to 5,000 same time last year," the stiff talking head announced. A few erect military types stood behind the speaker. One of them, a civilian, dipped his head at Nick.

"Who's that?" Ellie asked, curious.

"The uncle I mentioned. Retired military. Now in public affairs."

Correspondents raised their hands and called out questions, challenging the major, whose cryptic delivery quickly devolved into visible exasperation: red face, trembling hands, and rustling papers. He stuttered. An undercurrent of boos, caustic laughter, and mock applause serenaded the nervous song and dance act.

Oh, my, this is a joke, exactly how Ben said it would be: "Government theater blazing with persuasion, appeasement, and the attempt to win approval."

Nick leaned over to whisper in Ellie's ear. "No facts anywhere in these reports. Fiction. Thin veneer of falsity masquerading as truth."

As the briefing broke up, Nick anchored his palm in the small of Ellie's back and steered her toward the door. She shook him off; she didn't like being handled. "What's your hurry?"

Jenkins approached and Nick made the introductions, with reluctance, judging from his sour expression. "Ellie, this is the great David Jenkins," he said. "A legend here, or at least in his own mind." He waggled his fingers, à la Groucho Marx. "Jenkins, meet Ellie Ketcham, Ben Stryker's associate."

Jenkins rolled his eyes; they sparkled with delight when they focused upon Ellie, authoritative and confident. His whole manner suggested he was much younger than his forty-something years Ben had described. "Hi there, Ellie," he drawled in a voice as smooth as cream. "Glad to meet you. I'm sorry I couldn't make it to the airport to pick you up, but I just got back from Nha Trang. I look forward to facilitating your assignment."

Ellie opened her mouth to speak, but Nick was faster.

"I can see Ellie gets what she's looking for."

David's parried, "That's the least I'd expect. Whatever *we* can do for you, Ellie."

She noted the slight sarcasm and southern lilt in his voice. Matched the climate.

"I don't know about you guys, but I'm famished. Let's go back to the hotel for dinner," she suggested. "David, you'll join us?"

"I'm sure he has other plans," Nick cracked.

"Actually, I'd be honored. Celebrate the New Year."

A VIETNAMESE waiter in white dinner jacket seated them at a table on the open-sided terrace that ran along the front of the hotel. Ellie sniffed floral perfume in the twilight air. "Heavenly," she sighed. "Plumeria?"

"Also called frangipani," David said.

"Yes. First deep breath I've taken since I landed"— she glanced at the date on her watch with a look of surprise— "yesterday."

"Cocktail, Ellie?" David turned to the waiter who had appeared.

"Thanks. Scotch, splash of soda, twist of lemon, lots of ice."

"Bourbon neat for me. Nick?"

"Vodka soda lime."

While they waited for their drinks, Ellie absorbed everything around her: people drinking and dining alongside them on the terrace—she even caught a few words of Russian—and the noisy parade of military convoys, farting Lambretta and Honda motorcycles vying for space with *cyclo-pousse* bicycles on Tu Do Street just beyond the restaurant. Details were key in journalism. She turned back to the table.

"And I thought New York was a busy city."

"Drink to life and the passing show." David clinked Ellie's glass. "Old Southern toast. Tell me how you know Ben and Sarah? Are you from Aspen, too?"

She shook her head. "I met them in New York. I'm a photo-journalist. Never been to a war zone before, but I've never been good at resisting a challenge either, although the unknown can cause anxiety."

"I hear you, darlin'," David said. "From what Ben told me, you're more than up to the task he's given."

"I hear Stryker's got a reputation as a bully, but that he's a helluva storyteller," Nick interjected.

"You can't be a wimp *and* one of the most famous and admired authors in the world," Ellie parried. "Stryker's just warming up. Only eight bestselling novels, historical fiction with political overtones." She slid a sly wink at Jenkins.

"Well," David continued, "I can tell you Ben is high on your abilities, Ellie. He and I put together a list of reporters and photographers for you to talk to, so we can get started as soon as you're up to it."

"He gave me a list too. How soon is soon? I'm ready now. From what I've gathered, you might split for an assignment at any moment."

He snorted. "For sure. Helping you gives me a chance to honor the bond Sarah, Ben, and I formed in the early years when the war was not yet a war but the onset of a failing manipulation of a divided nation. I'd do anything for them, and I look forward to introducing you to the journalistic front line in Saigon. How long you planning to be here?"

"Ben figures a couple of weeks, maybe a month at the outside," she replied.

"Good luck with that," Nick quipped.

What was that about?

"Why don't I order for you, Ellie." He turned to the waiter who stood by their table. "The lady will have the Moules Marinières and I'll have the cheese soufflé. David, you like your frog's legs Provençale."

"Exactly so, Nick." David said as the waiter nodded.

"How do you know what I want?" Ellie blurted with a huff.

"Just wait till you taste them, heaven in a shell."

"So, why don't *you* have them?" She glanced at the menu and then the waiter. "I'll have the duck."

Nick grinned. "I like you, Ellie, you're straightforward. You pull no punches." He took a healthy swig of his cocktail. "How about if I order the mussels for the table?"

"Sure." Ellie shook her glass, which was practically empty, and upended the melting ice cubes into her mouth.

Nick modified the order and the waiter retreated.

"So, David, Sarah said you're with UPI. Might be a good place for us to start?"

"Aren't you the eager beaver," Nick said.

David responded, ignoring Nick's comment. "Yes, ma'am. I've seen a lot cycle through the UPI bureau since '62."

"Jenkins has the big job," Nick interjected again. "Senior correspondent. I'm a lowly stringer."

"Regardless, Nick, you're both doing the same thing: informing your readers of the truth. I hope." She glanced from David to Nick. "Where do you guys live?"

"I have a place on a street lined with old French Colonial villas not far from here," David said. "Big old house a passel of journalists calls home base."

"I'm one of them," Nick added. "Very grateful to Jenkins for giving me a room."

David went on. "Sarah tells me you're a good listener, Ellie, and insightful. That'll certainly serve you well interviewing reporters. We can be a garrulous bunch."

Ellie nodded. David took a sip of his bourbon. "And you're a photographer, too. We capture events and images with angles that words can only hint at, don't you agree?"

"For sure. Seeing things from two perspectives has taught me lateral thinking. When I interview, I look for what's not being said, which I try to catch in my photos, as well. Connects the two for a stronger piece."

"Might work back home, but the camera bares the ugliness of war." Nick set down his empty glass with a thunk. His nostrils flared. "I'm so tired of the high and mighty attitude of our country."

Ellie coughed. "That's some *non sequitur*, Nick."

He gazed at a spot beyond the table, rambling on like a tank over uneven ground. "Never acknowledging these people live by a completely different set of rules than we do. Hah!" He banged a fist on the table. "Whatever happened to championing the underdogs, poor fuckers? We act so superior. But I've seen firsthand what happens when you defend people's rights. You make a difference in their lives. I marched in Selma so Blacks could have access to good education. We achieved something there. Here, the only thing we're defending is our hubris. Imposing our beliefs on a people who don't want us and haven't wanted *any* of their centuries of invaders, for that matter."

"I've always thought war was a match between rivals, not David versus Goliath," she said.

"Hah," Nick said, his mouth pinched. "You've obviously lived a sheltered life. This is the Vietnamese David against the almighty American Goliath."

She threw a silent plea to David.

"Where's this coming from, Nick?" David asked, obviously catching her look.

"It's this war. You know it's fucked up. Everyone suffers except the few profiteers." Nick squinted, his eyes dark and flinty.

"Like whom?" she asked.

"You'll find out soon enough."

"The US government does seem to be using sleight of hand," David suggested, obviously seeking calmer ground. "As for the *official* reports issued by Public Affairs, they're not confirmed by the facts on the ground."

"Exactly," Nick agreed with a vigorous nod. "We're failing to tell the simple story of an imperialistic power occupying a third-world country with a corrupt government."

"Lot of smoke and mirrors," David said.

"A whole bone pile of corruption," Nick emphasized.

"Surely you can dig beyond the deceptions and find the truth?" Ellie looked from one to the other.

"You'd think so," David responded. "But when the news comes from our government, through its briefings and press releases, it's hard to ferret out the facts unless you venture outside the protection of the concertina wire. We use live sources as often as we can and balance them with government intel."

"And this so-called *enemy*," Nick said. "They're stronger than we'll ever be. We'll never beat them or even subdue them. You push one down, three more pop up. We have no idea how to fight them. They're guerrillas, and what do we do? Bomb the snot out of villages full of innocent civilians."

"Maybe we're piling too much on Ellie?" David suggested.

Ellie tuned into Nick's frustration. His intensity rose like bile in the back of her throat. She'd never considered this aspect of war reporting. Ben would sink his teeth into the challenge.

Hell, never mind Ben. I'm the one who's here.

"This is no time for blinders," Nick said.

She plucked a mussel from its shells, savoring it. "Never had mussels before. Delicious."

"Imagine that," Nick snarked.

Ellie registered the music of forks on china plates, the clinking of ice in Nick's vodka, the rise and fall of nearby conversations, the sweetness of plumeria.

Muffled gunfire sounded in the distance. How far away was

it? She darted looks around the terrace, but no one else seemed to notice. Were they ignoring it or were they used to it? Underneath all their words, Ellie heard, or felt more than heard, a drumbeat, low and insistent, signifying danger or excitement. She wasn't sure which, but the sensation was arousing.

If these two men were any indication of what the Saigon correspondents were like, she couldn't wait to launch into interviews. Taking the napkin from her lap and folding it, she grasped the table edge and leaned forward.

"How about starting tomorrow, David?"

Nick leapt up from his seat. "Gotta hit the loo."

Ellie watched him weave through the tables. Cocking her head toward him, she turned to David and whispered, "What's with your friend?"

"It's his passion to expose the faults of our nation. He has balls to speak out publicly."

"Isn't that foolish?"

"But that's Nick. He doesn't care."

"I get it. Listen, I'm a little nervous, David. How about a trial run, with someone less—"

"Not necessary. According to Ben, you're his top dog and he expects you to act like it. Just dive into the deep end of the pool. I'll check my schedule." He settled the bill for their dinner and rose, swallowing the last of his cocktail. "Happy New Year, Ellie."

"Happy New Year to you, David." She leaned back, reassured. *Just first-time jitters.*

Nick returned as David walked away, radiating a lopsided grin at Ellie.

"May I offer you an after-dinner drink? Make up for my gloomy observations?"

She gazed into his hazel eyes. Clear now. His darkness had been replaced by another kind of appetite. She gave him a sleepy glance and extended her hand.

"Tempting though your offer is, jet lag's pulling me to my bed."

He took her hand, raised it to his lips, and brushed it with a kiss, meeting her eyes. "*A bientôt.*"

She trod up the stairs to her room on the second floor. What might have happened if she'd said yes?

Within the odd cocoon of mosquito netting, she flopped onto the bed, legs and arms spread out *à la* Leonardo da Vinci's Vitruvian Man.

"Tomorrow is a new day," she whispered and gazed up at her newly discovered mute seer, the ceiling fan, before she fell into a coma of sleep.

5

———————

Anticipation tickled her awake. Eager to begin work, charged by their dinner conversation, and curious about this fellow Nick. She wondered why she was so attracted to a man who was possessive without reason and had an attitude. The type of person for whom she would not have time. Was it the similarities in their backgrounds? Was he a wayward soul, his spirit apparently as free as hers? Or was it because he was a member of a war-time press corps? *Am I a groupie? Oh, Ellie-Belly, quit pretending. He's a hunk. Just admit it.* She sighed and polished off breakfast with gusto in the terrace restaurant. There was a rhythm in Saigon; she sensed a thrumming beneath the sounds of the city, as if there were an underground engine running the war.

On the way back to her room, the concierge handed her a note.

Ellie, and so it begins. Meet me for tea at the Cercle Sportif, rue Chasselloup-Laubat, this afternoon at 4. Not far from the Continental. Take a cyclo-pousse *or walk. DLJ*

Tranquility settled around her the minute she walked through the gates. Cercle Sportif Saïgonnais swooned with the romanticism of a 1940s movie set. She strolled into manicured and grassy gardens, imagining the gardeners morphed into Vietcong by night. She shivered at the idea, even as the hot sun beat down.

She was perspiring and glad she'd twirled her hair into a soft bun on top of her head rather than let it hang on her neck. Eyes closed, she savored the silence, gradually becoming aware of the pop of tennis balls and, way in the distance, the disturbing *thunk* of shells exploding.

"Just another country club," said a voice beside her. She opened her eyes to see David Jenkins nodding his head. "Quite another dimension, isn't it?"

"Well, as I recall from my study of the American Civil War," she replied, "spectators gathered from a distance to witness battles. What's occurring here is somewhat similar since war and normalcy reside in the same site."

"Mm-hmm. Astute observation. Good juxtaposition. And such a welcome respite from the bruisings of war. Shall we mosey on over to poolside? It's a pleasant place to sit and chat." He led her through the building and out back, where a swimming pool sparkled in the sun, and men and women sipped umbrella drinks on an expansive patio. Children giggled and shrieked in their play.

A shell exploded in the distance. No one even flinched. She looked at David for his assessment.

Jenkins winked. "I see your point about the normalcy of war."

Ellie gawked at the laid-back vision surrounding her. "Is this the general attitude of Saigon? Immunity to war? What happens outside the city limits is just a sideshow?" With a glance at David's jungle attire, including boots instead of saddle shoes, she was glad she'd worn the khakis Ben and Sarah had bought for her.

She followed as he walked among the tables until he

reached a round, umbrellaed table close to the pool's edge. Sliding her red knapsack off her shoulders, she took a seat and inhaled the nostalgic scent of Coppertone.

"Guess I'm already used to Saigon's culture. I smell the relaxing scent of tropical flora and hear the tinkling of cocktail glasses, the squeals of children playing, all enhanced by the distant sounds of war," she commented.

David drawled a smile. "You have the makings of an old hand. Your eye and ear for details will serve you well." He eyed her khakis. "If you put a few wrinkles in your duds and roll up those sleeves, it'll look like you've been around a while."

She glanced from her pressed duds to his well-worn clothing. "Aha, diminish the greenhorn."

"Reminds me how we used to take brand new jeans, trample them under our horses' hooves, and throw them in the trough until they were broken in." He laughed.

A white-shirted waiter approached and took David's order for two lemonades with mint. "Even though I suggested tea, lemonade sounds so much more refreshing, doesn't it?"

When the tall frosty drinks were served, David guzzled his lemonade. "Thirsty. I've been thinking about how best to proceed with your project," he said in a formal tone. She pulled a pen and notebook from her pack.

As he counted individuals and news outlets on his fingers, she became aware of a man standing patiently beside the table blotting out the sun. She glanced up. He looked close to Stryker's age. His tanned face, with its nose like the prow of a boat, was as wrinkled as his fatigues, which were smudged with dirt and smelled the least bit ripe. A hefty belly strained the buttons of his plaid shirt. His gray-streaked brown hair was mussed, and two bushy sideburns threatened to overtake his cheeks. She had the distinct impression that within this hulk of a man lay a forceful figure. There was something formidable about him. The vibe was irresistible.

He winked at her as if he heard her thoughts. "Hi ho, David, where'd you find this lovely nugget of gold?"

"Hey, Jerry, Happy New Year, you're right on time. I can always count on you showing up," David said as Jerry pulled out a chair and sat. "Ellie, you should know this man. He's a rapscallion of a reporter with the *Herald Tribune*. Jerry Forrest, meet Ellie Ketcham, photojournalist."

Jerry grasped Ellie's extended hand in both of his. "Always happy to meet a fellow outlaw."

"Take a seat, Jerry." David snorted. "Ellie's here on assignment for Ben Stryker. He's writing a book about the journalistic front line and how reporters strategize keeping their wits about them to stay sane."

"If you can keep your head when all about you are losing theirs...'" Ellie quoted.

"Amen," Jerry growled.

"I'm encouraging Ellie to also consider the challenges we face getting our stories printed or told in their original form."

Jerry sniggered. "That, unfortunately, is an age-old challenge."

She acknowledged with a nod. "I guess it's a given in any war, especially this one, from what I witnessed yesterday at the Follies. I've experienced editors changing what I wrote, sometimes altering the intent. Must be much worse here. Especially with editors so far off the firing line." She relished having taken the first step toward equal ground with these grizzled thrill freaks.

"You've got that right," David said to Ellie then turned to Jerry. "We're lining up reporters for her to interview. You interested?"

Jerry snorted. "Interviewing the interviewers. That's rich. We don't spend a lot of time analyzing what we do. Our heads are down; we're grunts fighting different kinds of battles than the servicemen. But doing our jobs for the people back home just the same, we hope."

Ellie and David were silent. She'd learned to trust the lulls that came up during interviews, how not to jump in with filler comments and thereby choke off some gem. She sipped her lemonade and waited.

The waiter returned.

Jerry looked up from lighting a cigar and eyed their drinks. "I'll have what they're having with a shot of whiskey on the side." He puffed, and, as the tobacco caught, heavy, aromatic smoke wreathed them. Ellie inhaled deeply. It was a smell from childhood; her father had smoked cigars.

Jerry squinted at her through the smoke. "I'm familiar with Stryker's work," he said. "But why send a lovely young thing to do his work? He's no chicken. He pull up lame or something?"

"He was all set to come, but his wife is pregnant," Ellie said, "and as much as he yearned to do this work himself, he didn't want to abandon her."

"Sarah O'Neill? She'll make a fine mother. Hell's bells. If I recall, she was always a nurturer. When she met Ben, in Hue, fireworks. Match made in heaven." He scratched a sideburn and turned bloodshot eyes on Ellie. "Well, if you're looking to chronicle some local propaganda and willing to tolerate an old sod like myself, happy to oblige if I can."

Sweet Jesus. David's smooth. He set this up as if it were meant to be.

She exhaled. "Terrific. I know David's been here a while. How long have *you* been here?"

"Oh, a few years, I guess. Easy to lose track of time."

"Jerry's being modest," David interjected. "He's the definition of an old hand, brought a lot of us novices up to speed."

Ellie flipped to a clean sheet in her notebook and picked up her pen.

Jerry waved a hand at David. "This war teaches a harsh

lesson. Our assignments should come with hazard pay. The rose-colored glasses I had on when I got here distorted the real picture. Like everyone else, I believed the US was here to save the Vietnamese from communism." He waved his cigar in the air. "We rode in on our white chargers, only to have our lofty sentiments trampled. The whole fucking war is based on lies. First domino to fall was the Gulf of Tonkin incident, as you might remember?"

"The trumped-up attacks by North Vietnamese on American ships?" she asked.

"Yeah, horrid manipulative lie. It produced the resolution that drop-kicked the conflict into gear. So, right off the bat there's a lie at the line of scrimmage."

The waiter delivered their drinks. "No iodine?" Ellie asked.

"Hate those things. They give me the farts. Next domino was propping up the corrupt Diem government because it served our cause, then, bam, replaced them. After that, the dominos started falling faster. There were the inflated numbers of 'successfully' pacified hamlets and provinces, in which the US converted North Vietnamese sympathizers into champions of the South's corrupt government. I love that one. Total fantasy."

He tipped the whiskey into his lemonade and took a long pull. "And who could forget the excessively inflated body counts we're force-fed by the military? Jesus, talk about misguided."

Ellie glanced at David, who nodded agreement. Her mind flashed on the ceiling fan, and she coughed into her hand. "Assuming it's a moral issue," she began, reacting to the disenchantment in Jerry's tone, "Why do you keep on doing what you do?"

"It's just what I do," Jerry answered. He crossed his arms over his chest, watched the bathers in the pool then turned to her as if the answer was obvious. "But I'll tell you what, I've kept my own notes on what I've seen. We all started out virgins, believed in everything from Mom to cherry pie. But then it spoiled, and we had to clean up the mess and figure out how to handle the lies while doing our jobs, defending liberty, keeping the lights on for the folks at home." He pointed with his cigar, deploying stray ashes, to punctuate his comments. "A delicate balance of cynicism, objective reporting, and whiskey. No problem." He tilted his head back and snorted.

She recognized a difference in tone from Nick's impassioned rants. Jerry's were several layers more sophisticated. He didn't seem as personally affected as Nick. Or he could be hiding it behind his buffoonish manner. Maybe because he'd been at it longer, could look at it objectively, and had made his peace with it. Or maybe he was grateful to be alive after his experiences, certain the nonsense was trivial compared to death.

The contrast in reactions to this conflict varied among the few journalists she'd met so far. Then there was David, who seemed the least troubled by it all. Maybe it was a laid-back Southern thing. He struck her as an "it is what it is" kind of guy.

The waiter approached and handed David an envelope.

"Intervals are so precious in this war," he said absently, glancing at the note. "Necessary breaks in the action, eh, Jerry?"

"You ain't just whistlin' Dixie," Jerry shot back. "Well, in your case ..."

"What is it, David?" Ellie asked, noticing the change in his expression.

"Here today, gone tomorrow. I'm going up to Khesanh. Something's brewing. Not sure what, but UPI wants photographic feet on the ground."

She crooked her head at him, hoping for more.

"North Vietnamese Army's been building its forces near the airbase north of here. It's in a big valley, and Westmoreland is probably scared shitless at the prospect of another Dienbienphu situation." He paused for a moment, looking toward the muffled mortar thunks in the distance. "This could be some kind of diversion. Hope it doesn't catch those grunts with their pants down."

"Something wicked this way comes," Jerry said.

"Ray Bradbury," Ellie murmured, looking up from her notetaking.

"Sci-fi." He waved his hand at the surroundings and took a swig of his doctored lemonade.

Her head swung from one man to the other as she absorbed every word. "No idea when you'll be back, right?" she asked.

"You catch on quick, girl," Jerry said approvingly. "Don't sweat it, David. I'll finish this conversation with Ellie. That is, if I'm not called away, too." He winked at her, taking a meditative toke on his cigar as he mulled something over.

David left. Jerry ordered another round. "Make mine a double." He scratched his back on his chair. "As it happens, I've known Ben Stryker a long time. He rambled around this hemisphere for years. Always suspected he was CIA. He was one of those daredevil journalists who dangled his brash invincibility in front of the communists. Afraid of nothing. Waltzed through fire without burning his feet."

Ellie enjoyed the way Jerry used his cigar as emphasis. He wore the scattered ashes like dandruff.

"Kept to himself until he met Sarah O'Neill. Come to think of it, it's a wonder he made it out of here alive. Got to hand it to him, Ben's the real thing. And me," he scoffed, poking his chest with a thumb, "shit for brains. Not smart enough to get out."

The edges of her vision fluttered the way they did whenever something monumental happened. She was in the presence of history. Not a pushy charmer like Nick, Jerry was warm in an enveloping way. She shook her head to bring her mind into sharp focus despite her excitement and asked the most obvious question. "Why do you stay?"

Jerry coughed. "No offense. Your question's a good one. Give me a sec to collect my thoughts." He rubbed his eyes with the heels of his hands. "The way I see it, there are plenty of topics a journalist can cover: battles, politics, finance, health, climate, and so on. In all these areas, a higher power says the total truth cannot be revealed. Ergo, the censorship that cloaks our ability as war correspondents to relate the total story."

The drinks arrived; he downed his whiskey in one gulp. "Journalists, in my estimation, are the tools that prevent a dictatorship from creeping into the fragile democracy of our nation. It's my duty to chronicle the events of this fucked-up war, hoping the guts of truth dribble out. I believe in what I'm doing, and I also believe I speak for many of my fellow reporters."

She'd never questioned truth. It was simply part of her makeup. "Truth is all important."

"Hard to find it sometimes. War is littered with lies. Alas, hope springs eternal."

This man has such fierce pride in his mission. Pay close attention, Ellie. She stopped her notetaking. A Pandora's box opened? She acknowledged her obligation to Stryker, which she wasn't about to ignore, but a new impulse began to trickle through her bloodstream. Could she see for herself the firsthand experience of a journalist in the field of battle?

"How do you keep it all in balance? Objectivity is key, but how do you maintain it here?"

He narrowed his eyes. "Become a duck bobbing at water level. Keep your wits about you despite the bullets flying around your head. You've got to tell your story." He snorted, eyeing the tennis courts. "A matter of keeping your eye on the ball. That enough metaphors for you?"

He scratched his ribs with both hands, snorting as he did so. His moves were comical, and yet his buffoonery seemed to conceal a great inner strength. He pointed a long, thick finger at her.

"Stepping into this quagmire of a career will suck you into a whirlpool of untidiness, disorganization, frustration, bureaucracy, and deception, and will confront you with walls you cannot go through. Still, there are those of us who are gripped by the challenge and can't resist its lure."

She followed the rhythm of his words, the gravel in his voice, and watched emotions move like clouds across the landscape of his ruddy face. With his tide of words and images, he brought her onto his island of war.

"I'm no fortuneteller, Ellie, but with your honorable intentions, you will engage, argue, and attack to uncover the truth. It will grow into a kind of lust, a fervor." He exhaled as if what he was about to say was a confession. "I see through your naivety and desire." He stubbed his cigar in the ashtray with what she thought was deflation. "I was exactly like you way back when, and I'm still here."

There's hope if you keep after it. This man cannot be defeated.

As the tension released from his stony face, she sucked in a lungful of air, surprised she'd been holding her breath. Ideas swirled in her head followed by confusion, followed by flashes of challenging downhills and other thoughts and plans. He had presented her with something that took her breath. *Stop.* She took several moments to calm, wondering if she was going to act on any of her instincts. What surprises would come next?

6

L eft alone at the table after Jerry departed, Ellie focused on bringing her breath and heartbeat back into normal range. She reflected on the past two hours. Jerry Forrest was a curious blend of fact hunter, adventure seeker, and truth monger. Not only did he remind Ellie of her moral duty, but he also ignited a fire in her belly and grounded her to the reality of the situation she had walked into. Not only did his words make sense, but they also shook her foundation. He had the objectivity Nick didn't, and objectivity mattered in war reporting, obviously, as it did in all journalism.

Damn, she'd forgotten to take his picture, she'd been so absorbed in what he had to say. He'd managed to elevate the majesty and importance of her calling. She had to share her epiphany. Tearing a sheet out of her notebook, she wrote:

Dear Uncle Julian, Here I am on the other side of the world. The Orient! Saigon is exotic. A river town with the elegance of Paris and all its French architecture and food. Must've been a beautiful sleepy place before this war. The sidewalks are filled with Vietnamese and American soldiers, a definite clash of cultures, and there's a nervous undercurrent beneath the pageantry like the rabbling drone of unhealthy air conditioning. As if everyone has chosen to ignore the possibility of an impending disaster, me included. I have to admit it's part of the thrill. It staggers me how much I anticipate the challenge. It's the chance to participate in something way beyond my experience. I can take part in exposing the cause and futility of war to the world. If I thought so before, I now know with absolute certainty I've found my mission. Granted, it's all talk so far. The desire is burning in me, but how to accomplish it is yet to be unveiled. I'm within the enclosure of Saigon and in the safekeeping of seasoned journalists so there's no cause for alarm. Which will please Ben. Love, Ellie

~

EARLY ONE MORNING a few days later, she woke to a sharp rapping. It took a few seconds to realize the sound was live and not part of her dream. She parted the mosquito netting, slipped into her kimono robe, a Christmas gift from Sarah, and moved to the door.

She opened it to see Nick Burrows framed in the doorway.

"Nick?" Half question, half groggy welcome. She flushed, and a giggle escaped.

"Top o' the morning, Lady Eleanor." He strode toward her as if he were going to take her in his arms. She stepped back. He smiled.

"Listen," he said, "I know you're here to gather material for Ben Stryker, but I get the hit you might be interested in seeing the war a little more up close and personal. Am I right?"

Was Nick some kind of mind reader? How could he be aware of her itch so soon after she'd been struck by the rash of excitement to wade into the unknown? "Could be," she said with caution. "You have something specific in mind?"

"Been talking to my contacts, and I managed to hitch us a ride with the Army, Ninth Infantry, down into the Mekong

Delta. Crawling with VC. We'll chopper in with the third battalion on a search-and-destroy mission."

She tried to corral her excitement, but she was buzzing. Hah, understatement.

"Exactly," he said in his resonant voice. "I can see you're jazzed. This is the real deal, let me tell you. Could be dangerous. Lots of swamps and rivers, enemy hiding in the elephant grass, invisible sonsabitches. I got you in as my assigned photog, and, if you follow my lead, I'll be able to keep you safe." He turned away then glanced back at Ellie before she could wipe the smirk off her face. "You've got to keep your head down. I don't want you getting hurt. Shit happens, Ellie, and it's random."

"Can't take many pictures with my head down."

He waved off her quip. "It's just another way to say, 'stay alert'."

Oh shit, that was one of the terms Stryker wrote down for me to memorize. She chafed at the control Nick was trying to exert over her but chalked it up to his concern for her rawness. She had to trust he knew what he was doing; he was experienced. He could be a good person to lean on, strong and knowledgeable. Not to mention the sexual tension that rode the air streaming between them.

She weighed her options: stay and bide her time while David Jenkins was up in Khesanh or go on Nick's patrol. How would Ben react if he thought she was considering going onto the battlefield? He'd storm the gates. No question but that *he'd* go on a mission if offered.

Nick was intoxicating. He took chances. Fuck it, so did she.

"Okay, I'm in. When do we leave?"

"Tomorrow. Meanwhile, how about we continue our New Year's Eve conversation because I can tell there's more to you than what you outlined." He sank onto the edge of the bed.

"What exactly would you like to know?" She sat in the chair.

"Childhood, college, your life." Nick rubbed his hands together. "Just trying to get to know you a little better."

She hesitated. Almost sounded like prying. *Oh what the hell.*

"The one big image I have of my childhood is skiing. My father taught me before I could walk and then coached me until I was sixteen. He was why I accumulated a suitcase full of ski racing medals. Until it all ended."

"You stopped? Sounds like you could have led the National Team to victory."

"Dad died," she whispered.

Nick's jaw dropped. "I'm sorry to hear that. Couldn't have been easy for you."

"Grief takes its own sweet time, but if I learned one thing from him it was how to reach for the far edges of things, how to face a challenge beyond the limits of my ability without fear. Thrill-seeking while keeping my brain from rattling in my skull, you could say, although I haven't met any physical challenges recently like I had in ski racing."

"Just wait till tomorrow. We'll be riding out on the steep slopes of thrill-seeking."

"All ri-i-ight."

"And photography? How'd you get into that?"

"After I lost my father, I kept on racing. I thought he'd want me to do that. My junior year at Middlebury, I hooked a tip on the second gate from the finish of a giant slalom and tore the hell out of my ACL. It ended my racing career."

"Ouch." Nick hunched his shoulders. "What's an ACL?"

"It's a ligament, major knee stabilizer. Pretty much a necessity in ski racing. And walking."

"What a bummer. And that's how you got started taking pictures?"

"I wasn't comfortable sitting around. I was restless. I started with my mother's old beaten-up Kodak Rangefinder. With a new telephoto lens, I propped myself up at the bottom of the course, aiming at the gates stacked up the hill, but I was too far from the action to capture any decent shots. So I limped higher up the fence line, using my ski poles, reaching for better vantage.

"At one point, the sun was blinding, and I saw a ghostly silhouette inside the fence. It was the photographer from *Ski Magazine*. "I've been where you are," she told me. "Looks like you've got what it takes. Go for it. Prophetic words, right?"

Nick nodded enthusiastically. "And now here you are." He stood. "I should let you get some rest before our patrol. See you tomorrow."

"Wait, Nick, what about you?"

He shoved his hands in his pockets and rocked heel to toe. "Not much to tell. I'm an overgrown hippie activist, champion of the underdog. Good way to get into trouble. When I was a kid, I saved every stray dog I could, which gave me something to occupy my time besides my dysfunctional family. Guess I've gone from rescuing dogs to trying to save all the world's under-dogs." He shrugged. "Enough for now. This is just the begin-ning. We'll have lots more time to get to know each other."

7

Military traffic at Tan Son Nhut whizzed by in organized pandemonium. Nick ushered Ellie onto one of several Huey helicopters without seats. They squeezed into the chopper with a dozen or so soldiers gripping their CAR-15s.

Holy shit, they're just kids.

Nick offered her an olive-green spray can. "Insects are fierce."

Ellie wrinkled her nose at the harsh industrial smell of it. "No thanks."

Nick shrugged, sprayed a dose on his hands then rubbed it on his face, neck, and arms.

When the slicks lifted off, almost orgasmic heat seared in her thighs. The same rush as being on top of a ski hill before a race. It excited her, being here, and she peered past the gunner manning the M60 that poked out the open door at the lush green landscape rushing away beneath them.

The noise of the rotors dizzied. The vibration rattled her teeth. Nick hovered, all business.

"When we land, follow the men. Crouch down and run as fast as you can."

The sergeant on Nick's other side jabbed a finger on Nick's chest and shouted in his ear. Ellie heard him over the roar. "I know your type. You'd piss yourself if Charlie took a shot at you, and you wouldn't have any idea what to do. Like this here girl you want to impress. So, stay the fuck out of our way. I can't afford any casualties, especially American civilians. I've been through enough bullshit with your uncle and you pain-in-the-ass journalists."

Nick saluted.

The sergeant jammed a plug of tobacco in his cheek and turned away.

Nick hoarse whispered into Ellie's ear, "Horse's ass."

THE NECKLACE of single-engine Huey helicopters touched down on the landing zone one after another, disgorged troops, and leapt back into the air. With her knapsack on her back, Ellie ducked and scooted from beneath the rotor blades, one hand on the cameras dangling around her neck, the other on her ill-fitting helmet; clearly made for a man. She turned her camera on soldiers leaping from the choppers before they rose again like giant noisy grasshoppers out of a cloud of Oklahoma dust.

"Follow me," Nick yelled, and took off running, not halting until he'd covered fifty yards toward the first village.

"Hey!" He snatched at her elbow as she raced past him. "Cool your jets, girl. Let the grunts secure the village first. Booby traps can be anywhere. The blow-you-up kind." They waited in a field of grass that waved in the hot breezes. Rice paddies stretched in one direction as far as the eye could see, bounded by jungle packed with tall palms and trees and bushes with leaves the size of her torso. They high stepped one behind the other through the thick undergrowth. Seconds elongated into minutes. Anxious, Ellie's gaze swiveled in case the enemy were going to burst out at them at any moment.

In a clearing, they came upon the first hamlet. It wouldn't take long for the jungle to swallow up the collection of grass shacks raised off the ground. Pens beneath several of the huts held stinking wallows of pigs in thick, oozing mud. Odors of manure and urine hung heavily in the humid air.

An eerie quiet pervaded the village. Ellie lifted a camera, looked through the wide-angle lens at huts lined up before her.

Click.

"Up north in Cu Chi, where there are tunnels," Nick whispered, "it's rumored the entrances are in pig sties. When troops get near a village, the VC disappear into those tunnels. Who knows where they disappear to down here in the Delta. Maybe they drop into the Mekong."

"*Lai dai, lai dai,*" a soldier commanded an old man in soiled black pajamas, prodding him with his gun into the middle of the village. On the packed dirt in front of the shacks, the man hobbled to the sergeant. He kept his head bowed and eyes glued to the ground.

"What's going on?" Ellie asked.

"It's the village chief. They're going to question him. Rarely yields anything. These villagers scramble to survive. When we're here, they kowtow to us. When the VC come, they say whatever Charlie wants to hear. That's how they survive, taking bullshit from both sides."

Click. Click. She swiped her hand, shooing off mosquitoes.

"*Không biêt,*" the village chief whined in a paper-thin voice.

The sergeant signaled Nick with a roll of his eyes.

"Sarge says it's cool," Nick said, turning Ellie by the elbow. "Old man said no VC here. This could still get ugly. Let's check out the rest of the village."

"Come on, just a few more shots."

"Let's move on," Nick insisted and pulled on Ellie's arm.

She jerked away as she slapped the back of her neck in reaction to an insect bite.

His eyes flashed dark. He put his lips to her ear. "Ellie, this is a fucking war, in case you hadn't noticed."

She cringed and let him lead her away.

"Gook's lying," someone said. "There's VC all over the place. I can smell 'em."

"Yeah, got to be here somewhere," another said.

"Fan out," barked the sergeant. "Find them."

Ellie tossed an apologetic look at Nick, who shrugged it off. He was the one with experience; she was a tenderfoot. She had to trust someone. Might as well be him.

The sergeant turned to a lieutenant. Despite the officer's slumped shoulders, there was a hardness about him. Nick moved his hand up and down her back. "That's Lieutenant Eaton. He lost half a dozen of his guys by trusting one of these villagers," he explained, his earlier outburst apparently forgotten as he offered a speck of comfort.

The men returned. Hadn't found any VC. "If they're around, there're only a few. If there were more, we'd be in a shitstorm," Nick said.

It was five klicks to the next village. Ellie and Nick walked side by side in the middle of the column. "VC could surprise us at any time," Nick said. The prospect made her skin crawl. Plus, palm trees didn't afford much shade, and it was claustrophobically hot. Sweat trickled down her forehead, back, and underarms.

"Break," said the sergeant, and the men dropped by the side of the road, reaching for canteens and the cigarette packs tucked into their helmets. The aromas of tobacco and pot smudged the muggy air.

The minute she stopped moving, she was attacked by a

swarm of black flies and mosquitoes. After swatting and doing a jig, she asked for the bug spray. He smirked at her. Didn't matter; she needed relief from the insect intrusions.

"What's with the dope?" she asked Nick as she squatted beside him.

"Makes the war go down easier. See that kid over there? I met him on the last patrol. He had three choices: Hide on the streets of Baltimore as a wanted felon and maybe get knifed or shot, serve a prison term, or join the military."

"Nice choices." She chugged water from her canteen. She was struck by the realization she could leave at any time, but soldiers couldn't. Did this mean she had power she hadn't even thought about? The power of choice?

"These guys have either enlisted, gotten drafted, chosen this life over a prison term, or are gung-ho dickheads who want to kill gooks. This war is a total clusterfuck. Anyway, regardless of why these kids are here, dope takes the edge off. I can't blame them, can you? War is no picnic."

In the second village, the patrol swept through, chasing residents out of huts. Some stood, others sat. Small children hunkered on porches, hands on their knees, staring at the Americans. Older kids, boys mostly, followed the soldiers with their hands out, begging.

Two old women squatted on the top steps of a hut. Tar-black hair, streaked gray at the temples, framed faces weathered to brown, dry husks. Black pajamas draped over their shoulders as if hung on wire coat hangers. Their clawed, wrinkled hands clutched the shoulders of children in front of them. Their nails were cracked and stained by dirt from working the rice paddies.

Ellie tried to make sense of what she was seeing. The emaciated old women and scrawny kids with blank dark eyes and bare feet covered in dried mud were worlds apart from the tall, well-fed soldiers dressed in fatigues, cigarettes dangling from their American lips.

Click, click, click.

A grimy hand fluttered to cover an old woman's mouth. Ellie wasn't sure if the woman was smirking or scowling. When she lowered her hand and smiled, Ellie sucked in an involuntary breath at the sight of blackened teeth. An image bloomed of Bloody Mary's teeth in the movie *South Pacific*, stained from chewing betel nuts. The Polynesian women were large and happy. This Vietnamese woman was the opposite: convex back, eyes sunken in her face like two hunks of coal in a wrinkled paper sack.

Click.

Nothing happening in that village.

They walked on. Ellie was antsy; she didn't know what she wanted. Action or a nice quiet day to take photos. She really had no idea how she would react if they were ambushed. Nick might think he could keep her safe from harm, yet it was her camera that created her demilitarized zone, a buffer between her and the mud, the stench, the lives crushed by war. The camera enabled her to be objective.

Click, click, click.

She reached one hand up to swipe at the sweat sliding into her eyes. Her head throbbed in the steaming heat. She stumbled. Nick caught her arm.

"You okay?"

"It's so hot. My head's about to explode."

"Drink." Nick lifted his canteen to her lips, and she gulped the lukewarm liquid noisily.

"Plech, what *is* this?"

"Pinch of salt to keep us hydrated."

"Nick, these women, they're so old. They must be grandmothers left to tend the children. They're skin and bones. How do they survive?"

The question drifted in the midmorning heat. "Survival is inbred," he said. "War is a way of life. There's been conflict for centuries. No exit."

More people who can't leave.

Ellie looked past him at a canal running with water at the edge of rice fields. "Not that I'd do it here, but it would feel great to tear my clothes off and dive into the water. Cool me off."

He grinned. "I love the idea of you tearing your clothes off, but the leeches would suck you dry."

"Leeches . . ." Ellie grimaced, ignoring the rest of his comment. ". . . insult to injury."

The morning stretched uncomfortably, and clamminess pasted Ellie's fatigues to her body. Nick walked slightly behind her, and she liked the feeling of his eyes sliding up her legs, around the curve of her butt to her waist. She shook her head. *Stop that.*

She saw a shot she wanted and moved toward the canal alongside the road, focusing her camera on soldiers walking above the edge of the murky water. She'd discovered the telephoto perspective when she filmed ski racing.

Nick seized her arm and spun her around.

She shook him off. "Don't ruin my shot."

He lost his grip on her and huffed in exasperation. "Stubborn broad."

Leeches forgotten, Ellie hopped into the canal and squatted low to get an angle on the line of soldiers above her. Before she could even take a breath, the sergeant yelled, "Mines! Get the fuck out of there! Wilson, get her out!"

Wilson reached down and grabbed the back of her shirt.

Another grunt, Driscoll, lowered himself into the canal.

Wilson pulled her up onto the road as Driscoll pushed her out of the ditch.

Misstep.

Driscoll exploded into the air. His curdling scream twisted Ellie's bowels.

A mist of water and blood rained down on her.

Bone fragments poked out of his leg where his boot had been.

Wilson dropped Ellie into the dust. "Medic!" he shouted.

Men rushed to Driscoll. The sergeant stamped forward, pulled Nick by the front of his shirt. Nose in Nick's face, he pointed at Ellie. "I told you to keep that cherry in line. You and that stupid bitch are on the next chopper back to base. I don't want either of you anywhere near my men, Burrows. Ever. I shouldn't have been swayed by who your uncle is."

He slapped at his helmet. "I should never have let you bring a clueless noncombatant."

He turned to the medic. "How's Driscoll?"

The medic looked up. "He'll live, but he's lost his foot. Medevac's on the way. He's going home for sure."

Ellie sat on the ground in shock. It was like she'd been dropped into the ocean. Couldn't hear a thing. Nick glared at her through her fog. Wilson squatted to meet her eyes. His face was splattered with blood, and his eyes were pinned like those of speed freaks she'd met. He had white crust and dried saliva caked at the corners of his mouth. He looked so young. He spoke but his words were muffled. He sneered at her and stalked away.

She rolled over and vomited.

The sergeant stormed over, yanked Ellie to her feet, and thrust her at Nick.

"She's in shock, probably has vertigo. Get her onto the bird and the two of you get out of my sight."

8

———————

The noise of helicopter rotors registered a dull ache in Ellie's brain. The ride back in the Huey was torture. Trapped with the man who'd lost his foot, self-reproach roiled through her. Couldn't think, couldn't focus. She had to grip the strap to keep the wind from sucking her out the door of the helicopter where she would be buffeted and torn apart by potshots at the chopper from beneath the jungle canopy. She registered the simple fact that her body was intact as she glanced at the morphine-sedated soldier. Thank God Nick held her tightly in the curve of his arm.

The vertigo of guilt and anguish swirled around her. She gagged when she saw blood and gore on her vest. *Being in an explosion is a heart-stopping, piss-in-your-pants experience.* Hell, the closest she'd been was fireworks on the Fourth of July.

The drive into Saigon from the airport was a total haze. She huddled in silence, a steely Nick Burrows at the steering wheel. But she did recall Ben's farewell words to her at New York's Idlewild Airport. "I know how seductive the sounds of battle can be for journalists. We're like Pavlov's dog. A bomb blasts, a mortar whistles, and we're off, tongues lolling, tails whipping.

Let me be absolutely clear, Eleanor. You are never to go out into the field. You're there for one reason and one reason only, to interview war correspondents for *my* book."

And now she'd blown it for both Ben and Nick, especially Ben. What kind of backlash would the press corps deal him for sending out such an inept twit. Surely she'd be spurned.

She leaned against her rucksack, cameras still dangling around her neck. She sat without moving or speaking, eyes vacant, siphoning deep breaths as late afternoon sun beat through the windshield, roasting her lap.

When Nick pulled to a stop in front of the hotel, she slid from the car and stumbled up the stairs. With each slow step, she was ambushed by the faces of the soldiers, heard the buzz of mosquitoes, felt the tepid water above her calves and the squish of mud under her boots, the outburst of orders, the blast, a soldier tossed into the air splattering her with blood and flesh, then men pulling her out of the canal, and deafness. When she reached her room, she stopped, not turning around, not dropping her rucksack, not closing her door or unstringing cameras from her neck.

A man lost a part of his body, as if a painting of the war had peeled off the wall and burst into gory, bloody life in front of her. She had caused it.

"Oh, that poor soldier." She unbuttoned her vest and shrugged it and her rucksack to the floor, then sank onto the edge of her bed. Talk about trapped. Now he was stuck in a life with only one foot. She moaned. What if she hadn't been greedy for that shot? But she didn't know how not to go for compelling shots.

She had no idea how long she sat there, head in hands, before Nick found her slumped on the edge of the bed, elbows on knees.

"Ellie? Can you hear me?"

She didn't move, didn't lift her head.

"Ellie," he said a little louder.

She raised her head slowly until her eyes met his.

He lifted her cameras from around her neck, placed them on the dresser, and settled beside her on the bed. "Aww, sweetie, this is hard, I know. How can I help?"

"Help?"

He put his arm around her shoulder. "You're far from the first journalist to step over an invisible line. Not that this will make you feel any better about your experience."

"That poor soldier. I've ruined his life." She curled toward him and rested her head on his shoulder.

"Can you talk about it? Might make you feel better, give you some perspective."

"Not yet," she muttered, "but thanks for being here."

She turned her face toward his. "Oh Christ," she moaned.

"How about we work together? Try to put an end to this stupid fucking war."

She couldn't believe he'd said that, but she let it dissolve into her sorrow.

WHEN HE LEFT, Ellie reached for the scotch in the night table drawer, pulled out the cork, and tipped the bottle to her lips. The peaty liquor seared her frayed nerves. She welcomed its sting. Tears flowed. Head in her hands again, she sobbed. "Oh my God, what have I done?" She bolted for the bathroom and heaved. The scotch burned a second time.

Dawn brought no peace. It swamped her, flinging her out of her dreams and onto the shores of Hell. Hot and clammy, she lay curled tight as a fiddlehead fern, tangled in the sheets. Her mouth was parched. The taste of scotch lingered at the back of her throat. A boulder of pain lurked behind her eyes.

"Shit and double shit," she moaned. Parting the mosquito net, she shuffled to the bathroom.

Thoughts rattled around her brain. Follow the rules, her father had admonished, meting out punishment whenever she didn't meet or exceed his expectations. She reeled backward through a crazed web of memories to a time when her father's harsh words lashed her. She was nine, standing in the frigid aftermath of a giant slalom at Mt. Snow, Vermont, looking up at the scoreboard, where her name was listed second. Not first. Her father, looming above her, pointed, his words pushing his breath out in icy daggers of anger.

"You didn't try hard enough. Your line wasn't straight enough. There was no reason for you to lose that race. You should have won." He left her in the finish area.

Ashamed and humiliated, she slid her skis to her shoulder, gripped her poles, and headed back to the lodge, goggles hanging under her chin. A voice called out. She turned to see the girls' coach squeak across the snow. "Saw you race. You've sure got what it takes." She looked up at the woman, who squeezed her shoulder. "Win or lose, young lady, be proud of who you are."

Ellie shrugged, but the fact remained: She hadn't followed her father's orders, and she lost. Her father expected her to play by the rules he'd established on the racecourse. He liked rules, kept things neat. Except his rules seldom jibed with her own sense of how things should be. They were like clothing she'd outgrown. She often rebelled, part of growing up and challenging authority. There was the time she defied him, refusing to go to a big race, and chose instead to go into Boston with her boyfriend for a Byrds concert. Her dad had been so angry. He went to the race anyway. Skidded on an icy road and crashed into a tree. She didn't believe it was a heart attack that caused his death. His anger at her had made him drive recklessly. She was racked with grief and guilt for years.

Having challenged Nick's authority, not only had she caused the soldier to lose a foot, but he'd told her they would be blackballed from the press corps. Once more she had learned consequences were harsh when she strayed from the rules.

Hard lesson to be sure. She was a rebel who ignored the necessity of experience. Ben would be disappointed, she knew it.

She washed her face, pulled a brush through her unruly hair, and re-braided it, noticing dark circles under her eyes. She would find a way through this. "Okay, enough self-pity!" she declared. "Seize the day."

Deep beneath the surface, her spirit beat against the walls of her heart. She was a problem solver. She could do this. Even after the surreal experience of the patrol. But deep down her heart bled for that poor soldier.

Leaving the bathroom, she pulled fresh clothing from drawers, blue seersucker bellbottoms white T-shirt, lapis earrings to keep away evil and a turquoise ring to protect her thunder. Superstitious? So what. Her resolve was resurfacing. Separate the wheat from the chaff, the professional from the personal. She would not allow this incident to distract her from her assignment. How had she drifted away from her purpose anyway? Had her stupidity thrown all her promise out the window? Her only fear was journalists wouldn't talk to her after what happened on that patrol, not even for Ben Stryker.

She shuffled down the hall to the stairs and took one slow step at a time on her way to the restaurant. It felt like a death march. Nick was waiting for her. Her feelings were conflicted: he was a source of both comfort and shame.

"What are you staring at?" she asked, as if he could hear her thoughts.

He took a step back. "You look like shit."

"You have such a way with words."

"C'mon, Ellie, let me buy you breakfast."

"Not hungry." Still, she let him lead her to a table on the terrace.

Hunger and nausea swirled in her belly. She craved a resolution to rid herself of guilt and return to calm focus. She was determined to move forward because she certainly wasn't about to move backward.

She stiffened.

"You're upset, but snap out of it," he said. "Relax, it wasn't your fault. It's this stupid, useless fucking war."

"Of course it's my fault and I know you think so too," she rasped at him. "Why are you trying to make me feel worse than I already do?"

He cringed. Seconds passed, the growling of her stomach the only sound. His brows bunched over his nose.

"Ellie, I've got a confession. I owe it to you—"

She glared at him.

"Ever since I picked you up at the airport, I've acted like an old hand, like I've been covering war since, since the French lost Dienbienphu. But the truth is, I've only been here a couple of months longer than you. I got here thanks to my uncle's good graces. I'm still green, but I'm looking into stuff no one else is interested in. I'm working on a higher mission. I could deal you in on this."

"I knew you were an asshole."

"Yeah, trying to impress you. Can you blame me? You came off that plane and shook my world."

She waved his words away. "After what happened, I can't do my job if no one's going to talk to me. If that happens, I can't help Ben at all. Better to cut my losses and go home."

"This sounds harsh but bailing now would make you a quitter. Doesn't suit you. You're better than that. Shit happens, Ellie. You're learning the fast and hard way about the down and dirty of this place."

Her stomach tightened.

"There're hundreds of journalists here. Some of the hot-shit ones are Euros. They're a horny bunch. You can use your good looks to your advantage ... not to mention your gorgeous mane of gold."

"For fuck's sake, what do you think I am? Any opportunity to put me down, is that it, Nick?" She slapped her napkin on the table and stood.

He grasped her arm, gently. "Please listen to me. Actually, that was a compliment. You might literally have saved the grunt's life. Okay, so he stepped on a toe popper. You have any idea how many guys shoot themselves on purpose so they can get out of this shithole?"

"You're saying he might have shot himself in the foot to escape the fighting, but I beat him to it?" She huffed. "So I should think he was lucky? You sick fuck."

"Simple fact, Ellie. Grunts do it every day. Maybe this'll lighten your load." He paused. "How 'bout we start over? As far as getting to the action, we can go out on our own."

"We? Together? Not a good idea."

"Look, like I said, I owe you for the dumb-ass way I acted." He waggled a finger at her. "I pegged you for someone who wants to stand up for the truth, ferret out the facts. Was I wrong?"

She sat back down. He'd struck a nerve. *Dickhead is right. The truth matters. He's relentless, this one.*

"Everyone covering the war for the US is doing just that, along with the political ramifications for each side: The Vietnamese do this, so the Americans do that. Same old, same old. All the real shit's censored anyway. It's not enough to simply *cover* the war; we have an obligation to try and save the people caught in the crossfire, casualties to a conflict they never chose, never wanted."

"Okay. I get you're trying to make me feel better."

"Yes that, but there's something more important. Look, Ellie, if you step back and scope the big picture, you'll realize this civil war the US has engineered is merely a veneer, only the most recent attack perpetrated upon an ages-old culture. What's important is not covering the war but *uncovering* the plight of the Vietnamese. Not a single one of the colonialist countries, not China, Japan, or France, has ever considered the native people. No, they all had self-serving motives, whether using the country as a buffer, or lusting after its natural resources."

He threw his arms in the air. "Sorry, I get all whipped up by this. You and I together can tell a compelling story about the inhumane treatment of the Vietnamese people. I believe this down to my toes. You and I are the team to make a difference here. We can affect the outcome of the war. What do you say, Ellie?"

"I'm intrigued, but I'll have to think about this. I do have responsibilities, after all. I understand you're looking at a higher purpose. And I really do understand." She rubbed her arms, sensing his anxiety. "It's certainly true the coverage of the Vietnamese side in the war is absent. Press coverage lacks information from that perspective."

"That's where we come in." Nick's voice rose in pitch. "C'mon Ellie, we owe it to the Vietnamese victims."

"How do you suggest we grab the audience's attention about the Vietnamese being trapped by the high moral ground of the Americans? News is news. It isn't anti-American; it's the truth, that's what you're saying, right?"

"So right. I've picked the right person. We're partners, Ellie."

His eyes were burning with conviction, but she hadn't yet agreed. It was Nick who was sold on their possible partnership. His naked delight in believing he'd won her over to his cause shone in his face. He was a man caught between the dazzle of celebrity and his lofty ambition with something to prove—to someone. Something rankled; she felt it in her gut. Regardless of his dedication to his humanitarian beliefs, he wore the scent of a schemer. *I better be careful.*

"How would one begin such a project?"

A great range of emotions played across Nick's face.

"I've got an important meeting with a source. I'll fill you in later."

9

———————

Not easy to follow Nick's jump-shifts. All that talk and she'd forgotten breakfast. The swirl of emotions growled loud in her stomach. She ordered a quiche and ate with gusto, chewing on the possibility of redemption by exposing the US's destruction of the Vietnamese culture in the name of freedom. It was also weird to consider Nick's contention that a certain percentage of soldiers injured themselves as a way to get away from fighting and safely back home. *I guess some people* can *decide to leave.*

Walking up the stairs to her room after her meal, her thoughts tracked back to Nick's determination to save the natives of Vietnam. Should she share his work to uncover corruption and unfold stories of the struggles of the Vietnamese people for sympathetic readers? Still plenty back home what with all the antiwar demonstrators. She'd been moved by Vietnam's plight.

She glanced up at the lazy ceiling fan expecting an answer. None came.

Jerry Forrest's words about purpose had given her a *raison d'être*: She would stay and help expose the corruption on all sides and denounce this useless war.

This appealed to her sense of morality. It would simply be revealing the truth. Which meant if she agreed to work with Nick, the facts would have to be verified. So, a little time off from Stryker's assignment might soften the press corps' possible ban on her. She hadn't heard anything about her status within the press corps ... yet. She made a mental note to telex her notes from Jerry's interview to Ben and inform him Jenkins was away on assignment.

A slight hesitancy vibrated, but she couldn't deny that it was a just cause.

The rules weren't clearly defined yet, so she needed to watch her back. Was Nick really being kind when he told her some soldiers would go to extremes to escape the war and retreat to safety in the States? She'd listened attentively to his posturing about truth and Vietnamese oppression. It was clear he had a fervor for upsetting the imperialist apple cart. There was no doubt how much he cared about the downtrodden.

Yet the specter of uncertainty intruded. *Is he such an actor, he has me snookered? What motive? He has nothing but satisfaction to gain by accomplishing his goal. If I do this, I have to trust him entirely, which makes me a little nervous. I guess I can always ditch if something's out of order. Humanitarian adventure. Right up my alley. Is it really a partnership, or would I be his scapegoat?*

She was dizzy and cautioned herself on the wisdom of seeking an opinion from the only person she knew well enough to trust: David Jenkins. But he had an issue with Nick. Shit, she thought, it was about time to take charge and make her own decisions.

10

Nick Burrows had work to do. He was on a mission to expose the truth about the oppression of the Vietnamese people by their own corrupt leaders and the colluding American government.

He dodged and weaved his way through Cholon, Saigon's Chinatown, on his way to an assignation with Lam Quang Thiep, his source who funneled information to him on South Vietnam's corrupt government. Rounding a corner into a street of low-roofed, shack-like structures, he heard distant muffled gunfire. He paid scant attention to his surroundings as he struggled to shake off thoughts of Ellie. He saw her as a truth seeker, like him, but wild and untamed. He snorted. He was used to throwing his power around, especially with Uncle Francis in his corner to back him up, but Ellie was something else entirely. Even though she'd put a dent in his control, he found her pluck sexy as hell. He had his work cut out for him.

Each footstep resounded with determination.

More gunfire and distant explosions. "Christ, is nothing in balance?" he muttered. "Everything in this country is off its rocker."

He fought his way out of his distractions, his prison of anguish, and the luscious Ellie. He needed a clear mind to focus on his meeting with the enigmatic Thiep. "Focus," he scolded.

Arriving in the hush of a Catholic church, Nick took a ragged breath and slowed his pace, quieting his steps. In front of the altar, he swung left through a hallway to a carved wooden door. He wanted to hammer on it but knocked softly instead.

Thiep creaked it open, peered around to make sure they were alone, and admitted him into the small, cramped sacristy. He stood, unruffled.

"This idiotic war has blown out of all control," Nick blustered. "My dumb-ass president's sending half a million more troops over here. Lambs to the slaughter. And for what?"

Thiep's stick-straight posture made him seem taller than his five-feet-four inches. Even though Nick towered above him, the man had a way of looking him straight in the eyes, his tiny dark orbs lit with a conviction that Nick found unnerving. He was wiry and bespectacled, with a round face beneath thinning black hair. He was professor of history at Saigon University, but Nick couldn't imagine he had many students who were not intimidated by his stern presence. The man certainly kept Nick off balance and guessing at the thoughts and passions beneath his calm exterior. At times, Nick suspected the man was toying with him, keeping him at the end of a leash. Not easy for Nick to accede to this, but he'd sacrifice anything in pursuit of his goal. Even if he had to give up his need to control the situation.

The professor moved to an ornately carved chair and sat, hands clasped in his lap, jaws clenched. He gestured in the direction of a bench covered in worn blue damask.

Nick took his seat, one knee bouncing in time with his inner turmoil. He spoke forcefully. "Look, Thiep, the sooner I get proof of your government's corruption, the sooner we expose my nation's equally corrupt support of it. The US can't prevent a communist takeover of Southeast Asia. What hubris to think they can."

Thiep narrowed his black eyes and spoke in a soft, unhurried voice. "You are correct. My country will eventually fall under the rule of communism. The die is cast. The Southern government will fall regardless of American support. I await this outcome."

"What? You're just going to wait it out? For the sake of your people, we must uncover all the corruption."

"What good will that do, young Nick? Corruption in government is an age-old practice. Must I remind you I am a history professor? I appreciate your dedication. With your work there was a sliver of an opportunity to limit the damage of this useless conflict, but—"

Something in Thiep's voice unsettled Nick. "Come on, let's take that chance. We could be saving lives."

"Danger lurks. Our work may have been discovered. You and I cannot meet again." Thiep spoke with a detached expression. "The process of removing opposition to official policy has always been in effect but now it has increased with a broad wave of arrests."

"What does this mean for us?" Nick asked warily.

"One must weigh the consequence of current loss against future gain. A new strategy must be developed with new operatives; therefore, dedicated as you are to our cause, your effort is no longer needed."

The weighty presence and resolute will of Thiep bound Nick to his chair. Shocked to his socks, Nick could only mutter one word: "Explain."

When Thiep said nothing, Nick managed to ask, "Why the abrupt change? Are you afraid of the sudden roundups?"

"I act out of caution, not fear. We are under direct scrutiny."

The two men were as still as a photograph.

Finally, the light dawned. Nick coughed a loud swallow. "Was Tam compromised?"

"Yes. You must know you are not invisible to those you seek to expose. This places me in danger. I cannot be suspected of revolutionary activity. Highest goal now is to keep our attempts hidden. You understand."

"No. I certainly do not understand," Nick spluttered. "I take every precaution. Who could be watching me?"

"Secret police and your own people. Bad joss. Hard to erase corruption. Even more difficult when your government subsidizes it."

"I know they do, but most don't know that. "What proof do you have?"

Thiep remained silent.

Nick bit his lower lip. He flushed with anger, fighting the urge to argue, and reached for logic. He was an interloper. Thiep would not make a flighty decision, and once made, he would not change his mind.

But Nick could not keep his exasperation from boiling over. Plus, he had a reputation to maintain. He shot to his feet and began pacing and ranting, one hand flashing through the air.

"This is fucked. I'm working on something vital, but without you there's no validation. The world won't know what's really going on here, all the corruption and greed in the name of freedom." He glowered at the man in front of him. He licked his lips; his mouth had gone dry. He studied his compatriot, as delicate and faceted as fine crystal yet steel underneath. "I'm just about ready to blow the lid off the American munitions that General Phan sold to the VC. You at least have the photos you promised me?"

Thiep shook his head sadly. "Tam had photos. Gone now." He paused. "You are in their eyes, Nick. Without proof, you have no story."

Nick sank onto the blue bench. "Jesus."

"There is a Confucius saying: *It does not matter how slowly you go so long as you do not stop.* For centuries, we Vietnamese have been at war. Many have tried to break us. We bend only, not give up." His voice lowered. "You, too, must find another way."

Outrage gnawed on Nick's insides. Its evil companion, anger, was raising its serpent head. He blinked, took a couple of balancing breaths, and inhaled the stuffy air of the sacred space.

"You're right." He reached for a smile but managed only a crooked grimace.

Thiep's silence was driving Nick crazy. Thoughts clattered against his skull. The serenity of the church, which usually soothed his nerves, grated on him. He sucked in a few breaths in an attempt to calm his jangled mind.

"If you must continue this crusade, you may wish to meet with a colleague of mine."

Nick's head came up. He waited for more. Thiep slipped him a piece of paper, folded small. Nick opened it, noticed the French name, and stowed it in a pocket.

"Now, Nick, you go. *Tam biêt*, goodbye."

Thoughts darting in wild tangents, Nick scuttled back to the villa, paying little heed to his surroundings, neither noticing nor caring if he was being followed. His footsteps hammered a drumbeat in his brain. Grasping the reality of his position, he questioned the diminishing possibilities for success. However, any available possibility had to start somewhere, and he could only start from where he was. Who could help? Could he find someone with his limited resources? Would any of the foreign journalists sympathize with him? Then he remembered Thiep's parting gift. He stopped and removed the scrap of paper from his pocket. As he read and reread the scrawled name, he rubbed his chin and thought the sly old man hadn't totally discarded him.

11

———

Ellie sent her interview notes to Ben but had no new meetings set up with David still away on assignment. She had nothing to do but wait, not something she excelled at. The walls of her hotel room were closing in and the inscrutable ceiling fan continued to turn in its hypnotic fashion.

She fled. Wandered down to the bar, hesitating when she saw David Jenkins perched on a barstool with his saddle-shoed feet hooked around its legs. Did he know what had happened? That she was a pariah?

She met his eyes in the backbar mirror as she approached.

"Hey, darlin', good to see you," he greeted.

"Back so soon," she said. "You have more turns than a revolving door."

David laughed. "You're not kidding. Buy you a drink? Scotch and soda, right?"

"With a twist." She slid onto a barstool.

Her fingers trembled as she lit a cigarette.

"So, Ellie, I was going to ask what you've been up to while I was gone, but the correspondent community here is small, and there are no secrets."

Her head drooped.

He lifted her chin with his fingertips, smiling warmly. "Nick took you in-country without preparing you. What happened was not your fault."

She gasped, siphoning air as she focused on his eyes and scruffy beard. "Not my fault? But it was. If I hadn't been greedy for a shot—"

"Ellie, darlin', listen to me. He did not prepare you. You mustn't be so hard on yourself."

"But Nick and I are now *persona non grata* with the press corps. Makes it hard to do my job."

"I told you there're no secrets," David said, "but I'll tell you one. Just between you and me. You're not the one the military and the press corps will watch out for. You're secondary in this issue for many of the press corps since you're new and lack experience. It's Nick. He's developed a reputation as a flash grenade, and you might be just the tonic he needs. Knowing Nick, this incident will only fuel his foolish behavior. He needs someone to show him how he's seen by others. He's so focused on his mission to save the world he has tunnel vision."

So, she thought, David believed Nick was true to his mission.

David held up his glass, signaling the bartender for a refill. "That, and some distance from his oppressive, testosterone-saturated family. He doesn't do well under anyone's thumb, constantly rebelling to get back at them. That's why he's here. Francis Burrows got Nick the job as a stringer for UPI. It's Uncle Francis who will no doubt smooth over this fiasco Nick engi-neered. The man's got clout and a soft spot for his nephew."

"Why are you telling me this?" Ellie asked, color returning to her face.

"Perspective," he said. "It's not easy for Nick. He's struggling, and I'd like to see him find his own way. I gave him a room in the villa to give him a little autonomy. Plus, you have a positive effect on him."

"So you're telling me to look past the obvious and develop a little compassion?"

David shrugged. "Couldn't hurt, darlin'." He lit a cigarette and drew deeply on it.

Ellie mulled over David's comments about her being a balancing influence on Nick. She had to make sure his quirks wouldn't affect their work together since she had pretty much committed to following through with Nick.

"Well," David said, snapping her back to the moment, "I'm impressed by your tenacity. I must say you've got what it takes. Emotion has no place in this business. Skews the facts. I've been wondering how the incident would affect your assignment for Stryker. Say, how did your spur-of-the-moment interview with Jerry Forrest go?"

"Great. What a good guy. And he knows Ben and Sarah from their time together here."

He crushed his cigarette butt in the ashtray. "Care to go over to the villa and develop some film?"

"Far out. I was wondering where and when I'd be able to do that. I'll grab my film cans and meet you in the lobby."

They walked the few blocks in silence.

"Here we are," David said as he turned onto a walkway off Cong Ly Street that led up to a large, elegant house.

Ellie whistled.

"You should have seen this street a few years ago," David said. "It was lined with tall, graceful elms."

"What happened to them?"

"War progress you might say. The South Vietnamese regime cut them down so American military vehicles could pass." This house dates from the French Colonial occupation in the last century." He opened the door for her. A wide foyer led into a dining room on one side, drawing room on the other. Between them, an elegant stairway led to upper floors. She gazed at the elaborate decorative plaster ceilings and Empire furniture and whistled again.

"Walk this way. Out of fantasyland and back into reality." He headed through the kitchen and down a hallway. He turned, walking backward. "Follow the smell of chemicals."

When she entered the converted bathroom where a counter extended the length of a side wall, her nose crinkled at a whiff of developer chemicals, and she inhaled an early memory of her mother's darkroom.

Under the glow of a red light, they got to work. David slid the negatives into the chemicals. Ellie lifted out proof sheets with wooden tongs and clipped them to a clothesline above the bathtub. Before long, the proofs looked like Tibetan prayer flags.

"Please, use this darkroom anytime, Ellie. Front door's never locked. None of us can seem to remember our keys."

"Thanks, David. There's something very satisfying about printing my own photos."

"Cigarette break." He switched on the overhead light, shut off the red glow, and opened the door.

Nick was leaning against the wall outside the darkroom, arms crossed over his chest.

"Nick." She smiled.

"Isn't this cozy," he snarked.

David stepped close to Nick and whispered in a clipped voice so that Ellie couldn't hear what he said.

Nick's lips twitched. "Don't patronize me, Jenkins. While you're wasting time in the darkroom, I'm going over to UPI. Pyle's got an assignment for me."

With that, he left, footsteps reverberating through her brain.

"What in the hell?" She watched him stalk away. He had

issues, for sure, which cast a further cloud of doubt in her mind about working with him, despite what David had said.

"That's Nick for you. No telling when he's going to fly off the handle," David said with a tilt of his head. "Not to mention the jealousy."

"Jealousy? Really? No."

"He's wound tight, needs to be in control. Keeps him calm. Told me once that keeping a rein on his emotions was the only way he survived his father's abusive tirades." He cast a sidelong glance at her. "Sorry, got to go. Get my proofs over to the bureau."

"I don't mind walking back to the hotel. I could use some time to digest what you told me."

David nodded. "Doesn't hurt to have all the facts, right? Even so, might be a good idea to move slowly on the interviews while the heat dies down."

"Yeah, I get it." Questions about Nick continued to bump around in her brain. She opened her mouth to speak when she heard her father's words: "Silence is the most necessary ingredient in the learning process."

David's footsteps echoed down the hallway.

12

Like a murmuration of starlings changing direction, the mood shifted in Saigon. Preparations were being made for Tet, the Vietnamese Lunar New Year celebration, on January 31. Curiosity pulled Ellie into a study of Saigon neighborhoods. She found women sweeping out their houses, removing any bad luck that lurked within. Men repainted facades and trimmed trees, hung banners, and made everything fresh again to welcome good luck in the new year. Flower sellers were doing a booming business, furnishing bright blooms to decorate homes. Men strung garlands across streets. Families cooked, visited relatives. A busy, bustling, cheerful time.

On the cusp of evening, upon freshening up after her rambles, she stopped into the Continental terrace for an early toast to the Tet new year. She ordered appetizers and took them to her room, anticipating Nick's arrival. He'd slid a note under her door apologizing for his abrupt departure from the darkroom and inviting her to wander through the firecracker celebrations, but when he didn't appear by midnight, she went to bed.

"Coming," she called groggily when she heard banging on her door. She checked the travel clock as she parted the mosquito netting and got out of bed. Slipping on her kimono robe and snugging the sash as she opened the door, she wondered what amusing excuse Nick had fabricated.

But it was David Jenkins, wavering from foot to foot, cameras dangling from his neck. "David, it's past three in the morning."

"Grab your gear. Time to meet the war," he croaked, hands cupped around his mouth.

"What are you talking about?" He smelled of bourbon.

"The Presidential Palace and the US Embassy have been attacked." He slurred.

"Holy crap."

He straightened his posture. "If you want a piece of this action, get dressed and grab your gear."

Ellie pivoted an about-face into her room, snatched her camera bag, and bolted for the door.

"Might work a little bit better if you hustle yourself into some clothes and meet me in the lobby."

She glanced down at her robe and snorted.

"Seriously, Ellie, never walk out the door without your credentials, or your clothes." He smothered a laugh and walked down the hall in a loosey-goosey gait. "Hurry," he whispered hoarsely over his shoulder. "Time and the war wait for no woman."

She pulled on her wrinkled khaki shirt and pants, tightened them with a belt, slipped into her photographer's vest, which she'd had laundered after the grunt had stepped on the toe popper, strung her credentials around her neck, and shoved her feet into loafers. Taking a minute to load film into a camera with a long lens and one with a 50-millimeter lens, and to stuff more film rolls into her vest pockets, she did a fast shuffle to the lobby.

Outside, the year of the monkey wasn't off to a great start. Limp banners sagged across Tu Do Street. Noisemakers and confetti lay discarded on the sidewalks. The reds and yellows of Tet costumes had faded along with the celebrations. People scattered all over the street, looking like scared rats.

David scrutinized the shadows as they hustled up Tu Do Street in the direction of the cathedral. He kept his hand at her elbow.

"You have any details?" Ellie asked, scanning the strangely lit night.

"Couple handfuls of Vietcong sappers blew a hole in the wall around the embassy, crawled in and shot up the place."

"Shit! Did they kill any Americans?"

"It's war, darlin'."

Tracers ribboned the darkness. The sky blazed a spectral neon pink from a fire several blocks away. They made their way through crowds of frantic people, passed the cathedral, and turned right onto Thong Nhut Boulevard. Army tanks rumbled down the broad, tree-lined avenue. The vibration rattled Ellie's bones. Voices rose, shards of Vietnamese and English. Canvas-capped trucks belched diesel exhaust. Was the echo of guns she heard pop-popping an attack or Tet fireworks driving away evil spirits? She gripped her cameras tightly as they stole from doorway to doorway, keeping out of the line of possible gunfire.

"Pay attention," David said. "This is worth more than a handful of interviews."

"What's that smell?"

"Gunpowder, the scent of battle."

It sobered him up really quick. This is serious.

As they crossed Hai Ba Trung Street, the American embassy loomed before them on the left, a giant, new, startlingly white concrete fortress towering six stories above the tangle of houses, shops, and pagodas that had been a carnival earlier in the evening. Floodlights lit up the grounds as if it were surreal daytime.

Near the corner of the ten-foot wall surrounding the embassy, they found a gaping hole. Military guarded it. "Front door's superfluous when they can do that," she said.

David's sardonic glance told her she'd gleaned the obvious. Her chest was tight.

Suddenly, the noises and smells and the crush of panic muted. She was transported into the eye of an adrenalin tornado, her motor racing yet calm, her eyesight knife-sharp within the eddy of colors that streamed beyond her. It was her ski racing vision, the vision that gave her the ability to fly down a course with perfect focus, the rest of the world a blur. No fear, fueled by instincts, true and fast.

Chaos snapped into focus.

Sirens screeched.

Hot white floodlights rained down from the embassy.

Red and blue military lights strobed the darkness.

TV lights and cameras nosed outside the front and side gates.

A cacophony of army vehicles crammed the street.

Ellie mimicked David's movements as they inched closer, crouching, back-to-back, shooting photos. A handful of nervous South Vietnamese police in white uniforms barred their way, guns cocked chest high, when Ellie ventured too close. She swept her ID card from the chain around her neck and held it up. The police called out warnings and poked guns in her direction. She shot her hands into the air, still gripping her camera, clicking on motor drive until a policeman barked an order in Vietnamese and nudged her backward with the butt of his gun.

We're outta here," David commanded, his hand in front of her, backing them away. "No telling what could happen. Not worth the risk. There are too many ways to die in Vietnam."

They passed a CBS cameraman on the sidewalk. "No clue what's happening inside, man, all the gates are locked, no way of knowing anything," he said. "This isn't the only attack. Just got word of coordinated strikes in other southern cities."

"You hear that, Ellie? It was just a matter of time until the war finally crashed the neighborhood." David glanced at her. "My God, darlin', your eyes are big as two full moons. You okay?"

She ignored him, still holding her camera in front of her. "Let's check out the back of the embassy!" She started moving in that direction.

Police raised their weapons.

"That's it. We're gone. Come on. You don't want to mess with the white mice."

"The who?"

"The police. They're called that because they're cowards, but don't underestimate them; they're corrupt bullies when it comes to civilians." Grabbing her arm, he yanked her away. "These guys have mush for brains. You don't want to piss them off. I wasn't thinking. Shouldn't have exposed you to this danger," he muttered. "I'm as careless as Burrows."

She broke his handhold when they'd gotten a block away. "Damn those police, you know there's more happening in there. We should stay."

"This is how it works, Ellie: You get the shots, and you leave. You don't hang around. Simple matter of survival." He was quiet for a moment, watching the turmoil. "You don't want to get reckless. Won't end well. Come on. My place is just the other side of the cathedral. I've got to call the bureau, check in."

"I can go back to the hotel."

"Better if you don't go on alone, and I don't have time to take you."

Ellie glared at him.

He grimaced at her. "You've caught the fever. Just like an old hand. Great instincts." He walked so fast she had to trot to keep up.

She cocked her ears, listening to explosions and short bursts of automatic gunfire. Some of it sounding from behind them. Embassy, she thought. She inhaled deeply and followed David into the villa.

"I've got to call the bureau. Join y'all in two shakes. Darkroom."

The scent of developer calmed her. She stood for several minutes thinking about her mother, wondering how her World War II experiences as a Marine photographer compared with Ellie's own.

"Shit on ice, darlin'," David said, coming up behind her. "VC hit five main targets in Saigon, including the presidential palace, radio station, and naval HQ, as well as the embassy. Commandos backed by a battalion with heavy weapons."

"We only saw a fraction of it?" Ellie flashed on the palace she'd seen on her arrival ride into Saigon. "Shit. We missed the real action."

"It's not over. We were lucky we made it through in one piece. But now I've got to hightail it down to Cholon. Big battle between the Seventh Infantry and the VC."

"Cholon?"

"Chinatown."

"Yessir." She saluted. "I'm ready."

"Sorry. I've got to be free to move around and not watch out for you."

"But I can help you. Besides, aren't you still high?"

"Goes with the territory." He fished in one of his photo-vest pockets for a bottle filled with small white pills. He shook it and unscrewed the top. "Want some of these?"

"What are they?"

"Forget it." He emptied a few into his hand, and popped them into his mouth, swallowing them dry.

"I'm bummed. Guess I'll print the film we shot."

"That would be a big help." He unloaded film cannisters into her palms. "Contact sheets, yeah?"

"Yeah."

Sirens wailed.

"I'd better get moving. You'll be fine here. Best to stay put until daylight, only a couple of hours before you can go back to the hotel. Stay safe." David rested a hand on her shoulder before gripping the cameras around his neck.

"Don't worry. There will be plenty of action for you. You've got the goods, Ellie. Ben was right to send you here."

13

<hr>

She worked her way through the film.

"Jeez, these suck," she grumbled, eyeing her contact sheets in the red glow of the darkroom. She hadn't gotten close enough to the action. Her images lacked engagement compared to David's gripping shots. The insistent sliver of an idea wedged into her brain. She dropped the contacts on the counter, turned off the light, and made tracks for the US Embassy, cameras and credentials around her neck, notebook and pencil in a vest pocket.

She bobbed and weaved along the route she and David had taken earlier. Gunfire punctuated the night. At the embassy, military police stood guard. Pacing along two lengths of the wall, she eavesdropped on reporters who were speculating on rumors that flared as brightly as gunfire: VC on the first floor; VC all the way up to the sixth floor; no one even knew how many Americans were inside the building. It was a weird kind of stalemate with the Vietcong supposedly inside and a US show of might on the outside, but no one really had any idea if Charlie had breached the building or not.

A US Army helicopter swung in and tried to land on the

roof's raised platform but gunfire from inside the embassy wall sent it backpedaling into the air without offloading any soldiers.

She turned her camera on the reporters and photographers who gathered in small groups. She studied their stances, slouched and alert at the same time, and watched their eyes constantly scanning the scene. Restless and anxious, she glanced around, figured she was clearly visible among the frantic South Vietnamese and Marines barking orders, but no one paid her any mind.

As she approached the high concrete wall near the corner of Thong Nhut and Mac Dinh Chi, she eyed the jagged rupture the sappers had blown. No guards, no cops, but VC inside.

Fuck it.

Her downhill race mentality kicked in.

Pick a line. Stay on course.

She clutched her cameras close to her chest, looked both ways, dropped into a tight tuck, and ducked through the three-foot hole in the barricade like a stealthy thief. Floodlights cast eerie shadows. Her pride at making such a bold move evaporated when she tripped over a dead Vietcong body. Ellie's fist found her mouth. She froze.

This was her moment of truth. Was this it for her or would she be tenacious enough to become a reporter in this war? Wanting to be a war correspondent took more than the desire to be one. She had to control her emotions to accept that death, carnage, and reek of war would become constant companions from this point on if she continued. A slight dizziness took her back to the memory of her most frightening downhill race at Stowe, Vermont. The starting gate was above the octagon warming hut on a steep pitch fifty yards above the first left turn on the icy nosedive course. Three racers ahead of her had missed the turn and crashed into the frozen mattresses tied on the massive pines on each side of the course. All three suffered injuries. Moment of truth. She put aside all her doubts when the starter counted down, "Five-four-three- two-one-GO!" She went.

Her focus returned to the present. "Five-four-three-two-one-go" she rasped. She aimed her camera on what remained of the Vietcong's head that lay in a pool of blood, skull fragments, and brain matter.

Click.

The image made her sink to her knees and retch. She jerked her head back up, swallowing an urge to flee. Bodies splayed in and out of oversized planters. She gawked. Moved in close.

Click, click.

Pools of blood and exposed organs had already drawn flies. Another spasm ripped through her. "*Welcome to the stench of war,*" Nick had told her on the patrol. *Guess I'm not quite ready yet, but this will not stop me, no sir.*

Click.

Holding her breath, she hugged the wall and stayed low to the ground. The sight of dead bodies flashed her back to her mother's WWII Marine photos: surreal shots of dead and bloated Japanese. The embassy lights shed a strident, ethereal aspect to the spectacle she viewed through her lens.

Gunfire raked the wall alongside her, spraying her with fragments of concrete and grit.

The odor of spent gunpowder hung heavy in the air.

She scrambled out of the hole and collapsed on the ground against the outside wall, hyperventilating, lips pulled back over her teeth in a grimace. *Holy Shit.*

The sky was lightening, gelling the eeriness in momentary stasis. She changed film and grabbed her notebook, needing to jot down her stark and grisly impressions of the assault.

Her hands trembled too much to write.

An MP pulled her up by the elbow. "Clear the area, lady."

She offered up a glazed stare.

"Move. Get the fuck out of here."

As if on cue, dawn broke. US Military police shot the locks off the front gate and then rammed it open with a Jeep. She heard more choppers. Looked up. Ellie merged into the gang of reporters rushing into the embassy behind the Jeep, her Nikon on motor drive. David's words rang in her ears: "Get the shots and leave." Okay. She had the shots. She hurtled back to his darkroom to print the film.

The inevitable crash after the surge of excitement depleted her reserves, but by ten o'clock in the morning, the busywork of developing film had lowered her adrenalin levels and returned her heartbeat to a steady cadence. She'd gotten some jaw-dropping shots, a few of which she left among David's contacts, and picked her way back to the hotel, clutching her proofs in a yellow photo cardboard box.

Fatigue scratched the edges of her eyelids. "I broke on through to the other side," she sang wryly, mimicking Jim Morrison as she stepped into the shower, propping herself against the tiles as tepid water streamed over her.

Revived and in clean clothes, she headed for the terrace restaurant downstairs and slid into a rattan chair at a table for four. Her skin was sticky with perspiration, shower or no shower. The Continental was an island of mid-morning sanity in the madness that had descended on the city in the middle of the night.

Little had changed. People moved at the same tropical pace. She glanced at the Vietnamese waiter in his starched white jacket and saw dead VC in his black eyes. She cringed, looked away, mumbling her order for an omelette and a strawberry daiquiri. The first sip slipped down her throat like silk, a little sweetness against the horror.

Here she was, smack in the middle of a war. By choice. *Who'da thunk?*

The omelette came. She'd lost her appetite. That was a new wrinkle. Never happened before. As she drank a second daiquiri, her muscles unknotted. She picked at the eggs. A deep breath soughed through her body. She'd be able to sleep now. Her middle-of-the-night foray with David had been a surprise diversion from her nightmare of the Delta patrol. That horrid incident was falling into perspective. With David, her instincts had taken charge, and her desire to seek action kicked in. Head down like a bloodhound on a scent, she'd plunged back into the fray a second time.

Her hunger to capture the drama with her camera had become her sole focus. Confronted by the grim realities inside the embassy wall, war refused to remain in the background and had taken center stage. Her uncertainty diminished in a pouf like cotton candy on the tongue, and her confidence swelled.

Damn, she'd gotten some awesome shots. Ugly and disturbing, the dismemberment of human life without emotion resonated like nothing she had ever experienced. War. The thrill freak incubating inside her had burst out in spades.

She wanted more.

She chuckled. Life was a ski race: Straight down the fall line, over the bumps, through the compressions, tight turns, banks, and jumps.

Her mind was moving a mile a minute, but she was crashing. Back in her room, she fell into a deep sleep, only to wake again at noon. More sleep was not going to happen.

Up in the Caravelle Hotel's rooftop bar, reporters and photographers milled around, coffee or cigarette in one hand, shot glass in the other. Time of day didn't matter. Chatter was at a high pitch as they compared notes on the various attacks: the embassy, the old French national cemetery, Ton Son Nhut airport, and the main Saigon radio station along with attacks in Hue and Nha Trang. Sporadic fighting continued across Saigon.

She recognized an AP reporter she'd seen in a *Newsweek* photo of survivors of a chopper crash in the Central Highlands.

She sat down next to him at the end of the bar. He was thick and brutish. His eyes were wide and bloodshot, yet cunning, with dark circles below. The rest of his face was hidden behind a thick, growth of beard. He glanced up at her with no expression and looked away.

Man of few words.

"Max Kelly?" She stuck out her hand. "Ellie Ketcham."

He nodded. "Guilty, mate," he said with an Aussie accent. He took a sip of his whiskey before turning to her.

"Mind if I ask you a few questions for a book on wartime reporters?"

His slight annoyance didn't faze her; it wasn't exactly the right time to broach the subject. She was about to launch her first question when a shiver of energy vibrated through the journalists, causing them to buzz like a hive full of bees.

They began swarming out of the place.

Kelly bolted out of his seat and queried a TV reporter.

"What is it?" she asked when he returned.

"Cholon. Heating up." He scraped his chair back fast as he sat down. "Word just came in. Two battalions of VC are taking over the Phu Tho racetrack."

"Racetrack?"

"It's the only LZ for US choppers in Saigon. Can't let it fall. 'Scuse me, gotta go. Can't miss out on this."

"I'll come with you."

"Wrong."

She had to think fast. "I see you don't have a camera." She held up her red knapsack, which she'd automatically grabbed when she left her room. "I'll share my photos with you. What do you say? Come on."

As he walked toward the door, he turned back and shrugged. "Well, get a move on, mate."

They jumped into a cab with a couple of guys from Reuters. "Phu Tho," someone said to the driver.

"Taking a taxi into battle," Ellie mumbled. "Outrageous."

The guy in the front seat turned around. "Last I heard, the Seventh Infantry's mobilizing along with some ARVN South Vietnamese soldiers. All facing a shit storm."

"What's with the Seventh? I keep hearing about them," Ellie asked, her interest piqued. Stryker and David had mentioned them too.

"The Seventh is fabled," explained the guy in the front seat. "Been everywhere important in every war, starting with the American Revolution."

When the sounds of battle amplified, the driver stopped. He refused to go any closer to the racetrack. The reporters piled out. The Reuters guys took off down the main street.

Max led her in and out of alleyways. They crept along streets bounded by wood, corrugated metal, and paper shacks. They moved in a kind of dance. Max was a new partner, and she followed his lead.

Nearing the killing ground, deafening gunfire pierced the acrid, smoky air. It was like trying to navigate a fun house where floors and walls constantly moved.

Heads down, they burst out of an alley into the chaos of a street crowded with Seventh Infantry and ARVN fighters. Frozen faces, soldiers on autopilot, attack mode.

Click. Click. Click.

"Don't know if we can move any closer," Kelly shouted. "Get whatever shots you can, and we'll wait for an opening."

Saigon might have been Paris of the Orient with its genteel manners, but Cholon was something else entirely, a densely populated Chinese-Vietnamese ghetto. Turned-up roofs, chockablock slat-louvered ramshackle buildings, and residents scattering like pick-up sticks.

They finally poked out of an alley. Armored personnel carriers rumbled past in a convoy.

"Must be headed to the racetrack. If Charlie captures it, troop and equipment movement will screech to a halt. C'mon, let's join the convoy. You game?"

She nodded for him to move out.

Explosions split the air. Ellie darted like a water strider to avoid being hit by shrapnel, the way she'd believed she could run between raindrops and not get wet when she was a child.

A rocket-propelled grenade destroyed a storefront, so close it nearly broke her eardrums. She was numb yet conscious enough to follow Max. This time she was prepared for the vertigo and muffled hearing. The Aussie ran a haphazard obstacle course through Saigon's Chinatown.

Vietnamese MPs slumped dead over steering wheels, bodies, blood, and severed limbs littering the streets. Armored personnel carriers rumbled past in a convoy.

Max led her in and out of alleyways. Kinetic in an awkward dance, they crept along streets bounded by wood, corrugated metal, and cardboard shacks. Heads down, they burst out of an alley into the chaos of a street crowded with Seventh Infantry and ARVN fighters. They marched forward. Frozen faces. Attack mode.

The noise of battle ratcheted higher.

Whistles arced into explosions.

Metal tore with grating whines.

People screamed as they were hit.

Ellie took deep breaths to manage her pumping adrenalin, camera steady, motor drive whirring. The ocher fog of smoke from explosions and gunfire offered limited visibility.

She bent over to load a new roll of film.

A mortar round crash-landed across the street from her. A flying length of twisted metal sliced into her thigh, almost knocking her to the ground. She stared at it as if it were happening to someone else. She yanked it out. Pain hadn't reached her.

Max turned and pointed to blood soaking her pants leg. "You're lucky, mate, looks like a superficial wound. We're outta here. Get you cleaned up."

She watched the blood staining her jeans then looked up at Max. *Guess this is a band-aid kind of scratch in his mind.* Woozy, she took off the shirt she wore over her tank top and wrapped it around her upper leg. She shivered as if sitting on ice and broke out into a sweat. Hyperventilated. Stumbling, her eyes began to slide shut.

Max put his hand on her shoulder. "Stay with me, girl. You did great. Think you got some good shots?" He looked around. "We're not getting any closer to the racetrack."

She grinned as they stutter-stepped their retreat to the beat of gunfire and explosions.

They hitched a ride in a taxi filled with reporters. When they exited a cab in front of the Continental, Max thanked her. "Listen, I'm in room 308. I'll be writing my story. If your shots are as good as you say they are, bring them to me as fast as you can and I'll file them with my article, give you credit."

"I'll go print them now."

He looked at her as if for the first time. "What did you say your name was?"

"Ellie, Ellie Ketcham." She sped back to her own room and spied blood caking on her forehead as she passed the mirror. She cleaned the wound and hastily applied a couple of Band-Aids. Pulling off her pants, she cleaned and bandaged the shrapnel wound, stepped into clean pants, and limped over to David's, anxious to see what she'd gotten in Cholon. Disappointed he wasn't there, yet relieved to find the darkroom unoccupied and the prints untouched, she got to work.

14

She'd shot much more film in Cholon than at the embassy. Printing her own film was a chance to digest the experience, and she always discovered more in the images than she'd seen while shooting. Magic happened in the darkroom. She developed several of the best shots from her contact sheets and rushed back to the hotel to get them to Max.

"Nice work, Nellie," he exclaimed in his gravelly voice, after scrutinizing her shots.

"It's Ellie. Ellie Ketcham, K-E-T-C-H-A-M. Please spell it right when you give me credit."

"Course, Ellie. You caught the down and dirty, just what I needed. Watching you work today, I expected no less. You're good, mate. You don't deserve the bad rap you got. Shit happens. When I have some down time, I'll give you that interview. And I won't forget your photo credit."

"Thanks, Max, I appreciate it." She wouldn't mind working with Max. No sweet talk, no attitude, all business.

Back in her room, she flinched as she yanked the Band Aids off the hairline shrapnel wound above her left eye. She leaned closer to the bathroom mirror. Still bleeding. Her red badge of courage, she thought wryly as she cleaned the wound then smoothed a fresh bandage onto it and skittered to her desk. She repeated the action with her thigh. More blood than wound. Reflecting on her short experience with Max Kelly, she coughed. *My red badge? What a joke. This is no time for accolades and bullshit, Ellie.*

As she examined the contact proofs through her loupe, she saw their drama. She'd used a telephoto lens when she couldn't get close enough to a subject. The results were astounding. After an hour, she turned to the last contact sheet.

"Holy shit," she said. "No wonder Max thought this would be a good shot. I don't even remember taking it." She bent over the image of an American soldier hit in the chest by a sniper. The telephoto gave an eeriness to the shot, intimate yet remote. The soldier's face was one of surprise, arms splayed wide, rifle in one hand, not unlike Robert Capa's *Falling Soldier*, the famous image from the Spanish Civil War. Stryker had pulled a photo of the painting from his wallet to show her. "A naked and telling portrayal of the human tragedy of war," he'd commented.

What would Stryker think now? He'd pegged her right when he chose her for this job. And she had certainly gained a different perspective to bring to his project.

She stood at the window for a while, thinking back on what she'd experienced so far, then drew an air-mail letter form out of her desk drawer, and started a letter to Stryker. Before she wrote her first word, she realized she'd broken her promise to Ben about stepping into a warzone. "The truth, nothing but the truth," she muttered.

~

AND ... action! This world has fallen apart. A disaster a minute. Went on a patrol with Nick Burrows, a journalist friend of David Jenkins.

Eye opener. I'm sure you've heard by now that the South Vietnamese and the Americans got to play defense on the Vietnamese New Year, when the North Viets coordinated attacks on cities all over the southern part of the country. Jenkins was covering the American embassy, one of the sites that was attacked. I tagged along.

A small Vietcong assault unit of nineteen men, entered the embassy grounds through a big hole they blasted in the wall. Several Americans were killed or injured. I never expected to see dead bodies littering the grass. Blood and guts everywhere.

Then I went to Cholon with Max Kelly of AP, and I saw more fighting. I'm sure you know Cholon is Saigon's Chinatown. Now I'm beginning to comprehend your zeal to reveal a journalist's fixation on war. I'm sure each one has a different take. Of course, there is common purpose: to expose what is occurring. I am now aware of the obstacles journalists face: being in the right place at the right time, overcoming the fear of death or injury, the pressure of deadlines, and enduring the frustration of censorship. War correspondents are a rare breed. I applaud the true value of your project. I now have a better perspective from which to ask questions.

I know I defied your instructions to not cross the line into battle, but the firsthand experience of observing journalists in the field adds another dimension for me to explore about their strength, character, and devotion. Please understand. It was nothing you wouldn't do.

I'm good. That's all for now. I just wanted to keep you posted on what's going on. Hope things are good with you. Love to Sarah and her belly. More soon.

15

As a sultry Saturday evening hung in the air, the Caravelle rooftop bar percolated with the sounds of hard-driving, hard-drinking Saigon journalists who soapboxed their opinions, raising voices and cocktails in emphasis. Ellie listened from a table where she sat by herself, ears twitching like antennae. The ranting was beginning to make sense, a kind of self-preservation that enabled reporters to move back and forth through the veil of their battle-torn stories.

Was it really true they could leave at any time or were they as captive to the war as the military men? Perhaps journalists got so hooked on their subjects they sentenced themselves for the duration. Jerry Forrest came to mind. Hooked on a purpose.

She respected these reporters who plumbed the war's double-edged confusion. Balancing acts, with details in one hand, big picture in the other, not fitting together in any kind of proper jigsaw puzzle. It was a challenge to find what the *Washington Post* reporter Ward Just called a "trustworthy angle of vision." All while keeping the irony out, or at least on a low simmer, and without pointing fingers at the hubris of the planners in Washington and the editors back home. Ellie had landed exactly where she belonged. Her being an outcast was a mere wrinkle in the bigger picture.

She nursed her scotch, enjoying the glow of evening and afterglow of danger. Her experiences at the embassy and in Cholon surfaced in the forefront of her mind. Was she repulsed by the death and destruction or calloused and so focused by ambition that she was becoming cavalier? No, more like paddling a kayak of sanity through rapids of emotion.

Something made her look up. Nick. Rushing toward her. In one swoop, he grasped her hands, pulled her out of her chair, and gathered her into his arms, kissing her long and hard. She pushed him away and sat back down. His eyes darted around.

"What the hell, Nick. You can't just invade my personal space like that."

"Couldn't help it, Ellie-belle. You're irresistible."

What? The good Nick shows up having shed the skin of the other Nick who'd stalked her to David's darkroom?

He slid into a chair opposite her, crossed his arms, and extended his long legs out to the side, ankles stacked. He wore a mint-green Oxford shirt, sleeves rolled above his elbows. Interesting, her blouse was the same color.

"You do have such a way of disappearing. You stood me up. Where've you been?""

"In case you weren't paying attention, there's a war out there." His eyes shined. "Ellie, Jesus Christ, I've missed you. Any time away from you is too long. War makes strange bedfellows of us, doesn't it? You arrived in a bolt of lightning as if it had been aimed." He gazed at her shirt and her eyes. "That color brings out the green in your eyes. Amazing."

"You shaved. What else have you been up to?"

He rubbed his chin. "It's getting dicey out there. Charlie has upped the ante."

"Tell me something I don't know."

"You shouldn't be out there alone dodging bullets. A camera is not a defensive weapon."

"You heard about my visit to the embassy? I just caught the tail end of the attack." She decided to play down her part. "It was riveting, the little bit I saw." She watched his face watching hers. "Besides, I wasn't alone, I was with David."

"Pfft. I should've had your six."

She ruffled. "Hey, I did okay. I don't need you to cover my backside. And from what I saw, it was every man for himself out there."

He bristled. "Not if I'd been with you. We're a team."

Such bravado. A bluff for his insecurities? That wasteful jealousy David told her about?

Think fast. Should I tell him only he thinks we're a team. Nah, better to avoid the other Nick.

"Listen, Nick, you're making sounds that make me think you're looking for a relationship. This is neither the time nor the place for that. I'm here to do a job and a relationship would be a distraction. One I don't need or want. The work is what's important." As she spoke, darkness descended over his eyes like the extra lid of an raptor.

"You're right. I'm sorry. Our work is vital. He snapped his lighter to a Marlboro, inhaling deeply. He spoke deliberately. "We *are* a team. We're working to liberate the Vietnamese from an imperialistic takeover. Last time I checked, that had nothing to do with romance. Think you might be misreading my signals?"

His voice was even but his eyes remained veiled. *Change the subject. Quickly.* "Anyway, I had a couple of good interviews today," she said. "Wally Beene from *Stars and Stripes* and Peter Arnett; that was kind of a coup. David must've convinced them to talk to me." She didn't add that the men's responses had been cryptic at best. "And Max Kelly said he'll talk to me, too."

He rolled his eyes at the David reference. "So, you're making your way despite being blackballed. Good for you."

"Speak for yourself. I was never blackballed, to my knowledge. Keep on truckin', I say."

"Way to go, Ellie. You've been reading Zap Comics?" His voice sounded lighthearted but the light in his eyes remained shadowed. "Never dwell on what happened. Always move on. Eyes on the horizon."

16

―――――

Glancing around at the clusters of correspondents, she noticed their camaraderie. She saw that they ignored Nick; he was clearly not part of the press corps fraternity. He was an outsider. Ellie, however, had no doubt she was part of that fraternity, even if the men might consider her fluff. That had more to do with her being a woman than any misstep she'd made. She'd win them over.

"See you, Nick." She rose and walked away, heading for the Continental.

Squinting at the spread of contact sheets and prints on her bed, she reviewed the angles of battle she had captured with her camera lens. Would her photos stack up against what the veteran photographers shot? Damn straight. As she moved from frame to frame, her focus blurred. Images leapt off the paper to surround her. An eerie light flooded the room in a green-tinged jungle luster, and a stroboscopic vision of the soldier flying into the air flashed against the wall.

She swept the photo sheets to the floor and fell onto the bed, tossing restlessly until she dozed off into a fitful slumber.

"Race Day!" Her father's voice echoed down the hallway. He

shook the bed and threw open the blinds on a perfect icy-cold New England morning.

"Racer ready ... five, four, three ..." She was deep in an egg-shaped tuck, gliding through the gates, spiraling down the fall line, over compressions, legs burning, faster, faster ... finish line, cartwheeling into a ditch full of khaki-colored muddy water. World erupted into a fountain, turned the sky dark. The cloying, humid stink of jungle rot suffocated, the ditch stained red with blood, the air a cacophony of shouts and panicked voices.

A boy hopped on a bloody, mangled foot, closer, closer, a grimace on his Pinocchio face, teeth like Chiclets, black eyes searching an unseen future, jaw smooth as a baby's cheek, his disembodied voice. "My foot, my foot, oh God ..."

Her throat constricted. Tears welled.

Men in bandoliers gripped M-16s, crowded around the boy dancing on one foot. Marionettes, a chorus line of Army Rockettes, high kicked in garters and fishnet stockings. They streamed hatred at her, lips carved in wooden anger. They veered as one, a school of barracuda changing direction, leering at her.

Nick Burrows sat in a tree, sinister, grinning Cheshire Cat licking his paw. The tree tilted over the bloody canal; punji sticks and porcupine quills covered its banks. He jerked the chorus line's strings into a higher kick. The boy out front did a one-footed jig.

Ow ow ow. Her body was being pierced by their fear and loathing. She opened her mouth to scream. Nothing came out.

A gaggle of women sat on bleachers following the action. They watched, indifferent, their grimaces showing black, rotted teeth, their laughter discordant, hysterical cackles. They spat betel juice from between scabrous lips.

Ellie tried to run but couldn't move. She looked down. Her ski boots were sinking into mud. It oozed over the boot tops and rose up her calves.

Screams strangled in her throat and woke her. She pushed

herself up, caught her breath, as the dissonant beating of her heart gradually evened out.

"He's better off; he's out of the shit." With one foot, said her internal voice.

She thought she'd left the wreckage of the patrol behind and moved on, but she'd been ambushed.

Nick knocked and peered into her room.

"Ellie, you okay?" She looked up at him from the edge of her bed, rigid, bug-eyed. "Holy shit, what happened?" He entered.

"Nightmare. Soldier with one foot."

He walked to the bed and leaned down to brush hair off her face. She cringed, put her hand up, palm out. He peered into her eyes.

"You're safe. I'm here," he crooned.

She fled into the bathroom and splashed water on her face. When she emerged, he had switched on the lamps. She was grateful; light shrank monsters into mere shadows. He picked up discarded prints and examined the images. He poured scotch into one of two glasses on the dresser and held it out to her as she reentered the bedroom. "This oughta help." He sat on a corner of the bed.

She took the glass in a trembling hand, downed the scotch, and sank down beside him.

He took her empty glass, set it on the floor, and put his arms around her.

"I just saw some of your images," he said. "Exceptional. Way too good for you to even think about leaving. Obviously, Stryker sent you here to do his dirty work, but it's clear you've got a greater purpose."

Pushing away, she scowled. "You watch what you say; not only does Ben have more war experience than you, he can also back it up with his dispatches. Besides, where'd you get the idea I'm leaving?"

"Just keeping you safe is all. And don't you remember when you told me you might as well cut your losses and go home?"

She cocked an eyebrow at him.

She got up, returned the contacts and prints to their box, and sat on the desk chair. She poured more scotch and slugged it, her face relaxing a bit. "I'm not a quitter." She frowned at him and squared her shoulders.

It had taken until now for her curiosity to vanquish her hesitation to work with Nick. She had to know if his effort would truly be honest. "Okay, how am I going to assist you in saving Vietnam?"

He smiled. "That's my girl."

"I'm not your girl."

"You're the only person I can trust to work my Viet source. And it will give you something else to think about. Despite our barbed relationship, you're eager and smart."

She frowned.

"You do have more thorns than a rose bush, Ellie. You might not recall, but I suggested you could research the history of Vietnam, find out how they got into this mess."

"I remember. But history pales in the face of current events."

"Just listen a minute. I've arranged a meeting for you with a historian, a professor at Saigon University named Thiep. He'll make a great interview. He's stoked by the idea of your interest in his people and their traditions."

She resisted his eyes boring into hers. She wasn't going to rush into the fray. Yet. *But an interview with a Vietnamese scholar? Interesting. You surprise me, Nick.*

AFTER NICK LEFT, Ellie gazed around her claustrophobic room. From within its mosquito netting, the bed invited her to sleep, but she had no desire to revisit the minefield of dreams.

What could have caused a nightmare, the implied threat in Nick's eyes at the Caravelle? It had unnerved her that his voice was light while his eyes were dark and ominous.

She paced. Nick was a knot of contrasts. David had shone a light on his background, things Nick hadn't divulged, and provided at least some of the reasons his anger rode close to the surface. A wave of compassion pulsed through her. All he needed was to focus on the positive, as Pollyanna as that sounded, and find an outlet for his commitment to champion the underdog. He was persistent, she had to give him that. He kept showing up as if she were a magnet, trying to secure her agreement to join him in his mission to save the Vietnamese underdog. She continued to wonder if his offer was genuine, or if he had an ulterior motive.

Benefit of the doubt. He'd shown her a charming, caring side, with kindness that touched her. Did the good Nick make up for the other Nick? Okay then. There's nothing to lose or to risk except time, maybe.

~

THE NEXT AFTERNOON, she took a cyclo to Saigon University and waited outside Professor Thiep's classroom while his students streamed out. She walked in, and, assuming she was following the proper protocol, she bowed.

He returned an amused stare, remaining upright.

Her face heated. "Er, Professor Thiep, I'm Ellie Ketcham, a colleague of Nick Burrows. Thank you for seeing me."

He didn't look much older than his students. Lean and sinewy, like a tennis player. His cheeks bore the faint scars of acne. He wore big, round, wire-rimmed glasses.

"Welcome, Mademoiselle Ketcham," Thiep said with severe

politeness, gazing at her with intense eyes. He turned two chairs toward each other and indicated for Ellie to sit. He remained standing, his face composed. "How may I assist?" He spoke in a monotone.

"Nick might have told you I'm intrigued by your country, your situation." She folded her hands in her lap. "I'm interested in learning and communicating the history of your people to Americans."

He nodded and sat down, erect in his chair. "We are a centuries-old culture," he said. "We live close to the land. Spirits and fairies bring us good fortune. It is humans who bring bad luck. Our mythology is simple: Honesty is rewarded, greed is punished. Despite thousands of years of suffering and fighting invasions, we remain a simple people with uncomplicated needs."

His voice was soft and mesmerizing. She watched expressions pass over his face like fast clouds until he stopped speaking.

"What is the heritage of Vietnam's centuries-old culture?"

He unhooked his glasses from his ears, extracted a folded handkerchief from a pocket, and cleaned the lenses methodically. *Is he challenging me?*

Securing his glasses on his nose and ears, he spoke. "My nation's location has always been strategic in Southeast Asia. Many have felt the need to colonize us. The Chinese, so close by, wanted more land. Cultural assimilation, they called it. Very convenient, yes, to insulate their southern border with Vietnam from invasion.

"For the imperialistic French, our rubber and rich natural resources filled their banks with abundance. As easy to pluck as blossoms from a cherry tree. Each bloom turned to gold." He chuckled deep in his throat. "For them, we were the Southeast Asian Raj."

He narrowed his eyes at Ellie. "I do not wish to offend, but in the case of the American lion, do you honestly believe it possible to stop the spread of communism throughout Southeast Asia?"

He paused, as if to let the idea sink in, then continued forcefully. "We are merely one of many nations that fall into that political category."

"But sir," she blurted, "you do not think communism is a threat to your nation?"

A sudden stillness suspended the moment. The veins in his neck pulsated and his eyes turned totally black.

How in the hell had he done that? A sudden chill and sense of darkness enveloped her. Claustrophobia threatened to strangle her. As she gulped a breath of air, she wondered if she had violated some sacred privacy, a guarded secret?

The stillness faded, but not the darkness or the cold as Thiep's squirrelly narrow eyes returned to normal. He spoke in the monotonous drone of an academic.

"We have been fighting for thousands of years. We are a warrior nation. We survive. Simple matter of time, plentiful as rice. Time speaks truth."

She gathered up the last of her remaining fortitude. "Excuse me, but you didn't answer my question."

"I am not the one who has a say in the outcome of this conflict. I am merely saying that whatever the result, whether it be South or North that will reign, Vietnam will survive."

WHEN SHE GOT BACK to the Continental, Nick was sitting on the floor in the hallway across from her room, leaning against the wall. "Hey, El, how'd it go?" He jumped up.

She poked him on the chest. "You're pushing your luck, Nicky. First of all, you hide a communist sympathizer inside a history lesson? Your idea of a joke?" She rooted her hands on her hips, planted her feet apart. "I'm not laughing."

"Jesus, Ellie, what did he tell you?"

"It's what he didn't tell me. He didn't implicate himself in anything, but he sure as hell convinced me of what he really is about. There's nothing there I can take to the authorities, but you put me in jeopardy without a thought for my safety."

Nick snorted. "Christ, I'm offering you some meaningful work."

She raised an eyebrow, failing to suppress a laugh. "Thiep knows his stuff," she admitted. "And such conviction. He tried to convince me American firepower is pissing in the wind."

"It is," Nick said.

"So, you're colluding with the enemy?" She turned on her heel and entered her room.

He followed her and made himself comfortable on the bed, balling up a pillow behind his head and stretching his legs out full length. Ellie stood with her back to the window holding her hair away from her neck and hoping for a cooling breeze.

"Suffice it to say Thiep and I are on the same mission," he said. "If the United States really understood Vietnam, we'd abandon this absurd war."

"Sure, Nick, you and Thiep are going to end this war with diplomacy and politics? Take off your rose-colored glasses." She twisted her hair into a braid. "What's your angle?"

He reddened.

"I'm waiting, Nick."

"I'll fill you in over dinner. I know a great Chinese restaurant where they don't serve dogmeat."

"You trying to make me gag?"

"C'mon, what do you say?"

Ellie leered at him. "You're dodging my question."

Nick tossed back the gaze and pursed his lips.

"Okay," she relented, "but only because I'm hungry."

17

Enticing aromas of garlic, peppers, and mushrooms lured her into the French-Chinese eatery. Their round table had a lazy Susan in the center that spun like a roulette wheel. Nick ordered a sampling of dishes while keeping up chatter about the importance of *their* connection with Thiep.

He stepped all over his own words, repeating himself, almost buying back his pitch, which amused her to no end.

"I'm ravenous." She helped herself to a variety of Cantonese soul food: lotus root soup, steamed pork belly with salted vegetables, green leeks with pig's blood, Tong Kong salty chicken, and roast duck *lo mein.*

She crunched on something crispy. "M-m-m. Tastes like potato chips. What is this?"

"Deep-fried intestines," Nick said with a straight face.

"Really? Delicious."

His eyebrows lifted, telling her she'd batted down his attempt to unnerve her.

"So, listen," he said. "Questionable foods aside, you can get good information from Thiep, and we can follow that with articles that call out the US military. That's one way we can expose some of our own military's aggression."

She thought about his words. "*I* can get good information from Thiep? Why just me?"

He gazed off into the distance. "I had hoped you'd want to work with him, since he and I are not on the best of terms."

"Oh, now you and your source are not speaking?"

"Look, Ellie, I'm being honest. He wanted me to do something I'm not comfortable doing—"

"Hold on. You're not comfortable so you enlist me, so I can be uncomfortable?"

Nick thrust his arms up, hands out, annoyance flaring in his eyes. "Jesus, Ellie, I just want to unveil the truth without anyone getting hurt, physically, I mean. You'll only be extracting information. There's no risk in that."

She gave it a thought. "Your plan is to get this information and get it published."

"Shine a light in the darkness."

"There has to be proof, you know that. You can't print a word without it."

"Thiep will not provide information without backing it up, whether it be photos, documents, or witnesses."

"Look Nick, it's not hard to understand every publication has an agenda, either through censorship or manipulation. The best you can hope for is a communist propaganda sheet. Or will your uncle wave his magic wand at a respectable publication, and you, at least, will have a byline?"

Nick stopped eating, placed his chopsticks on the side of his plate, and met her eyes. "Low blow, Ellie. Leave my uncle Francis out of this. I'm here on my own merits, and don't you forget it."

She'd touched a sore spot. "My point is who's going to publish us?"

"French newspapers, for one. They'd love to see us Americans fall on our faces, since the Frogs failed to tame the Vietnamese in their seventy years of imperialism."

Ellie concentrated on the food, washing it down with jasmine tea, and laid her chopsticks on the rim of her rice bowl.

"I really don't see how I can help." She demurely dabbed the corners of her mouth with the napkin. "And isn't there a risk, you know, like collaborating with the enemy?"

"Okay, first of all, you're not collaborating. Secondly, for Chrissake, you're a journalist, much more than just a photographer. I know you. I see how you grasp things. It's facts that are key. You don't *take* sides, you cover them, all sides, in this war. Come on, Ketcham, get a grip. You're hooked. You can't fool me. Like you said, you're no quitter."

"Interesting list of justifications, or placations," she shot back. "This is not why I came to Saigon. Besides, you haven't given me assurances that I wouldn't face a firing squad for treason."

"Haven't you got a vivid imagination," he cracked.

She glared at him, cleared her throat.

He lit a cigarette. "Okay, okay." He raised his hands in surrender. "I'm getting the definite drift you're not interested in the Thiep connection." One eyebrow crawled up. "Okay, Stryker's work is important to you. Besides, I've seen your photos. You have a unique style. There's more to you than being someone's lackey. I don't want you to get lost in the shuffle, that's all." He beamed his best smile on her.

"I'm not someone's lackey. I am on a purposeful assignment." She protested but registered some truth in what he said. She might be playing with fire, but she trusted her ability to ride the knife edge as she'd done in ski racing. Racing had a physical edge; this edge was emotional. She wanted to choose her own fire. Thiep gave her the willies.

Between their sparring, and the edge of fire their conversation had sparked, the groundwater of sexual attraction had been stirring throughout dinner. As he walked her back to her room, pheromones flew wildly in the air. Nick's eyes shone. No mistaking what he intended. He put his hands on her shoulders and kissed her. She kissed him back. They stumbled into her room and onto the bed. His lovemaking was gentle yet intense. She gave in to the sensations and reveled in their new connection all night long. He left before dawn.

WHEN SHE WOKE, exhausted yet vitalized, she turned her attention to preparing for an important interview with the renowned correspondent Henry Lord. She was grateful for her ability to compartmentalize thoughts, move them around like chess pieces and bring the most important pieces forward. Thinking about Nick would have to come later.

The interview with Lord exceeded her expectations. She couldn't wait to tell David about it. She rushed to the villa and rapped on the door but couldn't wait for an answer and burst inside. David was reading a book in the living room.

"David, I met the most amazing guy from the *Washington Post*," she said, unable to contain her elation. "I found what Ben's looking for: a correspondent who's down in the trenches with the soldiers, telling their graphic stories."

He grinned at her and patted the sofa cushion next to him. "Come, sit down."

"Henry Lord." She remained standing, too excited to sit.

"I know him. He was wounded a year or two ago, caught some shrapnel from an exploding grenade. He left Vietnam."

"He just got back. He says he takes on the pain of every soldier who's ever been injured. He was glum, like he couldn't figure out how he got here or what he was doing yet couldn't stay away. Thinks the war is unwinnable."

Ellie ran her hands through her disheveled hair. She was still vibrating from the high.

David stared at her. "He's probably right. Really made an impression on you, didn't he?"

"He sees the big picture and concentrates its power into a detail. The drama of soldiers marching through mud, for instance, not knowing what's beyond the next rice paddy. I could hear the mud sucking at their boots as he talked."

"It's good to see the big picture, but I find it more useful to narrow focus." "For me, it's tight focus that tells the story." He alternately spread his arms narrowed them, bringing his hands together. "So, how'd you land this big fish?"

She chuckled. "Lucky, I guess. He sat next to me in the bar the other evening, and we started talking. It rolled on from there, and he agreed to meet me for an interview."

"Lord's honorable, not the kind to pay heed to gossip and rumor in this swamp of manipulation, lies, and deception. He won't write anything he can't verify."

She sank onto the sofa beside him but rose again just as quickly. "He told me about a French journalist he'd known years ago and said he could try to put me in touch with him."

"Does this reporter have a name?"

"René Jalbert. Ever hear of him?"

"Jalbert? Sure. Been around since the first Indochina war. I don't know him myself. A loner. Doesn't mix with the American Press corps. He's bound to be a fascinating interview; the man walked the *Street Without Joy* with Bernard Fall."

"What street? Who?"

"Bernard Fall was an incredibly perceptive war correspondent. His book, *Street Without Joy*, is about the French Indochina war. He warned of a protracted and horrid war if the Americans engaged."

"This could be an interview with depth. Perspective on two wars. What do you think?"

David shrugged, silent for a few moments. "Could be, Ellie.

Go for it." He clapped his book shut and laid it on the coffee table.

"Have you got a minute?" He stood. "I want to show you something."

"Sure."

He led the way to the second floor and entered a spacious bedroom dappled in sunlight. It was a study in rose: the carpet, cabbage-rose curtains, and a sitting area with two chintz-uphol-stered chairs and a Queen Anne writing desk. She looked at him questioningly.

"A change of pace, perhaps?" he suggested. "I thought you might like being in a houseful of reporters, and since I told Ben I'd watch over you when I could, the villa is more pleasant than the hotel."

"Did I hear you right? You're saying I can crash here?"

"Yes, ma'am. This room reminds me of my grandmother's living room in Natchez, loud yet comforting."

"Far out."

"You'll be safe and comfortable here, although we all spend more time out of this house than in it. But it's a good home base and your share of rent will be much less than your hotel room. That should please Stryker. There's also a lock on your door. I suggest you use it. Here's the key." He winked. "Our staff puts out decent food and keeps the place clean. So, no responsibili-ties other than your work, and you're closer to the darkroom."

"For as long as this job lasts, I'm grateful. I mean, I don't know how many more journalists are going to talk to me. Even if I'm totally stoked by my interview with Henry Lord, I'm real-istic. I'm still *persona non grata*."

"It's not quite the end of the world, darlin'." He paused, something he often did, as though editing his words before he spoke. "You will find your way. Jalbert may open the gates."

Hustling to the Continental, she cast her eyes around her room, slaying her dragons of fear, banishing the horrors of the patrol and the penumbra of nightmares. She shook off the lurking shadows the way a dog shakes off the rain. With renewed optimism, she threw her things into her duffel, slung her camera bag over her shoulders, saluted the ceiling fan, checked out, and waved goodbye to the concierge. Forward into a brighter light.

As she unpacked in her new rose-filled bower, she thought about Henry Lord's offer to connect her with French journalist René Jalbert. If the butterflies in her belly were any indication, an interview with Jalbert could take Ben's book to a new level. Balance had come to her right when she needed it.

18

There were almost as many typewriters in David's villa as lamps. They rested on tables, sofas, and chairs, as if abandoned in a rush. Ellie camped out at an electric Olivetti on the dining room table and typed up the notes from her interview with Henry Lord. She didn't often have the luxury of formalizing her notes. It gave her an opportunity to add reactions to a subject's comments. She hadn't been expecting Lord's observations about the Vietnamese people's irrepressible nature to mirror Thiep's declarations of their resilience in the face of imperialistic interference.

Thiep's words about the sturdiness of the Vietnamese rose in her thoughts. Up to that point, she hadn't seriously acknowledged that the United States was an imperialistic power. Nick and Lord both believed the US had no regard for the people whose country it had come to defend from communism.

She wanted to delve deeper. What made the Viets so resilient?

Abandoning her Nikons, she set out from the villa to scrutinize with her small, hopefully unnoticeable Rollei. She tried for invisibility, not an easy feat for a strawberry blonde in a throng of dark-haired Asians. Little kids huddled around her, reaching up to touch her hair, sticking their grimy hands in her pockets, hawking cigarette butts, and practicing their limited English.

She recorded the raw images, hungry to study the contrasts of street life that floated between commerce and war, between doll-like girls who played to the GIs and the gaunt crones she'd seen in jungle hamlets. She squinted through her lens at the layered charm of the flower sellers and sidewalk vendors, imagining their habits of survival, desperate and burning, inbred through centuries of oppression. Contrast provided a kind of balance. She moved as if pulled on a string beyond the downtown area and into the slums. Refugees crowded there, drawn in from villages by the American promise of work in the city.

The ground was shifting under her as she looked beneath the surface of this mysterious culture. Despite his leftist sympathies, Thiep had opened her eyes to the reality beyond propaganda; her perspective shaded from black and white to color, illuminating the sharp angles and raw edges of the evolution of the Vietnamese heritage. It was a case of a one-time sophisticated culture helplessly self-destructing at the hand of foreign oppression. With all his bluster, Nick hadn't been able to articulate the situation clearly at all.

Once you get a glimmer of what to look for, you can see.

That evening, she arrived back at the villa to be met by the cook, who handed her an envelope. "Very big man come here, look for you. He sorry you no here. Name René Jalbert."

Thank you, Po." Ellie bowed. To her, it was an honor to respect the ritual of Asian courtesy, even if Thiep rejected it.

She opened the envelope as she walked up the stairs. Smallish, square writing. "*Mlle. Eleanor, I am the journalist you have been told about. Shall we rendezvous? It is possible we share mutual interests. Tomorrow, 16:30, at the Oriental Star on Le Loi Street.*"

The plot thickened. And why not? This was the inscrutable Orient.

~

THE ORIENTAL STAR was tucked away through a kitchen and up a set of steep, narrow stairs. A couple of Vietnamese men in jeans, T-shirts, and flip-flops sat at a long bar extending down the right side. An American GI wearing a big splashy-flowered shirt, and a petite Vietnamese girl in a tight, shimmery dress lounged in one of the booths that lined the opposite side. A narrow gutter of an aisle separated them. Mirrors lined the walls. The smells of cleaning solvents mixed with greasy food hung in the air.

"Mademoiselle Eleanor." A sixty-plus-year-old man swiveled his head from his seat at the end of the bar. Quite distinguished looking, a little stooped, a cross between Beau Geste and Charles Aznavour. He stood, stretching several inches over six feet by Ellie's guess, and bowed. "I am retired Colonel René Jalbert."

She looked around. "I guess I am pretty easy to identify." She slid onto a barstool around the curve of the bar. That way she could face him almost head on.

"What is obvious is that you are a most attractive young lady."

Was he hitting on her? No. He seemed a no-nonsense type. Black hair peppered with silver receded slightly at the corners of his temples and his eyes were dark brown, almost black. They actually glittered. He lifted his empty glass.

"May I offer you a brandy and soda, or something else?"

She said nothing.

"Oh, drinking in the middle of the day is inappropriate behavior in your world," he said with a trace of sarcasm. "It helps me compensate for all the time I lose when I'm in-country where there are few sources for good brandy. It might be a little early in most parts of the world, but this is a war zone. Here it is never too soon for a cocktail."

"Brandy and soda will be fine."

He signaled the mamasan bartender, pointing to his glass and then to Ellie, and held up two fingers. He waited until their drinks were served.

"I will not waste your time or mine." He locked his eyes on hers. "Not a single member of the American Military Press Corps or a Western journalist in Saigon will associate with Nick Burrows since that ill-fated Army patrol. Not even Francis Burrows can help him. Because you are associated with him, you are, pardon the pun, bad news. Guilt by association. If anyone had any trust in you two, it has evaporated."

Although she'd suspected as much, especially from the clipped, abbreviated answers of the few who'd agreed to be interviewed by her, excepting Max Kelly, the magnanimous Jerry Forrest, and Henry Lord, his words stunned her like a slap across the face. She'd been swayed by Nick's assurances the shunning wouldn't last long. She honestly believed it would have dissipated by now, but, alas, it hadn't, according to this Frenchman.

She swallowed hard. "I did expect some of that. It's not fair—"

"Fair plays no part in politics and war. The US political powers do not wish for the truth about this war to reach their public. Your blunder on that patrol gives them easy opportunity to cast doubt on the press. They view every incident that discredits journalism as beneficial. You and Burrows have scored a few points for the prevaricating American general Westmoreland."

Ellie regained her equilibrium. "Interesting interpretation

that I have become a tool for US propaganda. How come *you're* not afraid to be seen with me?"

"Why do you suppose I chose this hole in the wall, as you might call it, eh?"

This guy pulls no punches. The pit she was wallowing in got deeper. "What's in it for you?" she asked, an edge in her tone, and waited for the punchline she was sure was coming.

"Allow me to backtrack for a moment. Since no one walked in the door with you, I must assume you are the principal actor in your research assignment for the American novelist, Ben Stryker. Am I correct in my assessment?"

"How do you know about my business?"

"It does not matter how I know. What is important to you is what happens next—"

Before he could continue, a Vietnamese urchin galloped into the bar, bare feet slapping on the floor. The mamasan chittered at him as he raced to the rear, stopped, ogled Ellie and Jalbert, then turned around and trotted out the door and back down the steps.

Ellie watched the show then shrugged at the Frenchman whose ramrod posture at the bar had a military bearing. He bolted off his stool to the exit and peered down the stairs after the boy.

He returned to the bar and turned his attention back to her. "One must practice caution. Youngsters such as that one are messengers, voyeurs who gather information for whomever pays them."

"Oh my, that never occurred to me. I'll be more alert."

"May I be so bold as to suggest being ostracized raises a unique opportunity for you to research your employer's book in your own way? If he does not like the result, you will have your own piece, or at least a byline that will restore and propel your career." He laughed, a deep, rich sound. The laugh stopped abruptly, and his voice grew serious. "Even if your spirit is willing, you don't have access to enough sources to help you complete your assignment."

"I'm not sure I like your attitude, Colonel." She made a move to slide off the barstool. "I'm not as helpless as you assume."

"So sure of yourself, but perhaps not," Jalbert said.

She stayed where she was, her curiosity irresistibly kindled.

He shook the ice cubes in his glass, swigged the rest of his drink, and signaled the mamasan for another round. "You will not regret making such a change in direction for your career. I offer you the opportunity to turn a negative into a positive."

"How? Go ahead, wave the magic wand."

"How?" he parroted. "I have seen much history, since before the first Indochinese war, through an alternate perspective. Allow me to give you some insight into this perspective. Please, do stop me if you already know this."

He paused, while the mamasan mixed drinks. When she set their glasses onto the bar, Jalbert shook his, distributing ice throughout, and held it up to Ellie in a toast. "Magnificent invention, ice." He took a sip and leveled his gaze at her.

She sighed to signal her impatience.

Jalbert ignored the slight. "Years ago in Laos, French military intelligence financed our war against the resistance with the sale of opium." He leaned in close to Ellie and lowered his voice. "When your President Kennedy took office, Monsieur Eisenhower told him Laos would be the location of the next major communist takeover."

"How long ago was this and who was the resistance?"

"In 1954, the French were defeated by the very same people whom the Americans fight now: Ho Chi Minh and company."

She reached for her glass and downed the remains of her brandy and soda. Thiep had not mentioned his people won one, even though she knew they had. Maybe Nick wanted a piece of their next victory. It was certainly in the wind.

"The Americans sent a small expeditionary team to Laos in the late 1950s, and they more or less stole the Hmong mountain people out from under the French, turned them into guerrillas, and used them to fight their own war against communism."

"You're saying Americans are still in Laos?"

Jalbert's eyes narrowed. "Now we get to the heart of this meeting. A secret war rages in Laos in which you Americans are deeply involved." He took a deliberate sip, held the glass up and looked at it, sipped, and replaced it on the soggy bar napkin.

"Okay. You have my interest now. Please continue." She was curious as hell and impatient with his serpentine manner. He was as opaque as Thiep. Clearly, if one spent enough time in the Orient, one became inscrutable.

He went on. "If you desire, you can have some very exclusive reporting to do. This is a rare opportunity for a probing journalist. The information you uncover will be highly censored by your government, but it will certainly find an outlet in the French press and be welcomed by the rest of the world."

"What's stopping *you* from covering it?"

"Let's just say I have everything to lose, whereas you have everything to gain."

"I'm a little slow, and you're very roundabout. You'll have to explain."

Jalbert picked up a half-empty pack of Gitanes from the bar in front of him, pulled two cigarettes out, and offered one to Ellie. She accepted, and he lit hers then his with a battered lighter. He tilted his head and exhaled smoke upward.

Ellie took a deep drag of the rich, black tobacco. She coughed.

When she'd recovered, Jalbert continued. "My family has

been in Vientiane, the capital, for generations. I was born and raised there. All we have left is a meager business, the Constellation Hotel, and I cannot afford to lose it. Your government can drop the hammer, as your saying goes, whenever it wants. Revenge could be a swift kick in the derrière from your Central Intelligence Agency. Yes?"

"Okay," she said slowly. The French accent that filigreed his words was mesmerizing. "So, what *is* the major issue in Laos?"

"Your government, via the CIA, is involved in the drug trade. With the opium and heroin that flood Saigon, Western Europe, and the United States, *this* is the issue." Jalbert cocked his head toward the booth where the GI had nodded out on the shoulder of his companion. "The addiction rate is very high among your soldiers."

Goosebumps shivered her flesh. If what he said about the CIA drug involvement was true, he was digging her a gold mine.

"You hesitate," he went on. "It is all well and good for you to question my intention for your career advancement, but believe me, it will only be downhill for you if you remain in Saigon."

She tilted her head. Downhill had always been a positive for her. Now it was a negative? "Who wouldn't hesitate without solid proof of what you say?"

"I understand you require proof." Jalbert signaled for another round. "Your association with Nick Burrows sank your boat before it even hit the water."

"What's Nick got to do with this? Your statement makes no sense. Why have you changed the subject? I'm asking for proof about CIA involvement in Laos."

Her gaze locked on her glass. Her heart pounded in her ears and her defense of Nick rose. She ground out her cigarette in the ashtray.

Jalbert paused. "For the moment, you have only my word. But the incident I'll have you witness will provide all the satisfaction you need to proceed in this venture. Now, bringing up Burrows is a means for you to accomplish this mission. First, a little background: For weeks, he was provided with information he believed to be true, which supports his naïve zeal to end this conflict by exposing American mismanagement of the war here in Vietnam. He was targeted by the South Vietnamese government when he landed in Saigon. His background and intentions were more than suitable to spread disinformation."

Her throat constricted.

"However, what transpired was totally Burrows' fault. He was incompetent, reckless, and he became the laughingstock of the intelligence community."

"You make him sound like inspector Clouseau. Do you have proof? How did he mess up?"

"With his obvious training from spy novels and his total disregard for discretion."

"Who knew this?" she asked brusquely, not liking his tone.

"Everyone. The British, French, Germans, Russians, Chinese. And, of course, the CIA."

"Yet he hasn't been harassed or interrogated. I need more proof than your word."

"Herein lies the humor. To start with, he was taken in by the South Vietnamese government to mask one of their capitalistic endeavors, one the Americans unknowingly handed to them."

"What are you driving at?"

"I am assuming the Americans are ignorant, although they could be smarter than I give them credit for. Maybe they want the South to presume they don't know their pockets are being picked. Truth can be a movable feast."

"You're so oblique, Colonel. Please just tell me straight out."

He cracked a half smile. "Pretending to be communist sympathizers, government agents offered to provide Burrows with mocked-up photos and false proof that US supply sergeants had a flourishing business selling war matériel to the Viet Cong. But it is quite the opposite; it is the many high-ranking South Vietnamese officers who profit from the sales. French journalists have been exploring this issue, and their reporting had to be countered."

"I get it now: Enter Nick Burrows." A feeling about Nick that had started to grow a while back now came into maturity with Jalbert's revelation. Seemed as if everything was handed to Nick, effortlessly, without him ever having the awareness of modesty or hard work, often relying on Uncle Francis's intercession. Wasn't that what David had said about Nick in his forgiving and softhearted manner?

"*Precisément*, although he has now become useless to the South."

Her belly tightened as the veracity of what Jalbert implied dawned on her.

"When his contact, Thiep, alerted him that he was being followed by US Intelligence, it was just a ploy to drive him away, to make him believe his contact was in jeopardy for passing him this valuable information. *Théâtre de marionettes.*"

"Puppet theater." *That bastard lied to me.*

"Yes, and when the buffoon sent *you* to meet with his contact instead, the Vietnamese saw through that like a thin negligee. No one will give Burrows a byline, not even the Ugandan Daily Monitor."

The full force of Jalbert's accusation descended heavily on Ellie's conscience. "He'll never believe me if I tell him this, that's for sure."

"Knowing Burrows, he will only deny it." Jalbert shrugged. "Do what you wish." He dripped the comment into the air like water. "I have some negatives that support my claim involving Burrows." He tapped the breast pocket of his jacket.

"How did you get them?"

"The how is not important."

"If I understand what you're saying, Nick's not guilty of any collaboration since he never published anything?"

"That's right, but he doesn't know this. Remember, he believes he's reporting for the communists. In truth, he's a nonentity, a shiftless dreamer who is not fixed in the real world."

Ellie heard a ring of truth. "You've backed up your story about Nick if those negatives are what you say they are, but it's really of no interest to me."

"Now comes, as you say, the punchline. All of what I have revealed puts this fool in a position to be useful to you. You could use him as he has tried to use you. Acknowledge that you have no friends or associates who have the time or inclination to become involved in a fact-finding mission to Laos. This would be difficult to undertake alone, especially for a young woman."

"You've been denigrating Nick, and now you're suggesting I use him to get me into Laos?"

"He is motivated, needs a place to put his zeal. Although he may be as ignorant as you about the country, he can at least protect you in awkward situations. Furthermore, he is but a stringer, with no regular employer, thus, available. Two sets of eyes are better than one."

"I see your point, but how do you suggest I manage it?"

"If he thinks the CIA is about to nab him, it will spook him enough to leave Saigon. I will provide support to verify this if need be."

Ellie held her head between her hands. "My head is spinning; I don't understand all this spy stuff. No one's up-front about anything."

Jalbert's voice softened a touch. "Ah, but spies are necessary in this dramatic theater we're a part of. You are not alone, mademoiselle. This war is mired in the underworld of politics, economics, nationalism, and many other issues highlighted by self-promotion and personal gain. If you survive long enough in the Orient, you might one day be able to distinguish one from another."

She rubbed her face with both hands.

"My suggestion to you is to start a new life in Indochine," Jalbert said.

19

———————

Less than an hour after meeting with Eleanor Ketcham, René Jalbert strolled alone in the falling darkness of rue Legrand de la Liraye, north of the city center, passing beneath tall plane trees that stretched high over the road. Plans were coming together. He checked his watch as he lit a cigarette then quickened his pace as he approached high whitewashed walls and entered through the open gate of the old French cemetery. Gravestones had crumbled into dust craters in the grassy knolls since US rockets and machine guns had followed Vietcong who tried to hide in the cemetery grounds during the Tet Offensive.

He followed a pathway lined on both sides with the resting places of French soldiers and colonial politicians. At an intersecting track, he turned right and walked through an area thick with trees and shrubs, finally stopping at the mausoleum of one of the cemetery's celebrated residents, Paul Blanchy, mayor of Saigon in the late 1800s.

Two Corsicans deep into their sixties and dressed in wrinkled tropical suits stood waiting, both smoking heavy-scented Gauloises.

"*Salut, Jacques, Emile, ça va?*" Jalbert greeted. "You are prospering?"

"Ah, Jippie, we have been well. It's a nice surprise that you asked to meet us here," Jacques Lescan, the portly one, replied.

The nickname Jippie derived from Jalbert's real name, Jean Pierre Piallit. He was not Parisian but a proud Corsican through and through.

"So many memories this sacred site brings back despite the recent attack." Lescan sighed.

"*Oui*, I, too, have many fond memories of friends who rest here," agreed Emile Basti, a wiry, excitable man who chain-smoked.

They puffed in silence, opaque cigarette smoke twisting around their memories of the 1950s when they were agents with French intelligence, known as the SDECE, who operated against the nationalist Maquis bands in the jungles of Indochina. With fewer and fewer funds coming from the French treasury, they had created their own organization, the Black Box, to keep assets liquid.

"We three were in the right place at the right time, *n'est-ce pas?*" Jippie said. "We had a fat slice of the lucrative French opium trade."

"We did well, didn't we," Basti reminisced, "for a time."

"The war might have been lost," Lescan added, "but we thrived until the CIA moved in with its gorilla purchasing power to sweep up the Hmong and their crops as a trade for joining the American fight against communism."

"I believe we may yet have an opportunity to get justice on the greedy bastards who stole our business in order to wage their own battles against communism," Jippie said in a whisper, "which is why I am glad the Black Box is in good shape. We will equal the profits our brother syndicates are reaping in Europe, or even surpass them."

"What? Are you crazy? The three of us against the American CIA?" Basti asked, his voice tight.

Jippie lit a Gitane and inhaled deeply. "Twenty years ago, we were clever enough to revive our opium traffic to supply Marseilles in abundance." He stared hard at the two men. "I have stumbled upon an opportunity equally as profitable. Another bright future rises for us on the horizon."

Lescan leaned toward Jippie. "Just remember, we are still above water. Not as affluent as in days past. The accounts of our secret Black Box Organization are not overflowing, but they are substantially filled."

"You were always a wishful thinker, Jippie." Basti extracted another cigarette from a crumpled blue package and lit it.

"Maybe so," Jippie agreed. "But this time there is real hope. Isn't the purpose of the Black Box to fill our coffers beyond capacity?" He clasped his hands together. "I just met with a hungry and naive American photojournalist who I believe will follow my lead. If this silly woman has any journalistic skills, and I sense she does—she's smart and curious and headstrong —she will find me in Vientiane. From there I will send her to Long Tieng to uncover the Americans' collusion with the South Vietnamese government's heroin industry. I will lay out for her the CIA participation in providing opium to the refineries in Saigon."

"What is your motive?" Basti asked.

"To expose the CIA. A *soupçon* of vengeance," Jippie replied. "And she has an accomplice, a wannabe agitator who fancies himself a champion of the underdog. He is a simpleton, but we can harness his passion to right imperialist wrongs for our mission of revenge. And it doesn't hurt our cause to know his uncle is with the CIA. Bargaining power, possibly."

"Both he and the woman will help you blow open the CIA's alleged hush-hush flow of drugs to GIs and beyond?"

Lescan patted the air with his hands to relax the excitable Basti. "Where does our bright future lie in all this?"

"When the news gets out, if the two of them are any good, there will be a worldwide outcry, especially in their own country, what with all the GI addiction here and in the US, not to mention the ongoing problem in Europe."

Basti narrowed his eyes. "You are hoping America will be disgraced and discredited and will wash its hands of any drug involvement—"

"Voilà, and the door reopens for us," Jippie finished the thought with a triumphant flourish of his hands, speaking without a trace of the sarcasm that had laced his conversation with Ellie. He expelled a plume of smoke and smiled.

"What keeps this pair from discovering your motives?" Basti asked.

"My motives are masked in truth. It will be a journalistic triumph to uncover what the Americans are doing." Jippie looked at his cohorts, who said nothing. "We have much to gain and little to lose."

"Are you asking the Black Box to finance this venture?" Basti asked.

"Yes, a meager sum, but I guarantee the most positive results." Again, there was no reply. He pressed on. "You will not regret it. Simply back my word to the one person I need to hire."

"Such as a bodyguard?" asked Lescan.

"No, a pilot, his plane, and his expenses in Laos."

"I'm worried there could be reprisals from the CIA?" Basti said.

"There will not be any."

"Since you are sure of that, Jippie, if this comes back to us, we will deny involvement, and we will point our fingers at you." Basti took a breath and continued. "We would be forced to expel you from the Black Box. Agreed?" Nods all around.

20

———————

Upon leaving the Oriental Star, Ellie imagined all her cells lining up at the edges of her body, little soldiers pushing her toward the thrill as well as the danger inherent in Jalbert's challenge. She could just feel herself dancing along a fence-top rail. She hailed a pedicab. The driver was a slight man with sunbaked skin, brown and wrinkled as a walnut. Ellie listened to the rhythm of his labored breathing as his legs pedaled round and round while she cycled Jalbert's words through her mind.

If she read between the lines, he was giving her a chance to leave the landmine disaster behind and to do something of consequence with her time in Southeast Asia. He was offering her redemption through a story no one else would have. Here was a chance to strike out on her own, not toil for Stryker or do Nick's bidding. Jalbert had turned her attention to the fact that she'd been taking her lead from the two men. She hadn't thought in terms of alternatives but in how to resurrect her situation. She'd lost her lateral thinking ability; Jalbert's timing was so propitious, any thought of going home fizzled like a rain-soaked sparkler, even if guilt over abandoning Stryker churned in her stomach. She had to be fair and tell Ben the truth. She'd send him a telegram.

She shivered. Odd man, Jalbert. Sardonic and stiff as a crinoline. Yet, there was something provocative about him, a disquieting undercurrent she couldn't put her finger on. Jeopardy? Was that why he warned her against traveling alone? She had no doubts she could seduce Nick into coming along with her. And really, what other options did *he* have?

She inhaled the steamy jasmine air and entered the villa, renewed optimism bounding through the door with her.

The house was dark.

She turned her head toward the living room, where someone breathed loudly, almost a snore.

"Hello?" she called.

A lamp switched on, and Nick stumbled into the foyer, blinking. He brushed the backs of his fingers along her cheek.

"Oh, hi, Nick, I was just thinking about you." A shiver razored her belly as the memory of their night of lovemaking rose.

"Ellie," he said dreamily. His breath nearly knocked her off balance.

"Whoa, you've sure tied on a whopper."

He sneered. "You're just like all the other broads."

So much for romance. He sped from zero to sixty in a burst. It was the booze talking. "Back off, Nick." She waved her hand, dismissing him, and walked toward the stairs, her mind on her new possibilities.

"Hey, I'm talking to you, woman."

"Not now, Nick," she said, straining to keep her voice light. Caution was knotting her stomach. She hastened up the first step.

He reached for her arm and pulled her back down off the step, spinning her around to face him, his eyes glazed. "Not so fast, Missy."

"Ouch. You're drunk. Get away from me. You'll regret this in the morning. Go sleep it off," she said, trying to move out of his way.

"I'm not finished," he spat, spraying her with spittle. "Just like all the other bitches. Talk nice. Start out all friendly and innocent. Then go meet a slimeball Frog at a whore bar. Thought you were different. Just another dirtbag."

"What?" Her mind raced back to the bar. "Wait, that urchin was your little *spy*? Cheap trick, mister. I thought it was odd that a child would enter that place to leer at me."

He grabbed her blouse near the neck and twisted, his face inches from hers.

"You're choking me." She pulled back. An upward thrust with her arm broke his grasp. "Get the fuck away from me!" She wasn't about to take his shit, even if she needed him for her adventure.

The light in his eyes flickered. He paused a second as if she was getting through to him, but then he recoiled and grabbed her shoulders.

"There you were, war virgin, landing in Saigon completely oblivious to the ways of war. I tried to teach you, protect you, keep you safe."

"Let *go* of me." Ellie wrenched hard out of his grip, but his hands were everywhere, grabbing, pinching. He gripped her shoulders and shook her. His eyes narrowed. Cold and hard.

She screeched, "Stop it!"

Nick pulled his arm back again, about to slap her. The sounds of their fight sliced the thick night air and brought one of their housemates to the top of the stairs.

"Lay off, Burrows," the man cautioned.

"You keep out of this," Nick snarled.

She took advantage of Nick's slight shift in attention, lifted her right leg, and stomped down on his foot with all her might, then kicked him in the shin with her left foot while holding onto the banister.

He absorbed the blows with a grunt and kept coming at her. His open hand had turned into a fist.

"Nick!" she screamed. "*Stop!*"

He stalled, rotated his fist, and eyed it like it wasn't his. He pushed her. She fell against the banister, hitting her right cheek. Her hand went up. A confused, surprised expression replaced Nick's snarling mask. "No, no," he cried, as if waking up to what had just transpired. He jerked his head around. "What have I done? Please no—" He reached for her.

"Stay the fuck away."

He lurched up the stairs.

She twisted her head and watched him go.

"Let me help you." The journalist started down the stairs to her.

"I'm okay." She fluttered a hand toward him and walked unsteadily up the stairs.

At the upper landing, he put a hand gently at her elbow. "You sure you're okay?"

"Fuckhead's out of his mind."

"Where'd you learn to defend yourself like that?"

"Dated a Secret Service guy once, thank you."

She closed her bedroom door behind her. *What brought that on?* The room whirled around her. The starch drained out of her muscles.

Trembling shook her body. She was stunned by the rage in Nick's assault.

Ellie stamped her foot. "Fuck no!" She refused to buckle under to his bullying. Jealousy again? Was that why he had had her followed? He had nothing to be jealous of; they were not involved. A one-night stand did not constitute a relationship. It took several deep breaths to steady herself. She was crazy to contemplate bringing him along on her adventure. Especially since he'd introduced violence into the equation.

Sometime in the middle of the night there was a scratching on her door. A note was slipped under it. She retrieved it, switched on a light, unfolded the piece of paper, and struggled to read the chicken scratch.

ELLIE,

I am so sorry for my behavior. I've struggled with my temper my whole life. Never really learned to rein it in, and sometimes I go too far, like tonight. My rage ties me in knots. I see nothing but the rage, red and pulsating, and then it dissipates.

When I marched in Selma, my loud, aggressive idea of how to run the protest went afoul of the organizers' vision, and I was black-balled. Had to scramble to get close enough with my Minolta to snap the drama. Vindication was sweet when UPI published and paid me for one of my photos. It was a lucky shot; photography isn't my thing. So many words ricochet through my head, writing is the only way to bring order to them and to use them to expose perpetrators of wrongdoing.

But words failed me that January day when you walked off the plane and shorted all my circuits. You're made of such tough stuff that you made me believe I was made of steel, too.

I'm ashamed I lost my temper. I was so drunk, I don't remember what happened. If only I could take it back. I hope you can find it within yourself to forgive me.

Nick

21

———————

Ellie held the idea of anger in front of her as if it were a conch shell, turning it around and looking at it from all angles. Where did Nick's anger come from? Not that it mattered. She was not there to rescue his ass.

Finally, sleep came.

Late morning light filtered through the cabbage-rose curtains. She heard five soft raps. Nick. She squeezed her eyes, willed him to leave.

He knocked again.

She got out of bed, slipped on her kimono, and opened the door.

All rumpled and looking like he hadn't slept.

Hah! Served him right.

He held up a tray, and the seductive aroma of dark coffee reached her senses.

"Room service." His grin was a mask, his eyes squinty. "Ellie, I can't believe I lost my temper. I'm so sorry," he offered meekly, taking a step into the room. "I don't know what came over me. I was drunk."

"That's a cheap excuse."

He tried another step forward.

"You get near me, and I'll scream," she growled.

He said nothing, hung his head like a hound caught sneaking a steak off the kitchen counter. Ellie looked away; if she dared look into those miserable hangdog eyes, she'd begin feeling sorry for him.

"So, you're here trying to get back on my good side?"

"I brought you breakfast in bed." A slight, hopeful smile appeared on his face then died. He held the tray out. When she didn't take it, he placed it on the bureau.

"What you did was bullshit. Unforgivable." She crossed her arms over her chest. He looked miserable, shoulders hunched, lower lip quivering. Her heart was beating hard against her ribs, yet she felt a certain kind of cold iron rising.

As much as she might want to skewer the asshole, she needed him. She lowered her voice. "You owe me, Mister. Big time."

"You're right, babe. I'm so ashamed. I-I-I said stuff I didn't mean. I don't know what came over me. Alcohol turns me into a lunatic. I become someone I don't recognize. I hope you can forgive me, and we can start over."

"Don't call me babe." He was so annoying.

"I brought you the strong black coffee you like, fresh-squeezed orange juice, and almond croissants. His eyelids drooped. Those eyes betrayed the truth of his soul.

"A flower, Nick?" She lifted a plumeria bloom with its big leaf from a glass and dropped it on the tray. It smelled heavenly, but he'd probably plucked it from the downstairs garden. "You can wipe that expression off your face; it's not going to score you any points." She sipped the strong brew, thinking it was better to forgive him, but she was unable to let it go quite yet.

"You spied on me, you asshole. That's creepy as hell, obsessive."

Nick had the decency to blush. His mood flips were faster

than the chord changes in Coltrane's *Giant Steps*. He took her hand, kissed it, started to walk to the door. He stopped and turned around. In his outstretched hand he held a yellow Western Union envelope. "Cook gave me this in the kitchen. Continental Hotel concierge brought it over personally."

He dropped it on the dresser and walked out the door.

"Oh, Nick, for God's sake!" She stomped over and locked the door, then got back into bed, leaned against the pillows, and sipped the coffee. She stared at the Western Union envelope, a shiver in her belly; it had already been opened.

APOLOGIES ... NO TIME TO WASTE ... MUST FINISH BOOK BEFORE BABY ARRIVES ... STOP ... SEND OR BRING YOUR NOTES TO ME ... OPEN FIRST-CLASS RETURN TICKET AT HOTEL WHENEVER ... STOP ... BONUS IN YOUR BANK ACCOUNT ... YOU ARE THE BEST ... STOP ... XOXO BEN & SARAH

"OH, MY HEART," she gasped. The telegram fluttered to her lap. "Infuckingcredible, Ben," she giggled. "Talk about coincidence. And just as I was about to cable you," she exclaimed to the telegram.

When René Jalbert opened the crack of possibility that Ellie could shed Stryker's assignment as well as reject Nick's Thiep scheme, she'd been battling uncertainty. Indeed, after listening to the Frenchman, who'd offered her an opportunity and laid bare the realities of her situation, she couldn't deny the probability that the Saigon press corps would continue to shun her because of her connection with Nick. Would that end if she weren't linked to him?

Her assignment for Ben had been accomplished, and now he had handed her a new beginning.

The telegram was a sign forward. She was sure of it. Best to put the negative behind her. Perseverance was her strength. Find the straightest line like a downhill, not a slalom that required skiing around gates to get to the finish line. Nick was a back-and-forth slalom. Laos would be the straight line of a downhill.

She hoped.

Her stomach twinged, goosebumps pebbled her skin, and her mouth went dry, just like before she crawled into the embassy grounds during a firefight. This Laos adventure was something she could sink her teeth into. It was hers alone, a real opportunity. No question that she was going to seize this chance.

She'd come to a crossroads, having entered her meeting with Jalbert anticipating an interview for Ben's book and exited the encounter with an unexpected new lease on life. And then Ben's cable galloped in from the West. "Thank you, Ben," she whispered. "I don't know how you knew I needed to be set free, but you did, and I'm grateful."

She leapt from the bed and danced a little jig, hands stretched out and twirling. Straightest line, she reminded herself. Make Nick an asset. Eyes on the prize: an exclusive story and byline.

She carried the tray to the dresser and swallowed the remains of her coffee, replaced the cup in its saucer, danced to the desk, and sat down.

The ceiling fan sent a whisper of breeze through her hair. She started a letter to her Uncle Julian.

The litany of odd things that have happened to me in the last few months could be debilitating if not for what they've taught me. The most recent was stubbornly going for an action shot, and I got a soldier blown sky-high.

She chewed on the end of her pen. She took full responsibility for the incident, even if she managed to sound cavalier in her letter.

What a gift Stryker had sent her.

I must have been born under a bright morning sun, Uncle Julian. Ben has released me at the very moment I lucked into an exclusive story in Laos. So, here I go, from ski racer to wartime journalist chasing a story deeper into Indochina.

Her only obstacle was Nick: elusive, slippery, temperamental. Not quite the shining star she'd thought he was. Nick had been put in her path to teach her a new strength. Sexy though he was, she needed to keep her distance.

Timing is everything, as Dad used to say. It's amazing how so many of his maxims can be applied to life way beyond ski racing. Timing saw me through Tet and a horrifying patrol incident, and enabled me to get some dynamite images.

Jalbert's words echoed in her mind: "Your own book, or at least a byline that will propel your career."

She folded and sealed the air mail stationery then addressed it. Her mind on the future, she twirled into the bathroom. The shrapnel wound above her left eye was fading, and her leg had scarred over well. She was lucky Nick hadn't hit her last night, although her right cheek was a little swollen where she'd hit the banister.

The reflection brought back a long-ago memory of a summer day. She was just a kid, ten perhaps, eating lunch with her mother at the kitchen table when the back screen door slammed and her aunt Harriet stumbled in, a huge shiner leading the way, skin around her eyes blotched and red from crying. Her mother led Harriet into the living room, giving Ellie a glance that said, "Stay out."

Ellie eavesdropped on their muffled words. Harriet crying, her mother soothing, telling her sister she'd done nothing wrong, that she had to pretend everything was all right, that it was important to preserve the sanctity of marriage and that wives were expected to put up with that kind of behavior.

"Our husbands have all the pressure of jobs and providing a living for their families. When the pressure boils over, they take it out on us. It's our role as their wives to support them, no matter what. It's in our wedding vows. We promised for better or worse, till death we do part. Love, honor, obey."

Totally cockeyed reasoning. Weird time, the 1950s. Women all dressed up, wearing high heels to push vacuum cleaners around the house, sweeping secrets under the rugs. Almost like slaves to their husbands. Women had been so objectified. Was that part of the reason they submitted to abuse?

As twisted as the memory might be, it spoke to Ellie. She would not be objectified. She was the equal of any man. Why were women raised to serve men? Made no sense to her, and yet part of her deferred to men; they knew more than women, right? Wrong.

Enough. She wasn't about to take abuse from anyone. She'd have to turn Nick to her benefit for this assignment. Take control.

First things first.

Like getting a flight to Vientiane. "No flights, commercial or private," said the Continental Hotel concierge when she entered. "Maybe you check out military transport? War going on, you forget?"

She bit her lower lip. "Yeah, forget." She turned away, paused a moment before stepping into a phone booth and placed a call to Jalbert at his hotel in Vientiane.

"*Moi, je suis prête*," she said when he came on the line. "I am ready."

"Well, well, well," Jalbert said, the connection sounding tinny. "So you have decided this little venture is worth your while, Mademoiselle Eleanor? You will not regret it. And have you inspired Monsieur Burrows to join you?"

She flinched at the sarcasm in his voice. "He may be more trouble than he's worth," she grumbled.

"Perhaps he deserves a second chance? Even with an unpleasant companion, harassment stays away when you have a protective male with you."

"I thought Orientals were reserved."

"I speak of your countrymen."

She coughed. "Well, I haven't, as you say, inspired him, not yet, but I know how. Can you find us a flight? Overland's out, right? You must know of a way."

"You are correct. Call me back in three days. No, I will phone you." He hung up.

Ellie looked at the phone. "Goodbye to you, too." She exited the close, muggy booth. Good thing she'd given him the phone number at David's.

She strategized on her walk back to the villa. A vague sense that she was putting her head in the mouth of a tiger passed through her mind. Was she that desperate for the possible reward? She rubbed the heels of her hands on her eyes. Damn straight!

She slipped a note under Nick's door.

Meet me at the Zoo at 7 p.m. in front of the tigers. Ellie.

22

———————

She sat in the glow of twilight on a bench across from the curved tiger enclosure.

Nick approached on cautious steps, his eyes darting around.

"Aren't they beautiful?" She pointed to the creatures pacing their barred jungle.

"What in the world are you up to, lady?" He cleared his throat.

She patted the bench and squinted at him. "Sit."

She'd dressed in a low-cut top and pulled her strawberry gold hair off her face and secured a barrette at the crown so waves would fall voluptuously. Nothing wrong with a little seductive fashion, kept at arm's length.

Nick lowered himself tentatively, as if sitting on a mushroom he expected to collapse. "I'm listening." His fingers beat a nervous rhythm on the bench.

"I'm going away. My assignment for Stryker has taken a left turn. I'm leaving Saigon, at least for the foreseeable future. I'll write a note to David, but maybe you could fill him in when he gets back?"

Without looking at him, she saw clenched fists.

"What the fuck!" he spluttered, jumping up.

"Sit down, Nick. I'm joining a French journalist on an assignment elsewhere in Southeast Asia."

"That Frog sleazebag from the bar? Now I know you're out of your mind. The French are reckless and thoughtless."

Ellie hoped she could ensnare him without inciting his temper, noting his long, choppy breath. "Elsewhere in Southeast Asia? That's awfully vague, Ketcham."

"Well, it's kind of hush hush," she hinted and leaned closer. "Can I trust you, Nick? It wouldn't do if this got out."

He licked his lips. "Of course you can trust me. I got you home safely from that patrol, didn't I?"

She rolled her eyes. "There's a secret war going on across the border."

"Oh, yeah, sure. Hard to hide a secret war. Cambodia's a scary place."

Sultry air swirled around them. "Not Cambodia. Laos."

"Yeah, right, that one too. So?"

"I'm going to Vientiane."

"Right on. Change of location works for me."

Especially, she thought, if what Jalbert said was true about the CIA's interest in Nick.

"You know," he purred, "we're a team, you and I, writer and photographer. I've got the ear; you've got the eye. Together, we can get a Pulitzer."

Ellie squinted.

"What are you waiting for, Godot?"

"I'm not sure I want to share a Pulitzer or any prize with someone so prone to hissy fits," she teased. "But I may be doing some work to help the Vietnamese people."

His eyes widened. "All ri-i-ight. Now you're talking." He swallowed hard. "I'll be an asset. We're more convincing as a duo. I can be ready in a flash. I travel light. You won't regret it."

He sat up straight. She gazed at the tigers.

"I don't know, Nick. I'll have to think about this."

23

——————

She stood, winked at the tigers, and walked away. Something about those big cats pacing off their pent-up power resonated within her. Nick was like the tiger; his smoldering good looks hid wild fury pulsing beneath the surface. She never knew which side he'd be showing. Danger ahead. Admittedly, she liked taking risks, but was she playing with fire? With the upper hand, maybe she could stop the anger before it escaped his cage.

Nick's expression amused her; a hound dog couldn't have done it better. His pleading, soulful eyes looked up from lowered head. She saw a man whose emotions were way too close to the edge. She must be looney to consider bringing him, especially if he was going to explode into a rage whenever the wind changed direction.

Odds were better than good he'd bitten, however. Smart move to hold back the fact she intended to photograph *and* write the story.

She speed walked back to her room in the villa. Fire surged through her body, tingling muscles, oxygenating blood. She stretched her arms high and then dropped into a tuck. Tension burned in her quads as she held the position. *Yeah, that's what it took to ski the fastest line and take home the gold.* She would hold her tuck throughout this assignment.

The groundswell of strength and power was heady. She didn't need to lean on people, not Ben and certainly not Nick. She was strong; she would lean on herself.

THREE DAYS STRETCHED into a week without word from Jalbert. Ellie's swagger wilted. She busied herself typing her interview notes and mailing them off to Ben in Aspen along with the portraits she'd taken and some of her images from the embassy and Cholon and the patrol. She expressed her gratitude and gave thanks for good timing. Another plus was that Max Kelly kept his word. Not only did he give her credit for her photos that were published along with his article, but he also sat with her for an interview.

In the lull of each afternoon, she lay on her bed, blood pulsing loudly in her veins like seconds ticking by on a schoolroom clock. Rain fell softly outside, streaking the window. The ceiling fan stirred the oppressive heat and humidity, ruffled the mosquito netting, and rippled over her exposed skin but succeeded only in making her believe she was melting.

The weather was toying with her, slowing time down to a crawl. The cloying heat hadn't bothered her during the embassy and Cholon attacks, but now it weighed heavily on her shoulders, like time.

Ellie searched for information about the current situation in Laos. No luck. She settled for some outdated guidebooks, mostly in French. The US's secret bombing in Laos wasn't Jalbert's focus. She rode the barstools in the rooftop bar of the Caravelle, hoping to glean some intel on Laos. Unfortunately for her, she was still "hands off." She attended the Five O'clock

Follies, which had relocated to the Caravelle roof, but learned nothing of interest.

"It doesn't even really matter anymore. I'm on to a different war," she rationalized as she walked back to the villa one night, listening to the muffled *thwumps* of distant mortars. She chuckled to find a note on the carpeting of her room. It had become the prevalent mode of communication at the villa.

"Eleanor, meet me at Tan Son Nhut. 16:30 tomorrow. Catholic Church, Northern Sector. Bring a long lens. Come alone. Col. J."

Jalbert. Finally.

She left the villa around three the next afternoon, peeking into the living and dining rooms, cautious that Nick the busybody could be lurking about, waiting to pounce. Po stood in the foyer near the front door.

"You haven't seen me, if anyone asks, especially Mr. Nick," Ellie whispered.

"Yes, miss. I not tell nobody."

With a Nikon and lenses in her knapsack, she walked down to the waterfront, taking snapshots with her Rollei as she went, listening and glancing back to make sure she wasn't being followed. She ducked into a side door of the Rex Hotel and walked out the front, where she hailed a taxi to the airbase. No sign of Nick.

How strange to find a church in the middle of an airport. Not in the middle, exactly. Outside the northern perimeter across the base from the main gate. The stone church was cool, hushed, empty.

Ellie wore khaki fatigues, sleeves rolled up high. She sat down in a pew, hauled out the Nikon, affixed the 300 mm long lens, and loaded film, setting the camera on the pew.

Steps resounded, echoing louder as they neared. She didn't turn around. Goose bumps rode her skin.

"Here you are." Jalbert sat in the pew behind her and dropped a flak vest near her on the wooden bench.

She held it up. "Is this necessary?"

"Just put it on."

"You don't waste words," she muttered. She slipped on the heavy, protective vest and cinched it as tight as she could, but it was still several sizes too big.

"What I'm going to show you, how do I say this, could be embarrassing for your government. This is what I mentioned to you the other day. You have your camera?"

She gestured at her camera beside her.

"*Bon*. Come with me." His fatigues were the color of coffee ice cream, pressed and starched. He wasn't wearing a flak vest.

She hesitated for a moment. Fuck it. She'd come this far. She wasn't chickening out. After a short walk past the Buddhist temple, the sentry waved them through the O-55 Gate, near the old French fort. They entered the Alpha sector of the base and paused behind a bunker. Ellie followed Jalbert as he tracked behind the Tango 2 Tower and ammo dump. He hugged the perimeter around the western edge of the base, toward the O-51 Gate, and jerked a sudden left along Runway 25-R and into the airplane graveyard.

"The runway is through there." He pointed to the south.

"You're not coming with me?"

"Would you rather walk away?" He paused then went on. "You can move around, just stay hidden. When a C-47 lands with South Vietnamese markings, you start shooting. This is Ky's personal air force. They'll offload bricks of heroin for distribution to Corsicans, Chinese triads, and street peddlers to sell to US soldiers on the street and at the bases."

Her jaw dropped in amazement.

"Tsk, tsk, close your mouth, young lady. The US has many addicted to heroin in its military as you witnessed at the Oriental Star."

"You mentioned Ky? As in the South Vietnam's vice president, Nguyen Cao Ky?"

"Don't take chances. Just get the shots. Move in and out of the shadows. Watchtowers surround us, and the base gendarmes are nearby. You will pay a terrible price if you are discovered. So, be quick, get good documentation, and then we leave."

"Where's all this heroin coming from?" she asked under her breath.

"This is all you need to know for now. You will have the photos as proof, but you can save your questions to find out how high in the South Vietnamese government this goes."

"What? It can only go one floor higher." The idea heightened her curiosity and excitement. *Landing a plane loaded with heroin in broad daylight? The Americans can't be that blind. News that will obviously be suppressed. Nick was right about the foreign press; it's the only place this can run.*

When she looked up, Jalbert had vanished.

The C-47 transport swept in for a landing, its two front wheels scraping the runway, tail dropping as it taxied. With propellers and wings up front, its fuselage stretched out to the rear.

Ellie sited the plane, focused, and kept her finger on the shutter. She wasn't using the motor drive, too noisy, but her monopod was essential with the long lens. She was one hundred percent zeroed in on her target, even while an awareness of her surroundings played at the periphery of her consciousness.

The South Vietnamese Air Force emblem of white star on a navy round encircled by red and banded by yellow and red stripes, a knockoff of the USAF emblem, was emblazoned on the back of the fuselage.

Crouching low, she duck-walked through tall grasses and between ghost aircraft to vary her angles on the Asian men who were unloading bales through the side door while others loaded them onto trucks. A small ruckus broke out when a bale was dropped, and its contents of small packages spilled on the tarmac. The clean-up took only minutes by men working at a frantic pace. With the telephoto lens, she could see their faces. No nonsense, no talking. Taking care of business.

A sudden rustling on her left stopped her cold. Her head whipped around to see a dove rising out of a bush. *Holy shit.*

Palm branches barely moved in the distance. The moment the trucks were loaded, they sped off. As she twisted to get a shot of the trucks making their getaway and their license plates, a rough claw grabbed her by the shoulder. Oh fuck, the police. Her pulse raced. She lifted her eyes. Jalbert's stone face stared down at her.

"That's enough. We leave now."

"Jesus, you scared me," she scolded. "I thought I was dead meat."

He threw her a look that said, "Pay attention," and took stiff, long-legged steps back to the sanctuary of the church. She quickened her pace to keep up.

"What proof do you have that load was actually heroin?" she asked in short gasps.

"Did you get photos of any individual packages?"

"In fact I did, one of the large bales dropped and broke open. I got a shot of the spilled parcels."

"Excellent. When you develop your film, you will see that each small package has a trademark: *Double UO Globe* brand. There is your proof."

"Proof of what?"

"The trademark for a brand of heroin."

She waited for more. Nothing.

"Okay, now what, Colonel?" she asked once inside the cool peace of the church. She exhaled hard, as if she'd been holding her breath the entire time.

"You can develop this film in secret?"

"Yes. What's next?"

"A colleague of mine, a Corsican pilot, will fly us to Vientiane. He's an old hand, highly skilled, and very much familiar with the skies and terrain of Southeast Asia."

This was it, she thought, finally putting her finger on the ghost of a question about Jalbert. He cast no shadow. No warmth, no personal engagement. Hardly looked her in the eye. What was in this for him? How much risk would he expose her to, to get what he wanted? Damn, fucker sure knew how to dangle a carrot.

24

———

"Goddamn," she said out loud as she studied a contact sheet through a loupe. "*Double UO Globe* brand. Jalbert's for real!" She felt a twinge in her lower belly and her temperature rose. "Holy shit, I'm sitting on a fucking powder keg! And there's more in Laos. This is as big as he said it was."

Let's see if Nick has grabbed the carrot I've dangled in front of him.

It was a few days later. She imagined him stewing in his room, maybe having second thoughts about joining her, especially when he wouldn't be in charge. That would be sure to rankle. But what else could he have going? She bent over her desk peering through the rest of the contact sheets from the airport, which she'd managed to develop without interruption at David's villa.

Nick knocked and opened her door.

Sweeping the proofs into the top drawer, she shut it hard then twisted around and glared at him. "Aren't you a nosy bugger."

His eyes pried into hers, lips pursed, no doubt curious as hell.

"What is it?" She stood to face him, hands on her hips and an edge in her voice.

"Uh, just wondering if Laos is a go?" His words were tight, spoken with noticeably less confidence than usual.

"I'll let you know as soon as I find out. We're waiting for word from my contact." She glanced at the open door.

"We?" He arched an eyebrow and took one step forward. "Does that mean me? I mean, we are partners, after all."

"I welcome your help. This is a major assignment, but only if you're willing to play by my rules. It's top secret and danger-ous, and it could change the destiny of Vietnam, something I know you're dedicated to."

He held his breath for several seconds then exhaled and waved his hands in capitulation.

"Can't say I'm not stoked about your coming around to my point of view."

"We need to talk about your temper, Nick. It's scary. You said you've struggled with it your entire life, and it sounds like you're pretty much helpless under its domination. How can I be sure you'll keep it under control on this mission?"

He looked like a mini storm was swirling in his brain. *Let's see how he reacts to this.*

"This is a very important mission. If you mess up, you'll pay the consequences. One misstep and we'll leave you behind."

He blinked. His mouth was working but no words came out. "We? Who is we?" he said finally.

"Those are the rules, and you do what I say. Are you in or out?"

"Of course I'm in."

Without a response to his agreement, Ellie pointed toward the door.

He left, closing the door behind him.

25

RENÉ Jalbert turned his ancient Willys Jeep onto Cong Ly Street and slowed to a stop in front of the address Ellie had given him. He swung his long legs to the ground and strode up to the villa. Nick Burrows stood on the walkway in T-shirt, shorts, and flip-flops, smoking a cigarette and scowling.

"Colonel Jalbert." Nick looked at his watch. "Awfully early."

Jalbert registered Nick's belligerent stance. His first impression, when Thiep had set up their first encounter in a clandestine meeting, had been right. This fool had no idea. Immature and volatile. He would need to be handled with care. In one sense he would be a buffer, a sacrificial cow. Jalbert chuckled to himself. He'd need velvet gloves to pull Nick into his confidence. He'd also have to exercise caution; Nick possessed inflated bravado as well as an exaggerated delusion of his capabilities.

"Monsieur Burrows," he began, "the time has come for our mission." He lowered his voice. "Confidentially, I must tell you it is of the utmost importance that you are a part of this venture. We must be vigilant, yet understated, and do everything we can to assist Mademoiselle Eleanor in securing the evidence we require."

He cleared his throat and went on. "Moreover, it must be said that your deep knowledge of US involvement will be a major contribution to her exposé. It is an angle she does not yet comprehend. You might think about how best to achieve this so that we surgically expose the corruption you and I know is there. Our goal is uppermost. I am confident you can work with her to this critical end."

"No worries there." Nick's nervous eyebrows betrayed his concern. "Ellie is one persistent chick, that's for sure. A bitch with a bone." He clucked at his comment, but when Jalbert leveled a sober stare at him, he deflated. "You can believe me when I say we're on the same page."

"Make no mistake: This will not be easy," Jalbert said emphatically. "To unseat the US government requires incontrovertible proof."

Nick sucked deeply on his cigarette. "Thiep was right to bring us together to help us accomplish our mutual goals."

Jalbert lifted a finger. "It is essential that we keep our shared goal quiet. Eleanor is after a good story and revealing photos. You must make yourself indispensable to her. Make sure she misses nothing. You and she are a team. You must allow her to believe she is in charge. Can you do that?"

"Well, yeah, 'course."

Jalbert skewered Nick with his intense scrutiny. "If all goes well, we will succeed."

It was clear Jalbert had reached Nick's ego. He puffed up like a bird in the cold. "I'm ready." He saluted Jalbert.

Jalbert's eyes narrowed as he appraised Nick. "An unnecessary gesture, perhaps, Monsieur Burrows, but I am gratified that you understand. Perhaps you should go collect Eleanor.

The plane awaits." Jalbert put his hand on Nick's shoulder with the faintest pressure. "It is imperative she believes you and I have just met. We have had no prior contact. Understood?"

Nick nodded, took a last drag on his cigarette, and flicked it to the walkway with his middle finger and thumb, twisting it under the sole of his sandal.

"You might as well come in and wait while I get her."

Nick left Jalbert in the foyer and walked up the stairs.

"WHAT'S GOING ON, NICK?" Ellie asked when she answered his knock. "You look very self-satisfied."

"A very serious man is downstairs. Says his name is Jalbert. Evidently, the plane awaits. So you might want to pack. Our mission is at hand."

"Far out!" Ellie chimed. She grabbed her red knapsack and smaller duffel, grateful for the trick Jenkins had taught her about being prepared: "Have a ready bag. Always be geared up to split at a moment's notice."

"I'll meet you downstairs." She shooed him out of her room, stuffed the prints and negatives from the airport shoot into an envelope and stashed them under the mattress along with her photos from Tet and the Delta patrol. A swift survey of the room and she dashed out the door, locked it, and skipped down the stairs, nearly running Jalbert over.

"Mademoiselle Eleanor, our pilot is waiting at the airport," he said drily.

Ellie tapped her foot impatiently as they waited for Nick. Po approached and handed her a sack containing a thermos of tea, dried fish, and rice balls. Nick clambered down the stairs and followed them out the door.

Ellie and Nick tossed their duffels into the back of the Willys. "Where are your bags?" she asked Jalbert.

"I have some matters to take care of. I will meet you at my hotel, the Constellation, in Vientiane."

An apprehensive quiver haroomed through her stomach.

At Tan Son Nhut, Jalbert parked near a motley gathering of planes and pointed to a rattletrap, single-engine transport nearby. The full force of the day's heat beat down on them.

The pilot regarded the trio from his open cockpit window. His face was deeply lined and weathered like crumpled parchment, and ice-blue eyes beamed out of its ravines.

"Whoa, well-seasoned plane," Nick cracked, cocking his head up toward the pilot. He shielded his mouth with a hand. "And *he* is way beyond seasoned. Face like one of those wrinkled Chinese dogs."

Jalbert angled a sideways glance at Nick then tilted his head up to the pilot. "Romo, *mon ami*, it is our profound fortune that you were available for this mission."

"When an old friend calls, Romo flies. I hope you have arranged an adventure for me? It has been some time since my pulse has raced," Romo said in a heavy French accent.

Nick rolled his eyes at Ellie.

"Meet your passengers, the photojournalist Eleanor Ketcham and her companion, Dick Burrows." Jalbert slitted his eyes at Ellie, who swallowed hard, too wound up to appreciate Jalbert's dig.

"*Nick. Nick* Burrows," Nick retorted, brandishing an arched brow at Jalbert.

"Excuse me. Of course. Monsieur *Nick*." The corners of Jalbert's mouth twitched. "And this daredevil in disguise is none other than Pasquale Romolino, the great Corsican aviator. We've known each other since de Gaulle had an *au pair*."

The two older men guffawed.

❧

AS Romo sat in his cockpit, his mind wandered back to what he considered his and Jalbert's odd friendship. Odd in the sense that Jalbert relied on him to take all the risks while never exposing himself to any. Regardless, Romo thought, they'd worked for years, always immersed in the mire of an unpleasant world, however exciting and lucrative. But transporting illicit cargo was boring; he only got shot at a dozen times. Plucking hostages out of the grasp of kidnappers, hah, now that took skill. Then sparing the death of the wounded by airlift during the heat of battle, well, that was Romo's specialty. He was the sacrificial lamb if the unexpected occurred, but where else could he seek out the thrills and elation of surviving life and death situations. *I am a man ravished within the joy of my own world of madness and chaos.*

He looked down at his compatriot. "Long live death, long live war, long live the Foreign Legion." The two men saluted each other.

"WHAT was that?" Ellie asked.

"Ah," Romo replied, "it is the toast of the French Foreign Legionnaires."

Are they distracting us with humor and glamour so we won't anticipate the danger in this venture?

Romo held his hand to his chest and bowed out the window in Ellie's direction then bobbed his head at Nick. "I'm gassed up and ready to fly. And Joelle," he said, reaching out to pat the chapped skin of the fuselage, "she is hot to trot, so to say."

"Your good luck charm, eh, Romo?" Jalbert ran his fingers over the name Joelle scrawled beneath the cockpit window in faded magenta paint.

"What kind of plane is this?" Ellie asked as Nick started for the steps.

"She's a Pilatus P6 Porter," Romo said. "S-T-O-L. Sturdy as a tank."

"That's short takeoff and landing, Ellie." Nick tossed the comment over his shoulder.

"Those were glory days, eh, flying all over this continent for the French?" Jalbert reminisced, ignoring Nick's comment. "There were many times you pilots barely escaped with your trousers."

"*Oui*, skipping between the bullets," Romo said. "We had the magic, *mon frère*." He frowned. "*Alors*, some of us did not. *C'est la guerre. C'est l'aventure.* Now, come aboard, *mes amis*, and close the hatch after you."

"*A bientôt*," Jalbert said to Ellie as she and Nick boarded. "You are in good hands. Romo will deliver you unharmed."

Unharmed? What does that mean? Ellie hesitantly took the navigator's chair. She gave the aircraft a quick survey. Anything could happen between here and there, like losing her gear. Without it, she'd have only her word. The proof would be in the photos she took. She dug out of her bag her two Nikons, one with a telephoto and the other with a wide-angle lens, and hung them around her neck next to the tiny Rollei she already wore.

Nick settled into the single seat behind her. The remaining seating had been removed to make a cargo area.

"Hey, no safety belt? No tray table?" Nick asked drolly.

Romo gave an exaggerated cough.

Ellie watched the pilot, whose khakis were as faded as his plane. He slid the cockpit window closed. The propeller chugged into a high-pitched hum.

"Do not allow the rattle to cause fear. It is Joelle's way of assuring us that we will indeed part with *terra firma*."

With clearance from the tower, he adjusted his beret atop thick, wiry white hair and pushed in the throttle. They taxied down the runway and lifted into the sky.

What was to come? Follow the *Double UO Globe*? The jungle landscape flowed past as the sun rose into the sky and washed the morning with light. Peter Pan could have flown past, and she wouldn't have been surprised.

"So, Romo, what's your background?" Nick shouted from his perch. "How long you been flying in these mountains?"

26

"What time is it?" Romo held up his wrist to check his watch and laughed at his joke. *Impudent little prick dares to question Romo? So I fuck up on occasion. That's how it goes when one flies in a war zone.* He could sense how uncomfortable Nick was. He also stank of ambition and self-importance.

"I've been in the Southeast Asian skies long enough to know the landscape," he answered with a chill in his voice. The cheeky little *merde* had no clue of what danger really was. A waste of time and breath to explain to one who had no point of reference about spending an entire adult life cheating death.

Pasquale Romolino lit a cigarillo.

"Romo is a fighter by nature." His thoughts drifted back to 1942 during the battle of Bir Hakeim in the Libyan desert with his detachment in the French Foreign Legion, surrounded by whizzing bullets, explosions, and wounded and dying comrades. He and his small band of legionnaires fought hard, exhausting all their weapons until they had nothing left but combat knives. Despite their efforts, they were overrun by Erwin Rommel's Afrika Korps.

Suddenly, pain shattered his memory. He grabbed his left leg with both hands and rubbed furiously. The aircraft rocked. Ellie grasped Romo's shoulder in an obvious effort to assist. She seemed more concerned about his discomfort than her own safety.

Romo turned to her and cooed, "Not to worry, mademoiselle, for your safety or for Romo's. This is a normal occurrence within Romo's flight plan." He threw his best grin at her.

"You've been injured, haven't you?" she asked.

"Probably crashed a plane when he fell asleep," Nick groaned from behind her. "I knew this was a bad idea."

Romo ignored Nick and directed his conversation to Ellie. "You are correct, Mademoiselle Ellie, but your companion Dick's—"

"Nick, goddamn it, my name is Nick!"

"Contrary to Nick's judgment as to the cause of my wounds, I was injured while I stood on firm ground."

Romo's memory flashed before his eyes of the doctor staring down at him with grave concern. "The nerves are shredded in addition to the many broken bones and shrapnel embedded in both your legs." The doctor took a breath. "I was briefed by your fellow survivors about your character, so I'll not paint any rosy pictures. It will take a miracle for you ever to walk again."

Romo shuddered at the memory. Brought back out of his reverie, he asked Ellie, "I am sorry, what was that again?"

"Were you wounded in war?"

"Ah, yes." He focused his eyes on his instrument panel.

She tilted her head slightly and gave him an engaging smile. "You give me the impression of someone who is very humble and doesn't care what others think."

Romo read an expression of pure compassion on the young woman's face.

"I'm sorry you suffered." In the next breath she whispered, "It must be difficult and unpleasant to be piloting a plane."

This one is worthy of the truth, he thought, and it would be a pleasant experience to relate to someone who I, Romo, consider to be genuine when there are not many I know or have met who give a shit. It is good fortune I excel in character judgment.

Romo dropped his cigar to the cockpit floor and crushed it. "What you say, my young one, is somewhat true. Sometimes Joelle gets the best of me, but it is because of my inability to have total control of my legs that I chose this vocation. I must confess that I cannot be an idle observer of the intrigue, adventure, and action occurring within my mistress, Southeast Asia, without owning some piece of it. When my legs were weakened, I learned to fly. I flew secret intelligence operations with 'Old Leatherface' Chennault and the Civil Air Transport just after the American spy agency bought the operation in the late 1940s. My cohorts and I also ferried journalists for the French at Dienbienphu and dropped supplies to them and to the nationalist forces in China. During the Korean War, I rubbed elbows with and won drinking bouts against former Flying Tigers— best men I ever met, wild souls with an extra serving of bravery.

"So. You are in good hands. Joelle, here, is my ninth plane. I've only been shot down twice. Crash-landed a few more times. Wheels are superfluous in this game." He chuckled, running his thumb and forefinger along a tracery of white mustache, the only straight line on his face, and rumbled out a laugh. When Romo laughed, he tilted his head upward in secret agreement with the clouds and the gods.

He pointed to the changing scenery, now an array of karst limestone-humped peaks, their hills and spiny ridges poking out through lush greenness, all floating in mist.

"My goodness, you were soaring over these jungles and mountains before I was even born. No wonder you're calm at the controls." Ellic gasped when the plane rocked hard to one side. "I'm just glad it's not antiaircraft fire that's bouncing us around like Mexican jumping beans. Thermals rising in the air over the mountains, right?" She met Romo's eyes and squelched a laugh.

"Down there, the Ho Chi Minh Trail snakes its way into South Vietnam." Romo pointed through the fog. "Americans bomb; VC rebuild. Supplies never stop moving from north to south—trucks, troops, tanks, bicycles, you name it."

Ellie ran off a few frames of the landscape below.

"I knew it," Nick exclaimed. "I knew the US was bombing the Ho Chi Minh trail. All those military denials, lies. And here we are, right now, flying over the scene of the crime!"

"Once we cross the spine of these mountains, the Annamites, we'll turn to the northwest and follow the Mekong to Vientiane."

Look at this woman. She loves every minute, every bump. For a woman, she's got des couilles grande.

27

———————

The plane dropped. Ellie's hand went to her belly. Nick had a death grip on her shoulder. *Why do I think this is the least of what we're going to encounter?*

"Exactly so, Ellie, mountain thermals," Romo said. "Merely air currents inviting us to land, but we are not quite ready yet. We will set down on a dusty airstrip just north of Vientiane."

Nick's breathing deepened behind her.

Ellie swiveled at the sound. "Nick, I didn't know you were afraid of flying."

"I'm not. I just hate those sudden dips that flip my guts around. Romo, isn't Wattay Airport right there at Vientiane? Much closer, man."

Romo launched a crooked smile that rearranged the wrinkles on his face. "I have been instructed not to attract unneeded attention. One cannot be too careful; there are many spies in Vientiane. Have you forgotten there is a war going on? And you never know where the NVA or Pathet Lao are lurking."

A sound like popcorn popping stuttered through the cabin. The plane shuddered. "*Merde!*" Romo checked the gauges. "Hold onto your hats—"

Small arms fire peppered the wings. He cranked the controls hard to the right, tossing Nick into the cargo area and Ellie against Romo; he elbowed her back into her seat.

"Not to worry," he purred, "Romo is at the controls." Gauges clicked insanely, indicator lights flashed, the altimeter needle dipped precipitously. "Ah, *mes amis*, this reminds me of when the Maquisards shot out both my engines and I had to belly flop into the Mekong. Sad to say, I lost my cargo, and it took ten days to march out." His voice remained calm even while he fought the controls as the plane lost altitude. "I am dumping fuel for good measure."

"We're a little close to the river?" Nick picked himself up and sat back down.

Images flashed across Ellie's mind: fragments of a countdown, catching an edge in a downhill, 70 mph and cartwheeling madly, wondering if she'd survive. Hyper-alive, she vibrated with excitement.

"Not time to worry. Romo is an old hand at this. You must relax now, my children. Hold on tight. We are going down. Our adventure is landing us quite a bit north of Vientiane. My apologies."

"Are you fucking kidding me? We're going to crash?" Nick shouted.

Ellie switched to automatic, her body tight with expectation yet coolheaded. Thoughts swirled into slow motion while trees slid closer, growing greener, the muddy river like a smear of peanut butter. She watched Romo, recognizing kindred calm in the face of danger. She bit her lower lip and clenched her fists, hoping the pilot was as good as he acted. She was surprised Nick wasn't venting anger. Fear, more like it.

More small arms fire whined past the plane like angry mosquitoes.

Ellie slid down in her seat as far as she could. She couldn't take her eyes off Romo. He gripped the stick tightly and worked pedals like he was dancing, trying to control the descent, while constantly scanning the landscape. "Soft landing, that's what we're looking for," he crowed. "I can ride the ground current and set Joelle down safely and without conflagration." He turned to Nick and grinned.

Ellie clutched her camera bag and duffel to her chest to protect her cameras.

Romo barely avoided splashing into the Mekong. He glided so close over the muddy river Ellie could see men in fishing boats and farmers in rice fields looking up, wide-eyed and probably terrified to see a steel dragon dive-bombing toward them. They scattered like frightened mice.

Romo whistled the '*Marseillaise.*' "Okay, Joelle, *doucement*," he crooned. Pulling back on the stick to lift the nose, he set his plane down in the soft, moist red clay earth.

Even with the blessing of the mushy cushion, landing was a shuddering, loud, terrifying contact with the ground.

"Courrez," Romo yelled. "Run! Vacate the plane!"

28

———

Ellie collapsed onto the red-clay earth. Thrown clear of the plane. Dizzy and confused. Her mind swirled with the happenings of the last few moments. Sudden fear, then the bone-jarring impact, then the noise, then the cameras around her neck swinging from their straps, pounding her flesh as if she were a punching bag, then Romo yelling, and then ... she lifted her head and peered at the surroundings. She held her gaze steady until her surroundings came into focus.

They'd missed the river. They hadn't hit any trees or people. The plane lay lopsided in the soft clay, one wing broken off. Somewhere nearby Romo was ranting, delirious.

"*La mort. Oui, je suis mort. Merde, merde, merde* ... I left without seeing my Jeanne ... Poor Helene will weep forever ... Not bad for sixty-two, eh? *Qu'est-ce que c'est?* What is this ... hell tastes like mud? Smells like mud and sewage?"

Ellie was grateful for the vast experience that had enabled Romo to set down his plane as gently as possible to avoid explosions and fire. Still, the landing was violent, and they'd all been thrown clear.

Nick was grumbling. She looked up to see him standing

over her, covered in clay, disheveled. "Ellie, are you okay?" He reached for a hand and pulled her up. She tried to straighten her clothes, to no avail. She was a mess. Clay in her hair, on her skin, in her teeth.

"Ellie, *chèrie*, you are in one piece?" Romo piped up from where he lay.

"Good as gold, Romo." She made an effort to disguise her shakiness. "We're all alive."

It seemed like outright magic that her gear was with her even though she'd had a death grip on her bags. Her Nikon F, 50 mm lens attached, was muddy too. She tried to clean the lens, and dropped to her knees, grimacing, panning the crash site with its scattered debris. The sound of the motor drive echoed in her ears. She framed the plane's fuselage, focused on the wide faces of people squatting at a distance and watching the drama. Her agitation eased once she got the photos she wanted, and she stashed her cameras in the knapsack. No need for them to get any dirtier or wet.

"Romo, any chance you speak Lao?"

"*Un peu.* But first, you must please to help me up. My legs are stubborn. They want to stay behind," he explained.

Ellie took a few rusty steps over to him. "Ugh, I need some WD-40." She winced as she stretched her arms and bent to touch her toes. "Every single muscle in my body is rusty."

She turned to Nick. "Come on, Nick, you get one arm, I'll get the other. Let's help him up."

Nick stepped over to help her haul Romo upright.

Romo wavered, found his balance, and noticed the curious people standing nearby. "*Bonjour, bonjour, mes amis, Sabaidee,*" he greeted, grasping Ellie's hand.

"Ellie, please hang on tight. I'm woozy as a drunken teenager."

He leaned on Ellie and asked the farmers who had gathered, "*Ruea Hang yao? Un bateau?*"

"*Jao, jao.*" One man nodded his understanding then trotted up the rise to a small village on stilts. He returned with a fisherman.

"*Sabaidee,*" Romo said, and repeated his request for a boat. Even through his obvious pain, it didn't take long before Romo, with his undeniable charm and mixture of Lao and French, negotiated for the fisherman to float them down the river to Vientiane. "*Khàwp jai lai lai,* thank you, *merci.*"

The Laotian turned away and ran down to the water on bowed legs, presumably to prepare their craft.

While they waited, Nick poked through the plane looking for his gear, and Romo rested against Ellie's bags. She fetched a couple of sturdy branches and cleaned them with her Swiss Army knife, fashioning rough walking sticks.

"These might give you some balance," she said, holding them out to him.

"How observant you are. You would notice a star shining through a cloudy night sky," Romo said, hand to his heart. He struggled to stand again, beads of sweat on his forehead. Ellie gathered her bags and the trio crept to the river's edge, where the beaming Lao in a conical hat motioned them toward a raft. He had just finished lashing two rafts together so they would accommodate the size of the Westerners.

"A raft? What is this, *The Adventures of Huckleberry Finn?*" Nick scoffed.

"Transportation is a luxury, is it not?" Romo asked. "Or perhaps you would prefer to swim?"

"Check it out," Nick said. "It's a jerry-rigged raft made of long bamboo trunks tied together with hemp, easily twenty feet stem to stern."

"Very common here," Romo said and pointed. "See how they bent the double bow upward? That's to keep the raft from flooding when it hits rapids."

Ellie saw they'd lashed three crosspieces of timber to the

long bamboo logs, and then built up the sides with more bamboo and a few rubber tires.

"It's still only six bamboos wide, each the width of an open hand, it'll be a snug fit," Romo said.

Nick moaned.

"Pretty clever engineering," Ellie agreed.

"Ask, and it shall be given," Romo said. "My Bible studies may be rusty, but this raft is a work of art." Turning to the fisherman, he praised, "*Ngam*—beautiful."

The fisherman's son, a boy about eleven years old, ran to the water's edge and hastened aboard, carrying a net bag of rice balls and smoked fish for the journey. Father and son picked up a couple of long poles from the shore and stashed them in the raft. They hinged a third rudder pole to the back. The man pointed and the trio made their way onboard, gingerly. Ellie helped Romo get seated, settling their bags as cushions for him to lean against, and knelt behind him. Nick, still stewing, stood in front of them looking out to the water, legs forked wide in a Napoleonic pose.

The Laotians dug the poles into the mud and pushed off from shore. Swift water caught them in its current.

Nick swatted at his face. "Oh man, land of giant bugs. Mosquitoes and some big squashy bug that stinks to high heaven."

"Termite," Romo said.

"Termites? Jeez," he winced. "Let's try a different subject. How far are we from Vientiane?"

"Not too far, less than 100 kilometers, about 60 miles." Ellie noticed the glance Romo angled toward Nick as he struggled to find equilibrium. He looked like he was about to boil over. Romo made a pretense of picking up his walking sticks and trying to stand. His movement jostled the raft and sent Nick over the side into the muddy Mekong.

Romo smiled at Ellie. "Just a minor attitude adjustment," he whispered and cupped his hands around his mouth. "Watch out for man-eating fish," he shouted, fanning the fire. Violent splashing ensued. Nick thrust his hand out of the water and grabbed a side of the raft, rocking it precipitously.

Ellie eyed Romo as she moved to the edge and clucked soothing comments to get Nick to calm down. "Relax, you're safe. No worries. Take it easy. No man-eating fish. Take my hands, Nick."

With the help of the boy, Ellie managed to lever Nick up and into the raft without capsizing it. He spluttered about leeches and water snakes and filthy-dirty river water.

"Fear is one thing, Nick," Romo's voice was deadly serious. "We learn to storm the gates of fear as we chase our goals but beware the anger. Anger is something else. It will take you down."

As if to prove Romo's point, all hell burst loose. Rocket-propelled grenades fired from the west bank and exploded on the opposite side of the river. Automatic gunfire spat back from the east bank. Foliage shredded. Tracers skimmed the water line. Cries and shouts pierced the air muffled by the rounds shrieking from both riverbanks.

Nick's eyes widened. He fell to his knees. Ellie tried to raise a camera, but Nick grabbed her and pulled her down.

"To the rear! Get down!" Romo roared at Ellie and Nick.

The five hunkered at the stern, which raised the bow higher. It was stitched by a volley of bullets, showering the occupants with bamboo splinters.

"Tell that guy to get us to shore," Nick yelled to Romo as the fisherman held tight to the rudder and maintained a steady course downriver.

"Captain knows what he is doing," Romo responded as more tracers zipped above the raft. "We must remain neutral. If we dock, they will think we are choosing a side. Then it is *au revoir, ma toute.*" He kept a firm hand on Ellie's shoulder as gunfire continued to catapult the Mekong.

"Let me shoot this." She failed to squirm out of Romo's grip.

Overhead, another wave of bullets whistled past. She and Nick covered their heads with their arms.

As the raft passed through the deadly crossfire and left the battle in its wake, Nick exhaled a sigh of obvious relief. "What was that about?"

"Just a skirmish, happens frequently. Royal Lao forces versus Pathet Lao communists," Romo said. "Everyone is groovy?"

The fisherman calmly steered the raft as if there'd been only a slight disturbance.

"Good photo op missed," Ellie groused.

"You didn't miss anything, Ellie," Nick said. "You can't photograph flying bullets, and the guys shooting them were hidden by the jungle."

He was right, she thought.

They sailed past dark green hummocks rising out of the water. She settled into the calm of the fairyland that had taken the place of gunfire.

Night was stretching toward morning by the time they arrived weary and sore at Jalbert's Constellation Hotel. Romo gave the captain plenty of kip in thanks for the ride.

Two blocks off the river, on rue Samsenthai, the Constellation was a five-story, modest ivory stucco building, with whimsical eyebrow carvings above its windows. The fading dowager was a shadow of the grandeur of Saigon's Continental Palace.

We are a ragtag trio of survivors.

"Greetings," said the Laotian desk clerk in heavily accented English as they walked to the front desk. "We expect you sooner. Please sign register. Monsieur Jalbert will be here soon. He ask that you please enjoy amenities." He gave them each a key.

In her small room on the third floor of the French Colonial hotel, Ellie set her bags on the bureau, the mud now dried and sifting to the tile floor. She sank onto the bed. She was wrung out but fought the urge to collapse fully into sleep; her sore muscles craved a hot bath. Only one bathroom per floor, and she let out a happy sigh when she found it empty. It was the small things that made a difference. Locking the door, she turned on the faucets, expecting the tepid water of Saigon, and gratefully watched the tub fill with hot, steamy water. Every movement involved in taking off her clothes was an exercise in pain. She examined her cuts and bruises. Small things. Big thing was being alive. She lowered herself in the tub, flinching as each scratch and cut met the water. The rhythm of the Mekong still rolled in her body.

Thoughts and steam misted around her as she retraced their journey from Saigon to Vientiane. Harrowing moments popped up like arcade targets from the surreal, improbable trip with its strange, mismatched companions. Nick with his quicksilver moods. Romo with his sharp-edged sense of the absurd and absolute, irreverent confidence. Not to mention the magical landing he was able to effect, saving their lives.

Deep down, she acknowledged the undeniable thrill. Had she become a convert to war? Was this bizarre, bloody, no-rules conflict in the jungles of Southeast Asia her calling? She might indeed be Ben's alter-ego. She chased the thought away and stored it in the back of her brain to explore later.

So far so good. She giggled. Plane crash, raft trip down the Mekong, Pathet Lao crossfire. She hadn't known she signed up for adventure travel.

Not to mention the roller coaster ride of Nick's temperament. She hoped he could keep focus on his deep passion to save the oppressed people of the world from imperialists' greed. The alternative was unpalatable. He could be charming and funny. Until the temper erupted. If she tried to jettison him, what would he do, backhand her into oblivion?

Through Nick she had learned how to maneuver a situation to her liking. Hadn't she gotten him to think it was his idea to come along on her journey? She would pay close attention, conservatively dole out information about her assignment while keeping him twisted around her little finger because he was a powder keg: idealist and hellion braided together.

Her thoughts turned to the pilot and his unquestioning command of his plane. Oddly enough, Romo, whom she'd known for the least amount of time, was the one member of their group she would trust with her life. He kept his cool in a crisis. His rowdy humor balanced his sense of the ridiculous. He was crazy brave. No wonder he was a war pilot.

Jalbert, as the most important piece of this puzzle, had not yet arrived. He was the leader, wasn't he, the man in charge of this crusade?

29

"*Entrez*," Romo replied when Ellie knocked on his door. He was in bed, weak and recuperating from the crash landing. When he saw her, he tried a closed-lip smile. "Come in, come in, I do not bite, although I would if I could." He nodded at a glass of water on the bedside table where his dentures rested. "The result of instrument failure in bad weather. A minor inconvenience," he lisped. "But what have you brought me? It smells like heaven."

"Espresso and croissants."

"*Alors*, first things first." He fished his teeth out of the glass and slid them into place. "The snapping turtle, he is back." He stretched his jaw. "I have overcome my embarrassment, Mademoiselle Ellie. Romo is what he is, no more, no less."

She set a cup and basket on the nightstand and propped pillows behind him so he could sit up. She handed him the coffee, moved the basket of pastries to the bed covers. "Exactly how many planes have you crashed?" She pulled a chair up to the bed and sat.

"The number matters not. Attitude is what carries us. It is the air beneath our wings if I may be so trite. This bruised body might be a shade slower on the rebound, but it still has the same hunger for adventure, still the great reflexes for solving a problem in midair. Still a few flights left in me. No need to fetch your parachute yet."

He waved his hand in the air, rolled his eyes, and dug into the croissants. "Impressive appetite, yes?" He unleashed a laugh and patted his belly. "But what about you, Ellie? You were jumbled around like my *grandmere's* old washing machine in that plane. And poor Nick, without a seatbelt."

"You reprobate." She laughed. "I'm stiff, but it's familiar, like after a fall on an icy racecourse."

"*Quoi?*" he asked, his mouth full of croissant.

She rose, struck a pose, knees bent, arms tucked like chicken wings. "I'm talking about ski racing. I was a ski racer."

"Ah, like Jean-Claude Killy."

"Yeah." She unwound from her tuck and sat back down. "Where's Jalbert? I thought he'd be waiting for us."

"He wields his magic somewhere, working out our next steps in this covert dance. I am sure I have no idea how he will manage that trick, but he has gotten me in and out of tougher places, *laissez moi vous dire.* Let me tell you!"

Ellie threw up her hands. "So we don't know when he'll show up?"

"Patience, *ma chèrie.* His ways can be mysterious, but he never wavers in his commitment, and always he gets the job done."

She slapped her hands against her legs. "What's your role in this adventure, Romo?"

He raised his palm to his chest. "You see before you a man without a plane, a cavalryman without a horse, a soldier without a gun."

"In other words, you don't know." She snickered.

"I will know soon enough. Cannot lie here one moment

longer than necessary. *Alors*, enough about me. Tell me about you. What is your part in this war?"

"I was challenged to reach beyond my comfort zone."

"Who was the crazy person who would send you to this godforsaken battle zone?"

"His name is Ben Stryker. Famous author. He sent me to Saigon on assignment to interview war reporters for a book he's writing."

"Ben Stryker? *Mon Dieu*, Ellie, I know this man. Crazy is the exact word."

Her eyes opened wide. "You know Stryker? How?"

He took a sip of his coffee and a big bite of a croissant. "We met back in 1954 when I flew him into Dienbienphu. My plane at the time was called Mireille. I always suspected Ben was sent under cover as a war correspondent by your OSS."

"Hmm, wasn't it the CIA by then?"

"Pardon, you are correct. Stryker, he did not act like a spook, but I think he was one. Romo, he knows of such things, but Ben was also a reporter to the soles of his American feet."

"Come to think of it, he did mention he kicked around Southeast Asia for several years. What happened in Dienbienphu?"

"Let's just say we got involved in our own little battle," Romo said. "It was the day I delivered another reporter to the bunker, Jack Robinson, 'JR'. That evening, Vietminh attacked out of nowhere like a swarm of angry bees. Down the ridges they came from the surrounding peaks. It was jarring—the noises, the acrid smell of fear and gunpowder, men screaming, shooting, falling—"

He closed his eyes. "JR was shot. He collapsed. I blasted my handgun like a marshal in your Western cinema, knocking Vietminh to the ground amidst dust and mortar smoke. Stryker shot too. We had to get JR to the plane.

"Stryker covered me as I helped JR to his feet and dragged him out of the bunker.

"Whistles blew, and men shouted as they charged the compound. One lobbed a grenade toward us but missed his mark. Ben scattered shot at the attackers. JR stumbled, moaned. I cinched my arm around his waist, and we speed-limped through a spray of machine-gun fire to the plane. I shoved the wounded man into the rear of my bullet-pockmarked aircraft.

"Surprising to say Ben was able to run between bullets, and he leapt into the co-pilot's seat. 'Nothing like a crisis to bring people together,' Ben cracked. His comment released our stress.

"The propeller of my Pilatus P6 coughed and sputtered to life. We bounced down the runway, grenades exploding behind us. It seemed an eternity to get enough speed, then I pulled back on the stick and Mireille lifted into the air.

"It is not time to worry, *mes amis*, I told them, over the sound of the engine and gunfire. I had done this flight so many times, I could do it blindfolded.

"JR crawled forward and stuck his head into the cockpit. 'I owe you guys. Thanks.' He was choked with emotion.

"Over my shoulder I saw the wounded man tying rags around his leg.

'One day, if we live long enough, we might ask a return favor from JR, eh, Ben?' I suggested.

'Yeah, possible,' Stryker mumbled."

Romo slurped coffee. "And then we were up and over the mountains and heading for safety. I tell you, Ellie, Ben Stryker was in thrall, in charge of all his faculties. I could smell his adrenaline."

Ellie hyperventilated. "Oh my god, a real action-adventure movie, the two of you." She looked up as if the movie screen were above her. "I can just see him. He never does anything halfway, does he?" she said, hand on her chest. "And neither do you. I'm so glad you all made it out alive. You, dear Romo, you are a born storyteller."

"Such is Romo's life, one long saga," he laughed, "between moments of greatness."

She snorted.

Romo cleared his throat. "We are at this moment on the edge of a new adventure. How much does Nick know? Not that Jalbert has enlightened *me* yet."

"Not much. That there's a secret war here in Laos. Other than that, we're all in the dark. She rose and replaced her chair. "Your eyes are closing. I'll come back later. Can I bring you anything? Do you want to see a doctor?"

"Already your medicine is working, and the rest is nothing a day's sleep will not mend. I urge you to be careful," he said. "Keep eyes behind your head as well as in front." He slid into a prone position, eyes closing.

She tiptoed out, left the hotel, and started walking. After only a few blocks, she realized she wasn't paying attention to the French Colonial city and its tangle of French and Laotian architecture. Her mind was a swirl of thoughts of Romo, Jalbert, Nick, Ben, Dienbienphu, and the upcoming mission. Without the clarity of knowledge and experience, the unknown stuck in her brain like a burr.

On her way back to the hotel, she spied a street merchant's collection of carved wood animals, birds, bowls, and walking sticks crammed into a space the size of a large closet. She pointed. The vendor pulled out a pair of native red ebony canes with gnarled and polished tree roots for handles that would fit the palms of Romo's hands perfectly.

When he didn't answer her soft knock, she tiptoed in and leaned the canes against the nightstand.

30

———————

Jalbert arrived in the night.

He met Romo for morning coffee at a quiet table in the dining room, their heads angled inward, drinking strong brew and smoking Gitanes. Blue air clouded around them, masking their conversation. In Romo, he had an ally; their Corsican bond was fast. Such a partner was essential because alone he couldn't run Ellie and also ride roughshod over Burrows. It would take a miracle to turn that idiot into a colleague. Hah, foolish thought; undisciplined, sloppy, and as dangerous as a grenade with a loose pin. Rather, he would need Romo's help for the smooth handling of this undertaking. He filled his friend in on the mission to expose the CIA for the drug runners he believed them to be.

"*Eh bien*, I have finally found what I was looking for," Jalbert confided. "An opium broker carrying the harvest of three villages down to Long Tieng by mule train. You, Ellie, and Nick will join them."

Romo nodded. "*Oui, compris.* Long Tieng. I have not visited that valley in some years. It will be nice to see my old friend, General Vang Pao."

"Ah, how unfortunate for you, my friend. I hear he is up north. Anyhow, it's the tail end of the harvest, so chances are good his second in command, Captain Khou Nao Torr, has already refined much opium into morphine."

"The Hmong general always transfers it to Vientiane," Romo said.

"Correct. If Vang Pao were smart, he'd build a heroin plant of his own in Long Tieng to process the opium into high-grade heroin."

The men looked up as Ellie approached.

"Good morning, gentlemen," she greeted. Jalbert stood, thinking she looked excited. Romo bowed his head to her, eyes sparkling.

"These walking sticks could be from no one else," Romo said to her. "*Merci, ma chèrie.*"

Jalbert stood and pulled out a chair. "Please," he said, gesturing for her to sit, and then raised his arm for the waiter. "Romo has been telling me about your escapade in getting to Vientiane. I am overjoyed to see you arrived safely. More than we can say for the plane, yes?"

"Romo's flying was genius," Ellie said, sliding into the chair. "We were diving straight for the Mekong, but somehow he managed to set us down in the soft loam."

"It was the simple fluttering to land of a large, prehistoric bird," Romo said with a bit of melodrama, his hands describing the action. "At this, I am practiced."

Ellie rolled her eyes and turned to the waiter to order breakfast: fruit, eggs, golden baguette with paté, and coffee. "I can hardly wait to find out what's next," she said, tilting her head toward Jalbert.

He eyed the people sitting closest to them then leaned in. "We're working on getting you up to the CIA's secret airbase," he said in a low voice. "And I hope I don't need to remind you that confidentiality is imperative."

"Secret airbase?"

"Long Tieng. Hidden deep in a pocket of mountains between Vientiane and Dienbienphu. We're chasing the dragon, so to speak. Our goal is to reveal that America's clandestine war has as much to do with drugs as it does with bombing raids on the NVA."

"The CIA are drug pushers?" Ellie asked. "We're going up against the US government? Interesting shit. Juicy story there."

"*Croyez-moi*, this is true, more or less," Romo said, wincing as he moved in his chair. "To get the Hmong to fight for them against the communists, the American agency funds the transfer of their opium from mountain growers to Long Tieng. And beyond."

Ellie shot him a glance.

Jalbert continued. "You have successfully documented the delivery of *Double UO Globe* to the South Vietnamese. Now it is time to expose the American involvement in the drug trade." The Hmong general, Vang Pao, works for the CIA. He converts the raw opium into morphine base right there at his headquarters, and then the bricks are flown to Vientiane on Air America to be processed into number four heroin."

"*La crème de la crème*," Romo said and kissed his fingertips.

Ellie's eyes widened.

Look at her reaction to Romo's delight for number four. What a naïve, ignorant, and gullible child I am manipulating. She knows nothing of the Orient, that opium, morphine, and heroin are staples and the currency of our culture. And she is not Burrows, thank the gods.

"Our challenge," Jalbert went on, "is to get you in there to take detailed photographs of their operation and to gather incriminating evidence against the CIA for your article. The secret is closely guarded, as you can imagine, which means Long Tieng is definitely off limits to civilians, especially journalists. So, we're scratching our brains to figure this out, but ideas percolate. My source tells me the next load will not be ready for transport for at least a week, maybe longer."

Romo wiggled his hands like a magician before the smoke hides his trick. "Very tricky to get you in and out without anyone being wise to your activity. You do stand out in a crowd, young lady. We must invent some sort of disguise."

"Dye my hair black?" she suggested.

"This will not be necessary," Jalbert scoffed.

"Well, whatever you come up with, I'm game. You're coming too, Romo?"

"This, Romo would not miss." He grinned, the wrinkles on his face changing course.

"The more the merrier," she crooned.

31

"Goddammit, where is he?" Ellie banged around her hotel room like a pinball. She was jazzed, finally able to feed Nick the details he craved about their mission. It was right up his alley, taking on the US Government. He had waved off her concern about Thiep and communist backlash, but taking on a top-secret division of the government? What were the possible repercussions? This could be dangerous, but if ever there were a need for facts, this was it. Nick might have considered her a liability on the Delta patrol, but she was now considering how much of a liability he might be. Was her twinge of concern about exposing the government or about Nick? Her focus had to be razor sharp; she didn't want Nick rolling around ready to go off at the merest provocation.

"Have a bath. Calm down," she admonished.

Shuffling back down the hall after a long soak, a verging-on-threadbare white towel wrapped around her body and clutching her clothes, she saw the door to her room gaping wide. She entered cautiously.

"Nick?" Irritation surfaced. No boundaries. He lounged on

her bed, legs stretched long, hands intertwined behind his head, goofy smile on his lips.

"Ellie," he said from low in his throat, purring like a sated feline.

She pushed the door closed, tossed her clothes on the bed, and tightened the towel that barely reached beneath her rear end. "How can you disappear like this, Nick? Two whole days without a word? Jalbert's here, and we're planning our strategy."

"Yeah." He held up his palms.

He had an irresistible smile, batwing eyebrows fluttering above bright eyes that radiated playful intelligence. Despite her pique, her knots of suspicion loosened.

"I have news about our assignment."

He was not paying attention. Not even reacting to the word "our."

"Later." He waved his hands, glided from the bed, and took her right hand in his left, sliding his other hand along the small of her back. He twirled her around the room in a slow waltz, humming in her ear. Then he was embracing her and kissing her and sweeping her off her feet. Her towel slid to the floor. He was doing his best to seduce her.

"Ellie, Ellie, your skin is like satin," he murmured, octopus hands roving her body. He kissed her neck and nibbled her ear. "I can't wait to show you what's behind door number three," he whispered. All the while she was trying to push away from him.

She finally succeeded in creating a little distance. "You've just stepped over the line," she snarled. "What is this, a quiz show? Christ, Nick, what's going on with you, you're different."

"As much as I ache to make love to you right now, I have something very special in store for you. Get dressed." He patted her rear.

She swatted his hand away and entered the bathroom, closed the door, and dressed. Unsure of what he was up to, she secretly enjoyed this side of him. It was the charming, seductive Nick. Maybe being away from Saigon and the heaviness of life there was releasing him from his demons. Maybe it would all be okay.

When she emerged, he went to her, twirled her around. "The mysteries of the Orient await you, my love. We will peel away the layers and discover the promise of the heavens." He breathed into her neck. He took her hand and kissed it. Pulled her out the door.

She grabbed her Rollei on the way out. Downstairs in the lobby, they ran into their comrades. "This is great. Nick, you stand over there with Jalbert and Romo. I want to document this gathering. We'll call it the *before* picture." Jalbert looked uncomfortable as she directed them into different poses: he and Romo, he and Nick, Nick and Romo.

"All right, all right, Ellie. Typical photographer. Shoot hundreds of pictures to get one good shot. Think maybe you've got enough?" Nick grumbled.

"Ha ha," she chortled. "Right on. Just one more. I want one with our pilot."

Nick obliged, in an obvious hurry, and then gave the camera back to Ellie.

"Okay, I'm ready to go." She hung the small camera around her neck.

Jalbert swung his arm around Romo's shoulders and the two shuffled off toward the bar.

Nick and Ellie strolled to a sleepy three-story white house in a quiet, leafy neighborhood of Vientiane not far from the hotel. Soft evening breezes whistled, as if beckoning them into a time tunnel. As they approached, the door swung open. A tall, regal woman stood there swathed in rich teal brocade shot through with golden threads. Ellie had never seen such fabric, more artistic than functional. She gaped at the long, many-hued patterned kimono vest over the teal gown that also shimmered with metallic filaments. The woman put her palms together in a *wai* and bowed slightly. Even the jeweled chopsticks anchoring her elaborate black chignon glittered. Was this a fairy tale?

"Welcome, Monsieur Nick, and this must be your Mademoiselle Ellie. You are my honored guests." Her French-accented voice was unusually soft and delicate behind thick makeup.

"Ellie, this is Madame Lulu, proprietress of this house," Nick introduced.

A faint perfume reached Ellie's nose, an exotic, hypnotic aroma that snaked around her, luring her. She had the sensation she was falling through the floor as if it were a cloud.

"Nick has arranged everything. He wishes to pamper you," Madame Lulu continued. "Please, come with me." She led them up a broad staircase of highly polished dark mahogany and along a hallway punctuated by several doors. At the back of the house, Madame stopped and turned a faceted glass doorknob, revealing an intimate room of bygone French Colonial refinement. Every aspect of the room was arranged to seduce—the smooth surfaces of the furniture, the sheen of dark wood floors, the muted greens, golds, and blues of the intricately patterned Oriental rug, the chartreuse damask fainting couch in a corner. Ellie ran her fingers over the silky finish of a Queen Anne table and thought here was a mystery of the Orient, a classic eighteenth-century European form carved from the exotic black and white ebony native to Laos.

"Ophelia joins you in a moment," Lulu murmured. "Please —" She gave a backhand swish at two burgundy-damask bolsters set on upholstered pads on either side of a low, brass tray table. Madame lit a candle on the table and left the room.

As soon as the door closed, Ellie raised the Rollei to her eye and shot the whole room with urgency. She inhaled deeply of the candle's aroma, an allure both headier and more seductive than fresh snowfall that promised unknown discoveries. She opened her mouth to comment.

"Sshhh, no more photos, no more words," Nick hushed. "You take the pillow over there." He pointed to one of the bolsters. "For you," he said solicitously and sat down on the other pad.

Ellie remained standing, unsure why discomfort needled at her.

Moments later, a Laotian girl entered, no more than thirteen Ellie guessed, innocent as a newborn fawn. She carried a tray that held two pipes and other paraphernalia Ellie didn't recognize, placed it on the low table, and knelt in front of it. She wore a royal-blue skirt that wrapped sari-style around her and crossed her chest to drape over a shoulder. Her shiny black hair was gathered into a dense beehive atop her head. The girl glanced at each of them and began preparing a pipe. She removed the lid of a porcelain jar and pulled out a viscous black ball. Choosing a thin metal stick, she pierced a portion of the gummy substance and twirled it through the candle flame until the dark ball softened. It gave off an alluring aroma. She then pasted it evenly, with precise strokes, into the bowl of a pipe. The process had the grace and formality of a Roman Catholic rite.

When Ellie's nostrils filled with the sweet and loamy aroma of the warming substance, the tug intensified. Wisps of pungent fragrance coiled around her, beckoning her to follow, to discover its secrets. The seduction of the bouquet alone could be addictive. "Opium." She formed the word aloud.

Nick shushed her, holding a finger to his lips. He spoke with drama. "The first gate of knowledge opens and welcomes you. Beyond the gate, a sliver of the perspective that sages, shamans, gurus, and healers have practiced in the Orient since the beginning of time. Come down here and join me, Ellie."

Her body stiffened. "Stop. No. I'm not going there. Not

doing anything to erode my focus," she declared. "I'm in Laos for a purpose. Not losing sight of that. I'll see you back at the hotel."

Ophelia held the pipe up to Nick, who gestured toward Ellie, and the girl held it out to her, balancing it in both hands, as if a prayer.

"Just take several, long, easy tokes," he cajoled. "You'll love it."

"I said no." She straightened her back, pivoted, and flounced out the door, down the stairs past a confused Madame Lulu, and out the door.

32

———

RENÉ Jalbert settled into a deep leather chair and rested his legs on the ottoman. He had a snifter of his favorite cognac and a fine Cuban cigar. The ritual of snipping the head off a Montecristo No. 4 and rolling the cigar around a few inches from the match flame until the foot glowed gave him immense pleasure. He sighed, grateful to be in the wood-paneled private quarters of his family's Hotel Constellation, one of the few places in the world where he found solace from the pressures of his life.

Basking in the headiness of cigar smoke and cognac, he closed his eyes and considered the formidable obstacles that lay ahead for his team. He couldn't keep them safe from all the risks they might encounter; there were too many unknowns, with the possibility of death topping the list. Regardless of the costs of his mission, gaining and exposing the damning information was worth the gamble; his redemption was at stake.

He and Romo had been through hell together. Jalbert trusted few people, but Romo was a man he could count on. With his snowy hair, face like a river delta, and lurching gait, Romo stood out in any crowd. A wild man with a daring, fearless soul and a pulsing heart of gold, he had the kind of extra sense, an inborn perception that lifted him above the masses. In the flying brotherhood, he was considered a phoenix, exceeding the nine lives of a cat.

If anyone could keep Ellie safe on the trek into Long Tieng it would be Romo, certainly not Burrows. Jalbert could kick himself for ignoring his misgivings and bringing the guy along. He'd smelled something off about Nick but had given him a chance because of his youth and possible usefulness, especially since this mission had so many variables.

Burrows was a powder keg. Jalbert would have to minimize him, keep him in the background. Including Romo on his mission hadn't been part of his original plan, but he needed someone he could trust. The icing on the cake was Romo's familiarity with Long Tieng.

With his knowledge and wit, quick reflexes, and deep experience, Romo was key to the mission's success; however, he was so immediately recognizable, especially to the American airmen who congregated in Vientiane's bars, his presence would only raise questions as to why he was there. Better if he stayed under wraps. But how? It would be like herding butterflies.

A little coddling of Jalbert's phoenix was called for. Time to play the adventure card. While this undertaking would certainly be a physical hardship for his old friend, the man was constitutionally unable to resist a challenge.

Jalbert reached for his cigar cutter and snipped the foot off his partially smoked Montecristo, laid it over the ashtray. Too precious to let it burn down. He rose out of the chair, reached for the vintage bottle of Pierre Ferrand cognac, set it on a silver tray with two crystal snifters, and carried it up to Romo's room.

Romo's eyes widened when he opened the door and spied Jalbert's tray of delights.

"Ahh, I see it is time for serious business."

Jalbert set the tray down on the bureau. He poured healthy measures of the golden ruby liquid into the bowls of the snifters. He offered one to Romo, whose eyes lit up at the sight of the label. They toasted each other and sat down.

Holding his glass aloft, Jalbert laid out the details of his plan. "Our mission is to trek down to the Long Tieng airbase to capture important photos. Together you and I will work out a strategy for reaching the jungle camp above Long Tieng where we'll join an opium caravan and follow their route down into the valley."

"What, may I ask, is my particular role in this venture?" Romo inquired.

"Not only will you be Ellie's guide in Long Tieng since you have extensive knowledge of the whole area, but you are also key to this entire venture. I trust you to keep everything in order."

"By 'in order,' I assume that I am to keep Mademoiselle Ellie from harm?"

Jalbert nodded. He and Romo were silent while sipping their cognacs.

"I'm sorry, for now I must keep you hidden away, old friend, but we mustn't take any chances of running into nosy acquaintances."

"It's not that there are legions of these men," Romo said, swirling the liquid in his glass and inhaling the aroma, "but they *are* critical to the Americans' success. And, yes, I do know many of them in Long Tieng, or shall I say *they* know Romo. Especially the veteran Ravens."

"Ah yes, swashbucklers of the sky, you call them," acknowledged Jalbert.

"These are truly brave men," Romo agreed. "Even this daredevil Romo would have an attack of skepticism flying single-engine Cessnas hunting NVA and Pathet Lao." He swirled his glass and inhaled the bouquet.

Jalbert shook his head. "With all the technology the Americans have, you'd think there would be a better way to call in air strikes against their enemy." Jalbert indulged Romo in his reminiscences. "Indeed, Ravens are vital to their secret war, intelligence gatherers, munitions experts, communications specialists, and combat search and rescue."

"Ah, search and rescue, my favorite." Romo tossed back his cognac as if it were a shot of whiskey. Tears popped from his eyes.

Jalbert's eyes blazed. "Easy there, *mon frère*. This is a rare and expensive brandy. Meant for sipping, not bolting."

"The first nip is to take the edge off. Do not lecture me on sacred protocol." Romo held out his snifter for a refill. "These legs of mine, they're hollow, not good for much else than holding the cognac. Where is Ellie? Should she not be here with us?"

"She mentioned something about a ready bag. Women, eh?" Jalbert shrugged. "Let's get down to business. What do you think is the best way to get to the rendezvous point with the opium train? We could go by caravan, 270 klicks from here, ten days, two weeks, maybe."

"What about Nick? Are you considering leaving him here?"

"I would like to, but no. He might be of assistance since there's a limit to your endurance. You'll want to keep an eye on him. He's not a fan of rules."

"Since walking is not Romo's ideal mode of transportation," Romo took a sip, put his glass down on the bedside table, and held out both hands, palms up, weighing options, "no question, I opt for wings."

"You are right, of course," Jalbert responded. "It's a time saver. I'll look for a maverick or old bush pilot. I might still have contacts from the old days." He swirled the exotic cognac in his snifter and swept the aroma toward his nose, inhaling deeply.

"Now, all we need is a cigar," Romo said.

"Ah, yes," Jalbert reached into his inside jacket pocket and pulled out a Cuban. "Will this do?"

There would be much time for relaxation later with the addition of more than cigars and cognac when Jalbert and his compatriots had returned the opium transport business to its rightful Corsican hands. "Speaking of comfort and getting things done, are you quite certain your legs will carry you? Once we make our rendezvous, I can arrange for a donkey to carry you down into Long Tieng."

Romo eyed him while sniffing the length of the cigar. "It's not like you to show such concern, *mon ami.* It tells me how important this mission is to you." Romo threw his head back and laughed. "An ass for Romo's ass? My legs will carry me where I need to go, but a ride they will gratefully accept."

Jalbert flinched when a rap sounded on the door. He cast a querulous glance at Romo and crossed the room, cautiously opening the door a few inches. "Eleanor."

"Ellie?" Romo called from his seat. "Come in. Join us." She pushed the door open and entered, coughing through the cigar smoke that clouded around the two men.

Jalbert brought a water glass from the bureau, poured a jot of cognac, and offered it to Ellie. "Let us drink a toast to a successful mission."

THE NEXT DAY while Romo slept off his cognac hangover, Jalbert went to Wattay Airport to find himself an airplane and a pilot.

It was midafternoon when he spied a ragged, late-World War II-vintage C-47 limping down the runway toward a hangar. Before the propellers spun to a complete stop, its scruffy pilot emerged from the door forward of the wings. Bulky as a dockworker, he tromped in heavy work boots toward a Quonset hut, reaching into the hip pocket of his dungaree overalls for a flask.

Before the man could take a snort, Jalbert ambled up to him. "Good day, sir. How's business?" Jalbert pointed at the plane.

"Who's askin'?" The pilot spoke with the chopped-off edges of a rough Bronx accent.

"You interested in some work?"

The man hesitated and tossed his gray mane behind his ears. "Like I said, who wants to know?"

"Ah, perhaps you are not the pilot I'm after." Jalbert pivoted away.

"Hey. I just wanted to know. Look, I'm always up for work, old man, legal or shady, don't matter to me. I fly for whoever pays me, I don't give a crap who, the French, Viets, or the warlords, they pay the best."

"You finishing up or in the middle of a run?"

"Takin' a load up to Pop Buell in the Plain of Jars tomorrow."

"Full load?"

"Livestock and seed grain but not everything he wants. I'm gonna get a ration of shit from the old bastard. He doesn't know yet."

Jalbert digested the pilot's comments. "Seed grain? I'm aware Mr. Pop feeds the hill tribes and refugees, but why seed grain?"

"A cover for the US crop substitution program," the man snickered.

This character is too good to be true. "Nothing will replace the poppies," Jalbert tsked.

The big man put his head back and tipped the flask into his mouth.

"How long have you been in Laos?"

"Forever. This fuckin' place don't know nothin' but war."

"You must like it if you're still here."

"You got me there. Name's Gus."

"René." They shook hands. "We who remain here are of a certain breed, Monsieur Gus. I have a proposition for you. It pays well."

"What risks will I be taking?"

"Just an extra landing and takeoff."

"I'm listening. But first." He rubbed his thumb and forefinger together.

"Perhaps you would share that?" Jalbert pointed to the flask then reached into a pocket.

Gus exchanged his flask for the wad of US dollars Jalbert offered.

Gus thumbed through the bills and dipped his chin in agreement.

"We have much to discuss," Jalbert said. He took a slurp of whiskey, wiped his mouth with a sleeve, and handed the flask back. In agreement, they walked to the Quonset hut.

Jalbert hunched over a map he spread across a card table and circled a spot with his pencil. "How close can you get me to this area?"

"This here's southwest from where I'm headin'." Gus pointed to a narrow valley in the general area of Jalbert's request. "There's an abandoned airstrip right there. It's overgrown by now, but I can set her down. This landing will cost you extra."

"We are agreed, then. I will make it worth your time for the extra effort." Jalbert refolded his map and extended his hand. They shook.

Returning to the hotel, he strode to Ellie's room. He pounded on her door. "Come, we have arrangements to make," Jalbert commanded when she answered. He marched off. Ellie ran to catch up.

He knocked on Romo's door with a series of urgent stutters

and entered without waiting for a response. Romo was jerkily pacing around his room. "Massaging the hesitant muscles," he said.

"We leave tomorrow." Jalbert closed the door behind them. "There are no worries. We simply disappear for a time. My hotel manager will say nothing about our whereabouts to anyone."

He unfolded the map he had shared with Gus. "Fortune shines upon us," he exclaimed. After pointing out vital locations, he launched into his plan. "The pilot who will drop us at this unscheduled stop is heading to the Plaine des Jarres to deliver supplies to a World Health Organization location. He pointed at Ellie. "Your cover is a journalist reporting on the crop substitution program the W.H.O. is sponsoring: The first organic step to eradicate the poppy crop. Unfortunately, our transport will have to make an emergency landing, here." His finger stabbed a spot on the map. "From there we will trek several kilometers to meet with an opium broker to join his caravan on its way to Long Tieng."

"Once we get to Long Tieng, how will my cover hold?" Ellie asked.

"This is where our pilot, Gus, becomes a vital element. His mayday call will be directed at Long Tieng, informing them he will have to land to unload half his cargo and W.H.O. passengers who will have to find their own way to Long Tieng to hitch a ride to Pop Buell's or back to Vientiane. Someone from the CIA will be expecting the stranded W.H.O. personnel and will have to accommodate you until they can deliver you back to Vientiane or up to the Plaine des Jarres, which will be highly unlikely."

33

———————

Jalbert's news of their imminent departure sent a morning-of-a-downhill-race thrill flooding Ellie's veins. No chance to preview the course; this time she'd be racing blind. Thoughts of Nick followed close on the heels of her excitement. He was going to miss out if he didn't leave Madame Lulu's and sober up.

"Er, great," she replied, "I'm ready."

"Indeed?" Jalbert asked, clearly sensing her hesitation.

"Do we wait for Nick?"

Romo cracked, "Since he's not here, I suspect he's been seduced by the tears of the poppy."

"It is simple, really," Jalbert said, voice firm, no room for nonsense. "He is here and ready by morning, or we leave without him."

She couldn't argue with Jalbert's logic. Nick had detoured to the dark side, more interested in getting high than participating in their mission. If he was such a dedicated journalist, why the conscious detour into opium? Well, better to find out now than in the middle of their trek. She would keep her eye on the assignment and not on Nick's quicksilver nature. In fact, she noted she felt safe and comfortable with Romo since she'd become weary of Nick's attitudes.

"I'll go look for him." She figured he was still at Madame Lulu's. His newly acquired affinity for opium was scary.

"Yes, you do that. I do not hold out hope, neither will I miss him." Jalbert executed an about-face and left the room.

Ellie gaped at Romo. "Stinging words."

"Jalbert's right, Ellie. Nick's commitment is mere dandelion fluff. Now, scoot your *derrière* out of here and find him if that's what you want."

Her brisk footsteps echoed, but her feet soon slowed until she came to complete stop. As Romo's final words sank in with a deeper meaning, she realized trying to bring Nick back was a futile gesture at best. If he was going to jettison his involvement and shirk responsibility, she wasn't going to launch a crusade to help him. She returned to the hotel.

A fleet of visions passed before her eyes of Nick lost in opium dreams, or worse. *Stop this.* She had to leave any worries about him behind. If she allowed concern to distract her, she'd be of no use to Jalbert. Not something she wanted to test. He could wield a vengeful response.

WHEN SHE JOINED Romo and Jalbert at an early breakfast, Ellie confessed she hadn't looked for Nick. "I'm not responsible for him," she replied to Jalbert's smirk. "Out of sight, out of mind." Grateful her rucksack was roomy enough for cameras and a change of clothes, she slung it over a shoulder, strode out to Jalbert's Jeep, and rode to the airport in silence.

"Ahhh, sturdy old girl, the Dakota," Romo said, rubbing his hands together when he saw the C-47 on the tarmac. "This plane has the bruises of time on her, been around at least since the French war."

Gus was leaning against the tail. Jalbert made introductions. "Sit anywhere," Gus called over his shoulder as he led them up the steps into the plane. "We're snug as bugs in here and the critters will be glad for the company."

The aircraft was a flying corral of goats, hogs, chickens, hay, grain, and dung.

Ellie gagged. "A flying Noah's Ark."

Jalbert shoved a few sacks of grain into an arrangement of beanbag-type seats and gestured to Romo and Ellie to settle in. "Careful where you step. We're lucky it's a short flight." The engines coughed and sputtered, caught and died, and then, after a couple of convulsive belches and a blast of smoke, they sparked and turned over.

"I don't know what's worse, the smell or the noise," Ellie said, holding her nose as they roared down the runway and lifted off. "One thing about Southeast Asia," she said, "It's aromatic."

Romo snorted. "Oui, it's the fragrance of this ancient continent, stronger in some places than others." He glanced at the livestock and winked.

After about forty minutes of flying over dense landscape, a shrill alarm emanated from the cockpit. Ellie jumped; the sound ripped at her insides like the tearing of a steel sheet.

"*Mayday, Mayday—*" Gus's international pilot's call for help was strained beneath the rasp of the alarm. There was no division between the cockpit and the body of the Dakota.

She covered her ears. "Can't he turn off that horrible alarm?"

Just then it stopped.

"Lima Site ninety-eight, this is Rogue Bird Transport three-five-six. My coordinates are nineteen-point-three-three-seven by one-hundred-two-point-nine-one-four, eighty kilometers north of Long Tieng. Damage to my fuel tank. Gauge reading empty. Must make emergency landing. Will update you. If there's no follow-up transmission, send recon flight. You have my present coordinates. Over."

The radio squawked but Ellie couldn't make out the reply.

"Small strip below, heading nineteen-point-two-eight-nine by one-hundred-two-point-nine-four-zero. I can squeeze this can in there," Gus bellowed.

More squawking.

After what seemed like forever to Ellie who was stewing in the confined barnyard, Gus banked and the plane fell out of the sky, landing on one of the myriad dirt strips that pockmarked Laos, bouncing down a runway barely long enough for the aircraft. Vegetation lurked at the sides of the strip, some of it scraping the wing tips. As the plane bounced and rattled to a stop, Gus yelled into his radio. "Lima Site ninety-eight, this is Rogue Bird Transport three-five-six one more time. Rogue Bird on *terra firma*. Sorry 'bout the mayday. I got just enough cans of fuel on board to get me to Plain a Jars, but I gotta dump half my load and two passengers. Over."

Gus listened to the crackling reply. "Just some yayhoos from the World Health Organization. One skirt and a cripple. Probably headin' your way, probably wantin' a hitch to Pop Buell's. Rogue Bird three-five-six, out."

Jalbert picked his way forward, clapping the pilot on the shoulder. "Thanks, Gus. Well done. You're the best. I will see you soon. Your bonus." Jalbert handed him an envelope of money.

"Roger that," Gus grunted and launched an elaborate wink. They shared a snort from Gus's flask. "Long Tieng can't get the W.H.O. people to Pop's but will fly them to Vientiane."

Jalbert patted Gus' shoulder. "Perfect. They fell for it." He lowered the steps. With her rucksack on her back, Ellie helped Romo down to the ground and handed him his canes. Jalbert led them off into the trees.

"We must cover some ground on foot to meet the opium

broker and his caravan," Jalbert shouted, as the plane noisily shot back into the air.

Jalbert must have noticed the furrowing of Ellie's brow. His voice took on a soothing tone. "Not to worry. Our objective is just at the base of these mountains." He pointed straight ahead. "Can you make it, Pasquale, or perhaps I should bring you that donkey?" Jalbert offered in an odd stab at humor.

Romo winked at Ellie walking by his side. "I can walk this distance to the camp," he barked at Jalbert.

Jalbert swung his arm around. "Hmong villages ring these mountains. These are friendly folk. They will accept us as their own."

After an hour's slow and gentle hike, she wrinkled her nose. "I smell more animals," she sniffed as they entered a small clearing. A rope pen held mules and ponies, their heads in feedbags, crunching grain. Large lumpy panniers on their backs were snugged in tarps. The odor switched from barnyard to the euphoria that had been so alluring at Lulu's.

Opium! *Nick would fucking drool.* Guilt tried to insinuate its way into her heart. *Fuck guilt. Asshole Nick puts getting stoned highest on his twisted pedestal.*

"The mules are already loaded. Presumably, the caravan is about ready to move out," Jalbert observed.

"If you don't mind, I will rest a while," Romo said.

"Yes, over there, not far from the fire. I'm sure the women will provide blankets," Jalbert replied.

A short distance from the animals, about a dozen Hmong men squatted at the tree line. In the clearing opposite the pen, three Hmong women prepared dinner at a fire pit.

Ellie watched them in their long black dresses tied at the waist with green and pink sashes. She giggled: these women could accessorize. Light but elaborate silver necklaces hung from their necks, and their heads were wrapped in simple turbans. They turned their warm smiles, which were filled with teeth stained by betel nuts, on her and chittered as they squatted around pots of rice and vegetables.

She retrieved a camera. The light was low, but the fire reflected in the glow of their faces. No need to use her pocket-sized Rollei here, no need to hide her big guns, the Nikons, and her array of lenses.

Waves of their talk and laughter washed over her as she moved around the group of women then the men, taking pictures. Men of all ages, also dressed in black, old and bent over, as well as some young boys.

Black was the main clothing color of Southeast Asia, Ellie mused, recalling the Vietnamese villages from the ill-fated patrol and the ubiquitous black pajamas.

A man rose from the edge of the group, also dressed in black. "Here is the broker," Jalbert said. "He speaks some French." He walked forward to meet the man and talked for a few minutes before he returned. "All arrangements made."

Ellie was enchanted by the simple beauty of the people and continued shooting until Jalbert cautioned her against using up all her film before she even reached the target. This day was done. They slept in a makeshift hut on stilts. Heavy horsehair blankets kept the cold away. Opium's alluring aroma scented her dreams and wafted Nick into dusty corners of her mind.

34

Ellie woke to birdsong. She lifted off the heavy blanket, finger-brushed straw from her clothes, and reached for her boots, shaking them upside down to expel any visitors. Stretching her arms, she gave thanks for the low humidity and rushed to join the day. Below, on the ground, Romo greeted her with a sticky rice ball and a compliment.

"The Hmong women commented on the beauty of your hair. It's not often they see burnished golden locks."

"You speak their language, Romo?"

"*Alors*, one doesn't live here for decades without learning a few words."

The Hmong moved through the misty morning. They had gathered up everything and extinguished the cookfire by drowning it in dirt. Nothing left but the lingering scent of the pack animals and their precious cargo.

They assembled, players in a convoy. The opium broker, with Jalbert and several Hmong, led the way. Jalbert had indeed arranged a donkey for Romo, and Ellie walked alongside him. Behind them, the pack mules, their sway backs loaded with raw opium. On a verbal snap from the broker, the caravan moved onto the single-track lane. Ellie recorded the twenty-mule-team caravan and the broker with her Rollei.

The trail was narrow, dark, and cold. It snaked through evergreen forests, up and down hills. She inhaled high-altitude pine smells mixed with the aroma of raw opium. She placed one foot in front of the other on the hard-packed earth, anxious, eager, excited, each step bringing her closer to her quarry. Ben Stryker flashed through her mind as she looked around, wondering what kind of fiction he'd turn the journey into. She couldn't wait to tell him about this. She envisioned an article and photos about traveling with an opium caravan. *How exotic. An easy sell.*

The rhythm of her steps freed her mind. One foot in front of the other. Best way to get anywhere. What an opportunity she had before her.

Atop his ass, Romo snorted. "You are thinking of the foolish one who is missing this trek? A certain waste of time."

"Actually no. I'm enjoying the forest," she replied.

High in the pines, daylight began to break. She bent her head back to see into the canopy, a hundred feet or higher, where sunlight sifted like dust to the trail below. Warblers and other songbirds kept time. Her footsteps marked the minutes. She was the sole American, lost in the drama of the jungle, marching to what? War, perhaps, but certainly the unknown. Everything familiar faded into the past. It was the unknown that telescoped ahead, serenaded by squeaks of leather pannier straps. Eventually the sun moved directly overhead, sending bright shafts of light to the forest floor. The Rollei hung around her neck. She shot sunbeams coming through the trees.

Up high, an aircraft engine fractured the silence of the jungle. "That's a T-28," Romo called out, turning in his saddle. "Weather reconnaissance." A few minutes later, a helicopter whop whopped. "Bell 205A," he reported.

"They're like a flock of birds," Ellie said, as other, smaller-sounding engines floated over them. "And those, Romo?"

"Forward Air Controllers in their Cessna O-1 birds. We must be getting close."

"They fly out of Long Tieng?"

"They're called Ravens. They're the ones who spot movement on the Ho Chi Minh Trail and call in the bombers."

Suddenly, Ellie clutched at her tummy. Without a word, she dashed off the side of the trail and into the jungle. She returned moments later, catching up to Romo with a blush of embarrassment reddening her cheeks.

Romo snickered. "Ah, something you ate?" He reached into a pocket and peeled a small glob off a large black ball of what appeared to be tar. "Swallow this." He handed the glob to Ellie. "It's the best cure for diarrhea."

"What is this?"

"The international cure for your condition. Opium."

She shrugged and swallowed.

The caravan crested a ridge. Several thousand feet below, a valley sprawled and a long, wide runway spined its length. "Oh my God," she gasped, hand to chest. "Look at that."

"*Oui,* the runway takes up practically the whole valley floor," Romo confirmed.

"Brigadoon," she whispered to herself.

"Not so different than the bird's-eye view I see from the cockpit." Romo chuckled, leaning back, and resting a hand on his mule's rump.

"This runway is four-thousand feet long," Jalbert said, having walked back to Ellie and Romo's position. "That's nearly a mile. Long Tieng is the second largest inhabited area in Laos, despite its remoteness. Headquarters of America's secret war."

Ellie barely listened; she was so taken with the view. A cacophony of planes, from frog-jumping two-seaters up to big transports, was parked in two bulges extending out from the main apron of the runway. A settlement of temporary shelters sprinkled between runway and mountains.

She jumped when Jalbert's sharp voice broke into her thoughts.

"Mademoiselle Eleanor, come with me."

They walked a short distance from the caravan. Jalbert shifted from foot to foot. He faced her, leaned in close, black eyes shining beneath frowning brows. Ellie's blood flowed with the certainty that this story of secret goings-on belonged to her; it was her fate. Everything in her life had brought her to this point. She owned the moment like she owned a downhill, especially with Nick out of the picture. She was ready in every way to plunge into this adventure.

"Listen closely." Jalbert squeezed her arm. "Do not underestimate the significance of this. Your job is crucial. Do not forget you are here to document the CIA's role in drug trafficking. This means we need detailed and complete pictures of everything—the Americans, both pilots and mechanics, the opium, Air America transport planes. For your information, the CIA owns Air America as well as General Vang Pao.

"I would tell you to beware of the general; he is key, and he is no fool. He has been battling communism since he was old enough to lift a weapon. He commands loyal troops who fight the Vietminh. But the general is away, and Captain Joua Vang Torr is minding the store. Keep your eyes open to everything. You need establishing shots that show the action but also where it is taking place. Context is key. Your photos must document the whole story." He paced several steps, turned, paced back. "Opium cooking in big vats with the mountains in the background and its conversion to morphine. Use anything to identify the location as Long Tieng: the runway, the planes. Context. Most important, the transfer of morphine bricks onto the planes. Get those CIA pilots on film. You understand?"

His hard stare declared this was no time for levity or

sarcasm, although she found his nervousness curious. After all, she was the one taking the risk, not him. She vibrated at the taut string between risk and treason. *I'm a journalist not a whistleblower.*

"I do understand, Colonel." She held his gaze. "I will do my utmost, but I'm not a fool either. You ask a lot, and I understand it will be to my benefit as well as yours. I've suspected you have your own motives, but they're none of my business. I do know what the word secret means, Colonel, and you can be sure I will get the best I can, given the circumstances and the danger."

Jalbert narrowed his eyes. "I sincerely hope your efficiency exceeds your arrogance."

"My only comfort will be your and Romo's support. I'm counting on the two of you to make my task possible."

As if she hadn't spoken, Jalbert placed both hands on Ellie's shoulders and looked directly into her eyes. "The opium broker will show you the way. I will rely on your ingenuity to secure a ride back to Vientiane for yourself and Romo."

"Hold on a minute. This wasn't in the plan. I need your help down there. Besides, how are you getting back to Vientiane?"

"Gus returns to our rendezvous point later today."

She smirked. His maneuvering was obvious. She still wasn't sure of his motivation, but she had no doubt she would figure it out. *What the hell. What matters is getting the story.*

Jalbert lit a cigarette, puffing compulsively for a minute, then dropped the butt and ground it into the dirt. He sniffed the air, leaned in close to Ellie, threatening. "You need me no longer. I count on you to complete this assignment successfully." He pivoted a neat military turn and walked away.

Just as she got to the edge of the caravan, a handful of Hmong tribal guerrillas climbed over the crest of the mountains. Fully armed, they wore short-beaked caps, chain necklaces strung with pointed bullets, and some wore strings of shriveled ears around their necks. Small round grenades hung from their belts. They carried submachine guns. Fearsome looking group until they recognized Hmong friends in the caravan.

She reached Romo as scattershot chatter broke out, accompanied by gesticulations and nods toward Romo and her. The broker stepped forward, speaking in Hmong.

Romo translated for Ellie. "This squad of General Vang's Irregulars has come to escort us to Long Tieng. It seems they heard Gus's SOS transmission down at the base. They were sent to provide cover in case of ambush. I trust them completely. They make the jungle safe. They're part of a larger guerrilla force fighting to keep communist warlords from taking over their villages. The leader says we're lucky we haven't been attacked by the Pathet Lao."

She thought back to the Pathet Lao crossfire on the Mekong. She and Romo might be less valuable to the general than his opium, but she was grateful for any protection.

With the new arrivals interspersed along the caravan, the parade moved straight down from the steep ridge over a well-worn trail. "They don't waste time with switchbacks," Ellie remarked. Her shoulders lowered from their perch up near her ears, and she relaxed within the safety of their guards. "Hey, Romo, how's your seat?"

"Indeed, this animal provides comfort and luxury for my legs, although a horse would be more cushy," he said, his face free of pain. "How's your tummy, better, eh?"

"Better." He wasn't kidding, she thought. The stuff really worked. *Considerate of Jalbert to get that mule. An act of friendship or merely part of his plan?*

She sniffed the air. The faint aroma of opium drifted past. How could a single trigger like the scent of opium mask all others, even the pungency of ripe donkey shit?

She kept her focus on her feet, moving one in front of the other. She heard faint rustling in the trees that pushed in on the heavily trodden path, and fantasized tigers and elephants moving through the forest. Something whizzed past her ear with the annoying buzz of a mosquito. A gunshot echoed. Another unsettling shot drew her head around. A Hmong went down.

"Nres! Embuscade! Ambush!" yelled the opium broker. The Hmong Irregulars positioned themselves to defend the caravan and raised their guns. Romo jumped off his donkey with surprising agility. "Get down," he barked to Ellie as he crouched behind the animal. Then, reaching over, he dragged her to hunker among several boulders. Four more shots rang out in succession. Startled birds came winging out of the canopied trees. Another salvo of automatic gunfire peppered the boulder nearest Ellie's head, spraying chips of stone.

A half-dozen Pathet Lao sprang forward out of the trees. Bullets exploded and sizzled. She breathed in the heavy stench of spent gunpowder the way some folks took pleasure in the smell of cigar smoke. Tet and the US embassy pierced her mind. She swallowed hard. Cold sweat ran over her skin. Fear and thrill twined in her belly, and she raised the Rollei.

"No time for that," Romo said as the Hmong returned fire. "We must move. Now." Without waiting for a reply, he grabbed her with one hand and retrieved the wounded Hmong's AK-47 with the other, yanking to get it out of the man's death grip. "I'll be back," he told the soldier in English, then in Hmong.

Blood pounded in Ellie's head. A rock shard propelled by gunshot grazed her lower jaw. Blood spurted and mingled with sweat that poured down her face. Stunned, she followed Romo.

They left the rocks, staying low, hustling off the trail and into the vine-tangled brush.

Behind them, groundfire trailed off into sporadic bursts and then stopped.

Ellie nudged Romo in the direction of two men hiding

behind a fallen tree, facing away. Pathet Lao looking for hidden targets, weapons pointed toward the path.

Romo wriggled forward, brought up the muzzle of the AK and squeezed the trigger, killing both men with a single spray.

Ellie cringed and gagged at the mind-tearing screams.

The communist guerillas were outgunned by Vang Pao's well-trained men. The skirmish passed and left attacking soldiers splattered on the ground while the Hmong calmly pilfered the meager belongings and harvested fresh ears. They tended to their fallen soldier, binding cloth around his upper arm wound to stop the bleeding. Romo returned the AK-47 to him.

She managed photos of the gory scene. Better late than never. She rubbed her churning stomach. *What I saw at the embassy was aftermath. This is the real thing. I don't know why there's a difference between seeing a man dead on the ground and seeing a man shot and his life ended. But there it is. Killing is brutal.*

"Ah, we must thank the communists for providing enter-tainment on this journey," cracked Romo behind her. When she turned to face him, his lips were pursed, and his eyes worried. He rushed closer and held her face in his hands. "You have been wounded, *ma chèrie.*" It is your badge of courage in combat." He took her hand and placed it on her jaw. When she looked at her bloodied fingers, she gasped.

Romo laughed, a deep rolling sound from his belly. "A mere scratch; it is the pace of excitement that accelerates the flow of blood. Not to worry."

She wiped the blood from her face with a strip of toilet paper. Her dad used to call TP mountain money, saying never to go hiking without it. That lesson paid off, especially this day. It was her second badge, the first having come from Tet. "This is life, right?" She leveled a grimace at Romo, who laughed again, and climbed onto his mule.

They resumed their march.

As they moved down in elevation, forest morphed into jungle, lofty hardwood trees and undergrowth replaced pines. Gradually the trail began to flatten out. She smelled smoke from cooking fires, the first signs of civilization. They skirted the airstrip. At its northwest end, hummocks of karst hundreds of feet high looked like they'd burst out of the ground in a fit of joy, and whose shapes had been weathered by water clustered around the runway.

The broker led them to a large, tin-roofed, open-air factory where Hmong unloaded the opium bundles from the mules. Ellie observed the assembly line operation and then crept along the perimeter of the structure as best she could. Using Romo on his donkey as a shield, she snapped photos with her Rollei of each stage: opium being boiled in large 55-gallon oil drums raised off the ground, fires glowing beneath them. Jalbert had described the process to her in detail as they'd walked from Gus' plane to the camp, and now it unfolded before her eyes: from adding slaked lime to the solution, to cooling it, to tipping the cooled solution through burlap rice sacks into more cooking pots, to adding ammonium chloride until a pH of 8 or 9 was reached, and then cooling it again.

The chemical smell was overwhelming. She sipped air to keep from gagging.

"*Carpe diem*," she said hoarsely. She caught it all on film, the cooking, cooling, and straining of opium, until they got the prize: chunks of morphine base, squeezed and dried in the sun and then shaped into coffee-colored bricks and loaded onto pallets for transfer to a plane bound for Vientiane. Heeding Jalbert's instructions, she shot enough background to identify Long Tieng. By the time she looked up, the broker, his men, women, and mules had scattered, and the Hmong dispersed. She tucked the camera into her bag. Romo beamed at her.

"That was lucky, wasn't it?" She winked. "You ever going to get off that donkey?"

"Perhaps never," he declared. "You would like to explore, or shall we look for Captain Torr?"

"Yes," she chuckled. "Both."

He dismounted and handed the rope to Ellie. "You can let him go. He'll find his way back to his caravan." He took stiff steps in a circle, canes clenched in his fists. "Might take just a few seconds to get the blood circulating in my legs again." He sighed. "A day of rest upon my ass." She wanted to hug him for his wonderfully level head. They strolled the single street chockablock with haphazard shacks and tin-roofed ramshackle buildings, electric lines strung randomly like decorative garlands.

Drawn by the sounds of celebration, they arrived at a festival of some sort. Ragtag Hmong Irregulars, dirty and smelling of war, Hmong women in traditional dress, ubiquitous black sashed with vivid hues, and children scurrying everywhere.

"That's the captain, Joua Vang Torr." Romo pointed to a man standing among his soldiers. Garbed in a dark-brown, short-sleeved uniform, he looked like the rest of the Hmong, with round face, high forehead, wide nose, and eyes that sparkled. He held a can of Lucky Lager beer above his head and made a toast. Romo translated as the captain addressed the men. She dug out her Nikon with the long lens.

"From our front line high on Skyline Ridge, we hold back the evil force of communism. You fight like the brave men you are. Together, we repel the North Vietnamese soldiers. We fight for our homeland. We live together. We fight together. And if we are meant to die, we die together." The tribal bond was strong. "Long live General Vang," he called out. A cheer went up, and men raised beers to their leader. The captain looked at each man as if they were friends, brothers, compatriots, members of a very special tribe.

"Wow." Ellie nudged Romo in the side. Her motor drive whirred.

"Torr and Pao are true heroes. Fighting communism." Romo winked at her. "Financed by the CIA."

As the captain scanned the faces of his fighters, he frowned when he spied Ellie and her camera and then his eyes landed on Romo. His face cleared, accentuating high cheekbones and chiseled features. He rushed over, his men parting for him, and stopped mere inches from Romo's wrinkled visage.

He clutched Romo by the shoulders and squeezed, leaning forward to kiss him on both cheeks. He spoke in a mix of French and Hmong. "What a surprise. I never thought a warrior like you would accept a civilian mission with the W.H.O. I have been expecting you, my old friend, since your forced landing. I apologize for the general not being here. He will regret missing you. You will join in our celebration of this army's great bravery and courage," he exclaimed and winked. "I trust your trek was uneventful?"

"Ah, Captain," Romo responded. "This is a great honor. You are just the man I hoped to see, but you are a magician. How did you know it was me?"

"The pilot in distress mentioned he'd dropped off a crippled Corsican guide. You must excuse his vulgar expression of your condition." Torr nodded at Ellie and eyed the W.H.O. ID tag that hung around her neck. "And this is your World Health photographer?"

"Yes, Captain. I am most happy to introduce you to Eleanor Ketcham."

Ellie put out her hand, which Torr took and lifted to his lips, his head tilting at Romo.

"*Mu pheuonkeoa,* old friend, you and your Eleanor must join me for dinner tonight."

35

General Vang Pao's house overlooked the military part of the base and the airstrip. Austere and oddly simple, it looked like a barracks—a large, U-shaped building of light-colored brick. Ellie and Romo were heartily welcomed by the Hmong brotherhood, who ate with the General every night. In Vang's absence, Torr was a magnanimous host. White Horse scotch flowed like Niagara Falls while they feasted on an unexpected American dinner of ribeye steaks, mashed potatoes, green beans, apple pie, and coffee. All sitting on the floor, like kindergarteners with milk and cookies.

Stiff from floor sitting for a few hours, Romo smiled when he saw their guide and his donkey waiting for them outside. Romo rode and Ellie walked, following the guide to a shack among many shacks huddled close in the Hmong sector. His family sat around a small fire eating a simple dinner of white rice, pumpkin, and a small portion of unidentifiable boiled meat. Ellie settled into a corner, feeling higher than the surrounding mountains, not sure if it was the thin air, the excitement of being in Long Tieng, or the scotch. Or could it be the opium Romo had given her much earlier in the day?

"I leave you here. You are safe with these people. No Pathet Lao," Romo said to her. "I shall return before the moon rises. Just a small errand."

She raised her shoulders, but he ignored her unspoken question and left. Was he going after a little opium relief from the constant pain in his left leg? She shrugged and lay on a brightly patterned blanket, going over the dinner in her mind. How lucky to have secured Joua Vang Torr's limited permission to photograph.

"Absolutely no photos of forward air controllers, our military strength, the airfield, or warehouses. All these are strictly off limits," he had warned, piercing a bite of steak in emphasis. "There is much local color in our Hmong community for your scrapbook." He mentioned nothing about opium; the warehouses being off limits covered what was not said. But his closing comments definitely gave her pause. He'd given her a scorching look. "We do not allow civilians here in Long Tieng, mademoiselle. It is because you are with my good friend Romo that I am making an exception in your case. Do not make me regret, as consequences would be dire for you both."

At the far end of a long day, she replayed the captain's warning. Eventually, she dozed despite her desire to stay up until Romo returned.

SHE jerked awake. Silty daylight sifted into the shack. In this deep crevasse of a mountain valley, the sun came up late and went down early. She sat up and looked around the dim one-room hovel. Romo slept soundly on a pallet near her. Around them women bustled, drank tea, and ate breakfast.

"Romo," Ellie whispered, but he was dead to the world. Her thoughts shone clear about the day's assignment. She had serious photos to capture. Deception was key. That piece of wisdom had been given to her by David Jenkins. It was one of the steps from Sun Tzu's *The Art of War*, which he'd loaned her.

Her strategy was "work the room." Schmooze past walls that had been erected.

Steps shuffled toward her and halted. Ellie looked up. A Hmong girl held out a steaming cup of green tea and a bowl of rice, mixed with a few unrecognizable vegetables.

"*Ua tsaug,* thank you." Ellie took the offering. Romo had taught her a few Hmong words. She nodded at the girl and scooped food into her mouth with her fingers. *Good timing is a battlefield maneuver, as per good ol' Jenkins. "When in the field, sleep and drink whenever you can."* The tea was hot and bitter and delicious.

Romo moaned, stirring.

"Let's get moving, Romo," she said, her mouth full. "Sun's aburnin'; time's awastin'."

"Such eloquence has never before passed Romo's ears."

"You slept in your teeth," she commented with a wink. "What have you been up to? Where did you go last night?"

"Perhaps I have been arranging our transportation back to Vientiane," he said. "And perhaps scoping out the base. It has grown since my last visit."

Ellie sucked her fingers clean before running them over her wrinkled clothes and through her hair. She retied her ponytail, fixed one Nikon with the 50 mm lens and the other with her long lens, snugged both in her knapsack, and hung the small Rollei around her neck.

She sipped her tea, eyeing Romo over her the rim of her cup. She cherished the closeness that had developed between them. It defied understanding. She was twenty-five; he could be her grandfather. She adored him. Loved him in a way that men who faced death together, fought together, bled together, depended on each other, and comforted each other on war-torn battlefields, could come together to love each other in a reverent, nonphysical manner. *Comrades in arms.*

She shook off her thoughts when he spoke.

"Help me up," he said, without a trace of embarrassment. "Let's make our way over to the runway. CIA HQ is there, in the shadow of those karst outcroppings."

She extended her hands and brought him to standing.

They walked slowly through the Hmong section of town, accompanied by Captain Torr's minder, who would enforce Ellie's promise not to photograph sensitive subjects. Side-by-side stalls held clothing, food, fabric, chickens about to meet their fate, water buffalo horns, and cooking utensils laid out on rickety tables. Patched and uneven pieces of corrugated tin provided shade in the open-air market. Ellie made a big show of photographing the local color, choosing her Nikon with the wide-angle lens.

People eyed her as if she were an alien.

A young woman sat in a kiosk set atop a couple of wood pallets laid over a gully in the street.

"*Nyob zoo.* Hello." The woman looked up at Ellie in surprise. A bright green umbrella shielded her from the hot sun as she watched over baskets of heavenly smelling bread, as if they were her children.

Romo stopped, breathing deeply. "Suddenly I am ravenous." He pointed a cane to a round loaf. The woman lifted it out of its basket and held it out to him. "*Bàhn mi,*" she said. He reached into his pocket and brought out a handful of kip, which he dropped into her hand.

Their footsteps slowed. Romo slung his canes under one arm while he tore off clumps of the crusty bread and munched while Ellie photographed. Behind the market, she could see huts being used as residences and businesses, some no bigger than sheds, no straight edges anywhere. More haphazard slices of corrugated tin topped the huts. Pretending to focus on market stalls, she took detailed shots of the background so that she'd be able to recreate the whole layout of the town. She was documenting a parallel universe. Without Jalbert's demand for confirmation of American criminal behavior, she sensed a novel, a kind of Laotian *Brigadoon*. She chuckled as yet another plane hurled itself into the air.

"Life in the key of noise," she commented. "It's as if Jalbert is watching from up there."

"Big brother does like to keep his eye on you," Romo observed, mouth full of bread.

Ellie moved from shot to shot, nervous energy fueling her sense of excitement. She switched to the camera with the telephoto lens and slung it around her neck.

If the minder should ask why she was photographing up close with a telephoto, she had an answer prepared. That answer had come as part of her first lesson in photography—a subconscious understanding of imagery—thanks to an Akira Kurosawa samurai movie in which the screen held the protagonist and the background in equal focus. The result was zero depth perception. Cynthia Woods, a photographer she'd known in New York, told her about the technique Kurosawa used and the effect he achieved with a telephoto lens. Ellie adopted the technique and used it often. She'd be able truthfully to claim her use of the long lens was a style issue, and she could explain the technique if challenged.

Thus disguised by style, she could capture the subjects directly in front of her, as well as the movement beyond of morphine bricks from the opium-processing plant onto trucks parked by the side of the tarmac. She photographed supplies, ammunition, guerrilla troops, and what she assumed were CIA personnel moving around. She also angled her camera to get shots of the pilots who waited in the cockpits ready to take off again after their gear had been offloaded and morphine base stowed. Even with the long lens, she couldn't tell if they were Vietnamese, Lao, Thai, or Westerners. True to her promise to Captain Torr, she stayed far away from the warehouses. He wasn't the kind of person she wanted to cross.

Finally, as the sun slanted its weakening rays onto the runway, Ellie photographed an unmarked C-47 as it landed and turned around. A dozen or so Hmong surged to the truck waiting nearby and shuttled morphine pallets onto the plane through the rear cargo door behind the wings. Fifteen minutes, and they were done. The truck returned to the processing plant, the men scattered, and the twin-engine plane took off.

Again, she couldn't get a clear shot of the pilot. It wasn't as if anyone wore CIA name tags on their clothing.

"This seems like a waste of time, Romo. I don't see CIA ID on anything; it's just people without labels. The Americans don't seem to be involved with the Hmong. No apparent connection between the two." Ellie loaded a new roll of film, advancing it to the first frame, and switched cameras again, returning the telephoto to her pack. "The transport planes have the markings of the Laotian Air Force. I see nothing definitive that shows CIA involvement. There's no decisive evidence of what Jalbert wants. Still, I've shot it all."

"What did you expect, *ma chèrie*, that they'd be wearing CIA emblems flashing with neon lights? You must look harder."

Ellie's head spun around. "You sound like Jalbert, but maybe you're right. Let's go into the CIA HQ. We can simply ask, 'Hey, you guys transporting opium?'"

"You must stop this nonsense, *ma chèrie*. Keep your eye on the prize," he cautioned. "The truth of the matter is you will not forgive yourself if you do not exhaust all possibilities. I know this about you. Jalbert knows, too. It is one reason he chose you."

She thought about Romo's comment, torn between her instincts and the specter of Jalbert's rage. "I admit I'm curious, even suspicious, but so far everything I've seen is out in the open, not hidden."

"No need for secrecy in a secret hideaway. But okay. Off we

go." Romo took the first step. "You may want to hide your big camera. Suspicion is rampant in the spy community."

She looked up and down the runway, stashed her Nikon, and scurried across to where CIA headquarters was hunkered in the shadow of the karst hummocks. She tapped her toe, waiting for Romo to catch up to her.

HQ was deserted. "It's as if they knew we were coming and took off," she whispered.

"*Alors,* our day has passed quickly. It might simply be cocktail hour," Romo answered, looking at his watch in the encroaching darkness then at Ellie. "*Oui,* it is time for Romo to take charge." His face crinkled.

"What do you mean?" Ellie asked.

He broke into a stride that defied pain. "Cocktail hour, *compris*? We are going to the American hooch for refreshment." He looked her up and down. "Perhaps you would prefer to drink your cocktail free of that donkey tail that sticks out from the back of your head? I cannot think of one thing that could outshine the welcome when the lovely Mademoiselle Ellie enters the room." He coughed into his hand. "That room is full of randy thrill-seeking warhorses."

She paused. "You're making fun of me, but I get it, Romo," she tugged at the tie that released her hair and feathered it out into a golden-red halo. Curious, she thought, the same remark coming from Nick would be offensive. All about the attitude.

"*Magnifique.* You might also wish to put your small camera away."

She secured all cameras and lenses in the foam-rubber dividers of her red knapsack.

They reached a ramshackle, thatch-roofed, tin-walled building from which she could hear music and laughter floating out of second-story windows. Romo eyed the steep stairway, took a deep breath, and marched up the steps, using the railing as a crutch, canes in his other hand. As he got to the landing, a couple of Americans were exiting.

"Boy, howdy," one of them said, winking at Ellie.

Romo entered the smoke-clouded room followed by Ellie, who stood by his side trying not to gawk at the American flyers in the bar. *Oh, be still my heart.*

"This is the Ravens' hooch," he said. "Come with me; cocktail hour swings by the vines."

"Hooch?"

"Over here, hooch is the same thing as a bar, a gathering place."

In his crooked gait, he walked over to a couple of vacant seats at the bar.

"Holy macaroni, will you look at what the cat dragged in?" a man with some miles on his face shouted from the other end of the bar. He raised a tattooed arm and pointed at Romo. "Guys, welcome a legend. This here's Captain Pasquale Romolino. He's logged more air miles than all of us put together. He's an honorary Raven; he's always flown straight at his targets. No jinking for Romo. Do not let him buy a single drink. His money's no good here."

"Hey, Romo—"

"You old aircraft jockey—"

Romo winked at Ellie.

"You're famous. I had no idea," she joked.

The bartender stood in front of them, wiping the bar. What'll it be, Captain? You heard Bruce. Your drinks are on the house. Yours, too, miss. Not often we get fame and beauty in the same visit."

"Do you have scotch?" she asked.

"Does a bear shit in the woods?" the bartender countered.

"No, he shits in his cage," a voice bellowed from deep in the room. Laughter.

Romo joined in, pointing at a corner of the bar. "Floyd and

Mamma are the Ravens' pet bears, Himalayan Mountain bears. They live in that cage back there and drink beer all the live-long day."

Ellie's eyes crinkled in fun.

"Sorry, ma'am, we don't get many ladies here, especially Americans. One scotch coming up. And you, Cap?"

"Beer is good," Romo said. "Perhaps also a small cognac?"

A TEAC reel-to-reel recorder behind the bar played Jimi Hendrix's version of "All Along the Watchtower." The bartender brought her a glass of icy scotch and a longneck Budweiser and cognac for Romo. First sip was always heaven, she thought. She sighed and settled in, as if she were just there for a cocktail and nothing more. She sat straight, keeping the knapsack on her back. Across the room a chair scraped, and a tall, skinny guy with acne scars and a head of wild ginger hair stood and walked to a point between Romo and Ellie.

"Are you Eleanor Ketcham?" he asked.

Her eyes narrowed. The guy looked vaguely familiar, but so did every man in the room. It took a minute for recognition to light.

"Chick Adler," she exclaimed.

Heads turned as she called out Chick's name. It was only a moment before the room returned to normal. She turned her focus back to him. "NYU. We both had creative writing class with Corney Chesterfield."

He smiled at her, eyeing her chin wound. "Then, as people do, you went off and became a journalist, and I resisted going back to Maine. I just wandered around a bit, you know." He turned his palms up. "I'd had my pilot's license since I was sixteen, so I joined up, and here I am. As far from New York City as you can get."

As he talked, she recalled his New England accent and tendency to blush. "You're the last person I ever expected to meet here."

"Yeh, how 'bout that?" Chick exclaimed. "We come halfway around the world, in a war, to run into each other again. In a place that doesn't exist. Go figure. How in blazes did you manage to find your way here? I mean, NYU to Laos is not your everyday route."

It wasn't time to revisit the past. "My good friend and guide here, Pasquale Romolino, and I were on our way up to Pop Buell's on a C-47 delivering seed grain when we had engine troubles. The pilot landed on a postage stamp of land and kicked us out. Had to lighten his load. There we were in the middle of nowhere high in the mountains. Somehow, we ran into a caravan heading down here." She sipped. "So, here we are. Small world, without a doubt, Chick." She sipped her scotch. This was unexpected. She wondered how much he knew.

Romo held out his beer bottle in a toast.

Once again, Ellie reflected on the good fortune that had left Nick back in Vientiane. His jealousy and temper would have been loose cannons.

"So, you're a Raven," she said.

Chick cast his eyes down and lowered his voice as if this was not a topic to be discussed. "Yup, guess I am."

Here we go. Let's peel the lid off this secret whatever.

The hooch suddenly got brighter. Ellie didn't know if it was caused by the scotch, the proximity of so much testosterone, or sensitivity to her assignment. Romo had brought her here on purpose, not as much for cocktails as for information. She leaned over and whispered in his ear, "I love you, you crazy Corsican."

"Chick, please join us." She moved over a stool so he could sit between them. "From what I remember, you were the most cerebral of the students in Corney's class and leaning toward becoming an educator. Interesting the turns life can take."

As Chick scanned the room, Ellie assumed he was seeking

help from his fellow pilots. None came to his assistance. He took a few more guzzles of his beer. "How did you say you got here, Ellie?"

"I'm a photographer attached to the World Health Organization. We're documenting the crop-substitution program. I'm sure you know about the Americans trying to get the Hmong to switch from growing poppies to cultivating seed grain. We're collecting data to see if this is going to work. Personally, I suspect not." Ellie shook her glass, surprised she'd finished her scotch. The bartender brought her another. "Thanks," she said.

She had Chick's attention. She was wading into unfamiliar waters and focused on her drink until she calmed. "So, Chick, I'm curious. We got here with an opium caravan. Uh, but what happens to the opium after it gets here?"

"Dunno. That's hill tribe business." He raised his longneck beer. "I'll stick to this stuff."

She winked at Romo and turned to Chick. "So, can you tell me if you transport contraband between here and Vientiane?"

"Holy crap, woman." He blushed. "Where'd you get such a crazy idea?"

"Oh, you know the rumor mills," she said, waving her hand. "With all the secret action here in Laos, it's no wonder people make stuff up."

"It's a matter of mathematics, getting two plus two to equal four," Romo interjected.

Chick feathered his hands through his hair and studied Ellie and Romo for a moment, creating a heavy silence between them. She imagined a light shining on Chick while he gave her the information she sought.

She nodded absentmindedly. She understood what the word *secret* meant. It would take a skilled interrogator to get Chick to reveal even his call sign. She abandoned her questioning to ease Chick's discomfort. Enough for the moment. A switch to small talk, a visit to Floyd and Mamma in their cages, more scotch, a dinner of pickled eggs, and Ellie and Romo practically rolled down the stairs and back to the Hmong quarters where they'd spent the previous night.

In the morning, an adjutant of Captain Torr's hustled them to the tarmac and practically pushed them onboard a C-47 Air America transport. Seeing the fuselage of the aircraft with "Air America" emblazoned in large letters—the first one she'd seen —Ellie resolved to photograph it when they deplaned in Vientiane. Upon boarding, she inhaled the smell of opium from the processing plant then saw the packaged bricks of morphine. She glanced at the American pilot. Her fingers itched to focus her camera once they were airborne.

Aha, the mountain comes to Mohammed. Did Chick arrange this?

36

As the plane lifted out of the valley, Ellie wasted no time recording the cargo with her wide angle. Out the window, she watched the limestone mountains disappear into the mist. Flying out of Long Tieng was waking out of a dream. Despite its being a secret island in the midst of war, it seemed untouched by the harshness of life. Images like clouds sped through her mind and gradually, reality encroached on her aura of wonder.

No sooner had she and Romo landed back in Vientiane than Ellie wondered if the place had been real, or if she could even find it again. Had it been a dream? Exhausted yet thrilled to have accomplished her mission, she heaved herself down the plane's steps, pushing through the heavy air. On rubber legs, she turned and shot a photo of the C-47, walked from the tarmac into the terminal, and slumped into the taxi Romo hired to take them from Wattay airport into the city. She almost cried with relief when the Constellation came into view.

She dropped her knapsack in her room and dragged herself down the hall to the bathroom. The tub had always been her place of renewal to think and unwind, and the deep porcelain clawfoot tub in this hotel made for good soaking.

Fragments of the past several days cascaded through her thoughts despite the fatigue that wilted the edges of her consciousness. Facts were as elusive as the steam rising around her from the hot bathwater. Images flickered on the ceiling: her old graduate schoolmate Chick Adler of all people in all the world; the zinging of Pathet Lao bullets, any of which could easily have ended her life; Romo's steadfastness, even when he goaded her because she needed it; the cold manipulations of Jalbert; and the unflappable, endearing Hmong.

She scrubbed her body with the rough washrag, cupping and splashing water on her face. "Ouch!" She winced when she washed her chin. God damn, that was more than a scratch. Her mind sharpened by the pain, she examined facts falling into place like jigsaw puzzle pieces. Her natural buoyancy surfaced, though she anticipated a rash of severe judgment from the obsessive Jalbert. Despite the hundreds of photos she'd shot, she had only a few of the interior of the processing plant and a few more of the load of morphine bricks on the Dakota she and Romo had ridden back to Vientiane. If she was honest with herself, it was an Air America plane, its name on the fuselage. Wasn't that proof? She had to make sure she worked with facts only. She had to keep from being just another scoop-hungry greenhorn.

Even if she'd captured factual proof with her photographs, the images were inconclusive. The pilot of the plane who returned her to Vientiane was frustratingly cryptic, answering her with one-syllable words and shrugging. He spoke not a single word of confirmation regarding illicit transportation. Why had she even asked? She'd seen the morphine for herself and wasn't surprised the pilot denied knowledge. She was an outsider. Amateur hour, she admonished. Promise turned mute. Moreover, even if he was an American pilot who transported morphine, she witnessed no furtive behavior, and he wore no uniform. In fact, the only uniforms she'd seen were worn by the proud Hmong Irregulars who fought the communists under General Vang Pao. Jalbert had indicated the CIA transported opium in exchange for Hmong fighters. She witnessed transfer of freight between Hmong and the Air America crews, and she tried to elicit information from Chick Adler, but he was as tight-lipped and circumspect as everybody else, old friend or not. *All secrets are safe and stowed away in this clandestine war, snug as grandma's attic. Even if Chick had verbalized an exposé, he would have been a single, uncorroborated source.*

So much for a bombshell exposé. She had to hand it to Jalbert, he was correct in his assessment of the CIA. It was definitely involved in drug transport. She had deduced that with her own eyes but couldn't back it up with facts. She hadn't gotten any photos of Air America planes being loaded with morphine. She had an exterior shot and an interior shot. Not connected.

Still, she could write a really good story based on what she saw. Heroism of the Hmong, fighting the forces of communism. And a story about the Ravens would grip hearts and minds back home. They were pirates, fearless and crazy as they dodged anti-aircraft spray while locating targets for the bombers. This was a heroic war story, even if it was part of the secret war.

Her thoughts drifted to the nebulous concept of communism. How had her country spiraled from fear of the Soviets dropping an atomic bomb on the US to rushing to defend the world against the Reds' imperialism a dozen or so years later?

Her own fear of communism had been fed from the time she was six, when duck-and-cover-like-a-turtle air-raid sirens sent her and her fellow first graders scooting under their desks, hands clapped over their heads. The whine of the alarm still raised goosebumps on her skin whenever she heard it.

The Americans' urge to save people's freedom was right. The tactics made her uneasy. Did standing up for freedom justify all the death it wrought? Was the US fighting a losing battle? Or was it, as Nick suspected, naked imperialism?

Dread insinuated itself under her skin, chilling her despite the hot bathwater. She turned on the hot water spigot. Where was Nick? Lost in opium dreams? Could he have slunk back to Saigon? He'd been storing up anger, most likely, waiting for his moment of revenge. She couldn't shake the nimbus of foreboding that had entered the bathroom.

Out of the bath, she wiped condensation from the mirror and inspected her shrapnel wound, which needed more than a Band-Aid to cover it. Back in her room, she applied a bandage. She pulled on a T-shirt over her panties, made sure the door was locked, flopped on her bed, and conked out.

~

"WAKE UP, BITCH!"

Her door slammed. The ceiling light came on, shattering the dark. "Huh?" She rolled over, peered through one eye. Nick loomed like a shadowbox figure, fuming, stealing all the oxygen in the room.

He ripped her from the bed.

His hand came out of a tunnel and slapped her face hard.

Blackness rose, pinpricks of light. She staggered.

Her palm flew to her scorched cheek. "*Stop it,*" she screamed. Tears welled.

"You fucking *left* me." His voice shrilled. His arms waved like semaphores. "We were a team. I was supposed to be there."

"That's choice. You blaming *me* for *your* fuckup."

"You can't stick me with this, you traitorous hussy." He twitched with fury, his fists balled, teeth clenched. "You ask me to help you. Then you stab me in the back. Judas!" he shrieked and let loose with a wallop, using his whole body, as if he were Rod Laver blistering a backhand shot.

She went down. Vision blurred. Thoughts jumbled. Hadn't she locked the door? Seasick.

He yanked her upright. Put a hand on her chest and shoved her hard. She fell on the bed and bounced off the other side. Rage blazed in his eyes; his brows flapped like hawk wings.

"Worried sick—" He spat the words at her. She cowered in a corner, arms up against the assault as she watched him let his rage out of its cage.

He stalked to the other side of the bed.

Jerked her up with his left hand. Slapped her face hard with his right.

Needle-sharp pain flared in her cheek. The wound on her chin opened. Blood spurted out from beneath the bandage.

She slid to the floor.

He dropped a key on her body. "I *will* get even with you."

He stormed out the door.

And slammed it.

Hot tears tracked down her face. Something crumpled within her. She crawled onto the bed, arms clutched around herself from the phantom chill. Nausea roiled. Blackness pushed in from the edges of her vision. She sobbed and rocked back and forth until she slid into an uneasy sleep.

Daylight filtered through the curtains. She hovered between sleep and consciousness, seeing his fist coming at her in slow motion.

Sometime later she heard her door open slowly. "Ellie?"

Fucking Nick. She grabbed a thick glass ashtray from the bedside table. "Don't you dare come near me."

She eyed him as he inched closer.

"I'm sorry I lost my temper; I don't know what came over me. Look, I'm really sorry, babe, it'll never happen again." His eyebrows lifted when he noticed the bloodied pillow and blood-soaked bandage on her chin. "Oh my God, did I do that? I'm sorry, really I am. I was so worried about you."

She struggled to restrain herself from attacking him as a wounded wildcat would: no holds or weapons barred. She was ready to strike.

"Worried? Don't make me laugh." He looked so contrite, as withered as an old man with all the marrow sapped from his bones. He made her gag. "Selfish, conniving bastard." She was beyond fearing him. She had to stand up for herself; otherwise, who was she? She sat up and cocked her arm, ashtray in hand, not in girly fashion but the way one would sling a sidearm fastball.

"Get the fuck out!" Her voice came from somewhere deep in her throat.

He fled.

37

A hidden, remote airbase in a secret war, Long Tieng shines like Brigadoon beneath mountain ridges that float thousands of feet above, she began. From the first words, the story streamed from Ellie's mind through her fingers and onto the page. Clacking away on an old Royal typewriter, she rolled sheet after sheet off the platen as she filled pages with details as sharp and crisp as a winter morning.

Mountain natives, known as Hmong, populate this pocket in soaring karst peaks that look as though they were lovingly shaped by a skilled old potter. Hmong farmers grow opium poppies on the mountain flanks. The pink, red or blue flower with its euphoric delights is the linchpin of their lives, although their annual income is a pittance compared to the riches gleaned by the narcotics trade once the sap of the flower is transported out of the mountains, transformed into heroin, and distributed throughout Europe and North America.

Hours later, she pulled the last piece of paper from the Royal and gathered the sheets into a pile. This was different than anything she'd ever written before.

"First draft done," she declared, lighting an unfiltered Gauloise from the crumpled blue pack on the desk. She had come to enjoy the dark, rich French tobacco. She leaned back and inhaled deeply, coughing out puffs of smoke; the first drag often seared her lungs. She sipped her tea and read over her draft, marking it with notes and ideas, adding details and quotes.

Then the clouds rolled in and covered her sun.

At least that was what it felt like to Ellie as the raw memory of Nick's pounding stole her attention. As long as she was involved in her story, she could remain focused, but once she'd written the first draft, he squeezed into her conscious mind. Not only her thoughts but her whole being, darkening even the air in her room.

"Son of a fucking bitch." Lighting another cigarette from the stub of the last one, she sucked in the harsh aromatic smoke with a vengeance. Her lungs didn't rebel this time.

His behavior was inexcusable. How could he treat her that way?

"Asshole!" she choked through tears, running her fingers over her swollen-and-bruised face. She wanted to pull his hair out, kick him in the balls. She was racked with pain. Her stomach churned.

She straightened her shoulders, stood, and marched around the room.

Enough. Back to work.

As she rolled a fresh sheet of paper into the typewriter, the doorknob rattled, followed by five small knuckle raps. She hunched her shoulders up to her ears. The prickle of fear undid her rationalizations of mere moments earlier. Perspiration beaded on her forehead, and she heaved a nervous sigh, not sure which Nick would show himself.

Five more raps.

She pushed her chair back.

Stood.

Flung herself back and forth.

No fear!

She went to the door and opened it a couple of inches. "Go away!"

An enormous bouquet of flowers filled the doorway. She gawked at the display of brilliant colors and inhaled the exotic scents, shaking her head slowly from side to side. Nick lowered the flowers and poked his head above them.

"Boo," he said. It was the playful Nick. He walked the flowers into her room and placed the large arrangement on the bureau.

"You think flowers excuse your behavior, Nick?" She held her breath, fearful she risked certain wrath by challenging him. "That we can go on as if nothing has happened? No. We're done. Over. I want nothing more to do with you."

"Now, now, Ellie." He waggled a hand. "You're wrong." His eyes moved from the cigarette in her fingers to the pile of butts in the ashtray to the Royal on the desk and the pile of papers beside it. "Chain smoking are we?" he asked. "And it seems you're writing."

Fear or no fear, a little payback was justified. "Yeah, doing *my* assignment, photos *and* story," she retorted, fighting hard to keep her face free of expression and clutching her fingers in front of her to quiet her quaking hands. Through her outrage, she managed a demure tilt of the head and reached for sweetness, coating her words with honey. "Of course, this might have been your story to write, if you'd bothered to join us."

His face changed immediately.

Uh oh. She could almost hear his smile splinter. His brows bunched together in the middle, and his eyes burned red like a Halloween mask. She'd crossed the line. Now he was a rabid dog.

She backed away.

He advanced.

"Mademoiselle Ellie-e-e." Romo's voice rang out as he

walked through her open hotel room door, rolling from leg to leg as if he were flying in stormy skies. He halted. "*Mon Dieu*, the air is so thick in here it would clog my propellers. I see I am interrupting a deep conversation." He stood where he was, hands gripping his walking sticks.

"Romo," Ellie sang, thankful as hell he'd chosen that moment to show up.

Nick razored a sharp scowl at Romo. "We're busy here," he snapped.

Nick moved in on Ellie, scowling into her face. She shrank back. He grabbed her chin and squeezed until she grimaced.

"O-w-w. Get away from me," she said hoarsely, reaching up to touch her bandaged wound.

"We're not done, Ellie, not by a long shot." His nostrils flared. He turned to leave, shoving Romo out of his way.

Romo thrust a cane outward. Nick stumbled but righted himself before he could fall.

"Listen, old man," he spat. "You stay out of things that don't concern you."

"Ahhh, I see you like fisticuffs." Romo put up his fists. "You would like some of Romo? This should be fun."

"Pfft, you're not worth it, you wasted old fart." Nick stalked out of the room.

Romo pointed at Ellie's cheek. She was shaking. "He hit you?"

She sank, the high of writing totally eclipsed by Nick's brutality. "His nose was out of joint because we left him behind." Ellie squashed her cigarette out in the ashtray. "It's how he copes."

"You are but a naïve child if you believe that excrement," Romo said.

She winced from the pain. "He's lost in his anger. Can't get out."

"Whatever good might have resided in him exploded,

blown away by the tornados of his rage," Romo said, quietly and gently. "Nick is the one who failed. This is not your fault."

Tears tracked down her face. Sadness moved in. "Enough," she said, wiping her cheeks. She straightened her shoulders.

"I assure you, you have no blame in this situation. Remember, it was Jalbert who insisted on our hurry-up timetable. Nick could not have known that."

Romo was bringing things into perspective.

He went on. "Now that we have broken the ice of discomfort, tell me what is going on. You have written something good about our adventure?" Romo asked.

"Maybe not exactly the article Jalbert is looking for, but the truth."

"*Bon.* I will leave you to it, then."

He put an arm around her shoulder and pulled her close. "Listen to Romo. The most important thing is for you to concentrate on your article. Do not think about the thug Nick who holds a grudge against the world. You are too good for him. I speak the truth."

Tears pushed at her lids, but she refused to let them fall. "Good riddance to bad rubbish."

Romo coughed a laugh. "So very American is that comment. "I leave you now. Lock the door after me," he added as he took his leave.

"Romo, will you please get rid of these flowers? I don't want them."

"Brava, *chèrie.* You are a phoenix just like Romo."

Tears dried; laughter rose.

38

____

"**N**o, no, no, no, no!"

Jalbert beat the ground with his feet back and forth in front of her, shaking the sheaf of pages in her face. "What do you call this?" he snapped, face flushed in obvious exasperation. "Unacceptable!"

Ellie looked up from the garden bench behind the hotel where she'd hunkered for most of the afternoon after entrusting her article to the front desk clerk. As the sun moved in and out of the pygmy date palms, she'd basked in the calming aromas of jasmine and gardenia that drifted through the soft humid air. Anything to keep out of Nick's way, and to avoid the hammer falling. Being furtive was a nuisance but a worthy step in preventive maintenance.

She gazed up at the tightly wound man who wielded strict control over his world. No soft edges anywhere on him. He resembled the crusty rind of a stale baguette. She chafed under his pressure tactics, the way he tried to twist her mind to get her to do what he wanted.

There's always a catch with this man. What is it this time? He obviously had a thing about power. _Bring it on._

"Colonel," she blurted out in a sarcastic retort.

He looked down at her, eyes narrowing. "What happened to you?" he said, pointing to her face.

"Nothing. Just fallout from the Pathet Lao attack on the caravan. After you departed."

He leveraged a sharp leer at her, as if he suspected otherwise. "You seem to have forgotten that the CIA is the critical element in this story. The culprit," he muttered.

One-track mind.

"The entire reason for this mission into Long Tieng was to expose their clandestine involvement in moving heroin to Saigon. Your only mention of Air America is of mere goodwill, troop movement, rescue missions, and saccharine Hmong. Where's the collusion with the South Vietnamese government? I thought you understood." As he spoke, his voice grew tighter.

"I understand"—she paused for effect, enjoying herself—"what I saw, and I saw no collusion. There were separate silos of activity. I got the opium processing, the loading of morphine onto planes, but none of those planes said Air America on them. Until we caught a ride back to Vientiane on an Air America jet that carried a load of morphine bricks. I did not see them loaded, and the pilot was not talking."

In the face of his fury, she relished her equanimity and took a deep breath of the dense floral air. "I documented everything, which you'll see in my photos. But the camera lens doesn't catch the invisible strings that connect images. Neither does it document smell."

"I do not want to hear excuses. I want results."

"I take it you did not understand me, so allow me to simplify. When my negatives are developed into prints, they will not have labels indicating that one photo is opium, and another photo is morphine being loaded onto an Air America transport." She crossed her arms and huffed.

His body language revealed he obviously hadn't considered

she was more than a camera lens, that there was a brain attached, and that she wasn't going to roll over for him.

"Truth, Colonel Jalbert, is what I saw in Long Tieng. It's what I wrote. It's what my camera caught. I forgot nothing of your instructions, I looked hard for what you described, yet it was all circumstantial. It was Hmong people doing the work, loading the planes. Air America flies the morphine to Vientiane where the South Vietnamese Air Force picks it up and carries it on to Saigon. I witnessed nothing that implicates the United States government. Believe me, I tried. I repeat, I documented what I saw. I'm not convinced that Air America is owned by the CIA. I saw nothing there to verify that. The fact that Air America uses the CIA runways isn't enough to point to collusion."

He flailed his hands, swatted at her words as if they were gnats, dismissing what she said. He took a breath and squeezed out his words slowly, sounding like someone with a lungful of pot smoke. "I've made notes for you in the margins. A few facts you neglected. Take this nonsense and rewrite it." He stood over her with a menacing snarl. She snatched the papers out of his hand and stared back at him, making no move to go. She was a journalist of high moral fiber. She would not be manipulated.

"You work for me, Mademoiselle Ketcham. Do not forget this." He scowled, voice squeezed higher. "We had a deal. I took you under my wing, brought you here, advanced you money, provided a typewriter and plenty of scotch, *and* kept you safe."

Safe, hah. Is that his humor?

He glanced at her injured chin and shrugged. "Make no mistake," he warned, wagging a bony finger at her. "You owe me the story we agreed to. You *will* deliver."

"Or what? Are you trying to intimidate me, Colonel?" Ellie's fingers brushed her cheek. She recalled Romo saying it was a matter of mathematics, getting two plus two to equal four. She glared at Jalbert. "I finally see why you want to expose the US for dodgy activities. I've asked myself for what purpose. Do you just hate the US and want to make it squirm? Or is it for some self-serving purpose?"

He glared at her, pivoted, and marched back through the French doors into the salon of his hotel. "You will deliver," he called over his shoulder. "Or else."

"We do not have a contract, Monsieur," she whispered.

39

———————

Ellie could almost see steam rising off Jalbert as he swept into the hotel lobby.

In a strange Vaudevillian changing of acts, Nick sauntered into the garden.

"Hey, El, what gives? Jalbert just blew past me like a gale-force wind." He sat down close beside her on the stone slab.

Nasty little fuck acts like everything's been glazed over with sugar. Got to watch what I say. She slid to the other end of the bench and frowned.

"What's going on?"

"Motherfucker lied to me," she snapped.

"This have to do with that article you were writing?" he inquired. "So, what's the problem? I'm sure it's a dynamite piece."

Ellie eyed him suspiciously. *Was that sarcasm in his voice?*

"I didn't write what he wanted," she mumbled, shaking her sheaf of papers at Nick. "It's a matter of truth. I couldn't verify his claim. Without facts, I have nothing. You can't write an article on innuendo." The words tumbled out of her.

"Ellie, Ellie, this part of the world is all about innuendo.

You should have figured that out by now," Nick said. "No real reason for war, just a humid veil of insinuation." He reached into his shirt pocket for cigarettes, lit one, inhaling and exhaling before holding the pack up to her. She nodded, and he went through the motions again before passing one to her. "What you have to do is weave the implications in with the facts." He paused and took a deep drag on his cigarette. "So it's seamless."

They smoked in silence for a moment.

"Want some help?"

"No. Absolutely not. I told you before, it's *my* story. Facts, not innuendo."

"Without Jalbert's help, where do you think you can get *your* story published?" Nick asked. "Have you forgotten you're a journalistic outlaw in this part of the world?"

"That doesn't worry me, and it's you who're the outlaw, buddy boy. My story's got integrity. Human interest. Stands on its own. And, I have great images." She flicked her cigarette onto the ground, clutched the papers to her chest, and flounced into the hotel.

JALBERT SAT ramrod straight at the bar nursing a brandy and soda. In the late afternoon, the room was as dark and quiet as a stodgy men's club. Nick slid onto the barstool next to him and ordered a vodka tonic. He drank it half down.

Jalbert ignored him. They were strange birds of a feather, both using Ellie to accomplish their individual ends. Neither had succeeded against a woman who was irresistibly charming but fierce as a Vietcong guerrilla.

"I can get you what you want," Nick said.

"Hmpf," Jalbert grunted.

"You may have forgotten I'm a journalist."

Jalbert examined his glass, sniffed, took a sip. "All right, Burrows, make it good," he said. The man was annoying.

"I happened to overhear your conversation with Ellie. She's gotten too big for her britches. You can wait till hell freezes over for her to rewrite her article the way you want. Not gonna happen. It's a matter of principle with her. Take my word; I know this woman." Nick paused for dramatic effect, taking a sip of his drink. "However, I can provide what she cannot."

"Because you have no principles?"

Nick snorted. "No. Because I understand how to massage allusions into facts."

Jalbert swiveled on the barstool and leveled a dark eye at Nick. "You're serious."

"Dead serious. I take her article and bend it the way you want it. To satisfy both our goals. No doubt her pictures tell the story you're looking for. We just need to manipulate the words."

Jalbert ordered two more drinks. "How, if this stubborn woman refuses to turn over her story to either one of us—" His eyes narrowed. He stuck out his chin. "I see. You have a strategy."

"I know how to manage her. I'm the one with the control." Nick lowered his voice. "Although she did force me to use a heavy hand the other day."

"*Quoi?* You raised a hand to her?" Jalbert bristled.

"I know how to keep her in line," Nick sneered.

Jalbert curled his lip in distaste and stared into the depths of his drink.

Nick lit a cigarette and inhaled deeply. "If I can get her to come with me to Madame Lulu's for an opium pipe, you should have enough time to find the pages and film in her room."

"That may provide enough time for me to take the article, but when she returns and sees it's gone, she'll be irate, like the caged lioness, to say the very least. No, a better tactic is required," Jalbert said.

Both men fell silent, staring straight ahead.

"Unless," Jalbert posited, "we give Lulu enough money to keep Ellie dreaming for a couple of days rather than mere hours." Jalbert recognized a solution, however distasteful.

"That's it. Perfect," Nick said.

"This will give me time to put a plan into motion," Jalbert thought out loud. "I charter a plane to Saigon where you perform the rewrite and I have the film developed. Then I send everything to Paris for immediate publication. This could work. You can rewrite with velocity?"

"In my line of work, as you know, if you can't meet an immediate deadline, you're out on your ass," Nick said. "Teach her a lesson. I almost wish I could stay and see the expression on her face."

Jalbert tightened his jaw.

"I know you don't like me, Jalbert, no matter. This is business. If you provide the money, I'll take her to Madame Lulu's tomorrow afternoon, and you can make all your arrangements. Sound good?" He reached out a hand to seal the deal.

Jalbert scanned the planes of Nick's face, the set of his mouth, the lust in his eyes. He ignored the handshake gesture. "You know, Nick, we really have no choice here. Our fight is greater than one woman's refusal to comply. We must make sacrifices for our cause. Unfortunately, Eleanor must pay the price."

"You're right. Ending the war, exposing the corrupt government—this is a dramatic moment that must be seized."

"I'm curious as to how you will effect our plan. From what I gather from Romo, Mademoiselle Ellie is not too pleased with you."

Nick waved a hand. "Not to worry. She can't resist my charms."

Jalbert narrowed his eyes to see through Nick's inflated ego. "No," he said, "you will not approach Eleanor. I will take care of the details. You take no action until you hear from me, understand?"

Nick glared at him.

"Going against me will not end well, Nick. Do you understand you are to do nothing until I say?"

"Okay, okay, fine."

"*D'accord.*" Jalbert held out his glass for a toast. "I'm curious, did you ever see Thiep again since he sent you to meet with me?"

Nick shook his head.

"Now, not a word of this to Romo, by the way," Jalbert added. "He is not a part of this venture."

40

Romo scoured the hotel and garden looking for Ellie, but she had vanished into thin air. For two days. This was not like her.

"What is going on?" The air had taken on a different weight; it was heavier. The skin on his head tingled. Something was up. He caught both Jalbert and Nick skulking like wolves with a scent. Whatever was afoot, it was not pretty. Stormy weather blowing up on the horizon. When he tried to corner Jalbert for information, his friend blustered some excuse and slithered away. "*Merde,*" Romo yelled after him. "*Tu es le serpent!*"

On the second night, he saw the pair sneak out of the hotel. Definite getaway.

Good riddance to Nick; he would not miss the ass. Not for a moment. And Ellie would certainly be better off without him. But the sudden vanishing of Jalbert was a surprise, though Romo had to admit behavior consistency was not his friend's strong suit. And those two together? Made no sense. None.

"Monsieur Romolino," called the front desk clerk as Romo walked out of the dining room on the way back to his room. "A message for you." He handed Romo a hotel envelope. Romo tore it open.

"*Mon ami*," Jalbert had written, "*I regret the unfortunate circumstances that force me to leave you behind. My mission holds more importance than the people involved. I regret it must be completed without you and without Eleanor. You are resourceful. I have faith you will find your way back to Saigon. You and the mademoiselle may remain in my hotel as long as you desire. We shall meet again. If I am not in Saigon when you return, present this letter to the Black Box Organization, whose address is written below. They will pay you for your services and reimburse you for the loss of your plane.*"

"*Merde!*" Romo snorted. He rushed to Ellie's room as fast as his legs could carry him. The door was ajar, the room vacant and disheveled. Drawers open, spilled of their contents. Where in this beautiful, fragrant world was Ellie? Feisty, gutsy lady whom he adored.

"It cannot be." He sank to the bed as realization punched him in the gut. He was a damn fool; he hadn't grasped the furtive behavior for what it was. Jalbert and Nick—that pair of blackguards had hooked up and stolen Ellie's work. He did not have the why of it figured out, not yet.

They must have hidden her somewhere. Or worse. Nothing they did would surprise him. They were ruthless.

IN THE DEEP *pillow of night, Ellie plummeted her snowmobile downhill into a snowy valley. As if she and the machine were one, she floated through weightless powder, following a pathway illuminated by panes of mirrors and prisms that glittered like white Christmas lights. She dashed through the downy snow beneath ski runs of rich crimson and brilliant yellow that sparkled against the backdrop of a black winter sky. Beyond the brilliance, purple shadows shimmered like storm clouds fringing the peaks at the horizon.*

Glacial fingers of cold reached inside her snowsuit, helmet, gloves, and boots, and caressed her skin with frost. Snow devils spiraled around her and cocooned her in a tumbling snow globe. When she reached the valley floor, the light of her headlamp splashed through the opaque curtain of snow and reflected a pair of slanted topaz eyes fixed on her.

She raised her goggles to her forehead and killed the engine. She stared at the vision: A bobcat. Sly hunter imbued with patience, the bobcat held her eyes until comprehension flowed through her mind: "Come along with me," it said to her.

She dismounted and followed on foot. The cat kept its distance from her, short tail twitching. It glanced back on occasion to see if she was behind and led her into a long dark musty tunnel. Currents of warm air swirled around her, and she caught whiffs of seaweed and salt. Then the smell was overpowered by juniper incense.

When she emerged at the other end of the passage, the bobcat was gone. A blinding orange sun hung in the sky. Before her on a hummock of green grass stood stone idols, chipped and crumbling elephant heads, tigers, and monkeys. In sandals and sundress, she followed the beguiling aroma of incense, strolling past the moss-clad monuments through a forest of rhododendron and ferns, and out onto terraces of rice fields that glistened alongside carefully tended canals. A spindly white egret teetered through the crops.

A trail appeared through a rice field. It was lined with rows of tridents, tall iron pitchforks stretching up to pierce the dome of sky. Some pointed straight up; others angled haphazard over the path. The scent of juniper pulled her into a trot, and she surged ahead, dodging gravestones through a church cemetery to the entry of a small stone structure.

Now barefoot and breathless, she crouched through a low doorway into a whitewashed room where a wizened old man sat cross-legged on a stone floor. He held a finger in the smoky air, beck-

oning her to sit across from him. His long gown puddled around him, a beaded necklace hung down his concave chest, and a crown of peacock feathers circled his head. Incense burned in a ceramic holder on the floor beside him, smoke from which he fanned into a cloud.

Dizzy, she sank to the cold floor. Crossing her legs in front of him, she put her hands together in a wai. He turned his palms up and entered her head, listened to her thoughts. She asked him to heal her confusion and depression. "For you," he crooned, "I will restore your equilibrium and strengthen your self-healing powers. I will call all my spirit helpers."

The shaman chanted his mantra and beat a hypnotic rhythm on his drum. His breathing slowed then sped up. He began to vibrate until his whole body shook.

Ellie watched his spirit release from his body, ascend upward, and float around the room. Through the twirl, she spied a large mystical peacock, royal blue, golden, and turquoise, rise up to the sky in a rush of rotors.

As his spirit collided with hers—

Her body was being rocked.

"Miss Ellie?" A voice spoke, muffled and indistinct. "Please to open eyes."

Ellie blinked once, caught a blurred image of Ophelia's face, squeezed her eyes shut, and reached for the dreamscape.

A rustle then a sharper voice pierced her brain. "Mademoiselle Ellie, you must wake now."

Ellie fought against opening her heavy-lidded eyes. She raised a hand and croaked, "Go away," and curled into a ball.

Madame Lulu shook her. "A very old and trusted friend bought you two days of dreams. That time has passed. You are in my guest room. You must leave now or pay for more time," she said in a huffy voice. Ellie heard the rustling of Lulu's elaborate brocades, the flinging open of curtains and windows.

Ellie covered her eyes with her arm. Too bright.

"Ophelia has brought you tea."

Muddled. Groggy. Captive far, far away in a spiderweb on a foggy night. She let herself be carried toward the brightening light, and then Ophelia was there, kneeling beside her, holding a bowl of aromatic tea.

"How you feel, Miss Ellie?" the girl asked, stroking Ellie's forehead. "You make longtime visit to dreamland."

Ellie thrashed. "No. Please. The peacock—"

"Mademoiselle, you are no longer in your dream," Lulu chided. "Now, you drink the tea Ophelia has brewed for you. It will free you from the dreams." Lulu leaned over and held the cup in front of Ellie's nose. "Your friend wished us to show you the many layers of opium mystery. I trust you have enjoyed the journey?"

Ellie struggled to swim up out of the depths of a thick, muddy swamp. Fog still hung heavy in her mind, but her body began to waken. Stomach acid rose into her throat. Her tongue was parched; it stuck to the roof of her mouth. She struggled to get up from her futon on the Oriental rug. A wave of vertigo pushed her back down.

"Too soon. You must drink." Lulu pointed to Ophelia's cup. She turned and said something to the girl. "Ophelia will help you with this sweet tea. Bring your strength back."

Ellie's head weighed rock heavy on her neck. "Got to get back to the hotel," she croaked. She tried and again failed to get up. Her body was not paying attention to her brain. The exotic aroma of the pipe circled her head like filaments of spiderweb silk, unbearably seductive. At the same time, she yearned for clarity. She couldn't keep from turning toward the dream, stretching for refuge. But her will to break out of the fog was stronger than the pull of the pipe. A low flame of outrage began to smolder in her core. How had she gotten there?

After the first sip that soothed her dry throat, she greedily gulped the sweet tea. She would drown the fog.

41

Romo had spent enough time in Vientiane to know that the proprietress of Madame Lulu's opium parlor held all kinds of secrets. The preeminent mistress of subtle gossip. He'd frequented her establishment himself whenever he needed respite from the agony in his legs. It was possible she might have news of Ellie, and there would be nothing wrong with securing a cache of opium dust to deaden the pain in his left leg especially.

Her place wasn't far. Worry propelled him to walk briskly. He ignored the pain. As he banged on the front door with one of his canes, it swung wide as if he were expected. The madame herself stood there in all her fancy silks, a smile painted on the mask of her face.

"*Bonjour*, Madame Lulu," Romo said.

"Monsieur Romolino. *Bienvenue.* You wish some relief today?" she suggested, her voice as smooth as merlot. She turned sideways and swept her arm toward the interior.

"Perhaps a small package of powder?"

"But of course. I save this just for you. *Un moment.*" She

walked to a rococo console table and lifted a small package out of the drawer before gliding back to him as if on rollers.

"*Merci.* He reached into his pocket for Laotian kip and dropped them into her open palm.

"By the way, I am looking for an American woman with golden-red hair. You are so well connected in this city, I think you may possibly have an idea where I might find her." He was killing her with politeness, hoping against hope she'd have the answer he sought.

"Curiously enough, Monsieur Romolino, she is here within our walls. Brought here by the French hotel owner Jalbert. Keep her dreaming for two days, he tells me. Pays much money."

"Take me to her," Romo said.

"*Suivez moi,*" she said, gliding up the stairs, skirts rustling as she moved. She opened a door. "*Voila,*" she said. At the sharp clap of her hands, Ophelia rose and left the room.

"Ellie," he murmured, concerned by the pale woman whose eyes looked disconnected from her mind and whose lips were chapped.

"Romo?" Ellie blinked.

He glanced around to see if she had brought anything with her, spying her red knapsack in a corner. He snatched it up, tucked his canes under an arm, and then lifted her as if she were a delicate Pietà. Wincing at the jolt in his left leg, he carried her down the stairs to where Madame Lulu, once more positioned in the foyer, opened the door for him. "A pedicab waits for you at the curb."

It took hours to bring her back to full consciousness, time Romo used to silence his indignation. He strained against his fury, vowing to find Jalbert and wring his miserable chicken neck. What part did Burrows play in this obscene performance?

Ellie gazed around her room. "What happened? Why is my room such a mess?"

"*Ma petite,* this is not a pretty story. Jalbert and Burrows are now partners in crime. Jalbert paid Lulu to keep you in the cloud of opium so he could steal your written pages and your film. This is why your room is disheveled."

"Those—" She clenched her fists and her jaw. The veins in her neck swelled. "My knapsack?" she gasped.

"It is here."

"Good," she breathed. "Then they didn't get all the film. Still some in my cameras." She leaned back against the pillows. "But it's as if they reached into my mind and stole my thoughts. We're going after them," she vowed. "That. Story. Is. Mine."

Her face paled. "Oh my God," she exclaimed. Her hand went to her heart. "Now I remember Jalbert's odd behavior when he invited me for cocktails in the bar. He said he wanted to apologize for his temper tantrum and talk about possibilities and angles for my article. I got really woozy and then the lights went out. He must have drugged my drink and taken me to Madame Lulu's."

"Cruelty such as these two have demonstrated must be punished. It is unconscionable, *merde*. We will catch these pirates and hang them by their toenails. Yes?"

Ellie's eyes narrowed. "I can think of another body part that would be even better to swing them by."

42

When Ellie's materials arrived on his desk, Ben Stryker could easily imagine himself as one of the people she'd interviewed. Even in her notes, her writing brought him into the action, to the point he could almost hear the whine of missiles and smell the cordite. Her work showed keen observation and perception of her subjects' commentary as well as their underlying emotions.

He was patting himself on the back for his good fortune in discovering Ellie Ketcham when his houseboy entered carrying a stack of English-language newspapers from around the globe. He lowered them onto the side table of Ben's reading chair and left.

Ben rubbed his hands together. "Talk to me, world press." Newspapers were how he kept current. News writers and their views of the world. He could disappear into them, taking note of trends, news quirks, writing styles, and opinions. He sometimes believed he was a spirit gliding with ease between the tenses of his life—the past of his books, the present of these newspapers, the future of his next book. One thing he believed was war correspondents were a unique breed. Their stories were like no others.

In the small kitchen to one side of his office, he poured himself a cup of coffee, spooned in cream and sugar, then settled into the down-filled cushions of his green leather chair and ottoman. After an hour or so, he reached the French newspaper, *Le Figaro*. Thumbing through, he paused at a two-page spread about Laos. A premonition vibrated. He read with mounting doom. His mouth hung open.

"This makes no sense," he said, shaking the newspaper. "What is going on?"

He moved to his desk, spread out the paper, and lifted the phone off the receiver. He spoke with urgency.

"Sarah, come over here. Right now—" He didn't like to disturb her baby preparations, but this was urgent. "I've got a situation."

"Notice anything unusual?" he said before she'd even closed the door.

She came up beside him and leaned over to survey the spread of the *Le Figaro* piece, one hand on her belly.

"These look like Ellie's photos," she said. "The style is similar to the prints she sent us from the embassy attack and the battle in Cholon. These must be hers, but where's her photo credit?"

"Read the text."

She read, but Ben was impatient and interrupted. "You see, Sarah? Some of it reads like Ellie's writing, doesn't it? The rest of it is sloppy and mediocre. Plus, the tone is belligerent. Is she collaborating with some incompetent? What do you think is going on here? Why the byline by someone else, some Nick Burrows character." As he spoke the name, a shadow scratched at his consciousness.

Sarah stood up straight, placing her palms in the small of

her back. "Wait. Isn't he the guy who picked Ellie up at Tan Son Nhut? I remember the name from one of her letters."

"Aha! That's it, Sarah. I thought the name rang a bell." He looked at her, suddenly worried. "She mentioned she was going to Laos in her last letter. But why does this say, 'Story and photos by Nick Burrows'? I thought it was *her* gig."

"We should call her." Sarah reached for the phone. "You have the number for the Continental?"

Ben opened to a page in his address book and slid it to her. She put the call through. Nodding, she hung up. "She checked out several weeks ago. Shall we try David Jenkins?"

Ben nodded, pointing to the phone number. Unsettling waves of worry washed through him. When Sarah reached Jenkins at 5 a.m. his time, he sounded muzzy. Ben put the phone on speaker.

"David, no time for niceties. Have you seen this article in the April 6 *Le Figaro* about Laos? The byline is by Nick Burrows, but the piece and the photos have Ellie's stamp all over them. What in the holy hell is going on? Who is this guy?"

Silence crackled down the line then David's hoarse voice croaked. "He's a wannabe journalist. All lies and fanaticism from what I can tell. His so-called concern for the underdog blinded Ellie to his real motives for a time. He seems to have manipulated her original Laos story into some vicious propaganda exposé. He's shaken up Washington, that's for sure. I can tell you the government is not happy. Burrows is in big trouble. You don't impugn the CIA and get away with it. But he's gone to ground apparently, disappeared."

Ben glanced at Sarah. Her face showed the horror he felt.

"But, David, where's Ellie?" Sarah asked. "The hotel said she checked out."

"I moved her into a room at my place. Thought I could keep a closer eye on her. But then she and Burrows left Saigon, obviously headed for Laos. She hasn't returned."

43

____

Time stuttered in Vientiane as Ellie made an effort to relax in her hotel room. Never one for waiting, even as a little girl, she had impatiently watched clothes going round and round in the dryer, urging them to dry faster. Her parents' generation rolled their eyes at her generation's craving for instant results in everything.

Life was a sine wave, up and down, a ship in rough seas. How many metaphors could she come up with to describe her situation? Where was her solid ground? She was drowning in the herbal tea Romo insisted she drink to flush out the intake of poisons from the past two days.

Her world had been pulled out from under her. After she'd synthesized the entire Long Tieng experience, placed it in context, and written her guts out, Nick and Jalbert betrayed her and ripped off her article and her undeveloped film. What a perverse reward. It was more like they'd filched her soul. Her story was good. They fucking hijacked it. She punched her palm with a fist. It took several deep breaths to calm her outrage. She stuffed her indignation just beneath the surface, fought to keep it from spurting like a Yellowstone geyser. And to top it off, she was constipated to the point of extreme discomfort.

Jalbert's greed she understood. He had so much at stake. But Nick was her ally. Or so he'd pushed her to believe. Despite his so-called affection for her, he impaled her with one of those tridents from her opium dream. Whatever mists had fogged her vision lifted, and she saw Nick in the stark glint of day. He was a miserable, manipulative, cruel loser, and above all a despicable abuser like the hunter who charms his prey then lets the charm slip once caught. A barnacle. He must have been stringing her along, riding on her coattails, just waiting for an opportunity, and she'd handed it to him on a silver platter. Sniveling slug, trailing his slimy deeds behind him.

She squeezed handfuls of hair, tugging to the point of discomfort. She clutched her pillow to her face and screamed in exasperation. "Ergh."

Romo found her in the garden later that afternoon, pacing back and forth in front of her favorite bench.

"This is driving me crazy, Romo. We're stuck here in Vientiane while those larcenous crooks are doing God knows what with my work. *My* work. We've got to get to Saigon, got to find them."

"Come, sit with me. It is true, you are in a difficult place. But you must look at the bright side—"

"Bright side? Are you crazy? My life has been shredded."

"*Oui*, but now is the time to untie the knots rather than tighten them," Romo suggested gently. He gave her a moment of silence. "We must talk about Nick."

Her stomach twinged as she struggled to bring order to her thoughts. She sat down on the bench. Romo wasn't letting her off the hook. He wanted to help her, agonizing as it was.

"Well, I've come to realize he has a Jekyll and Hyde personality: the charming, funny man with the soul of a zealot versus the tortured, angry man with a rotting soul." She lit a cigarette and blew smoke up to the sky. Romo was safe haven. Talking to him was better than being alone on the roller coaster of her thoughts.

"I see who Nick really is. The mask has dropped, and the monster has been revealed. Booze and drugs ate away any moral restraints until he was fueled only by his rage. There's nothing anyone can do to help or change him. In his mind, he's the victim and the world owes him a debt."

"You give him far too much credit," Romo declared, "but I see the light has dawned for you after the darkness. Romo bursts with pride for you. It's difficult to turn away. First impressions are strong, like waves on a white-sand beach. It has taken you much time and many waves to wash away your first impression of Nick."

He stood, grasped her hand, and kissed it. "I regret I must leave you to your thoughts while I seek a savior to return us to Saigon."

The next afternoon, wearing a conspiratorial grin, he crookedly waltzed into the lobby where she was waiting.

"You got us a flight?" she squealed, spying his grin, and jumped up from her chair.

Romo's eyes sparkled. "Shall we pray *this* pilot keeps us above the Mekong and not in it?"

Ellie threw her arms around Romo. "You are my hero."

"Flattery gets you every place." He beamed at her. "We leave with the sunrise. You would like some dinner first?"

"Thank you for the Aloe Vera; it did the trick. Everything that was stuck inside me is gone. I could eat an elephant right now," she said, the triumph of getting even whizzing through her veins.

~

THE PARTICULAR AROMATIC stew of Saigon settled around her when they deplaned at Tan Son Nhut. She breathed it in, her relief at being back mingling with jagged emotions. In the cramped back seat of a blue Renault taxi, Ellie fidgeted, pointing out the window at familiar markers. "I remember my first ride into Saigon," she said ruefully. "I was so excited by the promise of what lay before me." She frowned. "So naïve. Seems like years ago."

When they pulled up to David Jenkins' villa on Cong Ly Street, Romo helped Ellie out with her knapsack and duffel. He hitched up his pants.

"I apologize, but I must leave you now, *chèrie*, and turn my efforts to a search for the villainous René Jalbert." He reached out and ran his hands up and down her arms. "I will not be far in case you need me. The concierge at the Continental will know how to find me."

Her insides folded in on her. "But Romo—"

He escorted her to the front door, moving more smoothly now and without his canes. "I cannot depart without making certain Nick has gone," he said, hesitation in his voice. "The vermin could be waiting just inside to pounce on you."

He knocked. No answer. Knocked louder.

He opened the door and shouted, "David Jenkins."

He called again, and Ellie joined in. "David Jenkins!"

Moments later, footsteps skittered up from the back of the house. David appeared, wearing a black rubberized apron, and radiating the aroma of the darkroom.

"Ellie, thank God." He threw his arms around her, rocking her back and forth. "Ben and Sarah Stryker are worried sick about you. What in the holy hell's going on?"

Ellie gaped at David, unable to get words out of her mouth.

"They called from Aspen," David continued. "They saw Burrows' byline on an article in *Le Figaro* that impugned the CIA, but they recognized your writing style in some of it, and

Sarah identified some of your photos. You need to explain to them what's going on. They're frantic." He looked down, shuffled his feet. "Well, truth be told, we've all been worried about you. You disappeared with Nick, after which I heard nothing."

"What article? Oh Jesus," she groaned. "Don't tell me— Wait, didn't you get my note? I left you a note telling you I was going to Laos."

"No note," David said.

"Hah, Nick must have taken it." She spat out the words as if they were poison.

Romo stepped forward, feet apart, fists up. "Is Nick Burrows here?"

"David," Ellie said, pulling Romo by the hand. "Excuse me. This is my friend Romo. This man saved my life in Laos, twice."

David extended his hand, and the pair shook vigorously.

"Nick has vanished into the ether," David said. "God knows where. Come in, both of you. You've got to see this."

As she hesitated, David added, "It might hurt, but it's important you see it, Ellie." He led them to the dining room, where newspapers were open on the table. "French and English," he said, pointing to two newspapers. "I'll get us some tea."

"Perhaps you might have a soupçon of cognac?" Romo asked. He pulled back a chair for Ellie.

She gawped at the two-page spread, hand to her chest. Before her lay her article, completely sliced up and altered, filled with lies, suppositions, and accusations, and her photos of Long Tieng, from the karst mountains hugging the runway to shots of the opium refinery to aircraft taking off and landing. Romo read the French edition.

When David returned from the kitchen, minus his apron, he brought a tray holding teapot, cups, and a bottle of VSOP, which he set on the table. He poured tea and passed it around. The delicate floral pattern on the porcelain teacups contrasted with the heavy mood in the room. He extended the cognac in Romo's direction.

"*Merci.*" He poured a generous amount into his teacup.

"What the fuck. Story and photos by Nick Burrows? I could throw up I'm so angry." Ellie pinched out the words.

"I know your work, Ellie, and I know Nick's." David wagged a hand over the newspaper. "How did he get the byline? I can't imagine you gave it to him. And these photos. I'm sorry to say they're excellent. I know Sarah recognized them, but did you teach Nick your telephoto style?"

"No, goddammit. They're all mine."

She trembled with anger as she scanned the pages. "Now I get why Jalbert kidnapped me and locked me up for two days. He stole my work and made a getaway."

"What? Kidnapped you?" David asked, clearly startled.

"Got me out of the way so Nick could cannibalize my article and add whatever Jalbert told him to write. They basically accuse the CIA of being drug runners. No mention of the Air America middleman. Sleazebags. It was *my* goddamn story; these are *my* photos. I took the risks; I want the credit. Nick perverted everything I wrote. Made up lies. He wasn't even in Long Tieng. He'd disappeared into an opium fog, and we left on our mission without him. Aargh!"

David rested a hand on her forearm and pointed to the newspaper with his other hand. "This is some heavy shit. There are a lot of unfounded charges in the article with no backup whatsoever. And it exposes the secret of the Ravens. Head of station must have his boxers in a twist. That's got to be why Nick vanished. They get hold of him and he's a goner."

"Huh?" Ellie said.

"Your friend refers to your celebrated Central Intelligence Agency." Romo turned to David. "I fear this betrayal was the brainchild of René Jalbert. He is certain he sits on the right hand of God. He's been conjuring his revenge since 1954 when the Americans landed in Laos and snatched opium transport away from the Corsicans. He thought he'd finally found his redemption with Ellie. When she refused to bend to his scheme, he turned to the pandering Nick."

Ellie, holding the cup to her mouth, swung her head around, spitting tea. "Corsican? I thought he was French."

"Deception. The name of this game," Romo replied. "He is obsessed with getting the lucrative drug transportation back into his pocket."

"Holy crap," Ellie said. "I suspected something like that might be behind this."

"Not that Nick doesn't share in the blame, mind you," David said, scrubbing his cheeks with both fists. "He's been a greedy bastard as long as I've known him. A scavenger. Likes to sweep in and take credit for others' work."

He sipped his tea. "As hard as it might be for you, Ellie, you must back off for the moment. You might want to right this wrong, but silence and patience are required until you learn the true consequences of this article. We don't want you to be implicated. Very sensitive situation."

Ellie took a breath but before she could speak, David stood. "I call a time out, a mood changer. Why don't we skedaddle over to the Continental and have a little dinner. It'll give me a chance to cable Ben and Sarah that you're safe here in Saigon."

"It's going to take more than dinner to change my mood," Ellie spat. "I've been stripped naked." She balled her fists.

"Vengeance is mine sayeth the Lord," Romo added with a chuckle. "Pardon, it is my Catholic upbringing."

"I'm not leaving it up to God," she said.

"Is it not better to move forward than to dwell in the past?" Romo asked.

"You've learned a lesson about war coverage, Ellie," David said. "Bear silent witness to the atrocities but don't lose your humanity. You'll be fine." He patted her arm.

"Nick's true nature must be to betray and throw me into the fires of hell."

"Ah, *chèrie*." Romo frowned. "Do not worry. *Non*, we will make this right."

As they walked down Tu Do Street, Ellie wondered at the strange turns her life had taken. In front of her, Romo whispered to David, who stopped in his tracks. He turned and glanced at her, a horrified look on his face, and resumed walking.

David held the door open for Ellie and Romo. "I'll join you in a sec. Just let me cable Ben and Sarah," he said and walked to the front desk.

Despite her bedraggled appearance and the faded bruises, Ellie shed some of her agitation when she walked through the hotel and out to the terrace restaurant and inhaled the sweet scent of plumeria. She was thinking about the photos Jalbert hadn't gotten: the film she took of the South Vietnamese unloading cargo at Tan Son Nhut, the caravan down into Long Tieng, all the film of Joua Vang Torr and the Hmong.

"She smiles," Romo said.

"Determination," she said. "But it's going to take time and some vengeance. Hard to get spilled milk back in the cow."

As he joined them, David appraised Ellie. "Listen, darlin', I think it's best if you stay away from the villa until ... er ... this issue with the Long Tieng article blows over. I know of a handy little apartment you can use. Belongs to a colleague who's in Hong Kong for a couple of weeks." A look passed between David and Romo.

Dammit to hell, Romo told David about Nick's abusing me. Ellie bit her lower lip to contain her irritation and speared Romo with a rapier glance. He was distracted, looking past her to the street, appraising young Vietnamese women in their graceful *ao dais*.

Noticing her discomfort, David clasped his hands and broke

into her thoughts. "Nick's dangerous. You don't need to do this all alone, Ellie. Accept some help. This is bigger than you, although it's not all bad. I see the brilliant, poetic spark of your writing through Nick's bullshit, so in an odd way, he helped you. He's the one who bears the burden of treason. So there." He paused. "Not to worry about the future; I have assignments for you. With your eye and your talent, you're going places."

How curious that David's slow drawl could color his words with such optimism, she thought. A glimmer of light flickered in her brain. Working journalist. "I've still got some of my film," she said. "Under my mattress and more in my knapsack." David was right. She had to move on. But first things first. Reverse this despicable act by those dirtbags. She refused to be stained for even one extra minute.

44

"Champagne," David exclaimed as the waiter approached. "To celebrate your survival."

Ellie sighed. Her eyes brimmed with tears. "My survival," she repeated, barely above a whisper. "It's mind-boggling. I mean, just a few days ago I was lost in an alien universe. How insidious opium is: to float in a dream, completely unmoored, constipated, and drifting out to sea." She waved her hand, banishing the memory.

Romo laughed, reached for her hand, and squeezed it. "Ellie is a twentieth century Jean d'Arc. She has been through fire, and she thrives," he said to David. "May I tell you how we met? Through René Jalbert, one of the outlaws in this story."

The waiter returned, ceremoniously popped the cork, and filled three coupes, leaving the bottle in an ice bucket. David took a few sips. His blue eyes grew steely. "This story of mismatched serendipity really begins with me, and I am guilty enough for all of us. I'm the idiot who sent Burrows to pick Ellie up when she landed in Saigon." He emptied his glass and refilled it. "'What goes around, comes around.' I believe in karma. As soon as he's located, it'll be Burrows who takes the fall."

"David, you can't blame yourself," Ellie interrupted. "Nick's the dark force here. A user who attaches himself to the best vehicle to accomplish his aims. Come to think of it, this defines Jalbert too."

Ellie brushed her wounds. "Part of my attraction to Nick was connected to my excitement about being in Saigon, but I can't deny I fell for his line. Thing is—I still can't believe he's all bad. There must be some good *deep* underneath all the anger and rage and abuse."

"If there is good, it's imprisoned," David said.

Romo coughed. "So, your feelings for this despicable creature linger? This will dissipate. But let us get back to the story. When Ben and I were dancing around the Plaine des Jarres back during the French war, I also was flying opium for Jalbert and his Corsican friends. After many years, Jalbert found me again and asked me to fly two people from Saigon to Vientiane, hush, hush."

"Ellie and Nick," David said.

"*Oui.* Nothing is ever easy, *n'est ce pas*? On that flight, we took ground fire and crashed on the banks of the Mekong near Vientiane. I lost my ninth plane. It seems I have the lives of more than one cat, *oui*?"

He cleared his throat. "Once we reached Vientiane, Nick discovered the Laotian capital's most famous opium den that services non-natives. It was his quicksand. He lost touch with our reason to be there. On the morning we left on our mission to Long Tieng airbase, he was off in an opium fog."

"Your assignment?" David asked Ellie.

"To discredit the CIA," she said, her voice tight. "I was duped into it with the promise of an exclusive byline. Jalbert wanted me to take damning pictures and write an exposé to blow the lid off their involvement in heroin transport and sales.

In my naivety, I was blinded by the challenge of a story and not the lack of ethics in it."

She glanced at Romo, who gestured to her to continue. "This is still so raw. Sorry." She fought tears. "Long Tieng is deep in the mountains. It took a few days to trek there, up and down an opium trail. I photographed CIA headquarters and Hmong processing opium. What Jalbert said about government involvement was true. I just couldn't prove it even though I had images of raw opium and processed morphine that were nothing more than what they were: pictures. The rest would only have been my word, supposition."

"You're right about that," David agreed. "A she-said-he-said kind of squabble although the CIA would have the final say. No telling how it would end."

"Anyway, when we got back to Vientiane, Nick was beyond pissed that I'd gone off and stranded him. Socked me, broke open a wound I'd gotten from a piece of shrapnel. Black eye. Unleashed his fury at being left out."

She sipped her champagne. "You were right, David, he can't stand to lose control of, of anything." She fisted her hands.

David reached into the ice bucket, held up the champagne bottle, shook off the water drops, and refilled glasses.

"There is more," Romo said, giving Ellie a break. "Ellie could only write the truth of what she observed. So, here is the rub: This did not satisfy Jalbert's idea of the truth, so he enlisted Nick to rewrite her story into the one he wanted. I cannot help but wonder if they were partners all along."

"What?" Ellie gasped.

Romo shrugged.

"The article started a buzz throughout the press corps in Southeast Asia," David interjected.

"Why?" Ellie interrupted.

"Because there's no verification for the accusations within the context of the piece. The damage it did to the press corps is compounded by severe implications Burrows might face and probably will. That's the news that is going to be in the headlines. The message: *Do not fuck with the CIA.*"

"Is Nick still a threat?" Ellie asked.

"To himself, yes. For you, I have no clue, darlin'," said David. "He's obviously hiding. Response from the embassy is total denial, which means there will be reprisals if they catch him. There's precious little his uncle can do to help him. Now, the unofficial consensus of Nick Burrows by the correspondents is *persona non grata* with extreme prejudice." He raised his glass. "It might become official before we finish our wine."

He stole a glance at her. "What now, Ellie?"

"If I leave now, it would be running away. I'm not finished here." She looked directly into David's eyes.

"What is there to finish? I am curious," Romo exclaimed.

Odd question. Pride can lead to ruination.

David rested a hand on her arm. "I have assignments for you, if you're willing to enter a warzone, and it's not charity. It's what you need. Jalbert tried to silence your voice. He will not succeed."

A sudden spasm of terror twisted Ellie's stomach. She whipped her head around to the left then to the right. "Nick. I smell him," she said in a hoarse whisper, hand to her chest. "It's like a ghost just hissed in my ear."

David leapt out of his chair and dashed into the hotel from the terrace. "No sign of the bastard," he said when he returned and sat down, pulling a big white napkin onto his lap. "We must keep our eyes peeled; he could be following you. Let's get you to that apartment. It's not far from here. We'll take a roundabout route just in case."

Romo raised his hands, as if pushing back. "*Merde*, let us not make a 727 out of a Cessna," he said. "*Non*, I take it back. This *is* a 727. It is unfortunate he is a spineless coward. He is obsessed with Ellie. I have seen this in him, an addiction. There is no question that when his need explodes, he will strike out. We must not allow him to get near you, Ellie."

"Thank you, Romo. Nick hates you because you saw through him the minute you met him."

"You are courageous, young lady, like the daughter I never had. We will take good care of you. *Moi*, I remain here, with you, like glue." He winked.

45

In the utilitarian one-bedroom apartment, Ellie saw no signs of the person who lived there. Vagabond journalists often camped out rather than settled in. They spent more time on the go than kicking back. This place had a couch, a table with chairs, a couple of lamps and a few Asian knick-knacks. And the quintessential bottle of whiskey. The bedroom hosted a bed and clothing hooks on the wall.

Whenever she left, David or Romo shadowed her in lock-step. She was grateful for the brave, irreverent men who were grounded in sanity. Unlike the dark-world aura of her captors.

She spent her days at David's. Ben and Sarah phoned, expressing their worry and concern for her safety. Despite the static of bad connections, Ellie tried to put Ben at ease for his guilt in sending her to Saigon totally unprepared for the twists and turns of war and politics. She was deeply touched by their caring. What started as mutual creative sparks that past November had evolved into close kinship. Serendipity at its finest.

"You cannot blame yourself, Ben. I know I tend to be a bit headstrong, and that's what cooked my goose."

David left, reluctantly heeding the call from UPI to go up to Khesanh. The NVA had held the airbase in siege since late January.

Romo had plans to spend the night with an old love, Jeanne, a Frenchwoman who lived in an apartment above her café on Le Loi Street. He offered to cancel when David was called away, but the café was right across the street from Ellie's temporary apartment, and she waved him off.

"You deserve some fun, Romo. Don't worry, I'll be fine, and you'll be so close. We haven't had a whiff of Nick, so he's probably gone."

Romo looked skeptical. "*Non*, I must watch over you."

She jabbed her hands on her hips. "I said I'll be fine."

"I am fond of this stubbornness of yours," he said as he curled a piece of paper with Jeanne's phone number into her palm. "You call me if you need me, *oui*? I am in what you Americans call spitting distance."

Around nine that evening, Ellie stepped across the street to the café for some dinner, but she couldn't shake the willies. The events of the recent past weighed heavily on her, and it was the first time since returning from her opium captivity she'd been out alone. Goose bumps grazed her skin. She ate quickly and zipped back to the apartment, locking the door behind her.

She poured herself a glass of Mekong Whiskey and sat on the sofa in the shabby living room, tilting the lampshade so light fell onto her notebook as she made notes for a piece on traveling with an opium caravan, glad she'd stashed those photos in her knapsack. David's encouragement had sparked her writing fire, and words were beginning to kindle. Martin Luther King had been assassinated while she was in Laos. Talk about champion of the underdog. He was a real hero. She'd seen and heard him speak at a peace march in New York she'd covered for the *Village Voice* shortly before coming to Saigon.

A sudden knocking shook her to her bones. Five raps. Impatient, aggressive. Nick.

She didn't answer. He banged again, louder. She still didn't answer. He rattled the doorknob. "Ellie, goddammit, I know you're in there," he snarled.

Afraid he'd blast the door to splinters, she opened it. He stood there; shoulders hunched, hair disheveled like he'd slept on it and not brushed it. He smelled like overripe fruit and stale beer. His clothes were soiled and wrinkled. He looked like a bum.

"How did you find me? That was you at the Continental, wasn't it? You've been following me."

Nick swallowed and stepped into the apartment. "I was coming to talk to you, but a couple of White Mice got in my way."

"The South Vietnamese police?"

"Yeah, you don't want to get too close to those sleazeballs." Nick paused, clasped his hands behind his back, and took a deep breath. "Let me start over. I realize all the bullshit I've done. I'm here to apologize."

She grimaced at the hollow words. "I have no reason to believe you, none whatsoever. You have a lot of nerve coming here after what you did. You're a lying dirty rotten thief."

"Oh get off your high horse, Ellie. I told you Southeast Asia is all about innuendo. I simply employed it when you couldn't be bothered to."

"*My* high horse. That's choice."

She was being pulled into his sphere of manipulation and lies. Danger hung in the air. She'd seen this time and time again, the way his anger built up steam behind his mask of obsequiousness. She should slow down before he blew. Change the subject. No. Not backing down. Enough of his bullshit.

"Just get out, Nick. I never want to see you again."

His eyebrows were busy. What was he thinking?

"You do know this is all Jalbert's doing. I was merely his tool to get what he wanted. When you failed him, it was just his good luck I was there to pick up the pieces."

"That's a good one, Nick. Not interested in your lies. I'm moving on. You are part of the past." She eyed him, levered a comment she knew better than to do. "As a matter of fact, I'm on my way up to Khesanh."

The lights in Nick's eyes flickered then caught fire.

"With that asshole Jenkins? Fucking whore!" he rasped, his temper combusting. Anger blazed from his bleary red eyes in pinpricks of crazed rage.

Ellie stepped back as if struck. "You're the asshole, you thieving bastard! Get out of here," she choked out in a low, hoarse voice. Panic gripped her gut.

"Put one over on me, did you? Thought you could get away with it, did you?" His eyes were pinned, hazel irises vibrating.

"You're higher than shit," she said, blackness moving in from the edges of her vision.

He stormed her, sending her in a mad scramble around the sofa. "Stay away," she cried out, looking desperately at the door.

"No escape, baby. None of your friends can rescue you. No one here but you and me."

She backed into the corner, arms up. "Nick! Don't!" She seized a heavy metal Buddha from an end table and held it above her head.

He pulled his lips back over his teeth. Feral dog.

Her hand was shaking. She launched the statue and caught him in the mouth with a loud thunk. Eyes wide, he touched his lips and looked at smears of blood on his fingers. He spat out a chip of tooth.

"You don't scare me, asshole." She was unsteady. "Not your victim." Thoughts ran helter-skelter through her mind, bumping up against each other. A jumble of hurt, anger, and confusion until she was almost frozen with fright. She rose up against the fear, ejecting it with a ferocious shake of her head.

He snorted an evil laugh. "If this is the last time I see you, I'm gonna make it count." He lunged at her around the couch.

She sidestepped, clutched at the lamp, and threw it at his head.

He was ready for it, arms up, deflecting. As the lamp smashed to the floor, he grabbed her hard by the armpits and hurled her to the floor.

She landed on bits of broken lightbulb and screamed, a strangled sound like a wolf caught in a trap. She covered her face with both hands, smelled blood. Her father's words rang in her ears: "You don't win every race. Sometimes you hit the fencing. Get back on course and finish the race." Adrenaline flooded her system. She scrambled to her feet, scanning the apartment for another weapon or a way out, either one. Her nose throbbed. She stared up at him, swiping at the blood. "You're not going to win, no matter how hard you hit me."

"It's your fault I'm being deported tomorrow. The fucking South Viets have been chasing me for a week. I don't know why or who told them I was peddling smack, but I figure it could be no one but you." He took another swipe at her; she ducked. He almost pranced, as if enjoying his rage. "If it weren't for some embassy nerd, I'd have spent the rest of my life in a Saigon jail on a bogus charge."

"You're out of your mind," Ellie croaked.

"I had to sneak out of the embassy to settle things with you once and for all!"

"Fucking crazy."

"Oh yeah? Try this crazy on for size." He backhanded her. Her mouth gushed blood. He knocked her against the wall, threw her onto the sofa, overturning it, crashing her to the floor. She hit her head, hard.

The world went black.

When she came to, she was alone, no idea what time it was, blood spattered all over her blouse and crusted on her face. Her nose pulsed with such stinging pain, it had to be broken. Her teeth hurt and her whole body ached like she'd been pummeled by an ocean wave against a shallow reef. She raised her head slowly, heavily. She spied the whiskey bottle on the counter, crawled over to it, and pulled herself up. When she tipped the bottle to her swollen lips, she winced at the astringent pain. Pain meant she was still alive. A caustic laugh gurgled in her throat. Alive. She guzzled the raw alcohol. She might be battered and bruised, but he'd never destroy her spirit. Down but not out.

46

____

Romo licked his fingers as he polished off a chocolate croissant and lifted the porcelain cup of espresso to his lips. He and many in Saigon enjoyed the ritual of morning coffee. Jeanne's café near the waterfront, not far from Tu Do Street, had been established by her grandfather in the 1930s. Jeanne was known for her buttery, flaky, melt-in-the-mouth croissants and brioche, and strong French Roast brew served in delicate Limoges cups.

On this April morning, the heat was rising quickly, and humidity steamed, heavy with the promise of rain. The café was full, and people spilled outside to gather at the open-air tables and chairs. It was a favorite morning stop for Americans on their way to the embassy or military posts, chatting up a storm, sipping, munching, smoking.

As he took another sip, he spied a scrawny Vietnamese youth strolling through the café from the kitchen. The boy made a casual show of shrugging off his knapsack and placing it gingerly on the floor behind a table of South Vietnamese Army officers. He bent down, opened the pack, and removed a stack of postcards. He waved the cards until the officers shooed him away. The kid fast walked out the front door, leaving his pack behind.

Romo understood immediately. "Bomb! *Trái phá!*" he yelled. "*Allez, vite, allez!* Get out!" He jumped up and sent his cup clattering to the floor.

Startled patrons stared at him as he dashed into the kitchen where Jeanne was kneading bread dough. He grabbed her by a floury hand and plowed through the rear entrance to the alleyway behind.

An earsplitting explosion threw them to the ground.

Romo scrambled to his feet, helped Jeanne up, and made sure she was unhurt and safe then bustled around to the front of the café. Amid the chaos, he saw people lying like dismembered mannequins on the street. The coppery smell of blood mingled with coffee, the sulfurous smoke of the bomb, and the smothering aromas of Saigon.

Through the chaos, he spied Ellie across the street, bounding down the steep rickety stairs of her temporary apartment building and thrusting herself into the hysteria. She raised a Nikon to her eye, and panned the injured, screaming, bleeding, hysterical people.

She choked on the fumes then bent over and coughed bloody mucous onto the ground.

"Ellie," Romo called out, alarmed. She didn't hear him. She wiped her mouth on her arm and looked past it to the café. Chairs and tables had been splintered into kindling, mixed with broken glass. She made a dash for the smoking ruins and almost got hit by an ambulance.

Romo never moved so quickly. Yanked her out of harm's way. Stared at her, aghast.

"*Diu dannazione!* Goddammit!" he hollered in Corsican, picking her up off the ground. "Ellie! Great gods in heaven! What has happened to you?"

"Huh?" She wavered as if she'd sustained a concussion.

"Here is Romo to the rescue," he said gently, a cigar stub bobbing between his lips as he spoke. He cradled her face in his hands, peered into her eyes. "*Ma pauvre*, my poor little one, it is your face, purple, bloodied, and a brutal cut on your lip. Do you know this?" Romo stared harder into Ellie's face.

Ellie's shoulders sagged. Color drained from her face.

"Romo is here. You are safe now."

Her eyes opened wide as if she were seeing something beyond him.

"*Merde!* That asshole did it to you again, did he not?" Romo shouted in anger. "Last night? Oui, the blood on your face is dry, you were not in the blast. I must get you to hospital. Your nose, she is looking crooked."

"No, no. I'm fine," she said as her eyes closed and her legs buckled.

He caught her before she hit the ground.

47

———

David Jenkins burst through the open door of his villa and nearly knocked Romo over. "I came as fast as I could. How is she?"

"I mean no offense, but you run like a girl." Romo clapped David on the back, raising some red dust from his shirt. "You have run all the way from Khesanh? You must take your time, *mon ami*, catch your breath. All is well now. She is safe. It is I— I am ashamed to tell you, who is guilty. My fault. I left her unsupervised."

Hands on his knees and sucking humid air, David grimaced at the gnarled Corsican. "Where is she?"

"In here." Romo disappeared into the living room.

David followed.

The curtains were drawn. In the dim light, Ellie was propped up on a formal French-blue silk sofa, resting against a drift of bed pillows.

"David," she said.

"Land sakes, darlin'." David wiped an expression of horror off his face. A bandage encircled her forehead, her swollen nose was blue and purple and yellow, her eyes mere slits in her puffy face, lips cut and swollen. He'd seen front-line soldiers in better shape. He leaned over and looked for a clear place to kiss her. Failing, he straightened.

"The good news is Nick can no longer smack you around. He's been deported."

Ellie burst into tears, crying and laughing. "Owww, that hurts," she mewed, holding her head.

"Who has deported him?" Romo asked.

David opened his palms in front of him in a shrug. "I heard the South Vietnamese jailed him for dealing heroin to the GIs and then our embassy got involved and shipped him right out."

"Dealing heroin?" Ellie asked. "That's funny; he accused me of turning him in for that."

Romo ran thumb and forefinger over his mustache. "The American *embassy* you say, David? How certain is this information?"

"Who else could pluck him out of a Vietnamese jail?"

"*Adieu*," Romo snapped.

Ellie reached for David's hand and squeezed it. She spoke with a muffled lisp. "Thank you. I don't know what I'd do without the two of you." She absently touched her forehead bandage again.

"Prognosis?" David asked, turning to Romo.

"At first, the doctor was concerned about a concussion, but he examined and released her," Romo said. "No broken bones. Only her nose, which he reset. No teeth lost. Other than how you look, you are fresh as a warm brioche, *oui*?" he teased her.

"I've had better days." Ellie brushed off their worry.

"Perhaps a few glass splinters removed from her back," Romo added.

"Ellie?"

"He couldn't shake his demons. As Shakespeare said, he hoisted himself with his own petard."

David looked past the bandages into her eyes. She was

exhausted, completely deflated by Nick's beating. He tilted his head at Romo, seeking more information. He suspected there was more at play than mere surface wounds.

"Do not worry, David. I have taken care of necessities," Romo said. "I introduced myself to your cook, who has made a reviving soup. I went over and retrieved Ellie's clothes and cameras from the apartment. The door was open. She was very lucky no one looted it."

"Thanks. I'll check on the place." David swept his arm in a wide arc. "This is your home now. Both of you. You have rooms here for as long as you need them. I managed to get a week off, and that's pushing it, but then I've got to head back to Khesanh, big Army-Marine offensive. Operation Pegasus is finally lifting the NVA siege of the airbase. He paused and a slow grin appeared. "So, darlin', I was going to ask you to come along on this one, but you're in no shape for war journalism. Too bad. You might've gotten one hell of a story."

He watched as the crooked, swollen smile he was waiting for appeared.

"Nothing wrong with me that a visit to a battlefield can't fix."

48

Less than a week later, Ellie and David boarded a Chinook helicopter for the battleground.

"Khesanh's in Quang Tri Province. Once a bucolic plateau that connected the east coast of Vietnam with market towns along the Mekong and into Laos." David shouted so Ellie could hear him over the noise of helicopter rotors.

"Built as a small camp for special forces to train local Hmong tribesmen. I never imagined it would be the nexus of a bloody confrontation."

"So, what happened?" Ellie asked.

"The Battle for Khesanh started before the Tet Offensive probably as a distraction to draw troops away from cities and leave them exposed and under-defended.

"Twenty to forty thousand NVA surrounded and attacked six thousand Marines plus a few ARVN troops stationed there."

Ellie was speechless, astounded by the overwhelming odds.

"Charlie's not dumb. They used the same strategy as they had in Dienbienphu and hid a huge cache of weapons in the mountains surrounding the base. From there they snarled runway operations."

"They targeted the airstrip?"

"C-130s couldn't land, too dangerous. Remaining on the ground to unload would've caused direct hits, so they slowed just short of stalling, leveled out at about a hundred feet above the pockmarked runway then spewed a chute from the rear. Supplies landed while the aircraft goosed their speed and took off again in the blink of an eye. Never touching ground."

Looking out of the helicopter at the eerie landscape, Ellie sucked in a breath of disbelief at land that was being denuded and its people decimated. This still felt new: a crash course in war. Life was suspended, hanging in the air, like the helicopter, waiting for the next bomb or mortar to explode in fireworks. So, it's still raging?"

"Yes ma'am. Finally, by the end of March, thirty thousand American troops were deployed. Operation Pegasus began. Flocks of Chinooks deployed the first Battalion, 26th Marine Regiment and artillery into battle in the hills above this remote base. And here we are." David gathered his gear.

"This op may have been the last straw for President Johnson. He just announced he's stepping down. Not running again. He must have grappled with the futile nature of the fight, as well. I heard exhaustion in his voice when he announced he was suspending all bombing of Vietnam in favor of peace talks."

"How many times can you beat your head against the wall before you just walk away?"

Their Chinook hovered, waiting to land. What Ellie saw shocked her. The lush green jungle had been churned into harsh gashes of bloody red soil. She clutched a Nikon and photographed smoke and fires rising from the land. Marines scuttled through the pandemonium, running every which way, mouths open in shouts and orders, and diving into bunkers. Gunfire flashed like fireworks. The Chinook dropped down as if on tiptoes onto the strange hilly battleground, never completely stopping.

She jumped down, wincing from her injuries, following Marines who jumped, rolled, and scattered like ants on a mission. One hand on her helmet and the other stabilizing the camera, she dropped into a tuck, duckwalked behind David through dusky air filled with red dust stirred up by choppers, and followed him into a deep command bunker with stacked sandbag walls. Window slits let in light. The partial roof of wooden pallets was piled with more sandbags. She blinked, sniffing the tightly confined aromas of sweat, dirt, and cigarette smoke. Her eyes darted from bare-chested Marines who smoked and leaned against sandbags to the radio operator who connected his CO with other brass in nearby bunkers. She coughed, crunched on the fine powder in her teeth, and slid to the ground, reaching up to pull off her helmet.

"Keep your helmet on, flak jacket, too," David said with authority. She scanned her surroundings and realized that exposing any part of herself in a warzone was foolhardy. She squeezed herself closer to the ground and adjusted her helmet, grimacing from the latent soreness, tucking in the bandana wrapped around her hair, nearly the same color as the red soil. Her bruises were changing colors, and she was slightly woozy. She was glad David was with her; he was a comforting presence.

"Where are we exactly?" she asked.

"Straight north of Saigon, northwest of Hue, and inland. No offshore breezes to lighten the oppressive heat and humidity. Nasty place." David stood as the CO sidled over to them. "Ellie," David said, "this is Colonel Raynor."

Ellie rose and reached her hand out to the colonel.

Colonel Sidney Raynor ignored the gesture and glared at David. "You bring me an FNG? A virgin? Jesus, man." He squinted at Ellie.

Ellie squinted. *Jesus, he called me the fucking new guy?*

"You're too pretty to be here, even if you do brighten up the place," he muttered under his breath. "You may be an eager beaver, young lady, but I do not have time for you so you're in charge of your own welfare. No one else on this post has time to watch it for you." He lifted a pack of Winstons from his grimy shirt pocket, flipped open a Zippo, and lit a cigarette. He spoke as he blew out smoke. "Okay, here's the situation. The PAVN, NVA and the Cong have had a stranglehold on us since 21 January. Garrison's cut off. No exit. Now we're taking it back. Look around. Our B-52s are bombing the holy bejesus out of these mountains. Those damn gooks are persistent sons-abitches, hardy as beechnuts. But we're dug in, and we're not leaving. It's almost over."

A Marine captain called into the bunker. "Okay Jenkins, ready or not—"

"And away we go," David said.

"Keep your head down," the colonel barked, eyeing her with a sidelong glance.

They scrambled between bunkers over a surreal landscape. No defined front lines anywhere. Random gunfire arced between hilltops across the red, scarred soil of bombed-out valleys and cratered mountain flanks. Helicopters filled the air like flocks of migrating birds, hovering above the ground while soldiers jumped out, rifles in the air, and then took on wounded. Ellie's motor drive whirred as two Marines carried several injured men in a tarp to a helicopter, slid them in through the open door, and returned for more. She noted the urgency and desperation in their hotfooting it to load the injured so they themselves would avoid being wounded.

Just beneath the brow of a scorched hill, a missile launcher poked its snout toward enemy positions. Hundreds of missiles lay in a sloping field like sea lions lounging on a beach. Ellie high-stepped over the giant projectiles and photographed the tag-team of bare-chested, sweating grunts as they hoisted shells from the dirt and hucked them up to the launcher.

It was loud, dangerous, and smelly; flies were thick.

Her antennae quivered as she moved around, surrounded by continuous battle and the stench of charred earth. She leaned her camera into the faces of the fighters trying to capture the desolation. Some fear-crouching, some teeth-baring, mostly combat-weary men.

David pointed and motioned for her to hustle back to the command bunker, where he handed her a can of fruit cocktail. "Sweetest part of a field-ration packet. Let's sit."

She shouted in David's ear. "What kind of strategic significance does Khesanh hold? I mean, what is this battle for? King of the hill?"

"One of Westmoreland's brilliant ideas," he shouted back. "The man never met a skirmish he couldn't turn into a full-blown battle. Response from the military brass in Washington is to hurl more and more bombs and obliterate the opposition, even though it's done nothing to improve our position."

"So, you don't know why this fight is happening and countless lives are ending? That we're killing not only people but the land as well? Could it be a matter of saving face in the Orient?"

David squinted at her. "You may be too wise for your own good, darlin'."

"This is a completely different chapter of war than the embassy attack or Cholon or even that fateful patrol I went on with Nick." She looked down at the fruit cocktail, no appetite.

"I've been in this war long enough to grasp the fruitless nature of the fight. Military men heaving to the rules, rushing blindly into battle, as if victory is a simple matter of throwing enough firepower at the problem." He huffed. "On both sides."

Ellie bobbed her head. "It's a hard line to walk between fear and indifference. I'm learning to shift to a gear where I can focus on the war without becoming emotional about it."

"Amen to that," David said, "but that's the identical line the Marines walk. Look at them. Their eyes are vacant, their skin tattooed by the red clay dust. Fear is their constant companion. They're inured to death."

She eyed the fruit cocktail and took a tentative bite. "It's actually okay."

Night fell hard. Tracers flew like comet trails in the sky. The ground was unyielding and the air heavy and cold. Despite the repetition of shoot, reload, shoot, and the futility of the situation, Ellie was hungry for more action. Maybe it was the aroma of gunpowder that gave her a boost. She groaned at her sick humor. Still, she was grateful to be alive, especially after the wild beating Nick had dealt her that brought her a weird sense of perspective on her life. She dozed fitfully through the night, her sleep punctuated with questions David raised. She hoped she would never take death or fear for granted.

In the eerie predawn light, it was more of the same red clouds of dust. Chinooks and Hueys dropped fresh troops and took away wounded and dead. Claustrophobic heat. The aches and pain of her head and face were waning. She was too jacked up to feel hunger, but David insisted she eat to keep her strength up.

As she munched what passed for food, she listened to Colonel Raynor arguing on the radio with the base commander, who was squawking for a situation report in advance of an airstrike. In exasperation, the CO flung the radio back to its operator. "You," he barked to the radioman and a lieutenant, "come with me."

"What's going on?" Ellie asked.

"Observation post. Top of the hill."

Ellie jumped up and tugged the CO's shirtsleeve. "Colonel, let me go with you." She lowered her helmet onto her head with a wince she couldn't hide.

He looked at her like she was crazy. "Suit yourself, little

lady, it's your life." He frowned at her as he made his way out of the bunker, accompanied by his men. Ellie glanced back at David.

"Come on." She scurried after Raynor. David hustled to catch up. Single file, they followed a path that curved up the hill, ending at yet another sandbag bunker. This one was smaller and provided less protection. A single Marine hunkered there patrolling the ridges with his binoculars. He shook his head, indicating he saw no movement.

The post was exposed to the scarred hills but had a panoramic view. With binoculars to their eyes, Raynor and his lieutenant scanned the mountainscape while the operator crouched next to his radio set. Ellie got a shot of them in silhouette, perched like great blue herons on the skyline. They were seeking Front troop movement, any concentration of communist fighters, so the colonel could call in coordinates for the airstrike, but action had decreased somewhat, according to the spotter.

Raynor's head whipped around when a sudden mortar strike landed several hundred yards away. He pointed and shouted out coordinates to the radioman who repeated them into his transmitter.

As she panned her Nikon, Ellie spotted movement just below the rim of an adjacent hill. A handful of NVA were lit by the slanted early morning sunbeams, almost camouflaged by foliage. Like bushes swaying in the wind, except the air was still. A subtle motion alerted her. She raised her camera back up to her eye and focused on the lead man. He raised a long tubular weapon to his shoulder and aimed it at the US officers standing tall against the murky sky.

$\sim$

DAVID HEARD Ellie scream a warning as VC rockets screamed. He saw her launch herself into two of the men, knocking them down. David threw himself to the ground. Ellie was thrown as the lieutenant went down. The post crumbled in on the sentinel from multiple explosions. Stunned, Raynor called for medics.

"*Ellie!*" David screeched. He scrambled to her side. "Ellie, can you hear me?" She was on her back, mouth open, one arm stretched forward and the other back, one leg bent at the knee, the other underneath her body. He felt for a pulse.

49

Pasquale Romolino had fond memories of growing up in his large, close, loving family on the mountainous island of Corsica that floated in the cobalt Mediterranean Sea. Like Vietnam, Corsica had hosted marauding influences over the centuries. Its language might have been French since the eighteenth century, but its culture was Italian, and Romo had been raised to embrace the social code of *vendetta,* which required vengeance in blood for anyone who wronged the family honor.

Ellie was his family.

She had been wronged, assaulted physically and mentally.

She had a fighting spirit, something he recognized from his own rehabilitation experience during the second World War. It was part of their bond. Through the force of sheer will, they could accomplish anything.

He was consumed by the injustice of Jalbert's betrayal and Burrows' battering abuse of her.

Romo entered a small office on rue Paul Blanchy in a congested district of Saigon. The air was blue with cigarette smoke. He sucked in its aroma as if it were sustenance for his very being.

"*Bonjour, mes gentilshommes,*" he said to the two men sitting at a partners' desk.

The men rose out of their chairs. High-strung and wiry, Emile Basti grasped Romo's hand and pumped it until Romo's shoulder ached.

Jacques Lescan scooted around the desk and kissed Romo's cheeks. "Pasquale, what brings you here? It has been too long."

Romo chortled. "*Oui,* to see you two reminds me of days long past when we were fearless and rash."

"Exciting times." Lescan retrieved a bottle of cognac from the credenza and poured the deep golden liquid into three glasses. "This calls for a toast." He thrust the tumblers into waiting hands.

The three men raised their glasses and toasted in unison. "*Vive la morte, vive la guerre, vive le sacre mercenaire.*" Their foreign legion salute.

"Emile, Jacques," Romo said in a somber tone, "I regret that my reason for seeking you is no more elegant than the simple collection of a debt." He lifted a folded piece of paper from his inside jacket pocket and placed it in Basti's hand. He said nothing; the letter would speak for him. A heinous note in which Jalbert both justified his collusion and theft and guaranteed payment for Romo's destroyed airplane and his fee for the Laos operation. He had no need to parade Jalbert's betrayal; these men were no strangers to the Corsican *vendetta.*

Basti unfolded the letter, read, frowned, and passed it to Lescan.

Thunderclouds gathered on Lescan's face. "I thought it might have been you whom Jippie contracted for the job. It seems he failed in his mission. The article written by his journalist has caused heated response among the Americans."

The joy in seeing an old friend vanished from Lescan's eyes, and his expression turned dour in his pudgy face.

"Forgive my reaction, Pasquale, we certainly drape no blame on your shoulders. Jippie may not have involved us in any way, as indeed he promised, but we are not at ease with the situation," Lescan continued. "Above all, it will have turned out to be a costly operation, especially after you are paid." Lescan shook the letter in his hand. "Is this figure scratched on the bottom of the page the debt of which this letter speaks?"

"*Oui.*"

While Lescan took a large black checkbook out of the desk and wrote a check, Romo helped himself to another cognac. He threw it back, winced as it burned down his gullet, and placed the tumbler on the desk. "What action might you take if I expose Jippie in his attempt to discredit the Americans?"

Basti stiffened and stared at Romo for a minute then he, too, reached for another cognac. "We had a pact with Jippie. If there were any chance of a connection to the Black Box Organization, we would disown him and confiscate his assets. He agreed to these terms."

Romo smiled. "You are suggesting you might like to distance yourself from Jippie?"

Lescan tore out the check and handed it to Romo. "It is unfortunate he has become a liability."

"In that case," Romo said, "I will relieve you of that liability. I have photos that were taken in Laos of Jippie and the journalist who wrote the blasphemous article. They will somehow appear on the desk of an American agent; there are many such people working under diplomatic cover in the Americans' Saigon Embassy. There is no telling what might happen to René Jalbert."

A look passed between Lescan and Basti. Both nodded slightly.

50

Muffled voices penetrated Ellie's delirium. They reached her from a great distance, as if trying to squeeze through the eye of a needle in the center of her brain.

The voices grew louder. They resonated with familiarity. The deep, raucous bass notes of Ben Stryker's gunfire speech. She smelled his English Leather aftershave, as strong and outspoken as he was. Excitable, ardent. David Jenkins's voice was counterpoint. Musical and soft, between tenor and baritone. His soothing Southern accent sounded like the soft rustle of leaves.

A deep contentment spread through her body.

She pried her eyes open and saw the two men standing over her, blinking like owls. Somewhere beneath the fog, pain lurked in every punished muscle. She heard distant beeping, the artificial hush, and antiseptic reek of a hospital. Hospital?

"She's awake. Ellie?" Ben's voice was a whisper booming through a cotton ball.

David's hand curled around hers. "I'm happy as a locust in a cottonfield to see you awake, darlin'."

"What? Where the fuck am I?"

"Ever the wordsmith," cracked Ben.

"Welcome to the University of Colorado Hospital," said David.

"How—?" Ellie was confused as hell, peering around at the row of empty, crisp-white-sheeted beds in the large room. Only one other patient, two beds away.

"What's the last thing you remember?" David asked.

"Uh—" She cast her mind back. To where? *Right. Got it.* "Jumping out of a Chinook?"

"Very good. You and I flew up to cover the Marine relief operation in Khesanh. Do you remember any of that?"

Ellie tried to clear the murk clouding her brain and her ears. She looked up at David, not sure why she was so happy to see him there with her. "Nuh-uh."

Julian Duffy stepped between her two admirers, placed his hands on her cheeks, and kissed her forehead. "I'm so relieved —" He gasped and stepped back, unable to go on.

"Uncle Julian," she managed to squeak.

David filled the void. "We went with the CO, Colonel Raynor, and two of his men to the post near the command bunker. You must have seen or sensed something bad was about to go down because you screamed and knocked the men to the ground just as RPGs tore into the post. You saved three lives."

Ellie gaped at David and cleared her throat. "My God, but where were you when this happened?"

"I flopped on my belly when you threw yourself at them. Rockets zipped right over me. You saved my sorry butt, too. If you hadn't made that sudden charge and yelled, one of them would've taken my fool head off."

"Quite a time you've had, Ellie," Ben interjected. You couldn't buy a ticket for these rides at Coney Island. You've gone from interviewer to war correspondent to war hero." He held up two fingers in the peace sign.

"The force of the blast bucked you up into the air and landed you harder than a bag of hogs," David continued. "Punctured lung and eardrums, shrapnel tattooed all over your back, dislocated hip, not to mention concussion. And a couple of bruised vertebrae from landing on your camera. You've been in shock." He squinted into her eyes. "You were hit with a force that normally kills people. That's how strong you are."

"And you should see the camera!" Ben said.

"You'd think I'd remember something that dramatic. Did I get any pictures?"

"I'll say." David squeezed her hand. "And here's the thing. First you were flown to a medical facility just south of the DMZ where they stabilized you. Those docs are miracle workers. Amazing, considering the flow of wounded is never-ending. They treat them fast and send them back to the front. Colonel Raynor was so grateful to you he pulled some military strings and arranged for you to be flown here."

"Who—" Ellie couldn't keep her eyes open. She drifted off.

DAVID LOOKED at Ellie fondly as Ben launched into one of his trademark blathers. "Cheap bastards. The least they could do is give her a medal for bravery—"

"The military doesn't give medals to civilians," David said.

"I'm glad she's stateside, David. I'll take it from here."

"I know she'll be in good hands with you and Sarah," Julian said, still in a state of shock. "Keep me posted."

Ben rested his hand on David's shoulder. "I know how much you'd like to stay, but I'm sure you need to get back to Saigon."

"I'm sorry I had to pull you away from Sarah."

"Don't give that another thought. Sarah's a saint. She's got several weeks before she delivers. And don't worry about Ellie. I'll take her home with me. Got a plane standing by. She'll have every luxury while she recuperates. Don't worry about her. I'll keep you posted."

"She's been through so much. One gutsy lady. She'll come around like gangbusters, no question." He handed Ben a small, tattered notebook. "These are my notes from Khesanh. Maybe they'll goose her memory into gear. As soon as she's up to it, please give it to her and tell her UPI has promised her a byline for her story. A kind of Marines-are-taking-care-of-business-in-the-jungle piece, which could counter what I hear will come out soon about the massacre at My Lai."

"My Lai? Haven't heard," Ben said.

"Hamlet not far from Khesanh, smack dab in the middle of Vietcong-controlled territory. I don't know the details, but it sounds like a mess of Army soldiers went nuts and slaughtered a slew of unarmed villagers."

"Jaysus, Mary, and Joseph. God damn." Ben tucked the small notebook in his shirt pocket and patted it.

"I'm leaving her camera bag with you, with all the negatives, prints, and contact sheets Jalbert didn't steal. Even those she stashed under her mattress, not to mention her dinged-up Nikon. I think it can be straightened out." David extended his hand. Ben took it in both of his burly mitts, and they shook.

"I'd better get going, catch a flight back to the war," David said with reluctance. Julian leaned over and kissed Ellie's forehead. He and David left together.

～

WHEN Ellie and Ben landed in Aspen from Denver a few days later, Sarah tucked her into the big, cozy bed in their guest suite on the lower level of the house.

Peace wrapped its arms around her bruised body and muddled mind. She gazed through large windows that looked out on the snow-clad Elk Range across the Roaring Fork Valley. She exhaled, as though she'd been holding her breath since leaving Denver. Even though she'd never been there before, Aspen was homey. And so quiet. No mortar fire, no helicopter rotors.

She was drained to the bone. From her quilted roost, she relaxed and watched the sun ride across the breath-catching vista. Sarah encouraged her to lean into the comfort and allow the memories to gradually filter back into her brain. Strangely enough, she found Sarah's enormous belly a positive, optimistic sign that the future would be bright.

Over the next couple of weeks, she slept a lot, and, as she weaned herself off pain medications, the cottony sensation in her head began to clear. Once she was able, she and Sarah developed some of her film, and Ellie sifted through her proofs. Although her thoughts knotted up whenever she tried to remember Khesanh, partial memories came back as flashes of light, and, as time passed, she was able to gather disparate details into a cohesive recollection. Something deep in her brain tickled. She didn't know what it was, and she hoped it would work its way into her consciousness soon. She enjoyed the look of joy on Ben's face when she told him she'd met an old acquaintance of his who'd become her guardian angel. He'd slapped his knee and bellowed, "That old whipper-snapper Romo!"

With endless days stretching before her, she had time to think. It was one thing to heal her body, another thing entirely to resolve her emotional wounds. She called on her journalist's objectivity as she reconstructed her life since the fateful day Nick had entered the picture at Tan Son Nhut and scrambled it all to hell. What a trip. How could someone know if a man had abuse lurking in the bowels of his character? She'd been blindsided. Had it really been only four months? Hadn't he been deported? He was gone now, drop-kicked out of her life. Somehow, the cloud of opacity in the periphery of her mind had to do with Nick. If only Romo were there. He understood. It would be much easier if he were around. Meanwhile, she would focus on the physical, leave the emotional for later.

One morning in the middle of May, she headed for the breakfast room, still relying on a ski-pole cane for stability with her hip. Bright sunlight splashed through the stained-glass windows, casting prisms onto the table. Sarah brought plates of French toast and bacon to the table. She poured coffee.

"How are you still able to move, Sarah?" Ellie patted her belly.

"Not easy, that's for sure, but the end product will be worth it. Not far off now. It's got to be a boy, the way he kicks."

Ben, for whom nothing took precedence over the food in front of him, doused his plate in maple syrup. Then he paused and looked guiltily at Sarah and Ellie. He slid the pitcher to the center of the table.

"Sound the trumpets!" Ben sang once he swallowed a mouthful. "Got some good news for you, Ellie. Been waiting till you felt better, and that smile on your face this morning tells me you are tip-top sharp." He stuffed a huge syrupy bite into his mouth. As he swiped his napkin across his chin, he reached for a small notebook on the table beside his plate and handed it to her. "This is from Jenkins. His notes on your heroic visit to the battleground at Khesanh. He wants you to write the story from your perspective. Photos, too. UPI is waiting for them. There's a byline in it for you."

"I hope you don't mind, Ellie," Sarah said, "but I took the liberty of printing your film from the Khesanh proofs. You got some phenomenal images."

"I can't wait to see them."

Ellie held the rumpled notebook to her chest and tried to

keep tears at bay. "A byline. Oh, my heart. Wow," she managed. Salve for her wounds. "Gawd, I wish Romo were here." She bit off the end of a piece of bacon. "Do you know where he is? I haven't seen or heard from him since I left for Khesanh with David. Is he okay?"

"I'm sorry, honey, I have no idea," Ben said gently. I didn't even know he was in the picture until you told me."

51

———————

For more years than he could count, Romo had fit in the cockpits of his beloved single-engine prop planes like a hand in a silk glove. Anxiety tracked through his bloodstream whenever he was forced to be a passenger on a big jet airliner.

Nonetheless, he boarded one for a flight from Saigon to Paris. He had serious business.

Wielding one of the canes Ellie had given him, he strolled into the Luxembourg Gardens in the Sixth Arrondissement, just south of the Louvre. Hardly any pain today from that nerve damage he'd sustained in both legs back in World War II, which had been aggravated in the harsh landing near Vientiane. He chose a green slatted-metal chair among a scatter of chairs along a pebbled garden walkway. He parked himself, set the cane down beside him, slid a Caribbean Airlines tote bag off his shoulder, and placed it between his feet. He soaked in the pleasant atmosphere, gazing at the seventeenth century grand stone Palais de Luxembourg.

A man with the stiff gait of someone who spent too much time sitting at a desk approached Romo, a JAL tote bag slung over his shoulder. Same string-bean guy Romo remembered, but with a paunch and hair that was trying to escape his head. Same darting eyes. *Oui, definitely JR.* Romo's mood brightened as the man lowered himself onto a nearby chair.

Jack "JR" Robinson still wore his uneasiness like an ill-fitting suit; the fourteen intervening years since they'd seen each other had done little to erase it. Probably served him well in his post as deputy information liaison officer.

"I appreciate you taking time out of your day to meet with me," Romo said.

JR casually looked around as if he were admiring the gardens then brought his focus to Romo. "May I address you as 'old friend'?"

The request drew a smile from Romo. "Yes, my old friend. It is good to see you. We might have been friends for a day or two, but trauma binds us firmly."

"Absolutely. Many years ago, I told you I owed you a debt for saving my life. It's a debt I do not shirk, Pasquale."

The comment signaled to Romo that business must be expeditious. He studied JR for a moment before speaking. "When I flew you into Dienbienphu, I suspected you were not a journalist. *Alors*, recently, I heard through the grapevine that you're stationed at the US embassy here. When I called you last week, I hinted about a matter having to do with the nefarious Nick Burrows."

"Go on." JR ran his fingers down his tie and smoothed it against his belly.

"You see, I was in Saigon when the South Vietnamese arrested him. Then the embassy had him deported." Romo stole a glance at JR, who was staring straight ahead. "I assume Monsieur Burrows is being punished for his scandalous accusations against the CIA. What I don't understand is why you chose deportation over allowing him to fester in a Vietnamese prison."

"My apologies for delaying our meeting. It took a day to gather some highly classified information. What's this Burrows to you?"

Romo stiffened. His voice turned cold. "He has defamed a member of my family. The Corsican code of honor demands the head of the family repay such a foul deed in blood."

"In blood you say? Am I hearing vendetta?"

"Now that the ice is broken, so to speak, please to answer my question. Why not let Burrows rot in a Saigon jail?"

Romo watched JR gaze into the reflecting pools. "We made up a charge about heroin sales and used the South Viets to find him," Robinson said, giving weight to each word. "We couldn't afford our own manhunt. That would have been tantamount to admitting to the charges he leveled in his article."

"You kept this from his uncle?"

Robinson sideswiped a glance at Romo. "Not exactly. Cowardice seems to run in the family."

Romo stretched his left leg on the ground in front of him while digesting JR's cryptic response.

"*Eh bien*, I must now inquire if your organization plans to perform a dark mission related to the previously mentioned individual, which might compromise your regular operatives?"

JR stared straight ahead. "Only if one who is capable comes to the fore. You see, the information Burrows has is damaging to our efforts in Southeast Asia. We fear he may find another outlet for his accusations. We cannot allow this."

"Ah, I see." Romo clasped his hands together. This portended better than he had dared hope. "One favor deserves a reciprocal favor. I offer my services, free of charge, to take on this mission for you. All I need is the location of the principal."

JR scrutinized Romo as if trying to determine his reliability. "We didn't want this action to take place in Saigon, so we sent him to the US, although any incident in the states will be highly scrutinized. You understand it must absolutely appear that he caused his own demise."

JR leaned forward, resting his arms on his legs. "You should know he's heavily addicted to opiates," he said, tilting his head toward Romo. "Could be useful. If I can get this approved, we'll pay your operating expenses, since it's already been budgeted."

"If you insist." Romo smirked.

"I do."

"Do you have any suggestions for me since American soil is off limits?"

"Only one," JR said. "Research Mexico."

"Mexico?"

"Yes. Their investigative methods are quite moderate when it concerns foreigners; they're not really interested in the dross of visitors." JR flashed a smile of conspiracy. "I leave the extent of punishment to your discretion. It may go to the extreme if you wish, or not. But his ability to reveal his knowledge of our involvement in assisting our allies in their merchandising program must not reach fruition. *Comprenez-vous?*"

"*Oui, compris.*"

"Do you know anyone in Mexico?"

Romo searched his memory for past contacts. "Some years back, the laboratories in Marseilles were producing high-grade product when a man from a Mexican syndicate came to study the French methods of refining, since their own product was low grade. I was assigned by the Black Box Organization to guide him through the process. His name was Guzman. *Oui,* Arellano Guzman."

"Find him. He could be useful to you."

"*Mon Dieu,* this was twenty years ago," Romo said. "I hope he's still alive. He was, how you say, no spring chicken when I met him."

"It's a place to start, Pasquale."

Romo rubbed his chin and narrowed his eyes at JR.

JR rose to leave, paused, and bent over to whisper in Romo's ear. "I must get approval. Check with your hotel desk in one hour. Confirmation will signal lunch at *Le Bon Georges* at two o'clock. Negative means sorry, cannot meet for lunch."

"Do you know the exact location of Burrows?" Romo asked as JR strolled away.

JR responded over his shoulder. "Yes, we're following his every move. If we have confirmation, I will get you his location."

52

The snow had melted off Aspen's Bell Mountain, signaling the onset of gardening season. Memorial Day brought a shocking blue-sky day, a perfect time for Ellie to honor her reconstituted memory by hiking to the top of Red Mountain above the Stryker home and beyond, as far up Hunter Creek as retreating snow would allow. Besides, she liked leaving the Strykers and their three-week-old baby boy, Liam, to themselves without getting in the way.

She breathed in deep lungfuls of fresh, sharp air. Tentative breezes still redolent with winter's waning chill rode over her skin, yet she could almost hear the grasses and brush springing back to vertical. Holding ski poles Sarah had loaned her, she spread her arms in the bracing alpine air and twirled. What a switch from the suffocating heat and humidity of Southeast Asia.

Nothing was ever perfect. She'd worked hard at purging Nick from her system, but balance still eluded her. Why was it so hard to admit she'd been hoodwinked? As she placed one hiking boot-shod foot in front of the other, an aura like the one that signals a migraine wavered at the edges of her vision.

She stopped, started to shake. Her muscles went weak. She sank into the grasses alongside the trail. The world was spinning.

"Hoodwinked?" she shouted to the mountain peaks. "Try having the daylights beaten out of you and being left for dead. That motherfucker!" The memory that had been hiding swam into her consciousness. She saw herself being battered by Nick in that Saigon apartment. She watched the memory, as if it were a movie, in horror, living it anew. She covered her eyes.

Nick didn't care a hoot about me. He was so emotionally crippled by his own demons. How did I miss the signs? Jesus H. Christ, I am so lucky to be alive. No wonder I buried this in my subconscious. I was denying abuse? Easier to forgive than moving away, or admitting failure? Not my fault, goddammit.

She lay back and gazed at the clouds crossing the sky, aware of her position on the rim of the earth. Presently she stood, brushed herself off, and continued hiking. High places and less oxygen made for clearer thinking.

When she descended the mountain and got back to the Stryker compound, she was fired up to write her article for UPI. Her Khesanh memories had rebounded, as vivid as the scream of the NVA's RPG. True or not, she liked to think it was *his* slight hesitation when the NVA soldier sighted her through his weapon that had saved her life. They'd shared a kind of silent humanity beyond the bounds of battle.

David's notes had provided the last pieces of her memory puzzle, and her photos were riveting. Ben gave her an office to work in, a perfect cubbyhole with a view of the Elk Range and plenty of space to lay out her photos. With her head full of details of Operation Pegasus, she started writing.

Constantly struck by contrasts, she compared the omnipresence of the red dust in the hills above Khesanh to the red soil of the mountains surrounding Aspen. The battle surrounded her—the deafening noise, helicopter blades beating their ominous rhythm, the dust that singed the humid air, the mingled odors of sweat, gunpowder, disturbed earth, and death. She would adapt her telephoto technique into her writing, bringing this all closer to readers in a personal way.

Early summer breezes wafted through the open door as she tapped away on a blue Selectric. She rediscovered the rush of disappearing into the story. As she wrote, the tendrils of memory vined themselves around her thoughts and brought the whole episode to life beneath her fingers.

She'd been cleansed, whole, like the sun coming up over the serrated edge of the mountains or popping out of a tropical ocean, turning the sand coral, aqua waves lapping the shore. That was how good it was to write. All the cells in her body were in alignment. If being close to war brought amazing focus and lifted her out of her own life, writing the story brought her back to center.

She gathered the pages together and handed them to Ben to read, hoping for a less violent reaction than Jalbert's.

She needn't have worried.

That evening he, Sarah, and Ellie enjoyed cocktails in the hot tub. Liam was close by in the cabaña with the nanny.

"Ahh, don't you know the saints are all up and doing their dance of joy," Ben sang in his acquired Irish brogue. He reached for his vodka and downed a swallow. He went on, his voice like gunfire. "You have such a grasp, beyond your age and experience, uncanny really. And your journalistic voice enhances the rawness, doesn't coddle the reader. A convincing, terrifying look at the idiocy of this war. Such an innate grasp of moral clarity and the conundrum of being a soldier. Never lose this ability to untie the knots and straighten out confusion for a reader."

Ben sat tall, gazing fondly at Ellie. "We'll wire both text and photos to David tomorrow."

"High praise from the master of the universe," Sarah

quipped. "You also drive the message home with your unique lens work, Ellie. The images are so strong, they're almost blinding."

Ellie flushed. "Now, all we need is for people to read it."

"If we wrote just for our readers, we'd die from frustration," Ben said. "Take it from me, we write from compulsion. You tell the best story you can, and then it can go either way. If it has an audience, great. If it doesn't, it's their loss. Sometimes it feels like I'm shouting my message from a mountaintop, and no one hears it down in the valley."

"You're so full of yourself, Stryker," Sarah gwaffed.

"I see myself as a piece of *Kintsugi,* Ellie said. "It's the Japanese process of repairing ceramic bowls that have cracked or broken by filling the cracks with gold, which gives them new life."

53

———————

Romo landed in Culiacan, the lively capital city of the state of Sinaloa, which had been a hub for the export of narcotics to the United States since the 1950s. It took him a while to locate his old friend Arellano Guzman after the meeting with JR.

A taxi dropped him in the neighborhood of Tierra Blanca, where a formidable iron gate announced Guzman's ostentatious home. Behind the estate's high stone wall, armed guards patrolled with snarling dogs.

"Pasquale Romolino! However did you find me?" Guzman exclaimed in Spanish as his visitor was escorted out to a wide veranda. He motioned to the guard, who turned crisply and marched away. "You look just the same, maybe a few more wrinkles if that is even possible."

Guzman stood five feet four inches and had the build of a pit bull with hulking shoulders and a neck as thick as a fire hydrant. Beside him, Romo was a tall man. A slight stoop in Guzman's posture hinted at his age of seventy-one years. His black-framed glasses did little to diffuse his penetrating stare, which he could use to great effect with his enemies, although Romo himself had never been susceptible.

"As with you, maybe a soupçon less scrawny." Romo patted his belly. Speaking an awkward mix of French and Spanish and English, thinking of the inexperienced man he'd known, whom age had now carved down to almost gaunt, and whose thick hair was more salt than pepper. Romo noted the expensive gabardine trousers and cashmere sportscoat. "Time has been good to us both."

"Please take a load off those legs, my friend," Guzman said, gesturing to an ornate wrought iron table and chairs. "Since your Spanish is as rusty as an old iron pot, we speak English."

"I do not wish to bore you with trite details," Romo said, "however, I can tell you that if you are concerned about security, please to have no fears, my tread is light."

"But still," Guzman said as he poured two glasses of lemonade and handed one to Romo, "I take extreme precautions. One can never be too safe."

Romo's gaze roved around the grounds that spread out beneath them. "I have to be honest with you, Arellano, I asked at the post office, and they gave me your address."

After a suspenseful moment, both men laughed.

"Do you know, Pasquale, I have retired from the business unscathed, praise be to La Santa Muerte—she is the destiny of life." He crossed himself.

"No, I did not know. So why all the security?"

"One never knows who holds the grudges."

"Congratulations, Arellano. I had a sense about you when we first met, even though you were tight-lipped about your plans. I felt then, my friend, that you were different than those I knew in the trade who were as hungry as starving wolves. In you, I saw a patient man who approached your venture in a civilized manner and respected your competitors rather than warring with them. Was this not true?"

"As fate would have it, when I returned with the valuable information and techniques you shared with me, I was given the responsibility of hiring chemists and seeing to the welfare of the production facilities."

"You were the guard dog, so to speak?"

"Well put, *amigo*. However, it did not take long for El Patron to realize I had neither taste nor tolerance for blood and lacked the qualities required for my assignment."

"So, you were fired?"

"In a manner of speaking. He recognized my academic background and sent me to Mexico City to complete law school. So, I became '*El Abogado,*' the lawyer for the Federacion."

Guzman sipped his lemonade. "The years have been good to me. Now I have retired. Since truth is not often a commodity in this business, and rivals can carry grievances, I retain the security. So far, I have been left alone."

"Let us hope it remains this way, my friend."

"As it is, everyone knows how to find me, even my enemies, whoever they may be."

"So, you are saying that someone from your past might—"

Guzman shrugged, held up his hands, diamond-and-ruby-studded gold rings glinting on both pinkies. "You never know. It's the life I chose, and I live with it. It could change at any moment."

Romo waved his arm at the lavishly furnished house. Its pale-coral stucco glowed in the sunlight like a many-tiered cake. The main house, pool, and outbuildings were ringed by expansive green lawns. "Your security is an affordable expense, I can see."

"Enough of this chatter. What can I do for one who showed me much respect in my innocence?"

"Pardon, Arellano, I don't know if you can help me, but I must ask."

Guzman frowned at Romo. "Pasquale, no favor is too big between friends. And if it is perhaps beyond my capacity, rest assured, I will know someone who can fulfill your needs."

"My request is serious. It is one of vengeance. You must know I will not be offended if you refuse me."

"Do not concern yourself, Pasquale. That was one of my specialties."

"Indeed, I have come to the right man. Even though it has been many years, you are a true friend." Romo reached for his lemonade and proceeded to outline his purpose in graphic detail.

"Ah, here he is now," Guzman said as a young man strode outside and joined them. About thirty-five, handsome beyond belief, an Antonio Banderas. A gazelle in a three-piece suit. "Pasquale Romolino, meet my son, Luis."

Romo stood and extended his hand. Luis shook it.

"Don't let his cultured appearance fool you, Romo. Luis is the most capable man I've ever known. He is so sharp, he would have increased our business a hundredfold, but he has never crossed the line into my former enterprise. Luis is a banker and economic consultant. I believe we can trust him to make the arrangements for your mission."

"I do not mean to be disrespectful, but how can a banker assist with what I have in mind?"

"Ah, Pasquale, Luis is a strategist, a student of Sun Tsu's *Art of War*. Investing other people's money takes a skill similar to warfare. Also, my friend, the fact that I am retired does not mean I have lost all my contacts." Guzman leaned in toward Romo. "After dinner, you will inform Luis of your requirements. He will design a plan and orchestrate a successful result."

Romo bowed to both men.

"It is an honor to meet you, Señor Romolino," Luis said in perfect, unaccented English.

Guzman raised his glass to Romo. "Such a shame we lost touch after Marseilles. Later, I discovered it was you who suggested that an arm of the Corsican syndicate reaching closer to North America could be to their benefit and ours."

He twirled the ice in his lemonade. "Without your recommendation"—Guzman waved his arm around his living room — "none of this would have been possible."

Romo shifted in his seat, about to speak.

"Allow me to finish, Pasquale. Until I met you, I had only one point of reference. To be successful, I had to be a ruthless thug, even though it was a contradiction to my personality. You showed me how to be patient, to slowly build my empire to the satisfaction of a Corsican. As improbable as it seems, I accomplished this in the most sophisticated manner possible." He held up his hand to Romo, whose mouth hung open. "Now it is time for ..." He lapsed into Spanish as he turned to his son. "*Como se dice reciprocidad?*"

"Reciprocity," Luis said.

"Yes, Pasquale, it is time for reciprocity."

"Please excuse me," Luis said. "I must return to work. I'll see you at dinner."

They watched him walk into the house. "Family is precious," Romo said, turning to Guzman. "You are so very privileged."

The sun arced high overhead, eventually dropping below the horizon in a fiery display, as they transitioned from lemonade to tequila. As darkness claimed the last of the light, Guzman's butler/bodyguard returned. Guzman stood. "We will dine now. My cooks have prepared for you a superb meal."

Time took on a different dimension, without bounds, and Romo relaxed into the evening, having turned over the strategizing of his vendetta to Luis. With a glass of premium Añejo tequila, he exhaled cigar smoke and held the aromatic cigar aloft.

Guzman ensconced Romo in his guest cottage. "You stay here and relax, unwind." Two days later, Luis came to him and unveiled his plans for Nick Burrows.

Romo was astounded. "So soon? You have exceeded my expectations. You are truly an efficient organizer."

"Gracias, Señor Romo. "Because this Burrows is seriously addicted to opiates, my people can dangle the carrot in front of his addiction. It won't take much convincing to get him to drive deep into Mexico for a lucrative drug deal. We'll provide him with a car and money to trade for what he will think is marijuana. Who's to say what obstacles might present themselves to him and perhaps prevent him from crossing back over the border ever again?"

FOR THE TWO weeks it took to unroll "the project," Romo lounged near his cottage beside Guzman's Olympic-size swimming pool. Moving his legs in water was therapeutic. He would pull himself out of the pool, lie on his lounge chair until he was baked by the sun, and dive into the pool again, exhausting himself swimming laps. His legs had not felt so good in decades, and his heart almost burst with protective love for Ellie and the knowledge that she would now be able to live her life without the threat of that deceitful snake sinking his fangs into her.

He ended each afternoon joining Arellano for cigars and cognac. They relaxed under a red and white striped umbrella out on the wide veranda.

"I can assure you that your Burrows has disappeared. For good," Guzman said one evening. Champagne had appeared. "We toast to the success of this operation."

"I am not good with manners and small talk," Romo began, "but I wish to express my deep gratitude for all you have done."

"Not I. It was Luis's mastery. Not only is he highly skilled in his trade, but he can adapt his knowledge to any situation. A graduate of Harvard Business School, did I tell you that? I am very proud of my son. Not just anyone could arrange the journey for your Señor Burrows that landed the scoundrel in a notorious Mexican jail."

Romo couldn't keep his face from showing profound delight. "You should be proud. Your son is also quite a gentleman."

Romo snapped open his briefcase, brimming with American dollars.

Fire blazed in Arellano's eyes. "*Mierda*! Have you no shame? You insult me if you think I would accept payment from you. A favor between friends is a sacred gift. We are honored to have helped you accomplish your mission."

Romo was horrified to have insulted his friend. He opened his mouth to speak but nothing came out.

Guzman's anger vanished in a volley of laughter. He swept his arm around the grounds. "*Amigo*, surely you cannot believe I need the money."

Romo's eyebrows went up; he was still mute.

Guzman snorted. "Please, I do not wish to hurt your feelings, Pasquale, but as usual your behavior is, how the Americans say, way over the top, yet I know it is in good faith." He wrapped his arm around Romo's shoulders. "It is time to celebrate." The butler appeared, popped the Champagne cork, poured it into large flutes, and presented them to the two men.

"I did not mean to offend. I only wished to find an adequate way to thank you," Romo said, finding his voice again. He held up his glass to Guzman.

"Well then, I can provide the means for you to humble yourself." Guzman smirked. "You are the guest of honor for our feast. The women have been cooking for days. A few more days, and we'll be ready. I have planned this celebration to introduce you to the incredible team who accomplished this vendetta."

Romo wasn't about to give up. "Then, may we split this money among your team members?"

"You stubborn Corsican. We do not take your money. I accepted this challenge out of friendship, aided by members of my family. Family is everything, it's what gives life its salsa, *si*?"

"*Si, si si*," Romo agreed.

"Tell me, *amigo*, what was the reason behind this errand we have concluded?"

"I am surprised you did not ask before now."

"Reason was not necessary. It was simply your request to be fulfilled." Guzman guzzled his champagne.

Romo leveled a flat and open gaze at Guzman. "The man wronged my daughter."

"I did not know you had a daughter."

"Nor did I, until I met her."

"What is her name?" Guzman asked.

"Ellie, her name is Ellie," Romo said.

DURING THE FEW more days leading up to the feast, Romo rested and continued swimming laps.

Finally, a few afternoons later, enticing aromas wound themselves around his thoughts and tugged. His stomach growled.

"Hola, amigo," Guzman called to him over the railing of the veranda. "The feast begins!"

In the pool house, Romo changed into slacks, an open-collared shirt, and linen sport coat. He even added an ascot. This lifestyle suited him well, he thought. Tucking a pocket square in his breast pocket, he made his way up to the main house, where he found a gathering of people clustered around Arellano and Luis.

"Romo, *venga aqui*," Guzman said with hurry-up motions of his hand. "It is with great pleasure that I introduce you to the members of the most delightful and scandalous group of con artists ever assembled."

Romo looked around at the gathered people.

Guzman put his arm around a large woman in a tent dress. "First, I give you Cynthia Guzman, otherwise known as Caja Aguamala, who engineered your pigeon's journey deep into Mexico and led him into the dragon's mouth. She is my sister-in-law."

He then pointed to a big man with long arms. "Ernesto is my trusted bodyguard, and he provided protection for Cynthia. And no doubt cast a little fear for your pigeon. The Federale who arrested him and who could not be here today is Ernesto's cousin, Ramon."

He turned to a stunning woman with black hair and lavender eyes. "And none of this would have been possible without Ernesto's daughter Magdalena, who has a theater arts degree from the University of Southern California. She gave an award-winning performance in operating her puppet Nick and his addiction, driving him straight into the arms of the poisonous *Caja Aguamala*, which, you may not know, is the name for a lethal jellyfish."

"I am, to use an American term, blown away by the degree of complexity here," Romo said, flabbergasted.

"You can thank my son and his masterful strategizing talents." Guzman radiated pride as he gazed on each member of the team. "So, *amigo*, you approve of my family?"

"As you say, Arellano, family is everything. I am honored by your family's devotion and your hard work, for this could not have been easy."

Guzman shrugged. "It was an exercise to remind us that we

must keep our edges sharp. We cannot get soft. So, you see, we benefit as well." He raised a finger. "Forgive me, as long as we are rolling the credits, I must mention a former associate, Omar Fuentes, now of the infamous Sinaloa organization, who supplied all the goods that were necessary for this operation." Guzman raised his glass. "*Salud*, Omar. I wish you could be here."

Romo glanced around. Buckets of cerveza and champagne were parked on tables around the veranda. Huge platters over-flowed with delicious smelling foods—suckling pig and barbe-cued goat, rice and beans, soups, spicy grasshoppers, towers of hot tortillas. "This is quite the celebration. I am beyond grateful to you all. I salute you."

"And now we rejoice. Bring on the *tuba*," Guzman crowed.

Servers arrived with trays of cocktails. Arellano plucked a margarita glass and held it up. "Our regional drink, *tuba*. We ferment the juice from the coconut palm and flavor it with pineapple, lemon, and chili." He toasted, waiting until everyone had their glasses raised high. "To family, to friendship, to a job well done."

Romo joined in the hoots and *olés* that sounded around the small group. He smacked his lips at the taste of the strong, piquant cocktail and drained his glass.

"Now," said the magnanimous host, "we offer you foods of our region. Eat and drink to your heart's content, for tomorrow … tomorrow you will take your suitcase of money and buy yourself a shiny new airplane."

"How did you know I am without wings?"

"Ah-hah, loose Tequila talk has bitten your Corsican ass."

54

———

Was this the fucking Twilight Zone? Nick had been snatched from his life and flung into the shit-brown demoralizing dumpster of a federal prison in Iguala, Guerrero State. Vertigo whirled. He tried to reconstruct how this could have happened, from his uncomfortable ride from Saigon to Anchorage, to scrounging for drugs, and bumping into a gorgeous kewpie doll in San Diego who just happened to have what he needed to keep him straight, to his driving down to Mexico where obstacles turned lethal and landed him in jail. What a fucking cluster fuck. He ran his tongue over his chipped tooth and groaned.

Hopelessness settled over him like dust. The sun continued to come up, casting heat but no warmth and baking despair into his bones.

After months of festering incarceration, Nick showed the unmistakable stamp of a Mexican jail—hollow cheeks, angry bruises from daily fights, and open sores on his face and malnourished body. He was constantly harassed by inmates who thought all Americans were rich, but he had no currency with which to buy privileges. Neither had he been given a phone call, lawyer, or trial date. The most bitter pill he had to swallow was that no one, like no one, aside from his cellmates and the warden, knew of his predicament. Plus, nobody spoke fucking English in this pissant third-world shithole. Nothing he'd experienced in his life had prepared him for this. In much the same way children know their parents will save them from the disasters of childhood, so did he cling to the unrealistic expectation of release at any minute, even while his lifetime of entitlement gradually eroded into despair and then depression. He ground his jaw. *I've got to get out of here.*

Conditions were deplorable—almost non-existent sanitation, putrid water, and the fly-riddled slop they called food— and he'd been stripped of all human decency. Worst of all was the pervasive rank odor of filthy bodies, stale urine, and fermenting feces, not to mention his terminal dysentery.

He fantasized myriad possibilities that could lead to his release, but in reality, there was nothing he could do. He moldered among the murderers and habitual criminals, forced to face the fact that life had no value in this hellhole. So unfair. He did not belong there.

Without any way to communicate with the outside world, he gave up on ever breathing fresh air again. His mind tormented him with memories; they became waking hallucinations. And he ached for Ellie, whom he transformed from turncoat into his guardian angel. He resented being packed into this can of rancid sardines. Violent subhumans pushed at him from all sides. He could barely contain his outrage, but when he let it burst its bounds he was pissed on, raped, and beaten by cellmates. He spent much of his time curled in a protective fetal position.

"Oh great gods in heaven," he moaned to the rat that sniffed the floor near his face. "What have I done? Am I being punished for all the good I've done in my life?"

The rat raised its beady eyes at the sound of Nick's voice.

"Don't look at me like that. It's the truth," Nick spat.

He drifted from the harsh reality of his condition into delirium, where he was tormented by distorted images of his life.

"Anger is a disease. It festers and scars," he hissed at the rat, the only creature near him who understood what he was saying. Who had made that comment? Wasn't it Romo on that insane raft? Nick coughed on bile that hung in the back of his throat.

Hallucinations plagued him, twenty-six years of injustice.

Until he'd met Ellie, when his anger abated for a while but still steamed beneath the surface. She danced before his eyes, turning into a temptress, taunting him. The idea of love and hate spinning forever entwined choked off his heart and his very breath.

"Life is fucking unfair," he whined to the rodent. "I am lowered to this, am I? My only friend is a rat with privileges. *You're* free to roam as you please."

Clarity flashed. It was crippling. He saw that his rage had held him in a chokehold, a boa constrictor of a temper that had made him do awful things. He coughed. Suddenly he couldn't breathe. The air was being sucked out of the prison. Was this his karma? He could smell evergreens, feel the sudden shiver of cold winter air. He lost consciousness.

STEWING in this pot of skewed time, Nick spied a glimmer of hope when it appeared one morning or one afternoon, he didn't know which, like a shaft of sunlight on a dark, stormy day. The Mexican senorita who visited her Australian prisoner husband weekly agreed to smuggle letters out for Nick. He addressed his plea for money to Ellie in care of Ben Stryker in Aspen and prayed it would actually reach her, and she would come to his rescue. He wrote another to his Uncle Francis, who he assumed was at his post in Saigon, and a third to Jalbert in Vientiane.

He tried to keep track of time, counting ten days from the time the smuggled letters left the prison. He reasoned it could take another ten days for responses to come back. Who knew how long it would take for his uncle to receive his plea. He dreamed the messenger for his salvation was a white dove perched on Ellie's windowsill, patiently waiting for her to waken. In his reverie, he saw her rise, open the window, and take the precious item from the dove's beak.

He floated in his fantasy. It was the only way; reality just hollowed him out.

Throughout each week that passed, Nick clung to his last hope, sent off in three envelopes, and listened for the music of Ellie's voice to reach him.

~

OUTSIDE THE GUERRERO STATE PRISON, wind whirled dust devils into insane dervishes. Children played while their mothers waited to see spouses.

A gust of wind fussed with a swirl of papers. A girl squealed as she chased envelopes. She scooped them off the ground and dashed over to her mother, proudly presenting the spoils.

Her mother looked closely at the soiled, smudged envelopes. It was difficult to decipher the addresses since they were written in English, but she could tell one letter was meant to be delivered to a place called Colorado in America and the other to places she'd never heard of. APO Saigon and Vientiane.

She tore open the sealed envelopes, thinking they might contain money. No luck. Not even any stamps on them. She shrugged and threw them to the ground.

EPILOGUE
JUNE 1968

Ellie moved into a guest cabin at the far edge of the Strykers' property. It was snugged in a copse of aspen trees, the unique rustle of their leaves both comforted and sounded like applause. A welcome sanctuary, it held the peace she sought within its rough walls. Big comfy down-filled couch and weathered oak furnishings. Through the windowed front wall, she gazed out at unencumbered views of the Elk Mountains across the valley.

One afternoon, Sarah and Liam walked over from the big house with a basket of fruit and set it on Ellie's counter. "This is your special retreat," she said, taking Ellie by the shoulders and kissing her on the cheek. "Here you can focus on all the good things that lie ahead for you. You can restore your balance, find equilibrium."

Sarah released her and cradled her baby in his snuggly. "You're a champion, Ellie. We heard from David. UPI likes your piece so much, they're circulating your article and photos as a cover story. Well done."

"And," boomed Ben as he entered the cabin and rushed headlong into a speech, "you're going to set the world on fire."

He cast a glance at his wife and winked. "I'm just wondering if before you do that, you might like to join us for our book. Even though I've started the first draft, you bring an insight neither Sarah nor I have." He spread his arms wide. "Your perspective is unique." He peered into Ellie's eyes. "Of course, your name coupled with ours can do nothing but launch your career with fireworks. Your article is getting published in many, many papers. I was most impressed by your sidebar in which you tipped your hat to the journalists in the trenches."

"You helped me see we are each a cog in the wheel. I was only there for four months, and it was devastating. I have deep respect for the journalists who don't escape the war but dig down and find continuously renewing energy to translate it for the readers. I'm in awe of them. It's so important to be the eyes and ears of the general public. I understand that burning need to tell a story, a true story."

Sarah rolled her eyes. "Exactly so. That's what inspired Ben to write this important book. We three have each seen a different face of war, and together we can scale the mountains on the moon."

"Ach, the drama, Sarah."

"And this time we'd travel to Saigon *together?*" Ellie teased.

Ben laughed.

"I'm dizzied by your offer," she said. "You're going to have to give me some time to think it over."

AS DAWN POURED over the mountaintops the next morning, Ellie drove one of Stryker's Jeeps down from their Red Mountain home, through town, and across the valley to the Ute Trail. Good day for a hike. At the trailhead, a riot of pastel columbines, Colorado's state flower, greeted her, along with the rich aroma of pine needles warmed by sun. With each footstep on the series of switchbacks that corkscrewed up the eastern flank of Aspen Mountain, she gained spring in her step.

Such a sense of accomplishment in hiking the Ute Trail. She took off through the pines, zigzagging up the steep ridge. With every footfall, she shed the negative, as if molting a skin that no longer fit.

When she got to the top, she broke out of the trees onto a rocky pinnacle. It took her breath away to look down on the old mining town of Aspen, spread out so perfectly some thousand feet below her. The aspen leaves were beginning to catch the gold of autumn fire, a world on the verge of change, summer to fall. And her life as well. Optimism rose as she perched on the rocks for a few minutes, turning her face into the breezes that cleared her head. How free she felt without the specter of Nick's anger breathing hot on her neck.

As she inhaled into her diaphragm, emotions tumbleweeded. Whispers of the musical aspen leaves carried her away. She'd always been guided by her instincts, and now they rode free again. With each step she'd been soul searching to figure out why hesitation was her primary response to Stryker's job offer. No question it was a fabulous opportunity, and she could contribute a lot to the project, but it would mean staying in Aspen. Nothing wrong with that, except the yearning to be back on the edge raced through her blood.

"Yup, nothing like raw thrill," she exclaimed.

An image of Romo flashed in *déjà vu*. A brief image of a shiny plane. Then it was gone.

The sun darted behind a summer cloud. Ellie raised her head. She watched the clouds scooting through the blue, imagining each one held myriad possibilities. She could write a book on the Hmong people. In retrospect, it seemed prescient she had kept several film cans Jalbert hadn't found when he ransacked her room in Laos, photos she could use to illustrate such a book. Neither had he found the photos of Tan Son Nhut or Tet she'd stashed under the mattress in Saigon.

She jumped up, jogged back down the trail, and drove to her cabin. As she got out of the Jeep, the rich aroma of cigar smoke reached her nose. A man wearing an enormous grin waved at her from the deck.

"Romo," she yelped, dashing up the steps, through the cabin and out to the deck. She threw her arms around him in a tight embrace and kissed him with loud smacks on each wrinkled cheek. "I thought you'd abandoned me."

"*Jamais*, never." He held up a full glass of scotch and shrugged. "I could not find the orange juice," he confessed.

She laughed all the way from her belly. She'd traveled such bumpy roads since she'd last seen him, and he looked like he'd been lying on a beach somewhere. She took him in, the coppery tan, the crevices that seemed to have deepened, framing those intense blue eyes that always sparkled with promise, adventure, and fun. He'd shaved off the thin white line of his mustache.

"We have so much to talk about," Ellie said. "Come inside with me. I'll make coffee."

Once it was brewed, she spooned sugar and cream into his cup, carried their cups to the big, round oak table, and pulled her chair close to his.

She leaned close. "Where have you been, for God's sake, kicking back, catching rays somewhere?"

He breathed in the coffee's aroma and took a sip then tipped his scotch into the cup and sipped, twirling the cigar end on his saucer to shave off the ashes.

"Mmm, a holiday of sorts. The tying up of loose ends, *ma petite*. Choosing a new aircraft takes time and serious concentration, not unlike choosing a mate, eh? You too, you look golden and happy. It's clear you have survived your difficult journey, *n'est-ce pas*?"

She inhaled, filling her lungs with sweet alpine air, realizing the grip of fear was indeed gone. She launched into her tale, from Khesanh and waking up in the hospital with amnesia, to writing her article for UPI and entertaining Ben's job offer, to finally being able to accept that life lay in front of her, not behind. Best of all, Nick was gone from her life. She exhaled.

"You, *ma chèrie*, are far too special not to find love. Your prince will find you; he will shine with kindness and intelligence. This I know. Do not doubt Romo's wisdom."

She blushed.

Romo took a fortifying sip of his doctored coffee. "I must be frank with you. Your vision through the camera lens is inspired, clear and brilliant, but you had a blind eye when it came to Nick Burrows."

Ellie was grateful for Romo's insight. "Funny how it slips up on you, like quicksand."

She was thoughtful, drinking the coffee. "I realize I've been on a journey since my father died, a search for meaning, for myself. I can't really put it into words, but it has to do with the action and sense of belonging I found in Saigon, beyond all the bullshit. Also, I found there is a need, a burning to relate the truth to readers."

He reached for her hand. "We are all given a *soupçon* of wisdom when we are born. It is a small voice that lives just beneath the surface. It speaks or not, depending on how well we listen. You have listened well."

"You understand, Romo, thank you."

"You cannot know of my pride in you. You are noble. Your wisdom, your iron will, and your lust for adventure will carry you far. We are birds of a feather." Romo beamed. "You like this cliché? But I am serious. We, neither of us, gives up. It is the pain that creates more strength, *oui*?"

Ellie listened intently, basking in the force of his caring and the light from his blue eyes. He had supported her, championed her, and believed in her the whole time. "It is not magic that you have converted the evil of Jalbert and Nick into a new spirit of strength. It is resilience. You are a miracle."

He toasted her with his coffee cup. "Forgive another little taste of humor, but you are like the surefooted goat of the mountains who scrambles the steep cliffs without falling."

She groaned.

"You are also like the phoenix. Now, I speak of your courage —in Saigon, in Laos, in Khesanh."

"I'm an animal? A bird? All I did was follow your lead. You have taught me well, my mentor."

"Ah, *oui*, between us we have luck enough for entire worlds."

"And where will your luck take you now, Romo?"

"*Eh bien*, my new plane awaits my arrival in France. Then, I fly to Southeast Asia. It has long been my home, *oui*, and I miss it." He winked. "War is a kind of currency. It is a language in which I am fluent, and it provides me a living." He paused. "Also, I confess, it may be a habit."

They sat in comfortable silence. Romo broke it after a few minutes. "What about you? You will make Ben's book soar? This is your desire?"

"Well, in Saigon when he released me from my part in his war correspondents book project, I faced the fact that I'd just been marking time. To my surprise, this new offer was the impetus I needed to realize I am most alive when I'm in the middle of the action, the danger, as you say, and dancing on the edge, making a difference."

"*Alors*, shall we go dance in the danger together?"

THE END

ACKNOWLEDGMENTS

Numerous people have humored me, supported me, believed in me, and wondered how it could take so long to write and publish a novel.

I don't have an adequate answer. It's been a journey, on whose every moment was exciting.

No one has helped more than my husband. We embarked on this journey together. He to switch from screenplays to novels: Me to turn from journalism to fiction. When I began, I found it hard to make things up, but when I discovered the joy of creating characters who then snatched their lives and ran with them through my words, I was hooked.

I can't begin to adequately thank Ann Gimpel, an experienced novel writer and independently published author, for her unfailing advice and good-natured help. Her generosity has had no bounds, although I imagine she has rolled her eyes a lot.

To my writers' group, now disbanded, fractured by death and travel, I cannot imagine having gotten this book written without all the intelligence, love, and generosity I received from these people: Stacey Powells, Richard Hawk, Kirk Stapp, Jarrett Jackson, Peter Plantec, and Koji Kataoka.

And I'm indebted to my book group who bravely read a version that I'd thought was the final but wasn't. Their comments helped immensely.

Dee Dukehart, a PR maven whom I met when I was Leon Uris's researcher, turned me on to colleagues who took the time and energy to prepare proposals for me... Jane Dvorak, Polly Letovsky, Debra Fine. In the end, with limited funds, I decided to forge straight ahead into the publishing abyss.

To all my readers, especially my oldest friend, Michael Wood, I bow down in gratitude. So many different opinions, so many cogent and pertinent comments, criticisms, and praise.

Spending winter mornings in the gym playing pickleball on two courts marked with blue lines, I made friends. We chatted while sitting out a game on boxes along the wall. One of my favorite people was Lou Margulies, who read an early draft and gave me the best notes. She knew what rang true and what was being fudged over by the writer who wasn't sure about what to do in that instance. Her notes continued to help me through the next several drafts.

Not to mention the immense value of the internet and all the journalists' books, Wikipedia, and war memories I found there.

ABOUT THE AUTHOR

Writing has been a part of Diane Eagle's life always, a silk thread weaving through everything she's done. Whether running a ski racing circuit, researching books for the great storyteller Leon Uris (*Exodus, Trinity, The Haj*), serving as editor of magazines and newspapers, handling communications and marketing for summer music festivals, or being a paralegal, she has been constantly and continuously writing.

At nine, her first poem praised a stately horse standing on a hill, silhouetted in the sunrise. Her first novel followed.

She loves words. It's magical how many combinations of words float through the universe; it's plucking stars out of the night sky and lighting up a page with them.

Diane has published a poetry chapbook, *Snow Globe*. This is her first adult novel.